SHE
A
IN HIS ARMS . . .

It stirred images of how she had looked standing by the rain barrel yesterday, her corset lifting her breasts high, her chemise clinging wetly to her flesh. Desire surged through him . . .

Augusta pushed him away, her eyes defiant, her voice terse. "You shouldn't have bothered worrying about me. I might not be the hearty, fair-dispositioned wife you advertised for, but you'll never be able to accuse me of lacking good sense. It's the essence of my character. Some women are outrageously pretty. Others are outrageously sweet. *I* am outrageously sensible. What? What are you grinning at?"

He backed her against the wall, and when she looked as if she might flee, he blocked her escape. He whispered a kiss at hairline and tested the dampness of the fog on her flesh.

"I want to touch you." He breathed the words against her temple in a hoarse, husky whisper. He felt her palm on the back of his arm, as if in consent, and feeling her response, he smoothed a finger along the outer curve of her breast.

His breathing quickened. His fingers trembled. And in the swirling mist, lust overcame reason . . .

Savage Tides

Also by Mary Mayer Holmes

THE IRISH BRIDE
THE WHITE RAVEN

Published by
POPULAR LIBRARY

Savage Tides

Mary Mayer Holmes

POPULAR LIBRARY

An Imprint of Warner Books, Inc.

A Warner Communications Company

POPULAR LIBRARY EDITION

Popular Library® and the fanciful P design are registered
trademarks of Warner Books, Inc.

Cover illustration by Morgan Kane

Popular Library books are published by
Warner Books, Inc.
666 Fifth Avenue
New York, N.Y. 10103

 A Warner Communications Company

Printed in the United States of America

First Printing: December, 1989

10 9 8 7 6 5 4 3 2 1

To Kenneth Day—Whose loyalty, work ethic and dry wit capture the spirit of what Maine people are all about. How special you are to all of us.

To Leslie Keenan—Endings are not occasions for sadness, my friend. They're only beginnings in disguise. With thanks, and affection.

m.m.h.

—1—

**Philadelphia
July 10, 1831**

Augusta Mayhew fashioned a calm stitch in her embroidery while her sisters continued their discourse, raising composed but emphatic voices around her. It was a rare occurrence to witness her sisters fighting over her. It was an even rarer occurrence to find all five Mayhew sisters occupying the same room at the same time, but circumstances had necessitated their presence.

"I already told Augusta that I've made arrangements for her to spend the Christmas holidays at my house, Amelia. I think you're being mean-spirited insisting she stay with you instead."

Amelia sighed. "Lest you forget, Alberta, my chronic dyspepsia has left me in an extremely delicate state of health. If Augusta doesn't help me with holiday preparations, I'll be forced to hire someone."

"You and Charles can afford it, dear. But I made my

wishes known first, so she stays with me. Besides, my
guests are expecting to be served Augusta's Cape May
lemon pot pie as only Augusta can bake it. I wouldn't
want to disappoint them.''

A subtle breeze ruffled the parlor's crocheted curtains,
but Augusta knew it would require more than a hot summer
breeze to rid the house of the smell of decayed lilies and
roses. Four years ago, she had endured that smell for
months, for it had permeated the carpets and clung to the
horsehair upholstery. A humid day in Philadelphia often
conjured vivid memories of her father's wake. Five days
ago, the smell had invaded the house again, and beside
her father's memorial print in the parlor there now hung
one dedicated to her mother.

''I don't know why the two of you are creating such a
fuss,'' said Amanda Mayhew Crimp. ''We have twelve
months and four households to consider. Augusta can
spend three months a year with each of us. I want her next
June, July, and August. Godfrey and I have decided to
travel abroad, and naturally I wouldn't entrust the children
to anyone but Augusta.''

''You're going abroad?'' chimed Albina. ''Do you suppose I could borrow your Chinese crepe with the embroidered flounces while you're gone?''

''How can you afford a holiday?'' demanded Alberta.
''My Stanley said that your Godfrey's business has been
anything but profitable of late.''

''Ladies' corsets are always in demand, Alberta. Tell
that to your Stanley.''

Amelia sighed. ''I'd love to travel abroad, but I wouldn't
dare, not with my chronic headaches.''

Augusta continued plying her needle with quick, deft

stitches. At twenty-four, she was the oldest of the five girls—the oldest, the shortest, the only one without children, husband, or a flirtatious nature. She was also the only sister who wasn't a twin. Amanda and Amelia were a year younger than she was; Alberta and Albina two years younger.

Her sisters were possessed of flawless complexions, bright eyes, and beautiful children. Augusta was possessed of a great number of freckles. When their parents had paraded them all to church years ago, the twins had always been the center of attention. Their fellow parishioners thought it great fun to try to guess which twin was which, for the girls were as identically matched as bookends. The twins had grown more striking with age.

Augusta had grown more freckles.

When acquaintances spoke of the twins, they would employ words such as "stunning," or "fetching." When speaking of Augusta, they would usually comment, "Odd that a brunette would have so many freckles. Has she tried a treatment of lemon paste? It can work miracles." So one summer she smothered her face with the preparation and discovered that the paste did indeed work something of a miracle, but not the kind she was anticipating. Her freckles didn't disappear. Like the loaves and the fishes, they multiplied.

The incident proved to be only one in a long list of disappointments that had plagued her since birth. For instance, she had not been blessed with the extraordinary Mayhew red hair that made her sisters so attractive. Rather, her hair was black as a pot of ink, with not so much as a henna highlight to brighten its harshness. And it was not baby fine and straight. It was heavy and thick and it haloed her face with undisciplined ringlets when any hint of moisture crept into the air.

Her eyes were not the much-coveted Mayhew green. Their color hovered somewhere between green and brown. "A placid hazel," Albina had once said. "Sober and simple. Just like Augusta. It's a pity they're so big. I don't believe large eyes are in fashion this year." And not only were her eyes considered too big. Her eyebrows were so thick and dark that she thought they sometimes looked terribly odd against her pale complexion, especially when she wore powder to disguise her freckles. Her one source of pride was her eyelashes which were not red-gold and stubby like her sisters', but long and spiky black. "Rather like thorns," Alberta had been kind enough to comment years earlier. Augusta knew herself to be neither homely nor plain, but she also knew that matched against the unusual good looks of her sisters, she would always be considered rather ordinary looking.

"Actually," said Alberta, "if Augusta would vacate the house, we could decide a selling price and offer it for sale immediately."

"And then with our share of the inheritance, we could accompany Amanda abroad!" said Albina. "Just think. We'd be able to see firsthand the latest Paris fashions. Oooh, I'll be the envy of Spruce Street."

Amanda dabbed perspiration from her temples with a handkerchief made of the finest black mourning lace. "You seem to have forgotten one critical issue. What do you intend to do with the children? I already told you, I've reserved Augusta for my three angels."

Amelia sighed. "A holiday would be nice. Mama's condition caused me so much worry over the past years that I've developed chronic insomnia. I can't sleep anymore without taking a healthy dose of tonic bitters. Maybe a holiday would help alleviate some of the strain I've suffered.''

Augusta drew her sewing silk into a tidy knot and snipped off the excess with uncommon vigor. Seven years ago her parents had been involved in a carriage accident that had rendered them both invalids. She remembered well the shock, the grief, and then the inevitable acceptance that her parents would never walk again. The initial outpouring of sympathy for the family had been overwhelming. A day could not pass without a friend or neighbor stopping by to offer cheer or lend assistance to the five girls. Cakes and pies, stews and soups arrived without precedence. And when people couldn't pay their respects personally, they sent cordial little notes to Augustus and Isabel Mayhew, with wishes for a quick return to good health and with glowing praises for the Mayhew daughters who were providing such superlative care for their parents.

The girls thrived on the praise, for a time.

After a month, fascination with the Mayhew tragedy was eclipsed by fascination with more recent tragedies. That Isabel and Augustus Mayhew would spend the remainder of their lives bedridden became one more thread in the tapestry of the commonplace. The flood of wellwishers dwindled to a trickle. Notes began to arrive not daily but weekly, and then not at all. Praise for performing the extraordinary diminished to tacit nods of approval that the Mayhew girls were performing their Christian duty. Augusta's life took on a sameness that revolved around sickrooms and sick people, and as the weeks became months, the initial harmony among the five girls mutated into dissension.

As the head of the household, Augusta prepared a weekly schedule of individual chores. She'd never realized how unfair a person she was until the twins started to complain about their assigned chores. She was mean to make Amelia read to her mother when Amelia's voice was so easily susceptible to hoarseness. She was horrid to insist that they change her father's soiled bed linen and bathe him when they were unmarried and unaccustomed to the sight of a male body. She was despisable for dismissing their domestic and demanding that they cook and clean when they should be devoting their time to sewing caps and underlinens for their hope chests.

Augusta had no sympathy for her sisters' complaints, but she soon discovered it was counterproductive to argue with all four of them at the same time. As the months passed, she found it less exhausting to perform an unpleasant task herself than to try to convince one of the twins to do it. So what had started as the concerted effort of five gradually transformed into the sole effort of one. And the main ambition of the twins became to marry well and marry quickly.

Albina suddenly squealed so loudly that Augusta looked up, half expecting to find that her sister had been attacked by something with multiple legs and no discernible brain. "I have the perfect solution! If we gather the children together in one house, Augusta could care for all of them under one roof."

Amelia sighed. "They couldn't possibly stay in my house. What with all my medicines lying about, it would simply be too great a temptation for some of your darlings to resist. Alberta has the biggest house. I think they should stay there.''

''We're expecting to have several rooms redecorated next summer, so my house is out of the question.''

A knock at the front door interrupted their discussion. Both sets of twins peered at Augusta. ''Are you expecting guests?'' asked Amanda.

''As a matter of fact,'' said Augusta as she set her embroidery aside and stood up, ''I am.'' With a quiet rustle of black taffeta, she left the room. Albina threw a curious look after her sister.

''What do you suppose that's all about?''

Amanda smiled. ''Perhaps it's a gentleman caller.''

Amelia shook her head. Making sure that Augusta was no longer in view, she said in a low voice, ''That's highly unlikely. My Charles says no man with half a brain would ever take Augusta to wife. Men want women who are shy and biddable. You know yourselves that Augusta is none of those things. She's overbearing—''

''—and stringent—''

''—and she takes great pleasure in looking a man straight in the eye. My Harvey thinks it's appalling.''

'' 'Capriciousness gains a woman neither influence nor friends,' '' quoted Amanda in imitation of her eldest sister. ''If she'd thought to be a bit more capricious, she might have attracted herself a husband.''

Albina nodded her agreement. ''My Harvey thinks it was extremely selfish of her to spend these past years doing nothing but caring for Mama and Papa. You're right. She should have been trying to find a husband who could provide for her in her old age. Now the responsibility of providing for her falls on *our* shoulders. We'll have to feed her, board her, provide clothing for her. It's not fair, not when we have families of our own to support.''

"Godfrey says we should divide her share of the inheritance among us, since it's our four families who'll be assuming the burden of her care. Besides, she'll have no use for money if she's living off our generosity.''

Alberta smiled as if enlightened. ''And if she creates a fuss, we'll simply tell her that if she wants a roof over her head, she'd better—''

"It was so kind of you to come on such short notice, Reverend,'' came Augusta's voice from the hallway. The twins straightened their backs and collars and looked toward the doorway to find Augusta directing the Reverend Jerome Jordan into the parlor. The man nodded a greeting to the twins before waving his Bible toward the open windows.

"I'm not one to suggest improvements upon the Lord's work, but I would hope if He ever had thoughts of modifying Creation, we could convince Him to make Philadelphia summers less hot. How are you ladies faring with this insufferable weather?''

Augusta watched four lovely red heads bob daintily and four pairs of green eyes cast demure glances in the vicinity of Reverend Jordan's feet. She marveled how easy it was for them to effect the proper feminine gestures, to whisper the expected words. They had always done what was expected of beautiful women. They had flirted and smiled and snared husbands who had given them lovely homes and beautiful children. Augusta had likewise done what was expected of her, but she had little to show for her efforts except memories of the youth she had sacrificed to duty.

Next month she would be a quarter of a century old. By Philadelphia standards she was already an old maid, expected to spend her remaining years in the homes of relatives benevolent enough to keep her. She was expected to become a doting aunt who would do for her nieces and nephews what she had spent the past seven years doing for her mother and father. Without a husband, she possessed no identity of her own and was condemned to a social namelessness that was the bane of all spinsters. She would own nothing and would be beholden to everyone for even her most simple needs. It purported to be a dismal existence for someone who craved to recapture a few carefree moments from her lost youth.

Those moments were something for which Augusta yearned.

She wanted to bake a cake and eat it all herself. She wanted to play her violin for twelve hours straight in her bare feet and chemise. She wanted to learn to whistle, no matter how badly. She wanted to be surrounded by people who would make her laugh so outrageously that she would be overcome by hiccups and tears at the same time. She had fulfilled her duty to her parents. She felt it was her right now to do something that few Philadelphia spinsters had the courage to do.

She wanted to do the unexpected.

With a serious glint lighting her hazel eyes, she laced her fingers together at her waist and addressed her sisters. "Two months ago, when Mama took her turn for the worse, I happened upon an advertisement in the *Inquirer*.

I didn't pay it much heed in the beginning, but as Mama's health worsened, I began to think that . . . that . . ." She whipped the air with her hand, trying to think how to phrase it. "Oh, never mind." She shoved her hand into the pocket of her gown and withdrew a wrinkled square of newsprint. "I'll read it to you."

She unfolded the tiny piece of paper and set it in the palm of her hand. It was so worried from constant handling that it was limp as an unstarched hanky. She coughed to clear her throat and began to read. " 'Hearty, sensible, fair-dispositioned woman wanted to assume position of wife to resident wickie on Maine coastal island. Woodland pine and salt air aplenty. Must assist with light duties. Must be accompanied by cooking skills, and galoshes. Post response to: Elijah Payne in care of Haydon Crowley, Master, Ship *Windlass,* Portland, Maine.' "

"What, pray tell, is a wickie?"

"I think it means he's an Indian," said Amelia.

Albina shook her head. "Candle maker. He obviously does something with wicks. And what else can you do with a wick except make a candle?"

"If he made candles, he'd call himself a chandler," corrected Alberta. "A wickie is a person who makes use of wicker, which means, the man is a basket weaver. How quaint."

Amelia sighed. "Sea air can cause congestion in the lungs. I would advise the gentleman not to remain on that island any longer than is absolutely necessary. Is Reverend Jordan related to the man? Oh dear, are we about to lose the Reverend to an island community?"

Augusta refolded the advertisement and slipped it back into her pocket. "Reverend Jordan is here to marry me."

A sudden paralysis swept over the twins, except for Amelia, who stifled a squeal while motioning frantically for Augusta to come closer. "Reverend Jordan is *already* married," Amelia whispered into her sister's ear. "Good Lord, Augusta, his wife taught you to play the violin! How could you do this to her?"

Augusta straightened slowly. Even coming from Amelia, this was an absurd observation. "I am not marrying Reverend Jordan," she explained as if to a dull-witted child. "I'm marrying Mr. Payne. Reverend Jordan is here to perform the ceremony. By proxy. So "—she eyed each of her sisters—"which one of you would like to stand in for the groom?"

Struggling through their initial paralysis, the twins found their voices at the same moment.

"Marriage? You haven't even been fitted for a wedding gown!"

"You know nothing about his background. You haven't even been properly introduced!"

"This is totally irrational behavior, Augusta. I think you're simply overcome by grief at Mama's death. Pray, God, it passes quickly."

"How ungrateful of you! Considering all the sacrifices we were willing to make to draw you into the bosom of our families, I think it's mean-spirited of you to make a decision like this without even consulting us! Whatever has come over you, Augusta? Why are you doing this? Why?"

Augusta dwelled on the beautiful faces of her four sisters, knowing why. Because she wanted to manage her own home, not be a guest in someone else's. Because she wanted to cook for her own husband, not be forced to dote over someone else's. Because she wanted to bear her own children, not serve as a nanny to someone else's.

For seven years she had closeted herself with the smells of sickrooms and bed sores and decayed flowers. She had a chance now to purge her memory of those smells, to begin her life again on a windswept island where no one knew her, where no one would be predisposed to find fault with her appearance or disposition. She had read about Maine islands where whole communities of people lived independently of the mainland by catching their own fish, farming their own land, building their own dwellings, sewing their own clothes. She was hearty and sensible. She could make a positive contribution to such a community, and perhaps this time her efforts would be appreciated.

Perhaps.

She was a realistic woman. She knew there were people like herself whose every expectation in life had ended in disappointment. From her freckles, to her hair, to her eyes, to her parents' infirmities, to the young man who had once flirted with her only to gain an introduction to Albina— she knew that disappointments comprised a large part of her existence. She had learned to accept that. But there still burned within her one last glimmer of hope that she would one day be held in affection by a man who would not consider black hair inferior to Mayhew red, or hazel eyes inferior to green.

She hoped Elijah Payne would be that man. She hoped he spoke truth when he asked for a woman to be hearty and sensible and fair-dispositioned. Perhaps a man who lauded those virtues would be able to find within her something that no one had ever discovered. Perhaps somewhere, within the cocoon of her spinster's body, he would find a butterfly.

If only one existed.

But these were the secrets of her soul that she was loath to share with anyone. So in answer to Amanda's question of why she was doing this, she merely said, "Because I want to."

Amanda threw up her hands in disgust. "You see? My Godfrey was right. You care about no one but yourself. You haven't even the common decency to be civil about the whole thing. It would serve you right if this island was a thousand miles from nowhere so you could never socialize with decent people."

"You just wait! Your Mr. Payne will probably be poor as a church mouse—"

"—and short—"

"—and he'll look like a toad—"

Augusta sat down quietly as Reverend Jordan attempted to calm the twins' hysterics. Amid the screaming, wailing, and name-calling, she picked up her embroidery and plied a dainty stitch.

They were taking the news much better than she'd expected.

—2—

The knock that sounded at Augusta's cabin door was accompanied by a young man's voice. "'Scuse me, ma'am. Cap'n Crowley says to tell you we've dropped anchor. Standing by to row you ashore soon's you can make your way to the maindeck."

From where she lay on her bunk, Augusta rolled her head sideways, groaning when the compress on her forehead slid downward and flopped onto the bed. She had never been sick a day in her life, 'til four days ago.

"Ma'am? You hear me, ma'am?"

Augusta moistened her lips with the tip of her tongue and, rallying her last reserves of strength, croaked out, "Fine." But it wasn't fine. It hadn't been fine since she'd left Delaware Bay and headed into the open sea. The deafening clank of machinery aboard the paddle steamer hadn't bothered her. And the noxious fumes and soot belched out from the smokestacks did little more than sully her gown and burn her eyes. But when the steamer quartered into its first Atlantic wave, the resulting pitch and roll of the vessel created a motion so unnatural that she lost her appetite, her balance, and any desire to stand upright ever again.

During three days at sea nothing improved. She lost track of both her feet, having no idea if they were above her head or below her knees. She ached. She perspired. And when she boarded the two-masted ship *Windlass* in Portland Harbor, she entered her cabin belowdecks thinking this would be her final resting place.

She was heartsick to think she wouldn't live long enough to meet Elijah Payne. She had so wanted to meet the man who had found enough merit in her response to choose her over all the other women who had replied to his advertisement. But he had requested a woman who was hearty and sensible, not someone who would misplace her feet somewhere between here and Philadelphia.

She closed her eyes waiting for the benevolent hand of Death to deliver her from her misery. For a fleeting moment she imagined her sisters receiving the tidings that she had died from "terminal seasickness." They would no doubt feel extremely smug that they had predicted her failure. They would tell Reverend Jordan that she had received her due for her selfishness. And they would probably delight in parceling out her share of the inheritance amongst themselves.

One of her eyes popped halfway open.

Did she really want to be the cause of so much happiness?

The other eye popped open.

No. She didn't. By God, let the twins be disappointed for a change. She was going to survive long enough to meet her husband. If she still felt like dying after being introduced to him, perhaps she could expire in his arms. At least that might lend a more romantic mood to her demise.

From the maindeck she heard a clatter of metal accompanied by a singsong drone and creak of wood, and then a splash, as of a boat hitting the water. "All right, Augusta," she prodded herself. "Up you go."

She forced herself to her elbows, swallowed several times in rapid succession, and breathed deeply. Inhaling another deep breath, she swung her legs over the side and sat reluctantly upright. The shrill tone of the bosun's pipe prompted her to reach for her hat, which was hanging from a wall peg behind her. It was covered in pleated black silk, fashioned with a high rounded crown and wide brim that flared all the way around, and was bedecked with blackcock feathers and a black gauze veil. Without ceremony, she jammed it onto her head. After tying the wide satin ribbons in a fancy bow beneath her right ear, she lowered the gauze veil over her face and secured it behind with a silver hatpin. That done, she hoisted herself to her feet, grabbed her gloves, and with a determined half-shuffle, aimed herself at the door.

Captain Crowley found her hugging a section of the tar-blackened cable that ran from the top of the mainmast to its base, anchoring the mast to the deck. He grinned as he strode toward her. "If I hadn't a looked twice, I'da thought you were part a my standin' riggin', Mrs. Payne. Can I escort you to the Jacob's ladder? Looks to me like you could use a steady arm to steer you.''

Augusta leaned her body into the taut strength of the backstay. She looked up at the ship's master through the dark gauze of her veil. "How . . . far away is it?''

He laughed at her question and shook his head good-naturedly. "So that's the way of it, is it? Here I thought you were bein' shy hidin' yourself away in your cabin. Had yourself a bout with a slidin' stomach, did you? Should've sent word to me, Mrs. Payne. Pint a seawater and a few mustard pickles. Could've fixed you up slick's a whistle.''

Augusta forced herself to swallow. She suspected that mustard pickles would have done as much good for her seasickness as lemon paste had done for her freckles. "My husband advertised for a . . . *hhh*earty female,'' she choked out. "I'm off to a . . . dismal start.''

"You're on your feet, ma'am. That's a sight better than some what I've seen. I expect you'll get your legs back soon enough, and that bein' the case, maybe it's not real important that you tell 'Lijah what a despizable trip you had, him wantin' a hearty wife 'n' all. Sometimes what a man don't know don't hurt 'im one dang bit.''

"You call him 'Lijah,'' she mused, liking the abbreviated version. It sounded a gentler name shortened to two syllables. But his name wasn't her primary problem at the moment. "I don't want to . . . deceive him, Captain. But I don't want to . . . disappoint him either.''

"Man's not likely to be disappointed findin' himself spliced to a handsome woman, Mrs. Payne. Besides, so long's you can walk, talk, and cook, I doubt 'Lijah will have any cause for disappointment.''

Behind her veil, she glowed at his compliment. Over the years, gentlemen had found little reason to compliment her, though her father always had a kind word to offer about her levelheadedness and her extraordinary tolerance for cigar smoke. To have a virtual stranger insinuate to her face that he thought she was handsome was a happenstance she imagined never to experience. "Handsome" wasn't "stunning" or "fetching." But handsome was nice. To a Philadelphia spinster, handsome was very nice.

Captain Crowley extended his forearm to her. "Ready if you are, ma'am."

Uncurling each of her fingers from the backstay, she grabbed the captain's elbow and, still wrapped in the afterglow of his flattery, practically floated to the gunwale.

She wasn't able to view her new surroundings until she was seated on the stern thwart of the ship's boat, heading for shore. Four members of the *Windlass*'s crew manned the oars on the two center thwarts while Captain Crowley sat the bow, his head turned shoreward. Their rhythm through the water was slightly erratic, as if one man were powering his oar too vigorously and the others not vigorously enough, but this motion was less upsetting to her than the pitch and roll of a paddle steamer.

She looked to left and right, wondering where the mainland was. On the horizon, where sky and sea formed a blurred mirage of palest blues, she could see no dips or rises, nothing that would indicate a headland. She could see nothing other than the spit of earth that lay dead ahead. Elijah Payne's island. She didn't even know if it had a name, but she slid closer to the port gunwale to study it.

It rose from the water like a porcupine about to throw its quills. A crescent of beach lay directly ahead, but Augusta saw it was not a beach conducive to shoeless feet, for it was comprised of small rounded stones, like cobblestones, whose pinks and blacks and grays glistened wetly in the sunlight, like a mosaic of marble eggs. Driftwood and clumps of black seaweed littered the beach at the high-water mark. Above this lay a strip of white sand that was belted by a long rib of granite bedrock. A swath of grass undulated beyond the bedrock, sweeping toward a backdrop of towering firs with pointed tops—trees so darkly green they looked black.

At the near end of the beach a narrow set of wooden tracks led from the water's edge to a shingled building perched above the strandline, and roosted on the peak of the building's roof was a lone gull, his wings spread as if ready for flight, his head tilted to the side as if watching her. It seemed a place of quiet peace and tranquility, a place so untouched that if it had not been for the outbuilding and tracks, she would guess no mortal had ever walked its shore.

The boat's keel suddenly scraped bottom, jarring her, and she grabbed the gunwale to steady herself. Without a verbal command, the crewmen lifted their oars smartly, rattling the oarlocks as they hauled them aboard. The boat continued forward on the crest of a low wave, and when they were as far ashore as the tide would take them, Captain Crowley gave a nod. He and the four crewmen jumped the gunwales and with a great show of might hauled the boat higher up the beach to protect it from the rising tide. Augusta remained in the stern, tilted crazily to port, and as she sat, she turned her head slightly, listening.

There were no Philadelphia sounds here. No clackety carriage wheels or squeaky axles. No clopping horse hooves or voices hawking flowers, confections, or ice. She heard instead quiet, unhurried sounds. The wash of sea-water as it lapped the rocky shore. The click of pebbles as they tumbled together in the surging tide, rolling and somersaulting like dice in a cup. The almost imperceptible flap of wings as the gull perched on the rooftop caught an updraft and took flight. And the smells! Salt, mostly. Salt air and salt water, but she could also smell fish, and . . . and rocks, and sunshine. And she could smell the forest as the wind carried its fragrance to her—more aromatic than sachet, sweeter than perfume. Evergreen smells. Pungent wood and summer flowers. More evocative than the smells of baking bread or hot apple pie. Smells that touched her mind and her soul with a kind of primal pleasure. The smells of an unspoiled Eden . . . of paradise. And she smiled to think she had found a place so serene that she could grow intoxicated on smell alone, while listening to the whispered flap of a gull's wing.

Oh, yes, she was going to like it here.

"Help you outta there, Mrs. Payne?" Captain Crowley's voice intruded softly upon her abstraction, and she looked up, surprised to find him standing so close. Nodding, she grasped his outstretched hand, heaved herself to her feet, and clambered over the gunwale with as much grace as her flowing skirts would allow. She released his hand the moment her feet found purchase on solid ground, but finding a level place to stand was nearly impossible, for the rocks were bunched together like melons in a grocer's cart. They were wet and slippery. And she could swear that some of them were seesawing beneath her.

"This here's a right reg'lar island," said Crowley as he threw out a hand toward the bow of the boat to indicate they should walk in that direction. Augusta maintained an awkward pace beside him, staggering to port with one step, to starboard with another. She decided the rocks weren't seesawing. The whole island was.

"'Lijah keeps a garden the other side that stand a spruce," continued Crowley as Augusta brushed against the bow to steady herself. "There's a storm beach to windward. And 'tween here and there you got plenty a room to swing a cat. Hope it suits you."

Augusta leaned her weight against the side of the boat, planting her feet far apart to maintain her balance. "Does the island . . . have a name?"

"Used to have an Indian name." Using his hands as markers, he measured a two-foot space in the air. "Was about this long and didn't have a cussid vowel. Not a body alive could say it, so years back some feller changed it. Call it Devilstone now. Devilstone Island."

Augusta frowned at the godless name. She doubted Reverend Jordan would approve. She wasn't so sure *she* approved, but there wasn't much she could do about it. "And the mainland." She looked over her shoulder. "How far away is the mainland?"

"Fifteen miles as the crow flies straight over your shoulder there. Nearest village is a place called Lustre's Gate."

"Fifteen miles?" Considering what sea travel did to her, it might as well be the thousand miles Albina had wished on her. She prayed Devilstone Island did indeed suit her, for it seemed she was destined never to leave it.

"Mainland's not as far away as it sounds, Mrs. Payne. With a soldier's wind at your back, you could make landfall in 'Lijah's yawl in about four hours."

Augusta placed a soothing hand at her waist as the

ground swayed *baaack* and forth, *baaack* and forth.
"Throwing myself into the path of a . . . runaway flour
barrel sounds more appealing to me than the thought of
boarding another boat, Captain.''

Crowley laughed at her response while she scanned the
beach with a curious eye. Where were all the houses? The
people? Where was Elijah? She surveyed the tree line,
then cast a glance in the direction of the mainland, suddenly curious. "I hadn't given it much thought before, but
why do you suppose a man would advertise for a wife in
the *Philadelphia Inquirer* when he could hand pick his
own in a village only four hours away?''

Crowley's laughter faded as if chased away by an ill
wind. The muscles in his face tightened. He appeared
stunned, then uncomfortable, then worried that she had
thought to pose such a question. He gave his neck a long,
slow scratch and studied the polish on his boots, but no
explanation was forthcoming.

A knot of alarm began to tighten in Augusta's stomach.
"Captain? Is there something you're afraid to tell me?''
And then it struck her. "Is there something wrong with
my husband?''

"I, uh, I'm not sure how to answer that, ma'am.'' He
elevated his eyes, looking beyond Augusta rather than at
her, and in the space of a heartbeat he broke into a relieved
smile. He nodded toward the opposite end of the beach.
"Yonder's your husband now. Wait a spell, and you can
question him directly.''

Augusta pivoted around. Through the haze of her veil,
she saw the man making his way toward them with long,
steady strides, apparently unhampered by the fact that the
entire beach was listing like a derelict ship. And as he

drew near, she realized her sisters had been wrong about two things. .

Elijah Payne wasn't short. And he didn't look like a toad.

He was a big man, thick through the shoulders and chest, as physically rugged as her father had been spare. He wore a homely shirt of white cotton that was buttoned high to his throat, but the fabric seemed unable to contain the massiveness of his limbs. His breeches were not unlike seamen's trousers, wide-legged, unshapely, and rolled to his calves, lending him a freedom of movement that she imagined many a Philadelphia gentleman would envy. He wore neither hose nor shoes but allowed his feet to poke out naked from his trouser legs, a circumstance that, considering the composition of the beach, was either very brave or very foolhardy, she couldn't decide which.

"'Lijah, you ole bahstid!" Crowley stepped around the bow of the boat and extended his hand to Elijah Payne, who returned the greeting with a firm handshake and a clap on the captain's back.

"Been a while, Haydon, but you're lookin' fit."

Augusta watched the exchange with a racing pulse. It was so important to her not to disappoint her husband. She was prepared to accept the role of wife and all it entailed. She didn't even dread the act of physical intimacy. Indeed, once a woman neared the quarter-century mark, her anxiety over intimacy changed from the fear of experiencing pain to the fear of never knowing what the pain would be like. But she had anticipated this moment for so long that, now that it was upon her, she felt unsure, awkward.

Her eyes lingered on the hand that Elijah had clamped around Crowley's shoulder. She had expected that her husband would be possessed of all his limbs, but she hadn't envisioned the actual flesh. She had never imagined that his hand would be so finely formed, his fingers so shapely, his skin so brown. He stood straight as the *Windlass*'s mainmast, but he stood comfortably, with his weight concentrated on his left leg, and his hip angled slightly outward. Augusta tried to recall a time when she had ever been so comfortable with her own body, but could recall none.

His hair would not be well received in Philadelphia parlors. It was inches longer than fashion dictated, falling straight to his shoulders and tied at his nape by a black riband. Its color was shades lighter than her own, the warm brown of a lion's mane shot through with strands so blond they looked fingerpainted by the sun. It was clean, and untamed, and lovely to behold.

Captain Crowley slanted a look at her. "Seems kinda queer my introducin' you to your own wife, 'Lijah, but thar she blows, delivered to you safe, sound, and fit's a fiddle."

Elijah turned his gaze upon her for the first time, presenting to her a visage so appealing that she could do little else but stare in silence. Beauty had shaped his bones and touched the flesh that stretched tightly over them. His complexion was sun drenched with golden color, unblemished by freckles or stubble. His cheekbones rode high on his face, prominent and angular and slashed pink with health. His eyes were shaped like almonds, long and brown, almost black, and in them she saw little humor. He appeared a stern man, a jaded man, as if he had seen much through those dark brown eyes and had found most of it lacking.

She worried again that he would find her lacking, for indeed, his demeanor did not bespeak a man who would value good sense and a fair disposition in a woman. His demeanor bespoke a man who would appreciate a fair face and a shapely calf above all else. It was a discouraging revelation at best.

"Ma'am." Elijah tipped his head, squinting to perceive the outline of her face behind her veil, but she made no attempt to appease his curiosity by unveiling herself. This was not a propitious time to reveal the fact that the husband was prettier than the wife, not while Captain Crowley and his crew could be witness to Elijah's shock. She wondered if she would feel less daunted if he were a trifle more like herself. A trifle more . . . ordinary. She imagined she was supposed to feel exuberant right now. Instead, she only felt inadequate.

"We'll be fetchin' supplies from the *Windlass* for some time yet," said Elijah, "so you might as well head up to the house. I was thinkin' to have a chowder for supper. The fish is all cleaned. All you gotta do is chop the potatoes and onions and make the pumpkin bread. Supper's at five. That should give you plenty of time to get things on the table." That said, he turned back to Crowley, seemingly dismissing her.

Augusta's eyes widened in amazement. This was her greeting? No 'Pleased to meet you,' or 'How did you fare on your journey?' Just chop the vegetables and feed me at five? She'd seen more enthusiasm generated by her milkman when she'd ordered an extra pound of butter. His subdued reception galled her, but she found solace by telling herself that perhaps her husband didn't want to appear overly sentimental in front of his peers. Men, she realized, were sometimes embarrassed about such things.

"Excuse me," she said as she pushed herself away from the boat's support, "but where is the house?"

Elijah paused midsentence to regard her, surprising her once again with the absolute beauty that shaped the flesh and bone of his face. He thrust his hand toward the far end of the beach. "There's a path back that way. Follow it to the end."

Which was fine, except for one thing. "How will I know which house is the right one?"

Captain Crowley looked puzzled by her question, but Elijah didn't miss a beat. "It's the one with the cow in the dooryard. And if you wait for someone to let you in, you'll be waiting from now 'til kingdom come, so just let yourself in. The door's unlocked. Kitchen's to the right."

"The kitchen," she repeated, anticipating where Elijah Payne was expecting her to spend most of her time. "Of course." Feeling more irritated than fretful of a sudden, she nodded her head toward Crowley. "Captain," she said, then commenced to pick her way to the upper lip of the beach, where the rocks ended and the sand began.

Captain Crowley watched her go with something of a smile tugging at the corners of his mouth. "I think she was expectin' some fancy words from you, 'Lijah."

Elijah followed the man's gaze, watching his new wife weave left and right like a compass needle in search of a direction. "She walk like that all the time?"

"I suspect she's gettin' her landlubber's legs back."

They watched her in silence. Elijah shook his head. "Why's she wearin' that mosquito net around her face? No mosquitoes on Devilstone."

Crowley shrugged his bewilderment. "Why does a female do anything? Answer that and you'll be solvin' one've the grand mysteries of the decade."

"She doesn't see the path. Lookit that. Walked right past it."

"I dunno. She . . . she's comin' round now. Makin' a wide turn was all she was doin'. I bet that incline up to the path looks pretty damned steep to her, though."

"Probably wouldn't seem so steep if she wasn't looking at it through a damned mosquito net." Elijah frowned. "Why's she flappin' her arms like that?"

"She's—" Crowley bit back his words and grimaced. Elijah made a circle of pain with his mouth. Silence, then, "I suspect she was tryin' to keep her balance."

"Didn't work." Elijah shook his head. "Looks to me like she's gonna need some help untangling herself from all those petticoats."

Crowley nodded. "You'd think so."

Elijah stepped forward, pausing when he saw the figure at the end of the beach straighten her hat, untwist her petticoats, and roll gracelessly to her feet. "She's up." His voice reflected surprise. But what surprised him even more was the way she climbed the incline to the path, using her hands and feet, like a toddler climbing her first set of stairs. "Resourceful creature."

Crowley smiled his approval. "Got a lot a gumption too, for a Philadelphia lady. Wouldn'ta minded getting spliced to this one myself."

Elijah threw him a long look, saying nothing.

When the *Windlass* sent up a signal flag indicating that supplies were ready to be off-loaded, Crowley sent the ship's boat and crew back to the tender to begin the pro-

cess. He remained on the beach with Elijah, for he felt a
need to speak with his friend privately. Hunkering down,
he found a smooth, flat stone, then, rising, sidearmed it
into the surf. It skipped once, then sank with a *plop*. He
bent down in search of another stone. "The girl asked me
how come a man no more than four hours away from the
mainland had to advertise for a wife in a Philadelphia
paper."

Warming to the smell of competition, Elijah bent down
to find his own skimming stones. "So what did you tell
her?"

"Didn't tell her nothin'. Said she'd have to ask you
herself." Sporting a handful of stones, Crowley stood up
and skimmed another one into the water. It sank instead
of skimming, leaving a miniature wake circling around its
point of entry. "Damn."

Elijah came to stand beside him. He shot his first stone
into the water and watched it skip four . . . five . . . six
times.

"You've been practicin'," accused Crowley. "So, you
gonna tell her the truth?" He sidearmed another.

"No need to tell her anything."

"'Til she asks."

Elijah hefted a stone, got the feel of it in his hand, and
fired it into the surf. *Plink . . . plink . . . plink . . .* seven
. . . eight . . . nine. "You think she ever would've agreed
to come here if she knew the truth, Haydon?"

Crowley lifted his arm into position, paused, then
dropped it back to his side. Torn between truth and emotion, he shook his head. "I dunno. Maybe."

"Would you've come if you were a Philadelphia lady
and I'd told you the truth?"

Crowley searched the horizon with thoughtful eyes. "I think . . . I think I would've wanted to know more."

"And I wouldn't of been able to tell you."

Tiring of their sport, Crowley dropped his stones onto the beach in a cascading heap and rubbed his hands together, ridding them of sand. "I still say she deserves to know."

"I'll handle this," assured Elijah as he let fly his final stone, skipping it nine . . . ten . . . eleven times. "Just like I've handled everything else."

—3—

As she wended her way up the island path, Augusta pondered the sparse details her husband had included about himself in his one letter of correspondence to her. He had said he was twenty-eight years of age, had all his teeth and hair, was hardworking, and had been a wickie for eight years. She hadn't wanted to appear ignorant by writing to inquire what a wickie was. But having met him, she was thirsty for more details, for his brawny limbs and long stride did not lend him the appearance of candle maker or basket weaver. Hammer-wielding smithy or Mississippi keelboatman perhaps. But not a man who had spent eight years of his life molding wax or weaving twigs.

Her light-haired, long-eyed husband was thus something of an enigma to her. But one thing was certain. If there was a reason no woman in Lustre's Gate wanted to marry Elijah Payne, it was not his physical appearance. A more splendid-looking man she had never seen, but splendid in no way applied to his manners. *Pretty is as pretty does*, she thought, hoping that Elijah Payne's second impression would be better than his first.

She wandered past several deviant pathways in her ascent and questioned if they trailed down to the island's other residences. She thought it somewhat odd that she hadn't heard sounds of human activity, but the forest was so dense on either side of her that she surmised the trees probably absorbed whatever sounds were made. The seclusion of the path prevented her from divining the shape of the island, but she was sure of two things: Devilstone was big, and as steep as it was long. As if to evidence that fact, she stepped off the path and leaned against the trunk of a pine tree to catch her breath.

She hoped the house was near. Her nausea had subsided, but navigating this terrain on legs that felt sturdy as worn-out carriage springs was a near-impossible task. She craned her neck to look farther ahead.

The path was uneven and irregular, carpeted by moss and overlaid with pine needles that had dried to the color of ripe pumpkins. It tunneled beneath a roof of evergreens whose boughs twined so thickly overhead that they allowed only an occasional beam of sunlight to splash onto the ground, illuminating fern fronds that grew tall as her waist, and tree roots that poked up like skinny arms with ugly elbows. It was a world unto itself—a place where fallen trees played host to moss and mushrooms, a place of green haze, cool air, ancient boulders, and timelessness.

Blowing a lungful of air between her teeth, she readied herself and pressed onward.

The terrain leveled out after a while. The pathway broadened. Trees thinned. Augusta stepped out of the forest to be confronted by a sprawling stretch of grass, an L-shaped complex of buildings that sat near a precipice, and a conical tower that rose at least fifty feet into the air. She looked up and up, focusing on the glass cupola at the top of the tower. "A lighthouse?" She glanced curiously left and right to see if she had somehow found the wrong residence. But there was the cow, fenced within a rambling stone wall to the right of the house. She studied the tower as she walked closer. *No one mentioned anything about a lighthouse.* Was it still in operation?

It was a six-sided structure of white-washed shingles with only two windows embedded in its length to admit light, one at the base and the other closer to the top. A series of separately roofed sheds, all interlinking but of varying heights and lengths, snaked in an el from the tower to the main house. A rain barrel sat in the corner of the el to collect runoff from the roof. The main house was a tidy little structure, gable roofed and sided with rough shingles that had weathered to the gray of granite boulders. The only features brightening the grayness were doors and shutters that were painted a pale soldier blue.

There were no flowers, no flower boxes. A weather vane rattled atop a roof in the bend of the el—a carved whale that looked as if it was swimming against the current or trying to escape the greenery that was tangled around its crossbar. She thought she had never seen a place so severely simple . . . until she saw the inside.

She entered through one of the shed doors, finding the room piled high with wood. When she opened the door to her right, she discovered the kitchen and stopped short. The floor was so highly polished she imagined she could skate across it, but there were no rag rugs to add touches of color. The cook hearth was to the left, a zinc-lined sink and chopping block to the right, a small standing cupboard without decoration straight ahead. The walls were not bare. Above the cupboard there hung a wooden knife box, an eight-drawered spice box, a tin candle box, and a match box. But there were no embroidered samplers bidding a stranger welcome or expounding the virtues of home.

In the middle of the floor sat a plain trestle table flanked by ladder-back chairs with rush seats. But there was no centerpiece to please the eye, no crisp linen tablecloth to hide the wood's imperfections. To say the room lacked excess was the kindest thing she could say. It was bare, cold, sterile, and ordered with almost military precision. She wondered if Elijah's mother had ever occupied this house, for nowhere did it show evidence of a woman's touch. The man was obviously in dire need of a wife. How he had managed to survive this long without such amenities as tablecloths and dried flower arrangements was beyond her comprehension. She was confident she could change this house into a home in very little time. She could do good here, and that pleased her.

She lit on the two windows cut into the west wall. The glass panes sparkled with cleanliness, but— She cocked her head, trying to identify what was wrong, then gaped in horror. There were no curtains on these windows! She could forgive the absence of tablecloths, but no curtains? That was more than unacceptable. It was uncivilized.

With a spry step that belied her physical discomfort, she crossed the floor. She opened the door in the south wall and, grabbing hold of the jamb for sudden balance, peeked inside. The front room. Bare floor. Bare walls. Floor-to-ceiling fireplace made from rounded beach stones. A shelf of books. Two winged armchairs. Two side chairs. No curtains. Stepping into the room, she reached for the handle to the door on her immediate left and depressed the tongue.

The bedroom. Bare floor. Bare walls. Simple pine bedstead with trundle. Washstand bureau. No mirror. No curtains. Shaking her head, she removed the hatpin from her bonnet, lifted her veil, and untied the ribbons beneath her chin. Her new home wasn't austere. It was downright primitive! This might be Elijah Payne's house, but it was her domain now too, and she intended to make a few changes. It seemed she had arrived on Devilstone Island not a moment too soon.

For the remainder of the afternoon, between chopping, stirring, and baking, Augusta watched a procession of men burdened with supplies from the *Windlass* file past the house. She had no idea what the supplies were, only that they were contained in barrels and small crates that were deposited in the sheds closest to the tower. Last to be delivered were her three trunks, which she indicated should be placed in the bedroom. That done, the crew bade their respectful farewells and tramped back down the forest path. Captain Crowley and her husband remained conspicuously absent for another hour, appearing at the kitchen door just as she placed dessert in the oven to bake.

"Don't know what happened to that other gross a wicks, 'Lijah, but I can't leave you short. Have to make a trip back before winter weather sets in, seems."

Augusta snapped the oven door shut, latched it, then turned around to face the men. She had always prided herself on her ability to look a man straight in the eye, but she couldn't do that with Elijah, not when he was looking her up and down like a man judging a prize sow at a country fair. And for a moment she was fifteen again, standing outside church, and Peter Oliver was looking at her in the same bold way. She had blushed that day until Peter had quipped, "You don't look much like your sisters. Were you adopted?" She had willed herself not to cry that Sunday morning, but in reliving the moment, she felt a blast of warmth sear her cheeks and she turned back to her cooking, unable to bear the humiliation of that memory or the bluntness of Elijah's gaze.

"Smells better than Sunday dinner in here, Mrs. Payne," Captain Crowley offered. "If I didn't have to be hyperin' on up the coast, I might even invite myself to stay."

"You'll always be welcome at our table, Captain." She stirred the chowder. Not wanting the milk to boil, she swung the fireplace crane toward her and lifted the kettle off its hook.

"I might just take you up on that next time I'm in hailin' distance."

"Did you find the milk all right?" asked Elijah.

She shortened the iron trammel that hung from the crane and replaced the kettle on its hook. "I found it after a while." She swung the crane back. The kettle was a good eight inches higher above the flame now, so the milk would be less likely to boil. But she continued to stir it to give herself something to do. "I never would have thought to keep milk in the bedroom."

"No?" His voice sounded testy. "Where do you keep milk in Philadelphia?"

"In a cool closet in the dining room."

"I haven't got a dining room."

"Which, in inspecting your house, is the least of your problems."

Captain Crowley pulled on his jaw, thinking that the way this discussion was shaping up it was going to be a beauty. Too bad he couldn't stick around to catch the fireworks. "Gotta go, 'Lijah. Crew's prob'ly ready to have me keelhauled for takin' so long as it is. Take good care a the missus here, and I'll prob'ly see you in a few weeks. Nice makin' your acquaintance, Mrs. Payne."

Augusta lifted her hand in a gesture of farewell. She crossed a quick glance with Elijah to find him wearing discontentment on every feature of his face. But was he discontent because of their discussion or because he was disappointed with the way she looked?

He broke their gaze and nodded to Crowley. "I'll walk you back to the beach." He strode to the sink and picked up the two empty pails that sat on the floor. "You'll be needin' more spring water before the night's over," he said to Augusta, and without a word of farewell, he motioned Crowley out the door and left.

She peered across the room to watch the two men pass by the window. Elijah Payne was going to be trouble. She could feel it in her bones. But she wouldn't resort to batting her eyelashes at him to win his affection. "Capriciousness gains a woman neither influence nor friends," she muttered, giving the chowder a vigorous stir. Milk sloshed over the lip of the kettle and spilled onto the hot coals, filling the room with a terrible hissing that sounded worthy of the serpent that had tempted Eve. For an uncomfortable moment she eyed her surroundings, then, with a shrug of her shoulders, went back to work.

By the time Elijah returned, the chowder was ready, the johnnycakes were browning on the griddle, a sheet of gingersnaps was cooling in the pantry, and the table was set with the most hideous tinware Augusta had ever seen. It offended her sense of aesthetics to even dig the things out of the cupboard, but her own dishes were still packed away, so these would have to do. "Do you have any table linen?" she asked as he crossed the floor with the water-laden buckets. "Any napkins?"

He'd rolled his sleeves to his elbows, baring forearms that were solidly formed. Unclothed limbs were not a common part of Augusta's existence, but Elijah seemed unmindful of any breach of modesty. He hefted the pails into the dry sink, and when he did, the cords of muscle beneath his bare flesh thickened and slid in a display so purely masculine it commanded her full attention.

"Why do you need napkins?"

A whisper of sensation took root in the center of her chest and spiraled upward, bathing her with its odd warmth. Breathing deeply to dispel the sensation, she averted her eyes so he wouldn't catch her staring. "I've never sat down to supper without table linen."

Elijah shrugged his big shoulders. "I have." Making his way to the table, he pulled out a chair and sat down. He looked her full in the face, and this time she looked back.

"You might spill chowder on your trousers."

"Trousers can be washed."

"Yes, well . . . You'll need to wipe your mouth on something."

He held up both his hands, rotating them slowly for her inspection. "That's what these are for. If you don't wanna use yours, you can borrow one of mine. They can be washed too.''

One of her eyebrows shot up in an angry slant. "Indeed.'' She removed his soup bowl and plate from the table and strutted to the hearth. Table etiquette was not an area that was open to compromise, and she did not appreciate his making light of it.

She served him his chowder and johnnycake, and by the time she sat down with her own, he was halfway through his meal. She pursed her lips in exasperation. "It was kind of you to wait for me.''

"Don't have time to wait for you. I've got things to do.''

More important things than being polite to your new wife? she wanted to ask, but held her tongue. She slapped a dollop of butter on her johnnycake and watched it melt over the golden-brown mound. Elijah looked up at her between mouthfuls. She thought a few complimentary words about her culinary expertise might be forthcoming, considering the way he was devouring everything.

"Your face is awful white. And your eyes are red. You been cryin'?''

She lifted a finger to the corner of her eye as if in defense. Then she remembered. "The smoke on the paddle-steamer irritated my eyes. No, I haven't been crying. In fact, you will find, Mr. Payne, that I am not a woman easily given to tears.'' As for her face being white, of course it was white! She had to use a great deal of face powder to hide her freckles, but he didn't need to know that.

Elijah got up from the table to pour himself more chowder. When he sat back down, he rolled his sleeves higher above his elbows as if he were really getting down to serious eating. "I've never been on a paddle steamer."

"I would consider that a particular bit of good fortune."

"Why is that?"

He laid his left forearm on the table, circling it around his dishes like a protective wall. It was a casual gesture, but the allure of his bare flesh was distracting. "Paddle steamers make you—" She bit back the word "sick." She'd nearly forgotten that she wasn't going to mention her bout with seasickness to him. "They sully your clothes and burn your eyes." She paused, trying not to dwell on the soft, golden hairs that dusted his flesh from wrist to elbow. "Have . . . have you ever visited Philadelphia?"

"Never been off this island more than a day in my life. What's the matter? That surprise you?"

Shocked was a better term. She thought she'd seen such worldliness in his eyes. "I—"

"Not everyone has taken a fancy to locomotives and paddle steamers. The world's movin' so fast now I'm surprised it can keep up with itself. But it's not like that here on Devilstone. It's quiet here. The way it should be."

Augusta wondered if everyone on the island was as provincial as her husband. She toyed with her spoon, anxious to learn more. "If you've never been to Philadelphia, why did you advertise for a wife in a Philadelphia paper?"

"Philadelphia's as good a place as any. Got the results I wanted, didn't I?" He shoved his dishes to the side. "If that's gingerbread I smell coolin' in the pantry, I'll have some now."

She lowered her eyes to her own bowl to find it still full. He nodded toward the bowl's contents. "You plan on eating that?"

"Yes, I plan on eating that." Just because he'd wolfed down his own supper didn't mean he could start on hers.

"Good. You could do with a bit of fattenin' up. Looks to me like you probably have to stand twice in the sun to make a shadow."

She shot him a glacial look. "Indeed." If she was thin, it was all his fault. If he had thought to live someplace other than the middle of the Atlantic, she might have spent the past four days doing something other than avoiding the sight and smell of food.

Rising stiffly from her chair, she crossed the floor to the pantry, cut through the gingerbread, and slopped three spoonfuls of cream over Elijah's serving. When she stepped back into the kitchen, she found it hazy with smoke. Elijah had produced a cheroot from somewhere and was puffing contentedly, his eyes slatted against the enveloping mist as he watched her return to the table. She hadn't occupied a room with a cigar-smoking man for years—not since her father had died. The remembered smell struck a wistful chord within her, tantalizing her with a moment of quiet nostalgia.

"If the smoke bothers you, you can throw open a window or two." He didn't bother to remove the cigar from the crook of his mouth when he spoke, but his words were nonetheless distinct.

She slid the gingerbread across the table at him. "I'm fine." She remembered her father smoking his cheroots and sipping port in the sitting room after the evening meal. He would be dressed in a frock coat and starched neckcloth that elevated the art of smoking to an act of elegance. He never spoke while the cheroot was still clamped between his teeth and would certainly never think to light up in his bare feet with his shirtsleeves rolled above his elbows. Her father had smoked with dignity, with gentility. Elijah's enthusiasm for the habit seemed more basic, his enjoyment more sensual, more earthy.

She watched him dig into the gingerbread. A drop of cream splattered onto the tabletop, and without a care for propriety he wiped it up with a forefinger and licked the finger clean with his tongue. His teeth were even and strong; his tongue was dark and supple. He seemed to savor the taste of the cream in the same way that some men might savor the taste of a woman's mouth. It was too much to bear over cold fish chowder.

She fidgeted with the stem of her spoon before allowing her gaze to drift toward the window. "I've . . . I've noticed there are no curtains on any of your windows."

He shook his head while he chewed. "Don't need curtains."

"Blue and white gingham might be pleasant. Or maybe yellow. I could manage something presentable with four or five yards of fabric. Is there a dry-goods store on the island?"

"I just said"—he stopped chewing and speared her with his dark eyes—"we don't need curtains."

She disliked his tone but remained calm. "If you expect me to cook in this kitchen, Mr. Payne, I will have gingham hanging from those windows. Bare windows are an invitation to all manner of Peeping Tom. Perhaps the people of Devilstone wouldn't stoop to that kind of behavior, but I'd prefer not to place temptation in their path."

Elijah wiped his mouth with his fist, jammed his cheroot between his teeth, and angled away from the table on the back legs of his chair. "Haydon said he'd be back before winter sets in. You expectin' someone to pass by before then?"

Their eyes locked. Augusta's words were clipped. "Unless you have alienated the other residents of the island with your dreadful manners, I would expect you to be neighborly with them."

He grinned at that and blew a mouthful of smoke toward the ceiling. "We're it. There's you, and there's me, so unless you've got a notion about snoopin' around your own windows, you can stow the idea about curtains."

She stared at him, not quite comprehending his words. "There are no other people on this island?"

"Not alive, anyway. Caleb swallowed the anchor about three months ago."

"Caleb was . . . ?"

"My dog. Only a mongrel, but he was damn good company."

His face blurred before her eyes. She leaned back in her chair, too stunned for words. This wasn't what she had expected. This wasn't what she had expected at all. "You . . . you should have said something about this in your letter to me."

"What? Something about Caleb?"

"No! Something about your living alone here!"

"I did."

"You most certainly did not."

He removed his cheroot and frowned at her. "In my advertisement, I said I was a wickie. Have you ever known a wickie to live on an island where the population was more than one?"

"I've never known a wickie."

"No?" He clamped his cheroot between his teeth again.

"I suppose you wouldn't, bein' from Philadelphia. Not too many lighthouses in a big city."

"Lighthouse?" It fell into place with brutal swiftness. The tower outside. The pervasive quiet along the forest path. "You're a . . . a lighthouse keeper," she said, not believing her own words. There was no community, no common good, no one to appreciate her efforts. There was only her, and him, a dead dog named Caleb, and a fifty-foot tower. "Why didn't you come right out and *say* you were a lighthouse keeper?"

"The paper was chargin' by the letter! Wickie had fewer letters than lighthouse keeper."

"A wickie. How did you expect me to know what a wickie was?"

"If you didn't know, why the hell didn't you write and ask? I woulda told you. How the hell did you think I earned my livin'? Makin' candles?"

She hesitated. Color stained her cheeks. "That was my second choice."

"I'm not even gonna ask what your first choice was." The smoke from his cigar seemed to gather in an angry cloud around his head. The tip glowed like a fiery coal. "I said in my advertisement that I was lookin' for someone to help with light duties. What did you think that meant?"

"I obviously thought you meant light as opposed to heavy. Your phraseology was open for misinterpretation. You should have presented yourself as a lighthouse keeper on a deserted island."

"The island's not gonna be deserted if I'm livin' on it."

"But it's a clearer representation."

"Well, if that isn't a belch of claptrap. Anything else you wanna complain about while you're at it?"

"I'm not complaining."

"Seems to me you've done nothin' *but* complain since you arrived."

"Oh? Is that so. Well, perhaps if you'd done me the courtesy of greeting me with a bit more fanfare, I might have been better disposed to accept the situation here. I . . . I traveled a long way to get here, and you didn't even *inquire* how I fared on my journey."

"You were standin' under your own power and looked to be breathin'! What more should I of been interested in?"

She made an angry compress of her lips. "If you have to ask, I doubt my answer will make any sense to you."

"Lady, the only thing not makin' any sense around here is you. You blow in here like a nor'easter, jump down my throat for not askin' you the right questions, criticize my windows and my *phraseology*. Godfrey Mighty, I advertised for a creature who was fair-dispositioned. What did you think that meant? A woman who was disposed to attending fairs?"

"That is an extremely poor attempt at humor."

"Livin' on a *deserted* island, I haven't had too many people to practice on. Maybe that explains the problem with my phraseology." He stood up, nearly bumping his head on the lantern that hung over the table. "I've gotta milk Geraldine before I head up to tend the lanterns. You ever milked a cow before?"

"No. In Philadelphia—"

"I'll show you how tomorrow." He continued talking as he made his way to the door. "I eat breakfast at seven when I come down from the tower. Anything you wanna make. I sleep from nine 'til noon, then spend the rest of the day doin' chores. You have any questions, you can climb the

cylinder to ask, but it sounds to me like you have all the answers already, so I won't expect to see you."

The kitchen door opened and closed. She heard his footsteps fade. "You're welcome for the meal," she muttered
over her shoulder, unsure exactly what had just transpired,
but knowing that whatever it was, it had gone badly. She
didn't even know Elijah Payne, and already she'd managed
her first argument with him. She'd hoped her first day of
married life might have ended differently than this. She'd
hoped . . .

Oh, what did it matter what she hoped? She was living
on an island with a man who lacked all sense of aesthetics,
decorum, or modesty. The twins, no doubt, would be
delighted.

Propping her elbows on the table, she braced her chin
on the heel of her palms and sighed. "Welcome to Devilstone Island, Mrs. Payne."

It took her a little less than an hour to tidy the kitchen.
Afterward, she retreated to the bedroom to begin the work
of unpacking her trunks, but once the lids of all three trunks
lay open, she began to bristle with angry frustration. The
man hadn't even bothered to clean out a bureau drawer
for her! What was he saying, "I'll let you live here, just
don't let me see any evidence of it"? The slight cut deeply
into the veneer of hopefulness she had wrapped around
herself. Such a little thing, but it seemed to augur what
she could expect from Elijah Payne.

Overcome with sudden weariness, she sat on the edge of
the bed and smoothed her palm over the low post of the
footboard. She closed her eyes and bowed her head, and
when she felt moisture squeeze beneath her eyelids, she
dashed it away before it could wet her cheeks. She was

made of stronger stuff than this. But sometimes . . . sometimes she tired of being the one who was always strong. Sometimes the struggle just didn't seem worth the reward.

A gust of wind rattled the windows on either side of the headboard, prompting her to look toward the sound. Shadows had already formed in the north, swallowing the daylight. In Philadelphia she guessed that at this very hour the sun was still bright overhead. So, days would be shorter here on Devilstone Island. Drying her eyes on the back of her hand, she walked to the window.

Green grass carpeted the earth from below her window to the edge of the cliff, a distance of between some twenty-five to thirty yards. Beyond that she could see nothing but the evening sky dressed in shifting layers of mauve and blue. Another blast of wind hammered into the glass. In response she flattened her palm against the windowpane. Air rushed between the sash bars to bathe her fingers with coolness. She wondered how cold the room would become in a few months with the winds of winter blowing through the sash bars. The room didn't even boast a fireplace for warmth. "Neither fireplace nor husband," she whispered as she angled her head to glimpse the tower, but it was beyond her view from here. Did he stay up there all night long? He'd implied as much. He spent his nights in the tower, his mornings sleeping, and his afternoons doing chores. She wondered if he ever intended to spend any time with her, or if she was here simply to cook his meals. Perhaps she was simply too unimportant for him to fit into his schedule.

But it's not supposed to be this way. Life here was supposed to be different.

She wandered back to her trunks. Over the years, she

had hand stitched a considerable amount of linen for a trousseau which, until recently, she'd thought never to use—a dozen and a half nightgowns, a dozen chemises, a half-dozen nightcaps—articles she suspected would last her for the rest of her life. She'd sewn both plain and fancy pieces—some with plain cording, some with intricate embroidery—but she'd fashioned a special gown for her wedding night and on a whim, removed it from the tissue in which it had been wrapped.

It was made of fine white cotton batiste that flowed softly to the middle of her calves. The neckline dipped low, hugging the swell of her bosom, and the sleeves were the barest puffs of lace that fell daringly off her shoulders. Sleek lines rather than tiers of ruffles and flounces. She thought the style more suited to a woman of her advanced years.

She smoothed her fingertips over the cotton, thinking she would gladly trade all the nightgowns in Philadelphia for some sign of Elijah's affection. She would have welcomed the touch of his hand on her cheek tonight, the shared warmth of their body heat, but it seemed she was not comely enough to inspire any husbandly affection. He was obviously more interested in his lighthouse than he was in his wife. In Philadelphia she had always played second best to her sisters. Now she had the honor of playing second best to a lighthouse. She was no longer an old maid in Philadelphia, but despite the change in outward appearances, it seemed everything in her life had remained the same.

The room was quiet save for the intermittent rattle of window panes, so she stared out the darkening glass for a long time, thinking about what her wedding night should have been like, and wishing for the touch of a warm hand on her tear-stained cheek.

—4—

"Can you swim?" The voice was a harsh intrusion upon her slumber, as was the light that was suddenly thrust before her face. She threw her covers over her head to block out the glare, but Elijah was persistent. He whipped the covers off her face and held the lantern so close she could feel its warmth glazing her cheek. "Can you?"

She splayed her fingers over her eyes and wetted the inside of her mouth with her tongue. "Can I what?" Her voice was hoarse with sleep.

"Can you swim?"

"No." As she made to turn over on her side, he tossed all her blankets off her and grasped her around her upper arm.

"Doesn't matter. I'll tie a line around you in case you fall outta the boat."

"Boat?" The word hit her like a lightning bolt. Instantly awake, she struggled to sit upright while wrestling with Elijah for control of her arm. "Let go my arm. What boat?"

He dragged her toward the edge of the bed. "The rescue boat. Sit there and wake up. Where are your galoshes?" Not waiting for an answer, he hastened toward her trunks, ready to tear into one of them. "Which one?"

She shivered with cold and winced at the still-glaring light. "I . . . I don't know. One of them. At the bottom. But why are you looking for my galoshes at this time of night?" She thought she heard him curse. Adjusting to her wakefulness, she inched her nightgown over her knees and crisscrossed her arms over her bosom.

"There's no time to look." He hurried back to her. "You'll have to wear one of mine."

"One of your what?"

"Slickers. C'mon." He pulled her off the bed. She stifled a shriek as her feet hit the floor.

"You . . . *ahhrrr* . . . thefloorisfreezing!"

He herded her out of the room ahead of him. "This is nothin'. Wait 'til February."

"Wait a . . . Stop pushing me, will you! *Where are you taking me?*"

He set his lantern down on the kitchen table and let go of her arm. "Ship's foundering off the ledge to windward." He reached for a length of canvas that was slung over one of the chair backs. "If it goes down, we'll need to bring in survivors. You can help bail out the boat. Hold your arms up so I can get this over your head."

"But—" Numbed by what he was saying, she none-

theless stretched her arms over her head. "What ledge?
You never mentioned anything about a ledge." Which
made her wonder what else he'd never said anything about.

"Call it the Devil's Elbow." He angled the canvas
slicker over her head. She poked her hands into the arm-
holes and shivered as the rain gear slid down her arms. It
smelled damp and musty and thudded heavily onto her
shoulders. "Why did you think there's a lighthouse here?"
he asked.

Augusta shrugged. "Because it's dark."

He shook his head as he cuffed her sleeves. "The light
warns ships about the ledge. There." He finished rolling
the sleeves to her fingertips. She looked down at herself.
The slicker was so long that only three inches of cotton
batiste hung below. It was stiff as pasteboard and had to
weigh at least fifty pounds. She felt like a mast wearing
a sail. She fanned her toes for his observation.

"What about my feet?"

"Shoes'll only get wet. You'll be better off in bare feet.
Your hood." He threw the slicker's hood over the deep
frills of her nightcap, yanked hard on the drawstrings, and
triced up a knot under her chin. "You're all set. Let's
go." Grabbing her hand and the lantern, he led her out
the back door, hurrying her through the woodshed, a coal
shed, a toolshed, and finally stopping in a room that looked
to be glutted with foul-weather gear. He hung the lantern
overhead, snatched another slicker off a wall peg, and
threw it on over his head. On him the material fell to
midthigh.

"This way." With lantern in hand, he directed her to
a side door and flung it open. A blast of wind slammed it
back against the wall. Augusta startled at the sound and

with great trepidation peered into the blackness beyond the portal.

"It's raining." How could they attempt a rescue mission in the rain?

"You're lucky it's not ice. Watch your step." He forged into the darkness as if the night held no secrets for him. Augusta raced along behind him, her hand locked within his bone-crushing grip, her stride lengthening to keep pace. The lighthouse was at her back. They were moving eastward, away from it. She wished instead she were walking toward it. The night seemed an unfamiliar beast without benefit of sidewalks and streetlamps.

Rain sliced into her face, stinging like thorns. Bending her head, she angled her forearm against her brow and charged blindly behind Elijah. The wet grass was slick beneath her feet, causing her to skid once or twice, almost losing her balance. Elijah tightened his grip on her and yelled over his shoulder, "Stay clear of the cliff! Step off the edge and you're fish bait!"

It was the most endearing thing he'd said to her since her arrival. From the tail of her eye she tried to see the lip of the precipice, but it was obscured by shadow. She heard the thunderous boom of the surf below her, though, and felt the bedrock tremble as it absorbed the sea's fury. The sounds were alien and frightening, and they grew louder as Elijah put more distance between himself and the lighthouse. She imagined what she could not see— breakers hurling themselves into the headlands, the sea beaten into an angry froth. And everywhere the rumbling—as if some beast caged within the bowels of the island was growling its discontent.

"There's a walkway here!" shouted Elijah. He lowered

the lantern for her to see. "It'll be slippery! Watch your footing!" It was constructed of wooden slats and was indeed more slippery than the grass had been. It started as a ramp, but as it veered over the rocks, it became a series of steps that led ever downward. A hollow roar echoed back to her from a chasm below. The wind whipped into her body, flattening the slicker against her thighs. Her naked calves felt battered by wind and rain. Her toes were numb. She squinted into the darkness. Eerie shadows hovered around her like angels of death. Rocks. Above her. Below her. And in the light given off from Elijah's lantern, she saw another shadow. An outbuilding nestled among the rocks.

Elijah quickened his pace toward the building and threw open the door. He rushed Augusta in ahead of him.

The floor slanted away from her, sloping toward the opposite end of the building, which, much to her surprise, had no wall enclosing it. Elijah hurried in behind her and hung the lantern on a low rafter overhead. The building was about the size of their kitchen. At its center was a winch and a double-ended boat that was secured upon a wooden cradle. The cradle was positioned on a set of tracks similar to the trackway she had seen on the beach when she'd arrived. She glanced toward the open end of the building, eyeing the tracks as they snaked into the darkness beyond the boathouse. It was not a sight that inspired confidence.

Elijah directed her toward a bucket on a wall shelf. "Smear some a that on your feet and legs."

Walking over to the shelf, she peeked at the contents of the bucket. It was slimy and viscous and black and not a substance that she intended should come into contact with any part of her body. "What is it?"

"Axle grease. I use it to grease the trackways, but it'll go a long way to keep your legs warm."

Her tongue curled with revulsion. "Thank you, but . . . I don't think so." When she turned, she found him standing so close beside her that she shuffled sideways to allow herself space.

"Water in this part've the Atlantic is so cold, it can make your flesh feel like it's burnin'." With that he dipped his hand into the bucket, scooped up a black gob, and before she had a chance to react, he was on his haunches, slapping the grease onto her shin.

"Eechhh!" She hobbled backward and shooed him away with her hand, but he seized her calf, halting her retreat.

"Hold still, dammit! I don't have time to fuss with you." And because she couldn't go anywhere with his hand shackling her leg, she stood obediently as he smeared the grease from her toes to her knees. His manner was brusque and impersonal. He was touching her more intimately than any man had ever touched her, but he was acting as if she was just another piece of machinery whose parts needed maintenance.

"That should do you." He reached for a rag to wipe his hands.

Augusta braced her feet apart and grimaced at the unsightly slime blackening her legs. It clung to the hem of her nightgown like paste, staining the intricate embroidery she had spent so many hours stitching. A knot of emotion formed in her throat. It was ruined. Completely ruined.

But did Elijah Payne apologize for that? No. All he could say was, "Climb into the boat, Gus. We've got a night's work ahead of us yet."

"Gus?" Her face mirrored disbelief.

"Somethin' wrong with Gus?"

"Yes, there's something wrong with it. It's not my name."

Grasping a handful of slicker, he scooted her in the direction of the boat. "Augusta's too fancy. Too many syllables. Sit in the bow." She wrested her sleeve from his grasp with a self-righteous jerk. A small, movable staircase flanked the boat and cradle. Seething inwardly at the unsolicited mutilation of her name, she climbed the four stairs and stepped over the gunwale into the boat. *Too many syllables?* She fumed as she clambered over the center thwart to the bow. *How many syllables does he think Elijah has?* Sitting stonily on the bow thwart, she tapped her fingers against her slicker while her eyes darted about the interior of the boat.

Lashed to the side of the boat was a lance with a flat, barbed head gleaming at one end. A length of rope was attached to the opposite end of the lance, and this was paid out into a wooden tub that was fixed to the bottom of the boat. The lance fit her description of what she thought a harpoon might look like, but it made no sense to her to carry a harpoon in a boat unless you were in jeopardy of being attacked by a whale.

Her breath seemed to freeze in her lungs. *A whale?* Was this something else he hadn't bothered to tell her? Pivoting around on her seat to find him, she stabbed an accusing finger at him. "This harpoon is here for a reason, isn't it?"

He released a crank on the drum of the winch. The boat lurched backward, forcing her to brace her feet on the floor to prevent herself from being thrown into the center thwart. She gritted her teeth. A warning might have been nice.

Elijah bounded up the stairs and into the boat. He stepped over the center thwart and removed a coil of rope from where it hung around his shoulder.

"The harpoon," she persisted.

"Lift your arms out to the side. I wanna loop this rope 'round your middle."

She made a T of her arms. Her voice rose half an octave. "You're expecting to kill a whale with that harpoon, aren't you?"

"Could. If I see one." He circled the rope around her waist, knotted it, then roved the loose end through an iron ring at the bow and tied it off.

"So you admit there are whales in these waters?"

He bent over to retrieve something on the floor behind her. "Might be, but I've never seen one. Here, take this." He shoved a wooden piggin into her hands. "You can use that to bail."

She stared at the bucket. It was similar to a sap bucket and different from an ordinary bucket in that instead of being designed with an arched wooden handle, it had one stave longer than the rest that served as a handle. "How did you bail water prior to my arrival?"

He seated himself on the center thwart, facing her, and regarded her with eyes that seemed to burn into her skull. "I didn't. I did what I had to do with eight, sometimes twelve inches of water sloshin' around my ankles. So when I tell you, 'Bail!', you damn well better bail."

She narrowed her eyes at him, disliking him more intensely with every word he spewed. He was crude, and insensitive, and meaner than a blind spider. And if he continued in this same vein, he would be *wearing* the piggin he'd given her, not telling her to bail with it.

He readied his oars by thrusting them between their thole pins. Leaning to his left, he placed his hand on a lever that rose above the gunwale. "When I release this, we're gonna shoot down this slip faster than a go-devil. Hang on, lady, 'cause you're about to take a ride into the blackest corner of perdition."

He pulled back on the lever.

The winch rope creaked. The boat pitched backward. And then they were careening down the slip like a log sluicing down a flume.

The darkness struck her full in the face. The boat jolted and bucked. Her jaw rattled. Her breath vibrated in her windpipe. She hugged the piggin to her chest and choked down a cry as the boat skidded off the tracks and thumped headlong into the surf.

The vessel bobbed like a cork in a cauldron. Augusta crouched low on her seat to escape the wind, but it tore into her with relentless force, nearly ripping the hood from her head. Elijah was a dark shape consumed by shadow. She could not see him clearly, but she could hear him straining at the oars, could hear the oars chafing against their thole pins. His strokes were short and chopping, not pretty strokes, but powerful fisherman's strokes that muscled them through the heavy seas more vigorously than if the boat had been driven by steam. A wise man should have been daunted by the situation, but Elijah showed no signs of fright. She tried to find strength in his confidence. He had obviously done things like this before and survived, so perhaps she had no cause for worry. But just in case, she whipped off an abbreviated version of the Lord's Prayer.

Waves slashed into them—ten feet high and capped with foaming white. And like a man blowing the head off a mug of ale, the wind sheared the froth from the waves and sent it showering upon them, dousing them more thoroughly than the rain had. "Bail!" shouted Elijah.

Water sloshed over her toes. Bending over, she scraped the piggin against the bottom of the boat, scooping up what water she could, then in one motion sat up and heaved the contents of the piggin over the gunwale.

The wind spat every drop back in her face.

She let out a startled cry. Her mouth tasted of briny water. Her nostrils burned with it.

"Damn fool!" bellowed Elijah. "Throw it *down*wind!"

Backlit by Devilstone's beacon light, Elijah's face took on a ghoulish cast. She slatted her eyes at him. She didn't appreciate being called a fool. Glaring back at him, she clutched her empty piggin and slid across her thwart to the opposite side of the boat.

A wall of water rose behind Elijah. Augusta shrieked out an incomprehensible sound of warning, but the boat reared like a wild horse and rose high onto the crest of the wave, riding the summit for an eternal moment before plunging down the opposite wall into a waiting trough, prancing and bobbing until another breaker rose in the wake of the other.

"Keep . . . bailing!"

Disbelieving that they were still afloat, Augusta bent her back to the task at hand. Scooping and tossing, scooping and tossing. She clung to the gunwale as they climbed the face of another wave and suffered a pang of nausea as they swooped down its curved back. Spindrift sprayed over them. It stung her cheeks and numbed her flesh. She fought down her nausea. With less alacrity than before, she resumed bailing.

The waves were incessant, but Elijah was tireless as he powered them toward the foundering ship. Augusta couldn't gauge how far from the island they were, but in the light diffused from the tower she spied a solitary mast canting sharply. No ship. Only a single spire draped in a jumble of spars, lines, and sail. "There!" She flung her hand toward the specter.

Elijah swung his torso around to look. He nodded, then quickened the rhythm of his strokes.

The sea appeared calmer where the ship had foundered. Thinking her eyes were playing her false, Augusta squinted to see more clearly. But the image remained. The sea was less violent in a wide swathe around the mast. The swells were gentler. Their foaming caps of white were gone. It was an eerie sight, but a welcome one.

In a dozen strokes, Elijah guided them into the oasis. The change was immediate. He hauled the oars into the boat and leaned over the gunwale, dipping his hand into the water. When he straightened, he smoothed the pad of his thumb across his fingertips as if he felt residue there, then touched one finger to the tip of his tongue.

"Oil. Tastes like"—he tested his finger again—"palm oil. Probably what that rig was carrying. Looks like they dumped a few barrels after they hit the ledge to flatten the swells."

Augusta kept bailing, knowing she was losing the war with her seasickness. She didn't want to humiliate herself by retching at Elijah's feet, but if she didn't lie down soon, that's exactly what would happen. She hoped there were survivors from the wreck, but more than that, she prayed they would make their presence apparent so they could be rescued quickly.

Elijah unlashed his harpoon. Hefting it in his right hand, he eased himself upward, straddling the center thwart for balance. "Be still," he cautioned her.

Thankful for the reprieve, she stopped bailing in favor of angling her shoulder against the side of the boat for support.

"Ahhhoooy!" Elijah sang out. His eyes ranged over the oily surf. Water broke across the submerged ledge and dragged the mast farther into its depths. The night echoed with the sounds of screaming timber. But no human voice responded to Elijah's hail.

"Ahhhoy!" he called again. Augusta turned her face into the crook of her arm to escape the driving rain. It splatted against her slicker in an almost deafening staccato, but it was not so loud as to drown out the voice that cried out to them. She snapped her head up. Elijah heard it too. His body was suddenly straight as a gun barrel.

"How good are your eyes, Gus?"

"Not as good as that man needs them to be." She peered into the shadows.

"Say again!" Elijah called out, but the only sound that echoed back was the creak of timber.

Unable to see anything by looking straight on, Augusta sidled a glance from the corner of her eye, a tack that seemed to aid her night vision. A flat, dark shape bobbed some distance away, but it appeared to be nothing more than wreckage from the ship.

"Over there." She pointed toward it.

"Six points off the port bow. I see it." He paused as if studying the flotsam, then, "That's it. He's there. I can see him." He took aim with his harpoon.

Augusta's eyes widened. "My God, what are you doing? You'll kill him with that thing!"

He looked a mighty warrior as he drew back his arm and hurled the lance. The boat wobbled. The rope snaked out of the tub as it chased the lance through the air. There was a whooshing sound and a far-off thud, and then Elijah was pulling the rope slowly back toward him, hand over hand, as sure and steady as a clock.

"I hope you speared the wreckage and not the man." She watched in silence. In her lifetime she had never had occasion to keep company with men who were actively engaged in physical labor. Her father and his associates were bankers, accustomed to pushing quill pens across ledgers, not hurling harpoons through the air. The sophistication of the banking profession certainly had its appeal, but it suddenly paled in comparison to Elijah's untutored efforts. She watched his hands pull steadily on the rope. She watched his big shoulders swing easily beneath the strain, and she felt an emotion stir within her that was as unfamiliar as it was inappropriate, considering the circumstances. But she had never seen a man boast such physical prowess. To witness his exertions and his calm self-assurance was a heady thing.

She cupped her hands around her mouth so he could hear her next question. "What can I do to help?" Despite her nausea, she was inspired by his endeavors and felt the need to make a positive contribution to the rescue.

"There's a blanket stowed in a locker aft of the stern thwart! Dig it out for me! But stay low and go easy!"

Nestling the piggin behind the bow thwart, she steeled herself against the agony of movement and pried herself off the seat. She could not see that where the ship had foundered, water began to gush upward around the mast, rising higher and higher until only a yardarm remained, and then nothing at all. Elijah saw it and quickened his movements.

Augusta was maneuvering her way over the center thwart when she heard her husband's voice. "Bear a hand!" In a flurry of movement she scrambled to the side of the boat and looked down.

The man was lying atop a wide piece of planking, but he was so tangled in cable that she could barely make out his form. His legs were dangling in the water from his knees downward. Elijah had found the waistband of the man's breeches and was clinging with all his might. The boat listed ominously.

"Clap on to his breeches here! And don't let go! I can't get him free of the lines. Have to cut him out!"

She reached out her arm. He caught her hand and guided it to the man's waist, then snugged her fingers around the wet cloth. "Use both hands if you have to!" Elijah let go, and then there was nothing to prevent the man from floating away except the strength of Augusta's right arm. The wreckage bumped the gunwale. The collision jolted her elbow and twisted her wrist. Her grip slackened. She leaned farther over the gunwale and grabbed with her other hand. Elijah produced a knife from beneath his slicker and began to slice through the lines that fettered the man.

"Hurry!" pleaded Augusta. The current tugged at the wreckage. She could feel it drifting away.

Elijah sliced and hacked. Rope flew. The space between boat and wreckage widened. Augusta gritted her teeth. She saw Elijah throw the lines off the man and clamp his hand around the man's arm.

"I've got him! I'm gonna slide him this way and haul him aboard. Lever your hands under his thigh and lift!"

She struggled to lift him upward. Elijah gave a mighty heave. The gunwale dipped to within six inches of the water's surface. Seawater rushed over the side. Elijah muscled the man's torso over the gunwale. Augusta circled her arms around the man's thigh and wrenched backward on it. His leg thunked over the gunwale. She fell backward with its weight, but the man was safely aboard.

"I can manage from here!" shouted Elijah. "Get that blanket!"

Her nightgown was soaked. Her drawers were soaked. But the fact that she'd helped drag the man to safety filled her with exhilaration. She felt buoyant, invincible. Nodding to Elijah, she wriggled out from where the man's leg had pinned her to the bottom of the boat and boosted herself to her knees. She crawled over the other center thwart, then, with a cautious movement, stood up and leaned over the stern thwart in search of the locker where the blanket was stowed.

She didn't see the wake from the sunken vessel bearing down upon them. She heard Elijah yell, "Gi' down, Gus!" But in the instant that she twisted around to divine the cause of his distress, the first swell struck. The boat pitched to starboard, then lurched back to port. Augusta staggered left, then right. She threw her arms out for balance but found balance impossible. The next swell sent her reeling sideways. She slammed into the side of the boat. She felt pain, a rush of frigid air. She flailed desperately with her arms, but she was falling, falling.

The Atlantic drowned out her scream.

Cold. Paralyzing cold. The shock numbed her limbs, her senses. The water was dense and black and dragged her downward as if she were a plummet. Her knuckles were bruised. They screamed out in pain. Her eyesockets were so cold, she thought they might burst. Her teeth and gums began to throb. Her jaw seemed instantly frozen. Her muscles cramped. She began to thrash with legs and arms to save herself, but the blackness was so thick she couldn't distinguish up from down. She wrestled with the water, spinning around in her helplessness. Her limbs grew heavy. Pain shot through her temples. Her lungs began to burn. She wanted to breathe. She *had* to breathe. But there was no air, only images that winked cruelly in her mind's eye and voices that cackled in her ear.

Her throat constricted. She clawed at the water. She kicked. *I don't want to die!* But the blackness pressed down upon her, smothering, strangling.

The sudden tightening around her waist nearly sliced her in two. The rope. She'd forgotten about the rope. She was wrenched backward, and up. Her head broke the surface. She choked on her first breath of air. An arm manacled itself around her waist, and in the next moment she was lying in the bottom of the boat, looking up into the face of an angry Elijah.

"I *told* you to get down! What are you? Deaf?"

She coughed in his face. She sucked draft after draft of air into her lungs and made reply to his question by turning on her side and wheezing. Her limbs shook with emotion, with cold, and she suddenly wanted to retch.

"Women," spat Elijah. Leaning over the stern thwart, he threw open the locker and removed a wool blanket. He shook it open and dropped it over her. "Stay where you are, and *don't* get up 'til I tell you. Understand?"

She nodded weakly. Her teeth were chattering so badly, she was afraid she might bite through her tongue.

Elijah grabbed another blanket and draped it over the seaman, who was lying in the space forward of Augusta. He then climbed back to his thwart to man the oars. Augusta boosted herself up for a moment. She reached her arm across the seat toward the seaman and found his hand beneath the blanket.

He was so cold. So very cold.

She stretched his arm across the seat, and as they made their way back to Devilstone, she clung to his hand, willing him to live. Her touch was the only comfort she could offer him at the moment, but she knew that in some instances, a touch offered more than just warmth. It offered hope.

She remembered little of the return trip other than the chills and the cold and the burning in her windpipe. They didn't return to the boathouse. Elijah rowed them to the inner side of the island, and whether by instinct or dint of will, maneuvered the boat onto a narrow slice of beach that separated two massive arteries of bedrock. He hauled the boat above the high-water mark, then disappeared for several minutes, returning with a lantern, which he set on the stern thwart. With a steady hand he separated Augusta's fingers from the seaman's.

"Can you stand?"

She was still shivering so badly, she wasn't sure what she was capable of doing. "I th-think so." She forced herself to her elbows, and as she paused to muster her strength, Elijah slid his hands beneath her arms and lifted her high over the gunwale, setting her aright on the beach. She leaned against him as he unknotted the rope from around her waist.

"There's a path behind that outbuilding there." He grabbed the lantern and held it high so she could see what he was talking about. "It's a narrow dirt path and it hugs the rock formation that slopes off to the left. Follow it all the way to the top. The path to the house'll be right in front of you when you get there. You take the lantern." He closed her fingers over the metal handle. "I can find my way in the dark."

Her limbs were so stiff and her muscles so tight from shivering, she wasn't sure she could walk, but with warmth waiting at the end of the path, she knew it would behoove her to try. She managed two awkward steps before stopping to shine the light on the seaman in the boat. The blanket hid his face from view. "I sh-should stay and help you with him."

"I'll do what needs be done."

And she had no doubt he would.

Stiff-legged and wretched, she found her way back to the house. The lighthouse beacon still eyed into the blackness, but the house was dark as a cave. She entered through the woodshed and for a long, dazed moment stood in the doorway to the kitchen, not quite sure what to do, what to feel. The lantern weighed heavily on her arm. Her fingers felt as if they had stiffened permanently around the metal handle. Sick inside, she forced herself to move again, one foot then the other, one foot then the other. She had to build a fire. The seaman would need the heat from a fire when Elijah carried him back, and there was no one to do it but her.

Still dressed in her slicker an hour later, she was seated before the fire on a low stool, staring into the flames that leaped around the burning wood, when she heard a voice behind her.

"Did you have to track so much mud on the floor?"

She turned around to find Elijah standing in the doorway. He had removed his slicker and was toweling his hair dry. "I'm sorry. I didn't hear you."

"I said, did you have to track so much mud on the floor?"

She lowered her eyes to the footprints she'd left on the floorboards. She blinked dumbly. "The floor? You're asking me . . ." Rage suddenly devoured her lethargy. "I nearly drown tonight trying to help you, and you have the gall to ask me why I left mud on your floor?"

"You should've stayed low. I *told* you to stay low."

"You *told* me to fetch a blanket! And you needn't yell, Mr. Payne. Contrary to what you might think, I am *not* deaf."

"First rule of order in a rogue sea," Elijah persisted. "Don't stand up in the boat. How come you're still wearin' that slicker?"

"Because I've been too busy building this God-blessed fire to take the God-blessed thing off yet! That's why!"

"I don't remember advertisin' for a wife who had a notion to cuss."

"And *I* don't remember asking for a husband who would wake me in the middle of the night to drag me barefoot through the rain, truss me like a fowl, and tie me to the bow of a boat!''

"You're a bitter weed, aren't you? Squawkin' make you feel better?''

"No!'' Then hearing the shrillness of her own voice, she looked away self-consciously and shook her head. "No. It doesn't.'' She bowed her head, contrite for her outburst when she should be concerning herself with more serious matters. "Where is the seaman?''

"The same place you'd be if I hadn't trussed you like a God-blessed fowl and tied you to the bow of the God-blessed boat. He's dead.''

Something cold and leaden settled in the pit of her stomach. "But I heard him cry out. How could he be dead?"

"That's the way of it. He was pretty far through when we hauled him aboard."

Stunned, she drew her hand to her chest and cradled it against her canvas slicker. She'd held his hand to give him hope, but he had died even before she'd seen his face. It seemed a terribly cruel, a terribly lonely way to die. "I'm sorry," she whispered.

"Needn't be sorry on my account. I didn't know the man. He might a been a jeezly cuss for all I know. Mighta beat his wife and kicked his dog. I did what I could for him. That has to be good enough."

"But—"

"A man can't waste time feelin' sorry for every blighter who hears the angel call. And if you don't climb outta that wet rig, you're gonna hear that same angel singin' in your ear."

She regarded his face as he stood in the doorway. Could he be so lacking in compassion that he felt no grief over the loss of this man's life? Dear Lord, what manner of man had she married? "Would you have felt even a twinge of sorrow had I drowned tonight rather than the seaman?"

He bowed his head toward her legs. "You'd better wash that grease off before you crawl under the kelp."

"You didn't answer my question."

"You ask too many questions."

"Quite the contrary. I believe I'm guilty of asking too few."

He drilled her a look with eyes that were slate dark and resentful. "You do what you want down here, but don't come cryin' to me when your lungs get filled up with the pneumonia. I gotta head back up the tower." And head back to the tower he did, leaving her in a room that was unnaturally quiet save for the crackle of burning wood. For a moment she thought of the advertisement he had written for the Philadelphia paper. His words had made him sound such a thoughtful, caring man. But in truth, he was neither of those things. He was insensitive and callous, and his advertisement had been a lie.

"I've buried the seaman in the buryin' point. You wanna come down while I say some words over his grave?"

The volume of her husband's voice roused her from a sound sleep. Heart in her throat, she jackknifed upright, swiveling her head to find him standing calmly with his arms cradled around a milk pan. She exhaled her breath and fired him an exasperated look.

"Has it ever crossed your mind to wake a person with a simple 'Good morning,' or 'Hello?' "

"Can't say that it has."

"Do you suppose you might consider it?"

He shrugged. "Might." He set the milk pan on the dresser then lent a curious gaze to the rest of the room. Each of the room's four windows was wearing a flannel nightdress, spread-eagled over the glass like angels without heads. He tightened his lips then regarded her with those near black eyes of his. "You wanna come or not?"

He'd been up all night, but he looked fresh as morning itself. She wondered how he could command such vigor. She'd slept for several hours but felt as if she'd been trampled by wild elephants. She probably looked like it, too.

"I'll go with you," she finally said. "We might not have been able to save the man's life, but our prayers might do something toward the salvation of his soul."

"Hoist a stocking to your jib, then. I'll give you ten minutes."

She shook her head at him as he started to leave. "Is there a part of your life that isn't dictated by time restraints? You've been in a hurry ever since I arrived. Hurry and get supper. Hurry and get out of bed."

" 'The soul of the sluggard desireth, and hath nothing: but the soul of the diligent shall be made fat' Proverbs, Chapter 13, Verse 4. Nine minutes left now."

" 'Hurry is only good for catching flies,' " she recited to his retreating back. And when he broke his stride to glance over his shoulder at her, she flashed him a wry smile. "Augusta Mayhew Payne."

She dressed quickly, coiled her hair into a bun at her

nape, and dug out a pair of sturdy leather shoes for her feet. She splashed water onto her face to rid the sleep from her eyes, then, thinking to soften the effect of her freckles, she found her jar of facial powder and with her fingertips spread the cosmetic over her cheeks and nose.

Elijah was waiting for her outside the kitchen door, Bible open in his hand, his back flush against the house for support. "Not a second too soon." He slammed the Bible shut. "Your time's up." He gazed down at her, appearing as if he might say something else, but when he regarded her face, a look of such shock filled his eyes that she felt a self-conscious warmth crawl up her neck.

She brushed her knuckles against the ridge of her cheekbone. "What are you looking at?"

He looked stunned for another moment before pushing off from the house and nodding toward the woods. "Not lookin' at anything. You need to use the convenience on the way by?" He headed out along the path. Augusta took several quick steps before falling into stride behind him. The outhouse sat at the edge of the woods, downwind of the house, but it affronted her sense of dignity to think that Elijah would be waiting outside the door for her, knowing what she was attending to inside. In fact, it affronted her sense of dignity that he would even ask!

"Thank you, but I've no wish to delay you any longer than I already have."

"Suit yourself."

They walked in silence, listening to the *plop* and *splat* of raindrops falling from the trees. The water slickened the pine needles that carpeted the path, making their passage rather treacherous, but Elijah plodded onward, never turning his head once to see if Augusta was following.

She began to wonder if he'd stop to help her up if she lost her balance. As he set off down one of the side paths she'd seen the day before, she decided he probably wouldn't even notice if she failed to arrive at the burial point. Sighing her frustration, she raced down the path behind him.

She'd expected the burial point to be an actual point of land, but it wasn't. It was simply a small fenced plot of earth located beyond the tree line on the inner shore of the island. Within the fence there were several long mounds of stone, each marked by a wooden cross that bore the weathered inscription of the deceased. As she followed Elijah through the gate, Augusta tilted her head to read the inscriptions. One read:

UNKNOWN SAILOR
1825

Another:

DROWNED MAN
1816

She paused at the base of this mound and ranged her eyes over the congery of gray stones. The plot was well-kept, but bleak, seeming a terribly woeful place to lay men who had once been strong and vital. She thought of her parents' gravesite in Philadelphia, with its clipped green grass and potted geraniums. The site was surrounded by two generations of Mayhew markers and seemed a far kinder resting place. Indeed, she could never have countenanced her parents' bones being interred beneath a pile of rocks. But if she remained on this island, this is where she would be buried—beneath Devilstone granite, beside strangers without names. A shiver raced up her spine at this grim look into her future.

"It's over here," called Elijah. He stopped before a mound in the far corner of the plot and opened his Bible. Augusta hurried toward him, but he began to recite the psalm before she could take her place beside him.

" 'The Lord is my Shepherd; I shall not want—' "

She slid to a halt and bowed her head.

" 'He maketh me to lie down in green pastures: He leadeth me beside the still waters—' "

The stones were all neatly placed over the man they had tried to save last night. She wondered how Elijah had worked so quickly to bury him. He should be exhausted from lugging so many rocks. Where had he found them?

" '. . . Yea, though I walk through the valley of the shadow of death, I will fear no evil . . .' "

She shifted her gaze to regard his bare feet. Did the man never don a pair of shoes? The soles of her own feet were raw from going shoeless last night. His feet would have to be boot-leather tough to endure the rigors the terrain had to offer. It seemed fitting, though. His feet were tough as shoe leather, and his heart was cold as pond ice.

" 'Surely goodness and mercy shall follow me all the days of my life: and I will dwell in the house of the Lord for ever. Amen.' "

"Amen," she repeated.

He closed the Bible. "Didn't have time to rig up a marker yet. Have to do that this afternoon after chores."

Augusta made a half-turn away from him to peruse the other graves. "For a small island, you have an amazingly crowded cemetery plot."

"Tends to happen when people stand up in boats in the middle of squalls."

Her back stiffened. She supposed that was meant as a reprimand, but she was going to ignore it. She had no desire to start the morning off with an argument. Strolling away from him, she focused her attention on another marker. "Phineas Payne—1823. Your father?"

"The same."

"My father's name was Augustus. Augustus Bartholomew Mayhew. He died four years ago." A few obligatory words of condolence from Elijah seemed appropriate at this time, so she waited for his response.

"We all gotta go sometime."

She sighed at his utter lack of tact. "What a lovely sentiment. You should inscribe that on one of your crosses." Rolling her eyes with disgust, she wandered around Phineas Payne's grave to a smaller mound of stones. "Lydia Payne. I assume this is your mother?"

He shook his head. "Lydia was . . . family."

"A sister?"

"Why do you wanna know?"

She sighed again. "Odd as it might seem, I *would* like to learn something about you other than the fact that you're always in a hurry. So who was Lydia? Your grandmother?"

He hesitated, then, "No. Lydia was my wife."

Augusta pivoted around so fast, she could feel the bones in her neck pop. "Your wife? You've been married before?"

"You wanted to know, didn't you? So there. Now you know."

Her mouth worked soundlessly. She looked away from

him, unable to sort out the emotions that were suddenly riffling through her.

"It's a man's right to take himself a wife."

She could think of no response. "You've been married before," she repeated, sounding more dazed than when she'd said it the first time. "Why . . . why didn't you tell me sooner?"

"What difference would that a made? Lydia's dead and buried. I'm married to you now."

"Still, I . . . I had a right to know about your former marital status." She couldn't decipher whether she was feeling shock or betrayal, but whatever the emotion, she knew she was feeling overwhelmed. She massaged her brow, trying to clear her head. "How did she die?"

When there was no answer from Elijah, she peered into his face. "How did she die?"

He narrowed his eyes at her before looking skyward. "It's getting late. I've gotta catch some shut-eye. Forget about breakfast. No time to eat anyway. Just have dinner on the table at noon." He started to walk away, but her words chased after him.

"You can't run away every time I ask you a question you don't want to answer! I'm going to be on this island a long time, Elijah Payne. You're going to have to face me sometime!"

He broke his stride and turned around slowly to face her. His voice was deadly calm but filled with menace. "What happened to Lydia is no concern of yours. I have no reason to talk about Lydia, and neither do you. If you have a lick of sense, you won't mention her name to me again." Spearing her with a final look, he strode toward the gate.

The morning breeze lifted his hair off his shoulders. The sun highlighted its golden streaks, reminding her again of a lion's mane. But she cared little for the lion's roar. She studied the marker with Lydia Payne's name inscribed on it. What had the woman been like? Plain? Beautiful? Had Elijah advertised for her as well? Had he loved her?

This last question gave her pause. Was this the reason why Elijah seemed so ill-disposed to accept her? Was he still in love with his first wife? But if he was still obsessed with Lydia's memory, why had he decided to marry again? Perhaps he wasn't obsessed with the woman's memory. Perhaps he merely found spinsterish Augusta to be a poor substitute for a young bride.

"Lydia Payne," she whispered. How could she expect to compete with a dead woman for Elijah's affection? It seemed that nothing about this marriage of hers was working out. She was foolish to have thought that her life could ever change for the better. She was foolish to have ever come here.

Kicking the dirt with the toe of her shoe, she rubbed her nose and, with head bowed, started for the gate. She passed another marker, this one inscribed with the name "Eliza Payne," but she didn't stop to observe it. This would have to be Elijah's mother, but she wondered why the grave wasn't closer to Phineas Payne's, and why the year of death was marked on the crosses for the men, but not for the women. Considering Elijah's attitude toward her thus far, she would think herself fortunate should he deign to carve her *initials* on a marker, much less her year of death.

But she did wonder when the women had died. It would have to have been a very long time ago, for all traces of their existence had been removed from the house. Odd. It was almost as if he was trying to hide something. But what? Well, Elijah had obviously been named for his mother, so perhaps he would be better disposed to discuss *her* than he'd been to discuss Lydia. There was something amiss on this island, and she intended to find out what.

After returning to the house, she whipped up some griddle cakes for breakfast, then, while Elijah continued to sleep, she washed the kitchen floor, erasing the muddy footprints she'd tracked in the night before. She had a mind to start unpacking her trunks while the floor dried, but Elijah was occupying her room, so she would have to wait.

With more than two hours to spare before the noon meal, she wandered outside and, with the wind blowing full in her face, stood on the edge of the precipice that fronted the lighthouse. Seventy-five feet below her, boulders and rocks were strewn about like monstrous jawbones, and she realized that Captain Crowley had been correct to call it a storm beach. It looked as if it had been ravaged by storms and savage tides. There was no sand here. There was only a wasteland of bedrock and boulders that seemed to comprise the island's outer skeleton. It was an angry place. A frightening place. She stepped back from the edge, her palms clammy at the thought of how close she might have been to the edge last night. She considered what might have happened if she had taken one step in the wrong direction, then decided it would be best not to think about it.

With the cliff on her left, she continued to walk, retracing the route they had followed the night before. She kept her eyes skinned for wreckage from the sunken ship, but the rocky shoreline seemed free of debris. She paused at the walkway that wound its way down to the boathouse, but rather than descend into that chasm again, she continued along the path.

The terrain grew less forbidding as she walked. The rocks along the shore became longer and flatter, more like ribs than jawbones. The high plateau of the island began sloping downward. She passed by the deep, narrow beach where Elijah had landed their boat last night, but the only reason she knew it was the same beach was that the boat was still there. Beyond that, the pathway wended through trees and bushes and around a sharp bend. Once around the bend, she heard a covey of gulls screech out a shrill greeting and in the distance saw them softpedaling landings on a huge rock formation that jutted into the sea at a right angle to the island.

As she approached it, she decided that anyone with imagination might mistake the rock for a beached whale. It was entirely separated from the island save for a natural bridge of rock that formed a narrow connection between the two. The island was still a good forty feet above sea level at this point, so the bridge leading down to the rock was extremely steep and gave way to precipitous drops on either side of it. The rock was hump-shaped and low, and Augusta suspected it would be completely submerged when the tide was high. But the tide was low now, and where the face of the rock formed shallow craters, she saw pools of water sparkling in the sun. One tidal pool was small and rectangular, suitable for bathing. The other was long and elliptical. If it was deep enough, she might be able to swim a dozen strokes from end to end, once she taught herself how. In fact, this might be the perfect place to learn.

Excited with the prospect, she picked her way over the narrow bridge and with careful steps climbed down onto the rock. Its surface was irregularly shaped, like a stack of griddle cakes that had been sliced down the center and flipped sideways. Navigating over the rock made her feel as if she were guarding the ramparts of a medieval fortress, but she smiled at the analogy, for there seemed little of value to guard on Devilstone Island.

The rock was deeply scored in some places, jagged in others, softly rounded in yet others. Some areas were so white with barnacles that at first glance it resembled un-melted snow. Sea mosses as soft and green as velvet ribbon swathed the lower elevations, and close to the waterline gnarls of granite wore seaweed like eighteenth-century heads wore wigs. Augusta stepped down from a higher to a lower elevation to stand before the smaller tidal pool she'd spied from the pathway. It reminded her of a min-iature reflecting pond—no more than two feet deep but so inviting that she kicked off her shoes, rolled her stockings down her legs, and with her big toe, tested the water.

Cool, but acceptable. With the sun warming the surface, it might even become pleasant.

Lifting her skirt to her knees, she sat down on the edge of the pool, then, with legs outstretched, lowered her heels into the water. She suspected the salt would be welcome relief on the nicks and cuts she'd sustained on the bottoms of her feet last night. And in this she was not mistaken. The water soothed like a kind word. Leaning back on her palms, she dangled her feet languorously. She fanned her toes and felt the odd sensation of water gliding between them. She slackened her calf muscles and watched her feet buoy to the surface of the water, almost as if they had been inflated with something lighter than air. No gulls screeched. No wind howled. Other than the tranquil flow of the surf, all was quiet. Peaceful. Unhurried. Again she was struck by a sense of timelessness, and as she pondered the shape of her toes beneath the water, she wondered if Lydia Payne had once sat on this very spot, dangling her feet in this very tide pool.

Why was Elijah so reluctant to talk about her? He had to be hiding something. But as the peacefulness of her surroundings settled over her, she admitted there could be another reason for his reluctance. Perhaps the pain of Lydia's death was still too fresh in his mind. Perhaps it merely hurt too much to discuss the woman he had once called wife. Augusta could sympathize with those feelings.

After her father's death, she'd been unable to speak his name for months without a knot forming in her throat. She had loved her mother, but her father had captured a special place in her heart. He had loved her without reservation. He had loved her for what she was, not criticized her for what she was not. While her mother had fretted over her lack of suitors, her father had quietly assured her that fifty years was a long time to spend with any one person, so there was no reason to rush matters. While her mother had bemoaned the unmanageable waviness of her hair, her father had quietly assured her that there was a certain charm connected with hair that had a mind and will of its own. What her mother deemed calamitous, her father deemed laudable, so nothing was ever so horrible that Augustus Mayhew could not put it to rights with a single word.

He had made her feel special, never unpretty or unwanted. And all he had ever asked in return was that she tolerate his cigar smoke and refrain from batting her eyelashes in his presence. Her sisters subjected him to enough of that.

His death had devastated her. With his passing she lost father, mentor, companion, and friend. She'd never experienced that rare closeness with another person, but she wondered if Elijah had experienced it with Lydia Payne, and if he still suffered from the loss. If that was the case, she could understand why he had reacted so violently to her prying. A man's emotions might be kept under tighter reins than a woman's, but she suspected they were no less fragile.

She lowered her eyes in shame. Poor Elijah. Despondent over the death of his wife, and here she was questioning him as if he were a common felon. He had every right to marry, and she had no right to expect him to have lived his former life according to the guidelines she might have provided for him. She couldn't fault him for wanting a companion with whom he could share his life on this island. That would be unfair. She would prefer that he hadn't married before, that she be the first woman in his life, but she realized it was futile to try to dictate the course of events that were already past. Elijah had married before, and *she* would forever be cast in Lydia Payne's shadow.

She frowned at the thought as another notion crept into her mind—a notion that smacked of her father's optimism—and she suddenly smiled, realizing she had been looking only at one side of the coin. If Elijah's marriage to Lydia had been a good one, wouldn't he want his marriage to Augusta to be equally good?

It seemed natural that he would, which bespoke hope for their relationship as man and wife. Elijah had no doubt treated Lydia well. Perhaps since her death he'd forgotten how to practice kindness, but if he'd done it before, he could learn to do it again.

So maybe it wasn't so calamitous that Elijah had been wed before. Lydia might already have smoothed some of his rougher edges, so all that remained for Augusta to do was repolish what had grown dull from lack of use. She could restore him to acceptable form, and in doing so, she intended to prove that she could take Lydia's place. Maybe she wasn't as pretty as Lydia, or as fair-dispositioned, but she'd be willing to match her culinary skills against anyone sporting a prettier face or fairer disposition. There'd been no finer cook in the city of Philadelphia than Augusta Mayhew. If she couldn't dazzle her husband with her looks, she was sure to dazzle him with her Cape May lemon pot pie. She'd seen fresh lemons in the pantry, and there was still time before dinner to prepare it.

Removing her feet from the water, she swung them onto the bedrock to dry. Others might object to her thinking, but she was of a firm mind that the most direct route to a man's heart was still through his stomach. She sloughed water from her feet, and as she reached for her stockings, was struck by the feeling that someone was watching her. Without moving her head, she shifted her eyes from side to side, then slowly and calmly turned her face to cast a long look over her right shoulder.

The creature was basking on a narrow ledge of rock near the waterline. It was about three feet long and pudgy as a pork sausage, with a round sleek head, whiskers, and round eyes that were softly black. Its coat was predominantly brown with lighter spots close to the flippers, but the most amazing feature about the animal was its face, for it was neither brown nor spotted. It was white. Completely white. She was staring into the eyes of a white-faced seal.

Swiveling her legs around, she rose quietly, never removing her gaze from the seal. Its eyes held her in fascination. They looked vulnerable to her and so incredibly human that she felt as if the creature could read her mind.

She took a step forward, hoping to pet him.

The seal rolled over and slithered downward, and in the next instant it was lost amid the seaweed and kelp.

"Don't go!" she called out, but she saw a splash, and then he was gone. She watched the surf for a few minutes, expecting him to reappear, but he vanished as mysteriously as he had appeared. *Just like Elijah,* she thought, wondering if she would ever see the creature again. She hoped so. His was the friendliest face she'd seen on Devilstone Island thus far.

Just before noon she heard the thump of Elijah's bare feet on the bedroom floorboards, and when he opened the door, she could tell by the smell that preceded him that he'd already lit up a cigar. Sleepy-eyed, he sauntered into the kitchen, his shirt untucked, his hair in wild disarray, a towel thrown over his shoulder and a shaving mug and razor in his hand. He stopped short just inside the doorway to grace her with a rather startled look. "Forgot you were here," he mumbled before scratching his head and shuffling toward the side of the sink where his shaving mirror hung.

Unsure how to respond to his greeting, she gave the hash she was frying a whack with her spatula and said nothing.

"You got some hot water over there for me to shave with?"

"Bring your mug over. I'll pour you some."

Slapslapslap. He walked as though he were unconscious—head bent and cigar dangling from the corner of his mouth. She was delighted he looked so haggard. He'd looked so fresh-faced earlier after not having slept all night that she'd begun to wonder if the man was human.

"Do you never get more than three hours of sleep a day?"

He handed her his shaving mug, then linked his fingers over his head and stretched his arms toward the rafters. "Nope." She filled his cup. "Any man who sleeps more than three hours a day is worthless as a hole in the snow." He let out a great bearish yawn and stretched again, causing his shirt to ride up and his breeches to hang low.

Augusta saw a sliver of manly flesh appear in that gap between his shirt and his breeches. The flesh was pale and dusted with a soft matting of dark brown hair, and when he sucked in his stomach, she saw that flesh curve inward, molding itself to the shape of his ribs. He sported no gentleman's paunch. He was lean as a mountain cat and hard as Devilstone granite. She realized that anyone who could power a boat through ten-foot waves would need to be a man of physical superiority. But Elijah Payne was more than just physically superior. She felt her fingertips tingle as the space between his shirt and breeches widened. He was magnificent.

He ended his yawn and dropped his arms. Augusta

handed him his shaving mug without meeting his eyes, quite sure that it was the hotness of the mug that had caused the tingling in her fingers.

"You washed the floor," he said as he headed back to the sink. "Good. Have to keep this place all buttoned up in case Haydon decides to pop a surprise inspection on me. And speakin' a that"—he plunged his shaving brush into his mug and began to work up a lather—"how much longer do I have to stare at your underdrawers blockin' the view out my bedroom windows? Any boat sailin' close in will think I'm runnin' a bawdy house 'stead of a light-house."

Augusta felt her cheeks flame that he should mention what was normally unmentionable between a man and a woman, but she vowed not to sound distressed. "You've obviously forgotten a great deal about the cut of female cloth. Four of my warmest nightgowns are obstructing your view, Mr. Payne, not my . . . not anything of a more intimate nature. Would you prefer milk or tea with din-ner?"

"Milk. I don't care what the things are. I just want them down."

"They'll come down once I have proper cloth to fashion curtains. Chintz for the bedroom. Gingham for the kitchen."

"We'll see."

She didn't like the sound of that. She slapped his hash into a plate and set it on the table. She could hear the *scratch, scratch* of his razor against his face and saw that a cloud of smoke hovered above his head even as he shaved. How could he shave, smoke, and talk all at the same time? "How often do you sail into Lustre's Gate?"

"I don't."

She shot a look at his back, suspecting this was a devious half-truth. "There were fresh lemons in the pantry this morning. How did you come by those if you didn't buy them on the mainland?"

"A supply ship from the village brings sundries out once a month."

She thought for a moment. "Very well. I'll simply have to place an order for material the next time the ship arrives. When was it here last?"

He wiped the excess lather from his face with his towel and turned around to face her. "The day before you arrived. It won't be here again for another four weeks."

Four weeks to place the order and four more weeks to receive it. Eight weeks. That was simply too long to wait for privacy. She'd have to think of something else. She poured milk for Elijah and tea for herself, then served herself a portion of the hash and sat down opposite him at the table. "Why do you never sail into Lustre's Gate?"

Elijah set his cigar on a saucer, shoveled a forkful of the hash into his mouth, and swallowed. "Four hours in and four hours back. The weather breezes up on me while I'm owlin' about the village, I'd be stranded."

"Would that be so terrible?"

He arched one long eyebrow at her. "My job is tendin' lighthouse, not sandpaperin' the anchor in Lustre's Gate."

"I could tend the lighthouse for you."

"Right. If you're as good with lanterns as you are with boats, we'll all be in for a treat."

"I can learn, if you show me."

He took another mouthful, chewing slowly. Augusta

searched his face hopefully. "I could take window measurements today."

"Go ahead."

"Then you'll do it? You'll sail into Lustre's Gate?"

"Nope. But I keep a tape measure in the back shed if you're set on findin' out how big my windows are."

Her eyes lengthened to angry slits. "You delight in being so perverse, don't you?"

He narrowed his eyes back at her. "You better not be accusin' me of likin' boys better than girls."

"I'm *accusing* you of being self-willed, narrow-minded, and . . . and contrary! And your name is all wrong. You shouldn't spell it P-A-Y-N-E. You should spell it P-A-I-N!"

"That's enough!" A flash of emotion brightened his eyes. "I'll tell you this once, and once only. I'll not be gone from this island overnight, not for you or anyone else. You understand?" The intonation of his voice signaled that he expected the conversation to end here, but she wasn't ready to concede.

"Why? What in the name of heaven do you think is going to happen if you're absent from Devilstone for a single night?"

His fists came down so hard on the table that the tinware rattled. In his eyes there was a fearsomeness that transcended mortal anger. "This discussion has ended!"

Brown eyes challenged hazel. She could feel his anger. She could see it clouding his eyes. Could see it pulsing in his right cheek. It made her mouth dry up like old parchment. But since it had been her intention this noontime to dazzle the man rather than enrage him, she concluded that a partial retreat was in order. But only partial.

She lowered her eyes, seized her fork, and calmly stabbed the red flannel hash that sat on her plate. "I have a modest amount of sprigged muslin in my trunks. Until I can place an order with the captain of the supply ship, I'll simply have to make do with that. But I'm sure I can confect something suitable." She shoved a forkful of the hash into her mouth. "I'm surprised your Lydia didn't demand any feminine trappings in your house."

"Some folks have too much sense to fuss with things a man has no use for."

She smiled stiffly at the slur. "Indeed? Well, some folks simply have no sense of aesthetics."

"And some folks have no damn sense at all!"

She forced more hash into her mouth.

"Somethin' burnin'?"

"My pie!" She charged across the room, grabbed the long-handled oven shovel, and threw open the oven door. Smoke billowed out like ash from a volcano. *"Ohhhh."* Elijah shook his head as the smoke enveloped her. He heard coughing and wheezing, and when she finally emerged from the mist, she sported on the blade of the shovel the blackest thing he'd ever had occasion to look upon.

"What's that supposed to be?"

It was dripping and bubbling, so she dropped it onto the hearthstones and stood over it almost protectively, fanning smoke away from it with the shovel. "It was supposed to be my famous Cape May lemon pot pie."

"Looks like boiled axle grease."

That he should compare one of her culinary masterpieces to the grease he had slopped onto her legs last night did not sit well with her. "Had you been courteous enough to conduct a civilized conversation with me at the dinner table, I'm sure I wouldn't have allowed the pie to slip my mind!'' She rehung the shovel by the mantel and marched back to her chair. Elijah was nodding his head sardonically.

''Just like a female.'' He gestured to the room at large. ''*She* burns the pie, but it's *my* fault because I wasn't engagin' her in proper conversation.''

''That's correct.'' She rubbed the sting from her eyes with both fists. ''And if you find females so utterly offensive, why did you bother to advertise for a wife?''

''Sure as hell wasn't to bake me Cape May lemon pot pie. Never touch lemons. They give me hives.''

She stopped rotating her fists. She dropped her hands from her eyes to her cheeks and fixed him with a most bewildered look. ''Why were there lemons in the pantry, if you can't eat them?''

''I use 'em to wash the glass chimneys in the tower. Makes 'em sparkle.''

She sighed a long, frustrated sigh. He wouldn't have eaten the pie even if she'd managed to save it from incineration. So much for trying to dazzle her husband with her cooking. Leaning back in her chair, she slanted a forlorn look at the burbling mess on the hearthstones, wondering how best to dispose of it. ''You don't suppose flame-blackened lemon pot pie would kill the harbor seals, do you?''

''Nope. But I don't know where you expect to find harbor seals around here.''

Her face softened in surprise. ''I saw one this morning. He was sunning himself on that whale-shaped rock that angles into the water. The one with all the tidal pools.''

Elijah shook his head. ''I call that the Reef. And the

place where I landed the boat last night is the Gulch. But there haven't been any seals in these parts for thirty years.''

''Well, they must be back, because I saw one. He was about yea long''—she marked the length with her hands—''and he had a white face.''

Of a sudden, Elijah grew so still that he seemed not to breathe. The long angles of his face tightened. His eyes darkened with unease—and something else. But she couldn't discern whether it was desperation . . . or fear.

Stiff-limbed, he gathered up his dishes and carried them to the sink. ''Sun must've blinded you. You didn't see any seal.''

''Ex*cuuu*se me, but *I* was the one doing the looking, and *I* saw a seal.''

''You ever see a live seal before?''

''No, but—''

''And you didn't see one this mornin' either.''

She opened her mouth but was too flustered to form words.

''I'm gonna start my chores now. I've changed my mind about showin' you how to milk the cow this afternoon. I'd rather have you unpack your trunks and get things straightened around in the bedroom. I can't abide sleepin' in a room with all that female clutter.''

She found her voice with a vengeance. ''How . . . how arrogant of you to dispute me when you weren't even there this morning to witness what I saw! If I didn't see a seal, what do you in all your great wisdom suggest I *did* see?''

''How the hell should I know? Might've been some flotsam from the wreck last night, for all I know. Plankin' and shredded canvas.''

''It had long whiskers and huge dark eyes.''

"Might've been a dead body washed ashore."

She stabbed him with her gaze. "It blinked."

"Oh, well, it blinked. That explains everything. Dark eyes. Whiskers. What you saw was a mermaid in need of a shave."

"There are no such things as mermaids," she said crisply, enunciating each word.

"No such things as white-faced seals, either."

"You . . . you . . . *I saw it!*"

"You thought you saw it!"

She screamed so loudly that Elijah clapped his hands over his ears. Up she shot from her chair, fists clenched. "I have *tried* to be nice to you, but you won't allow it, will you? I cook for you, but never hear you utter a word of thanks. I nearly drown last night, and you accuse me of being deaf. I happen upon a seal this morning, and you accuse me of being blind. I've met many an ill-bred man, but none . . . *none* who delighted more in his own insolence than you. Did Eliza Payne fail to teach her son the basic elements of human decency? Or were you simply absent when the instruction was being given?"

"Eliza Payne never had a son!"

"No? Then how, pray tell, do you explain your existence?"

"Eliza Payne wasn't my mother! She was my"—his voice grew low—"my first wife."

—6—

Augusta blinked once, then twice, but the blinking didn't change the words that were echoing in her head. "First wife? Your *first* wife? You mean, Lydia wasn't your first wife?"

"She was my second wife."

"Second wife?" She stared dumbly. "You've been married not once before, but *twice*?"

"Three times, includin' you."

"Three—" She continued to stare. One former spouse was forgivable, but *two*?

"I've had some trouble with my wives so far," he said matter-of-factly.

"You've had trouble with your wives *living*, is what you mean. And I'm next in line. Oh, that's encouraging. I have a great deal to look forward to, don't I? Perhaps you should plan to expand your cemetery plot. From what

I saw this morning, you've just about run out of room. If you accumulate any more bodies, you'll have to bury them at sea, and frankly, the thought of aquatic creatures backstroking through every orifice of my body is not one that carries much appeal!''

''You're steppin' across a fine line, Gus.''

''Really? I suppose that's the same thing you told Lydia and Eliza . . . *before* they ended up in the family plot. But at least their orifices are safe from aquatic invaders. You lured me here with phrases like 'woodland pine and salt air aplenty.' You didn't mention the frequency with which people *die* here, most particularly your wives. I came here with the thought of trying to regain some of my lost youth, but it looks as if the only thing I'm going to gain is an unwanted slice of earth wedged between a nameless seaman and one of your former wives! You were wrong not to tell me that so many had come before me. You were wrong not to explain everything!''

''That's a bunch of bilge!''

''No, it's not! You deceived me, and you continue to deceive me! You tempted me with a taste of paradise, but you've served up nothing more than a bellyful of perdition. You and your rescues at sea, and dead sailors, and dead wives. I wanted to be the first with you! I wanted to be special. But I don't think you know the meaning of the word.'' She turned her back on him, unable to look at his face for another moment. ''I had something of value to offer you. I wasn't so naive to think you might treat me like a queen in a game of chess, but I had hopes you might treat me better than an ordinary pawn. I wanted to feel like a butterfly. You make me feel like a mole.'' Silence ensued as she attempted to marshal her emotions. She rubbed her nose and held her head high. "I want to know who those women were. I want to know how they died. And I want to know why you thought none of this important enough to tell me."

She felt the slight vibration in the floorboards as he approached her, but she didn't turn around. "I've got two things to say to you, Gus. Number one, that hash you made could grow hair on a wooden leg, but it could've used more salt. And number two, if I were you, I'd have me a long look in the mirror. Either your skin is peelin' off your face, or you've caught yourself one helluva case of leprosy. See you at supper."

She spun around angrily to find him on his way out the kitchen door. "I haven't finished with you yet!" she called after him, but he just kept walking, leaving her to stew in her own juices. She glared at the door. She glared at the dishes he'd carried to the sink. She lifted her hands and rotated them slowly before her face. "What am I? Invisible? Or do I simply speak a foreign tongue that he has yet to comprehend? I asked him three direct questions. I heard myself. I received not one answer." She stared at the doorway, then back at her hands. "That's it. I'm invisible. I'm only imagining I see these hands, just as I only imagined I saw the seal this morning." She flattened her palm against her brow to test for a fever. Her flesh was cool, but what did Elijah mean when he said her skin was peeling?

Frowning, she hurried toward the sink. Elijah's shaving mirror hung too high for her to peer into, even on her tiptoes, so she lifted it off its hook and, with mild trepidation, held it before her face.

"Oh, Lord." She winced, screwed her eyes shut, then

slowly opened them again, knowing why Elijah had looked at her so strangely earlier. She looked like a carnival freak, the result of having applied too much face powder this morning. This is what happened when you had dozens of freckles to camouflage, no mirror in your bedroom, and a husband who was counting off every tick of the clock. Her face was whiter than the face of her imaginary seal, except in the places where she'd rubbed her eyes and cheeks. In those places, the powder was streaky and caked with soot and moisture. She did look like a leper. The twins, she was sure, would find it terribly comical. She might have laughed at herself, but others had laughed too often in the past to allow her the freedom to laugh at herself now.

He should have told me, she kept telling herself that afternoon. With Elijah tending to his duties in the cylinder, she had free rein with the bedroom, so she began the task of unpacking her trunks. But thoughts about Elijah and his former loves kept intruding, and the more they intruded, the more annoyed she became. She unpacked the counterpane she'd spent years completing, but when it came time to throw it over the bed, she wasn't sure she wanted her handiwork gracing the place where Elijah had lain with his multiple wives.

Annoyance dissolved into curiosity and curiosity into suspicion. How had he come to marry those women? Had he lured them here with promises of woodland pine and salt air? *Three wives*. She knew of no gentleman in Philadelphia who could boast three wives, except . . . She sat down on the edge of the bed, remembering. Except that man of European descent whom she'd read about in the *Inquirer*. He'd amassed a considerable fortune, not through lawful channels, but by marrying heiresses and systematically poisoning them. The authorities grew suspicious when wife number four complained to a lady friend about the bitter spirits her husband kept serving her as a nightly tonic. The lady friend was the police inspector's wife, and the European gentleman now resided in a place where he could neither spend nor enjoy his ill-gotten gains.

Memory of the scandal caused the skin at the nape of her neck to prickle. It was frightening to think that on this earth there walked men who possessed neither morals nor conscience, men who would lure a woman to the altar for only one reason—to dispose of her and steal her money.

Nervously, she shifted her eyes to the center of the bed. Had Lydia and Eliza possessed any great wealth? "They couldn't have," she whispered aloud. Men who craved fortunes tended to spend fortunes. If Elijah had inherited money from his dead wives, how was he spending it?

She ranged her eyes about the room, lighting on the nightgowns that still covered the window glass. "He's certainly not spending it on window dressings."

And I'm not an heiress. I have a modest inheritance, but nothing substantial. Elijah wouldn't have married me for my money. But another voice reminded her that a wickie's concept of wealth could be less grand than the concept held by a gentleman of European descent. Perhaps in Elijah's eyes, she *was* wealthy.

Unable to abide the direction of her thoughts, she rose quickly and returned to her trunks. But her mentations would allow her no peace. Three wives, and two were dead. Would she be soon to follow?

"Stop it!" she railed, pressing her hands over her ears as if to prevent the voices from tormenting her. "Had he wanted me dead, he could have accomplished that last night without the least effort."

The voices quieted. She hesitated, then lowered her hands. "He doesn't want me dead," she persisted. Bowing her head, she touched a finger to the bolt of sprigged muslin that lay atop her belongings. "He can't want me dead." She gathered the muslin into her arms, prepared to fashion her curtains this very afternoon. But as the image of the burial point held fast in her mind, she stared at the muslin, then dropped it back into the trunk.

Perhaps she would postpone the sewing. After all, she might not be here very long.

She didn't trust Elijah Payne. She didn't trust him or anything about Devilstone Island.

She watched him surreptitiously at supper—over her shoulder while she was standing, above the rim of her tea mug while she was sitting. When she wasn't watching him, she had the distinct feeling that he was watching *her*. But he seemed much less obvious about it than she. *He's had more practice,* she told herself. She didn't offer to engage him in conversation, and he responded in kind. So supper was a quiet affair, punctuated only by the sounds of spoons clinking against tinware, loud slurping, and self-conscious swallowing. She had prepared pease porridge. Elijah wolfed down three bowls before she had finished her first, and he didn't wait for dessert. He carried his dishes to the sink once again, and with a curt nod before leaving, said, "Could've used more salt." The door slammed shut behind him.

"Maybe next time I should make it with seawater instead

of spring water!'' She flung the words at his head as he passed by the outside window, beyond earshot. ''Maybe that would be salty enough to suit your taste.'' Salty enough? She smiled wickedly. It would likely kill him.

By the next morning, killing him became a definite option.

She'd slept fitfully that night, alert to creaking boards and rattling windowpanes. The noises might not have bothered her had her mind been at peace, but there were too many unanswered questions floating in her head to rest. Unable to sleep, she rose before dawn to begin breakfast preparations, deciding on something simple—hardscrabble oatmeal pancakes with molasses sauce. She doubled the amount of salt in the recipe to spare herself having to listen to any more of Elijah's complaints. But to no avail.

''You people in Philadelphia ever come across somethin' called salt?'' This, as he licked molasses sauce off his lips.

''What a ridiculous question. Of course we use salt.''

''Well, you'd never know it from the taste of these pancakes.''

And that, as the saying goes, was the straw that broke the camel's back. She might have understood had he criticized her hair or complexion. She was accustomed to those kinds of comments. But this man had the audacity to criticize her cooking. No one *ever* criticized her cooking. The twins had even been forced to heap praise on her for her abilities. Her freckles might be unsightly, but her cooking skills were above reproach. Yet Elijah Payne had the nerve to criticize her not once, but *three* times.

''If my cooking is so unpalatable, perhaps you should cook your own meals from now on.''

"I don't wanna cook. I just want you to do it right."

"For your information, my instincts in the kitchen have *always* been right."

"Except when it comes to food."

"There is nothing wrong with my instincts or my food. It's your mouth that's the problem. You simply can't *taste* anything! You—have—no—taste!"

"In women maybe!"

The gibe stung, not enough to reduce her to tears, but enough to foment her emotions toward a single purpose. The time for verbal skirmishing was over. Elijah Payne had just declared war and, by God, a war was what he'd get. So he didn't like the way his food tasted, did he? Well, she was of a mind to give him something to taste. She would give him something to taste that he would *never* forget.

"Here, chick! Here, chick, chick, chick!" Augusta uncupped her hands from around her mouth and squinted to see farther down the path. "Ignorant bird. Where are you?"

Before he'd gone to bed this morning, Elijah had told her to spread feed for the chickens in the barnyard and collect the eggs in the henhouse. Grudgingly, she'd done so, but only because she realized she shouldn't make the poor chickens suffer because of her disenchantment with her husband. She'd had the feed almost all spread when one of the birds flew to the top of the stone fence and, in the next instant, escaped over the other side. By the time she was able to give chase, the bird had disappeared. But Augusta rushed down the forest path anyway, thinking it the only sensible route for the fowl to have taken.

"Here, chick!" she called again, knowing she had to get back to the house soon before her stew boiled over. And this was one stew she didn't want anything happening to, so the bird had better show its feathers and fast. "If you don't show yourself this instant, you're going to be a very sorry bird when I *do* find you!" She craned her neck this way and that, peering into the depths of the forest. "I have a wonderful recipe for fricassee!" She waited. "*Chicken* fricassee!" She crept farther down the path. Wherever the bird was, it seemed unaffected by her threat. She rounded a sharp curve in the path, then stopped dead in her tracks.

"Mornin', ma'am."

There were three of them advancing toward her—three men wearing knitted caps on their heads and loose breeches held up by rope belts. *Seamen*, she thought. But what were they doing here?

Elijah had implied that, other than the crews of the inspection and supply ships, no one ever set foot on Devilstone. Had he lied about that too? Unless . . . unless this *was* the crew of the supply ship.

"Good morning," she offered in greeting as they formed a semicircle around her. "Are, uh, are you from the mainland?"

The three men exchanged questioning glances with each other before one man, whose nose was big as a summer squash, gave his head a definitive nod. "When we're not gone to sea, you can find us on the mainland. That right, boys?"

The two men crowding around him nodded their agreement. One flashed a rather bashful smile to reveal the existence of only one tooth in his head. Augusta forced herself to smile back.

"Are you from Lustre's Gate, then?" Hope welled within her. She prayed they were. Elijah had refused to share any of the details of his past life with her, but perhaps some of the villagers would be less closemouthed.

The Nose shook his head. "Sorry, ma'am. We're from farther up the coast. Way north of here."

The Tooth looked confused. "North? I thought—"

"Don't think," warned the Nose.

"Why'd we have to bring him with us?" whined the third seaman. He was a dwarf of a man with a flat face and no lips.

Augusta sighed her disappointment. The men were obviously going to be no help whatsoever. They weren't even sure which direction was north. "Am I correct in assuming that you gentlemen are lost?"

"Not now, ma'am. But we've been . . . adrift. That's what we're doin' here. Need to fill our water casks. You have fresh water here to restock our supply? We'd be obligin' to you."

"We have have fresh water, yes, but I'm not exactly sure where the spring is. Elijah hasn't shown me yet."

The Nose cast a meaningful look at the Dwarf, which prompted Augusta to explain further. "I've only been here two days, you see. I'm newly married to the island's wickie."

The Tooth looked alarmed. "You're married to an Indian?"

The Dwarf grabbed the Nose by the elbow. "You never said nuthin' about Indians."

"She married a *wickie,* you peabrains. The man makes candles. Now leggo my arm."

"Actually, I'm married to the lightkeeper," she said, laughing. "But I do agree with you. Wickie sounds Indian. In fact, I didn't learn the meaning of the word until I arrived on the island. So you needn't feel silly about your mistake. I made the same mistake myself." She favored the Tooth with a benign smile.

He reddened with the attention, smiled back, and with his next breath asked, "What tribe does your husband belong to?"

Augusta stared at the man. The Nose ripped the knitted cap off his head and *whapped* it against the Tooth's shoulder. "Half-wit," he spat.

"Anyone on the island besides you and your husband?" asked the Dwarf.

"My husband says it's uncommon for a wickie to occupy an island where the population is greater than one."

The Dwarf scratched his head and appealed to the Nose. "Wha'd she say?"

"She said no!" yelled the Nose.

Taken aback by the trio's rudeness, Augusta leveled an imperious look upon them. "If you gentlemen are quite ready, perhaps you'd care to collect your water now." She looked from side to side, then behind them. "Did you leave your casks on the beach?"

The Tooth stared at the Dwarf, who stared at the Nose. They said nothing. Augusta cocked her head at them, unable to decide if they suffered more from deafness or simplemindedness. "Did you forget where you left the casks?"

"We didn't forget, ma'am," said the Nose, reaching

his hand behind his back to extract something from the waistband of his breeches. "We just weren't sure how much longer we had to go through the drill."

She had never seen an actual firearm before, but that didn't prevent her from recognizing the metal and wood object that materialized in the Nose's hand. She didn't know what kind of gun it was. It wasn't much bigger than the man's hand and was designed with only one barrel, but that barrel was aimed directly at her head. She took a slow step backward.

"We don't wanna hurt you, ma'am. But you've got somethin' on this island that we want, and we're not gonna leave without it."

She chided herself for having thought them simpleminded. They weren't simpleminded. They were armed, and dangerous. She forced herself to breathe evenly to dispel her fear. "What is it you're after?" She took another step backward.

"C'mon, ma'am. It's common talk what Bunker buried here."

"Bunker? Wh-who's Bunker?"

"If you wouldn't mind to stop backin' away from me, ma'am." He waved the gun. She stopped retreating. "That's better. Bunker's the fella who made off with all those gold sovereigns when that Limey frigate went down on the shoals durin' the revolution. Common talk is he buried those sovereigns somewhere hereabouts, and he died before he could dig 'em up again. They're worth millions now, and we aim to have 'em. That right, boys?"

The Dwarf and the Tooth nodded their agreement. Augusta slanted a disbelieving look at the three. "You're searching for buried treasure? Here?" The idea was so outrageous that, despite the danger and the gun pointed at her head, she felt herself begin to smile. "I'm sorry to disappoint you, gentlemen, but the only thing buried on this island are the remains of all my husband's former wives. And given the number of former wives he's had, that leaves very little room to bury anything else."

"You're wrong," said the Nose. He shifted his gun to his left hand, snapped his fingers in the air, and opened his palm before the Dwarf's face. The Dwarf reached beneath his knitted cap to remove a square of yellowed parchment, which he placed in the Nose's hand. "I got a map to prove you're wrong."

Augusta shook her head, unsure who irritated her more—these men for being here, or Elijah for not warning her that something like this could happen. "The only treasure on this island is one muleheaded man who lacks any pretense of manners or good taste. If you want to steal *him,* you're welcome to him. He's sleeping up at the house."

The Tooth shook his head. "I'm not stealin' no Indian."

The Nose unfolded the parchment and held it up for Augusta's viewing. "Here. Take a gander at this and tell me there's no treasure on this island."

Augusta took a hesitant step closer to the Nose. With a quick sweep of her eye, she scanned the faded scribblings on the parchment. "There is no treasure on this island."

"The hell there ain't!" He snapped the map around to view it himself. "This here is Devilstone Island. This is the beach where we landed. And *this*"—he stabbed his gun at an irregular inkblot in the center of the parchment—"is where we're gonna find the treasure."

Shaking her head, Augusta snatched the map from the

Nose's hand and slatted her eyes at the scribblings. "*This* is a child's rendering of the continent of Africa. *That* is a giraffe with no neck. And *this*"—she stabbed her finger at the inkblot—"is someone's dirty thumbprint." The Nose snatched the parchment back. Augusta laughed. "Just how did you happen upon that bogus piece of parchment?"

"None of your business how I come across it. All you gotta know is it's genuine and it's gonna make me rich."

Augusta folded her arms across her bosom. "You obviously have the wrong island."

"This ain't the wrong island! This is the right island!"

"Well, you'd never know it from that pathetic drawing!"

"The man had more talent for hidin' the treasure than he had for drawin' it!"

"Too bad he buried all the gold! If he'd had a brain in his head, he might have used some of that money to give himself art lessons!"

The Nose's face bloated with such anger that Augusta thought his ears might fly off his head. "Lady! If you don't stow the backtalk, I'm gonna force-feed you this gun for your next meal!"

Augusta didn't flinch. The gun would probably taste better than the stew she'd prepared.

"Where's the house? Back that way?"

"As of this morning, it was. But perhaps you should consult your map."

He scowled at her comment. "Why don't you take a round turn right here and march back where you come from. That husband of yours has got to be less ornery than you. Kee-reist, if you hack 'n' hammer like that all the

time, I won't have to steal the poor bugger off this island.
He'll be *beggin'* me to take 'im.'' He scooted her along
with the barrel of his gun. "Get movin'."

"You have the wrong island. You'll see." She fired a
haughty look at him before spinning on her heel and heading back in the opposite direction. But it smarted that even
the reavers thought her bold and overbearing. She thought
she had left those labels behind in Philadelphia. She
thought she had escaped the sharp tongues that were so
willing to find fault. So she had run from Philadelphia,
but it seemed she had escaped nothing.

—7—

As they approached the house, Augusta hoped that Elijah had been unable to sleep. She hoped he'd heard the commotion and would be waiting for them in the kitchen with his harpoon sharpened and at the ready. But he wasn't waiting for them in the kitchen. Nor was he anywhere to be seen.

"The bedroom this way?" asked the Nose, pointing his gun toward the parlor.

Augusta nodded, smiling inwardly. She wouldn't want to be the Nose when Elijah woke up to find that gun pointed in his face.

"You two keep an anchor to windward out here and don't let her outta your sight." The Nose stepped into the parlor and opened the door to the bedroom.

Augusta waited, eyes riveted on the portal. Any moment now she expected to see the Nose skating across the parlor floor on his face. She listened for the first telling sounds of the inevitable brawl. Elijah would be furious. The kitchen wouldn't be big enough to contain his fury. He would be maniacal with rage, wild with frenzy.

Wearing his breeches and nothing else, he shambled into the kitchen with his hands linked behind his head in submission.

"Keep your hands right where they are," cautioned the Nose, his gun trained on Elijah's naked torso.

Augusta watched in stunned disbelief. Elijah should have decked the man by now. What was he waiting for? She watched him yawn. *He's getting ready,* she thought. He wracked his shoulders from side to side and flexed every muscle in his arms so that ridges of sinew swelled tightly against his flesh. He looked bigger without his shirt. He looked shamelessly erotic with his face framed by the shapely bulk of naked forearms and biceps. And though she had reason to distrust him, she could not dispute his physical allure or her response to it. Lifting a hand to her breastbone, she tried to still the fluttering in her chest, but the sensation persisted, dancing beneath her fingertips like angels wearing toe shoes.

He stopped yawning. *Now,* she thought. And faster than she could blink, he thrust his arm toward the reaver, grabbed his gun hand, and began pumping it like a carriage jack.

"The name's 'Lijah Payne. I see you've already met Gus. What can I do for you?"

"Bunker's gold," said the Nose, as Elijah continued pumping his hand. "We know it's here, and we aim to find it."

"Fair enough. But you can put the gun away. We're sociable folk here on Devilstone."

Augusta's mouth fell open. He should be blackening the man's eye not shaking his hand! What was he thinking? She began tapping a slow, irritated rhythm on the floor with the toe of her shoe.

Elijah slung his arm around the Nose's shoulders and directed him toward the table. "Sit a spell. Don't see why we can't chew this over civil like." He pulled out a chair for the Nose.

Tap, tap, tap went Augusta's shoe. Her brows dipped into an angry vee. He was being more congenial to this . . . this *pirate* than he'd been to her. Next thing you know, he'd want to serve the man refreshments.

"Get you gentlemen a swig of somethin' wet?"

Taptaptaptaptap.

The Nose declined refreshment. Elijah continued with his discourse. "So, gentlemen, shall we talk gold? Do you have a map?"

Augusta smiled smugly. She could hardly wait to see the Nose's reaction when Elijah told him the obscure markings on the parchment represented something other than Devilstone Island.

The Nose spread the map out on the table.

"Yah, that's Devilstone all right," said Elijah.

Taptaptaptaptap.

"And let's see, if this dark stain marks where the gold should be, my guess is we'll find it close by the burial point. That's good. The soil there's good for diggin'."

Augusta rolled her eyes. *Why don't you offer to rent them shovels?*

"Did you bring shovels, or do you wanna borrow some of mine? I keep 'em in one of the back sheds."

Taptaptaptaptap.

The Nose threw him a sly look. "How come you're not denyin' Bunker buried his treasure here?"

"I'd have to be a damn fool to deny that, wouldn't I? Everyone knows this is where Bunker stashed his gold."

"Not everyone." The Nose directed an accusing eye at Augusta, who favored him with a scowl. Returning his attention to Elijah, he asked, "And just how come you're so willin' to help us? You have the island booby-trapped or somethin'? How come you don't want the gold for yourself?"

"I won't say I haven't looked. But you tell me. What can a wickie do with a cache of gold on an island in the middle of the North Atlantic?"

"He could buy curtains," said Augusta.

The Nose pondered the question before nodding. "I s'pose. But I still think it's kinda fishy, you bein' so co-operative and all. Makes me think you're up to somethin'."

"Just tryin' to make you feel welcome. Gus and I don't get many visitors. We're happy for the company, aren't we, sweetheart?"

Sweetheart? She stared at him agog. *He's up to something.*

A hissing sound rose from the hearth. Augusta swiveled her head around. Steam was spewing from beneath the lid of her kettle. "Ohhh." Racing toward the hearth, she grabbed a pair of mitts off the mantel, shoved her hands into them, and snatched the lid off the kettle. The smell of boiled meat and spices filled the room.

"Don't let her try nuthin'," bellowed the Nose.

Lid in hand, Augusta swung around to show him she was up to nothing untoward. "I'm not— Oh!" The Dwarf and the Tooth had already surrounded her, and though they were unarmed, their closeness startled her. "You might have made some noise, so I'd know you were standing there!"

The Nose was on his feet. "Put the lid back where you got it."

Augusta puzzled at the request. What did he think she was going to do with five pounds of cast iron? She sidled a glance at it, hefting it to waist level. The Dwarf and the Tooth jumped back a step. Perplexed, she knotted her brow at them. There was fear in their eyes, and as she hefted the lid again, she suddenly knew why. Five pounds of cast iron could cause serious damage if hurled into a man's chest. She tightened her grip on the ring in the center of the lid. They deserved to be taught a lesson. Maybe a solid thrashing with an iron lid was what they needed to get them out of her kitchen and off this island.

Indecision wrenched her insides. The Dwarf and the Tooth looked terrified. The Nose lifted his gun. And then she lit upon Elijah's face, and what she saw there held her spellbound. While she wrestled with inner turmoil, he remained serene, fixing her with a look that encouraged her to maintain a cool head. *He can read my mind*, she thought. *He knows what I want to do*. And with his eyes he was telling her that she had nothing to fear. He would protect her, if she would just remain calm. "Give me time, Gus," he seemed to be saying with those dark eyes of his. "Give me time and I'll take care of everything." And as she wavered with indecision, she thought how ironic it was that this man whose life was ruled by haste was now begging her for time. And she, who had mocked his quickness, was searching for a hasty way to end all this unpleasantness. But his message was well received.

"Here." She thrust the lid at the Tooth. "Hold this while I stir my stew, would you? It's heavier than I thought." As she made the transfer, she stole a peek at Elijah, who bowed his head slightly in approval. And in that moment she felt a connection with him that transcended mere physical attraction. Her husband was offering to bear responsibility for her well-being, and that was a kindness no one had offered for seven long years. It made her aware that she was truly sharing her life now. It made her shoulders feel wondrously unburdened and her arms so light that she guessed she had just sprouted wings, like a butterfly.

"We've got a long afternoon of work ahead of us, gentlemen," said Elijah, standing up. Augusta broke eye contact with him then, but it wasn't easy looking away when his eyes held such comfort. "I'll get the shovels."

"Wait a minute," said the Nose. "We'll all get the shovels."

"Even Gus?" Elijah looked skeptical. "No reason why she has to come with us, is there?"

"Doggone right there's a reason. I don't trust her. That's reason enough. I wanna be able to keep my eye on her while we're workin'."

Elijah shrugged. "Suit yourself."

"But what about my stew?" Augusta objected. "I should stay here to watch it."

"Watch it do what?" asked the Nose. "Look, hike that kettle outta the fire, crack the lid, and let the thing cook.

You don't need to watch nuthin'." He waved his gun at the Tooth. "You stay here with her 'til she finishes fussin' over her victuals, then meet us outside. You got that?"

"Got it." And when the three men had gone and the Tooth was alone with Augusta, he took a whiff of her stew and watched quietly as she gave it a stir. "I can tell you're a new bride," he said after a while.

She was listening for sounds of a struggle from the shed and had no wish to talk, but she forced herself to continue the ruse of friendliness. "How can you tell that? From the way I stir stew?"

"Nope. From the weddin' garland on the weather vane."

She stopped stirring to look up at him. "From the what?"

"The weddin' garland on the weather vane." And when still she looked confused, he explained further. "That evergreen bough your husband's got twisted around the crossbar of your weather vane. That's the same thing a seaman'll hang from the yardarm of his ship when the captain gets spliced. Means a new bride's welcome aboard. That's how I can tell you're fresh married."

She remembered seeing the evergreen bough hanging from the crossbar, but she'd thought its presence accidental—that the wind had probably ripped it from a nearby pine and blown it across the roof where it had tangled in the vane. "You think Elijah did that to welcome me?"

"Yes'um. I suspect so."

Musing over this revelation, she turned back to her stew. So maybe he hadn't cleaned out a drawer for her or asked her how she'd fared on her journey. He'd made none of the gestures that would have come naturally to her. But he *had* extended a kind of greeting to her. She smiled as she stared into the kettle. In his own quiet, unaffected way, he had bade her welcome.

"You best lift that kettle onto a higher hook, ma'am."

Her nerve endings prickled with sudden alarm. She couldn't serve this to Elijah. Not now. "The kettle is fine where it is," she assured him. And as for the stew, she hoped it burned.

With a shovel balanced atop each shoulder, Elijah led the way to the burial point. The Nose trotted close on his heels. Augusta, sandwiched between the Dwarf and the Tooth, trailed behind, but they maintained so quick a pace because of Elijah's long strides that by the time they reached the burial point, they were all gasping for air. All except Elijah.

Elijah was whistling.

The Dwarf glared at him. "What's he so happy about?"

Augusta leaned against a rock to catch her breath. "He's probably happy his . . . legs are so long. I wish . . . mine were."

The Nose crossed in front of her to observe the graves within the burial ground. "Lot a people unreeved their lifelines on this island." Turning abruptly, he walked back to where Elijah had driven the shovels into the ground. "You're clean outta space over there."

Augusta didn't hear Elijah's response, for the Nose's comment reminded her of her earlier misgivings about her husband, and she struggled now to arrive at some definitive answer. Her feelings had undergone such a drastic change in the last hour that she no longer wanted to think Elijah capable of marrying for unscrupulous reasons. She hoped he spoke the truth when he professed disinterest in any gold they might find on the island. If this were true, she could discount her earlier theories, and she very much wanted to do that. It would make no sense that a man who set so little store in wealth would plot to accumulate an excess of it by marrying women of means and doing away with them. It seemed a highly impractical pursuit for a man so preoccupied with practicality. She shook her head at her own foolishness. She'd succeeded in frightening herself half to death simply because Elijah couldn't bring himself to discuss obviously painful memories. Her accusations had been unfair and unwarranted, and she scolded herself for allowing her imagination to run amok. Murder and intrigue might be found on the pages of the *Philadelphia Inquirer,* but they certainly did not exist on the shores of Devilstone Island.

Having caught her breath, she climbed onto the rock she'd been leaning against, sat down, and tented her skirt around her legs so she could watch the proceedings. Elijah and the Nose pored over the map a while longer before the Nose grabbed one of the shovels and began marking off paces in a direction away from the burial plot. On his seventh step, he thrust the shovel into the ground. "We'll dig here. This is where it should be."

"Hope you're right," said Elijah.

The Dwarf grinned. "I hope he finds a whacking great jug of Jamaican rum."

The Tooth lazed his back against Augusta's rock. "I hope he finds a coffer of diamonds and rubies and pearls."

Augusta drew her knees to her chest and perched her chin atop them. "I'd settle for some yellow gingham."

Soil and grass flew in every direction as Elijah and the

reaver began their excavation. Augusta expected that Elijah might be planning to clout the man with his shovel at some point, but that point never seemed to arise. She didn't know how he intended to rid himself of the reavers without using force, but she decided not to worry the issue. From where she sat, he looked to be enjoying himself.

He worked faster and labored harder than the reaver, displaying the same vigor with which he'd manned the oars two nights ago. He hadn't shaved yet this morning, so his face was dark with stubble, but she didn't dwell on his face. Her eyes strayed lower, to the place where his collarbone formed a long ridge beneath his flesh. A tangle of soft brown hair spanned his chest below the collarbone, then funneled downward, forming a dense cover over heavy pads of muscle and thinning out where muscle turned to rib. Dirt sprayed against him, mingled with his sweat, then seemed to melt on his flesh, streaking him with rivulets of moist earth.

Augusta slid a fingertip into her mouth. It felt cool against her tongue, but she wondered if it, too, would melt when pressed to Elijah's flesh. Her face grew warm. She watched his muscles knot and slide as he heaved shovelfuls of earth higher and higher. The flesh at his hairline beaded with perspiration that dripped into his eyes, so he stopped for a moment to wipe his forearm across his brow, and when he did, Augusta stared, and knew desire. His pose was wholly innocent, but with his weight on one leg, his breeches sagging below his navel, and his arm raised to expose his underarm and side, he seemed to touch a part of her that was buried as deeply within her being as the treasure was buried beneath the earth.

To touch him would be to know the mysteries of the

universe. To feel beneath her palm the shape of his arm, the beat of his heart, would be a moment in paradise.

Elijah raked his fingers through his hair, drawing it away from his face, and when he seemed ready to resume work, he looked far across the way, found Augusta's eyes, and winked.

She dropped her gaze to the ground, her feelings alternating between embarrassment and disquiet. Embarrassment because of the lusty nature of her thoughts. Disquiet because Elijah had probably read her mind again. Embarrassment because she wasn't sorry for what she'd been thinking. Lifting her gaze, she slanted a look toward the burial ground and beyond, where the open sea glimmered in the sunlight. She wondered if she would see the white-faced seal again. Yesterday she'd sensed that the animal was capable of reading her mind, just as Elijah had seemed to do today. But having listened to Elijah, she questioned now if the animal truly existed or if she had indeed imagined it. Strange how this man whom she had known all of two days could affect her thinking. Strange how for the past two days she could think of nothing *but* this man. And angling her head away from her shoulder, she waited for a cool breeze to wash the heat from her cheeks.

The day wore on, and on, and on. Four holes, three dozen broken clamshells, and an Indian arrowhead later, the Nose threw his shovel to the ground. "It's not here. I shoulda known it was too good to be true."

Elijah leaned on the wooden shaft of his shovel. "You're not givin' up? Hell, we can dig a half-dozen more pits before sunset. If that map's authentic, the gold'll be here somewhere."

"If we haven't found it by now, we're never gonna find it."

Elijah shrugged. "It's a big island. Might be buried someplace else. Maybe we read the map wrong. Lemme see that thing." He climbed out of the pit he'd dug, grabbed the map from the reaver, then lowered himself to the ground, stretching out his long legs before him. Augusta slid off her rock and nodded toward Elijah.

"I'm going over there," she informed her bodyguards and not waiting for their escort, off she went.

"Look here," said Elijah, jabbing a finger at the map. "Maybe we started diggin' too close to the burial point. Another ten feet thataway"—he pointed toward the interior of the island—"and we might hit somethin'."

The Nose mopped the sweat from his face with the sleeve of his shirt. "Don't you ever get tired, Jack? We got four pits here deep enough to mine tin, and you wanna dig more? If you wanna kill yourself, go ahead. Me, I give up. I've had it."

Augusta suppressed a smile with difficulty. Maybe this meant they'd be leaving soon. Circling one of their many piles of dirt, she spied the arrowhead they'd unearthed and hunkered down to examine it. It was made of stone, and from end to end measured no bigger than her baby finger. But what fascinated her was the fact that it bore markings indicating where it had been lashed to a shaft. Picking it up, she brushed it off and held it up for Elijah's perusal.

"Where do you suppose it came from?"

"Came from the damn hole we just dug," snarled the reaver.

Augusta glared at him. Elijah held out his hand for the artifact.

"Bring it here, Gus. Let's have a look-see at it."

Hoping that the Nose might get inexplicably sucked into any one of the four pits surrounding them, Augusta stood up and crossed the short space to Elijah. She placed the arrowhead in his upturned palm, and as she stood over him, she noticed something she'd been unable to see from her rock.

He had freckles. Not in an obvious place like hers, but sprinkled lightly across his shoulders. He seemed not at all troubled by their existence and didn't rush to hide them from her, which indicated to her that he was simply unaware that freckles were the bane of every woman's existence. She envied him his unconcern. She pressed her fingers to her cheek, thinking it admirable that he didn't feel the need to hide behind layers of rice powder. She wished she could flout the dictates of fashion with such ease.

Elijah turned the arrowhead over in his palm. "Phineas used to say that Lustre's Gate was built on the site of an old Abnaki Indian village. Maybe this thing's Abnaki."

"But I don't understand how it got here."

"The Abnaki might've summered on Devilstone. Fishin' was probably better out here. Clammin' too. Come June, they probably loaded up their birch-bark canoes and paddled the fifteen miles out here. Might find more of these things if we dug a few more holes."

"*You* can dig more holes if you want to," the Nose piped up. "I've got enough blisters on my hands without wantin' to add to 'em. I think the missus was right. I think we got the wrong island." He wiped his hands down the length of his shirtfront, then motioned for his companions. "C'mon, you two! Time we weighed anchor."

Elijah flipped the arrowhead to Augusta and in the next moment heaved himself to his feet. "It's a damn shame you've gotta leave just as we're gettin' acquainted. That right, Gus?"

She lent her husband a quizzical look before she finally caught his drift. "A terrible shame. Just terrible. I probably won't be able to sleep tonight thinking what a shame it was that you had to leave."

Elijah nodded agreement. "In fact, why don't you stay and have supper with us?"

"No!" Of a sudden, her face became a bull's-eye that four sets of eyes targeted on. She colored at her own outburst, but she knew if the reavers tasted her stew, they would probably accuse her of adding something lethal to the pot. And who knew what would happen then? The excavations on the burial point suddenly looked an appropriate size for a rather small woman from Philadelphia.

"No?" questioned the Nose. "What's the matter? We ain't good enough to sit at the same table with you?"

She shook her head stiffly. "That's not it at all. I . . . we've been here so long I suspect my stew is probably ruined."

"That so?" said the Nose. "Well, maybe we'll just take our chances. Maybe there's a reason you don't want us to go back to the house with you. Maybe you got somethin' hidden in that kitchen a yours. In a flour barrel, or a dough box. Maybe that's why you got us all the way down here, so we'd be as far away from the house as possible. Maybe, just maybe, you got Bunker's gold in your kitchen."

"*Gold* in my kitchen? I don't even have curtains in my kitchen!"

"We'll just see about that, won't we?" He picked up

his shovel and hoisted it across his shoulder. "C'mon, boys. We're gonna victual up with the lighthouse keeper and his missus."

Augusta threw a glance heavenward. They were never going to be rid of these three. But she reminded herself that she was the one who had hoped the island would have a dense population. She shook her head. Sometimes you had to be careful what you prayed for.

To her amazement, the stew wasn't burned. On the contrary, the vegetables and meat were tender and the broth had thickened to a perfect consistency. She couldn't have created a more exquisite-looking stew had she actually been trying.

"Ruined, huh?" the Nose flung at her. "All right, boys, spread out. There's gold here. I can smell it."

Augusta crooked her mouth to the side, too smug to tell him that what he smelled wasn't gold. It was thyme.

While Elijah washed up outside in the rain barrel, the reavers searched the sugar bucket, the flour barrel, the meal barrel, and the dough box. They checked beneath the sink, in the butter churn, through the drawers of the spice cabinet, and in the oven. They knocked on every board in the floor to ferret out hollow spots, and finding nothing, moved on to the parlor. The more they looked, the angrier Augusta got. She didn't appreciate people upsetting the order of her kitchen. She didn't appreciate having to wipe floury fingerprints off her newly washed floor. She didn't—

Crash! Tinkle-tinkle. Crunch.

"Idiot!" It was the Nose's voice. "Now look what you've gone and done!"

Augusta looked toward the parlor, her temper on a slow

burn, but she refrained from crossing the floor to discover what they had broken. It didn't matter what they'd broken. The only thing that mattered was that these men had disrupted the tidiness of her domain and threatened her person, and she intended they should pay for the error of their ways. She gave her stew a loving stir. She'd had to tolerate ill-mannered guests in her parents' house, but this was *her* house now, and she would allow no one to be ill-mannered without suffering the consequences. No one.

They traipsed back into the kitchen before Elijah finished washing. "The place looks clean," the Nose complained. "Looks like you can serve us supper now."

Without saying a word, Augusta gathered together the needed hollow- and flatware, threw the spoons onto the table in passing, then proceeded to the hearth, where she began dishing out the stew. The Nose took a seat, then indicated that his companions should do the same. "How come there's only three spoons here?"

Augusta delivered the first bowl to the table and plunked it before the Nose. "Because only three of you are eating."

"What about your husband?"

She was hoping Elijah would stay outside so he'd be spared having to sample the stew. If he joined the reavers now, she wouldn't have any way of warning him. "Do you *see* my husband anywhere?" she snapped as she hastened back to the hearth.

"He's standin' in the doorway," said the Tooth.

She threw a look in that direction. He was standing in the doorway, his hair freshly scrubbed and dripping.

"You wanna dish me out a bowl of that while I fetch myself a shirt, Gus? I'm so hungry, my stomach's almost touchin' my knees. Wait'll you wrap your teeth around that stew, gentlemen. Gus is one helluva cook.''

She opened her mouth to say something, then closed it again, knowing there was little she could say to discourage him from eating. Poor Elijah. He was doomed to suffer the same fate as the reavers. She was sorry for it, but it just couldn't be helped. ''I'll get another bowl.''

With the men seated and the stew served, she removed the saltcellar from the cupboard and coaxed it toward the center of the table. ''Be forewarned, the stew is hot, *and* . . . it needs salt.''

The Nose swept his hand through the steam rising from the bowl. ''You got somethin' to drink?''

''The milk hasn't separated yet, and I used all the spring water to make the stew.'' In actual truth, she had pitched most of the spring water out the window so she'd have none available, but they didn't need to know that.

The reaver's expression turned sour. ''How do you expect me to eat when you don't serve nothin' to drink?''

''I expect you to use your spoon.'' She smiled stiffly. He looked as if he might fling a rejoinder at her, but he was interrupted by a loud slurp from the Tooth.

''No one ever teach you any manners?'' the Nose barked at the one-toothed reaver.

Augusta watched the Tooth's face contort with astonishment, then pain. Either his feelings had been hurt by the Nose's comment, or his tongue had just shriveled in his head from all the salt she'd added to the stew.

''This is great stuff!'' said Elijah, swallowing one mouthful and plunging his spoon into his bowl for another. ''But you're right, Gus. It could do with a bit more salt.''

Sliding the saltcellar toward his bowl, he sprinkled a liberal amount over the stew and began chowing down like a man on the brink of starvation. The Tooth gawked stupidly at Elijah, then dropped his gaze to his own bowl, staring at it in some bewilderment. The Dwarf ventured his first mouthful, then seemed to freeze in position with his eyes round as bandboxes.

"What's wrong with you two?" asked the Nose.

Elijah spoke around a mouthful of carrots. "They probably can't believe how good this is. Eat up, man. Eat up. Plenty more where this came from. In fact, Gus might not let you leave the table 'til you scrape your bowls clean. Like she's always tellin' me, wastin' food's a sin."

Augusta wanted to lean over and kiss him. This was working out much better than she'd imagined. She hadn't expected Elijah to pretend to like the food, but it added the perfect touch to her ploy. The dear. But she couldn't understand how he could consume so much of the stew without gagging. She winced at the torment he was suffering to indulge her.

The Nose shoveled a spoonful into his mouth. "That's the way," encouraged Elijah, noting that the man's expression digressed from sour to horrified, and that his cheek suddenly bulged with liquid he seemed reluctant to swallow. The reaver's eyes darted left and right, right and left, as if looking for someplace to dispose of the liquid that bloated his cheek. Elijah laughed at the man's contortions.

"It's not doin' you a bit of good sloshin' that stuff around in your mouth like that." Reaching out his arm, he delivered a friendly blow to the man's back. "Swallow it, for God's sake."

The Nose grunted. The bulge in his cheek disappeared,

relocating in his eyes, which seemed ready to pop their sockets. He paled; he reddened; he let out a little wheezing sound, and then his mouth twisted into the most impossible shape Augusta had ever seen.

"Kee-reist!" he yelped, shoving his bowl toward the center of the table. "Wha'd she use to make this? Seawater? You wanna listen to me, Jack. She wants to kill you, and she's not actin' like she'd mind takin' us along with you. If you care a lick for your life, don't eat nothin' else that creature serves you."

"Does this mean you won't be eating dessert with us?" inquired Augusta.

"Dessert? Kee-reist, wha'd you plan on servin' for dessert? Fishhooks?" Pushing his chair away from the table, he stood up and gave the blisters on his hands a gentle rub. "One of you tries to work me to death, and the other tries to poison me. I'm hyperin' outta here while I'm still able."

Elijah looked disappointed. "I was hopin' I could convince you to spend the night. We could smoke a few cigars, have a game of checkers."

"Hah!" Flashing a thumbs-up sign to his companions to prize them from their chairs, he began backing slowly away from the table. "If we was to spend the night here, we'd probably wake up tomorrow mornin' in one of those holes you made me dig today. Forget it, Jack. I've got more brains'n that."

Elijah shook his head. "Sorry you feel that way," then, rising to his full height, "but if you insist on leavin', at least let us walk you down to the beach."

The Nose rounded the corner of the table. "Forget it. We can find our own way back."

"Wouldn't hear of it," objected Elijah. Grasping Augusta by her elbow, he waltzed her across the floor in the Nose's wake. "It's only polite."

"You keep your distance," the reaver warned, thrusting his palm out before him as if to ward them off. The Tooth and the Dwarf hastened out the door ahead of him.

"Tell you what," said Elijah, "we'll escort you to the edge of the woods."

With fear etched on his face, the Nose suddenly showed them the back of his head and sprinted out the door. By the time Elijah and Augusta reached the doorstoop, he was halfway to the woods.

"Nice meetin' you!" shouted Elijah, waving his hand over his head in farewell.

"Stop by again when you're in the neighborhood!" called Augusta.

At the edge of the woods, the Nose turned and cupped his hands around his mouth. "You people are crazy! You hear me? Crazy!" And saying that, he charged down the path as if the Devil himself was about to give chase.

Elijah seemed taken aback. "That's never happened before."

"What? That someone has come looking for Bunker's gold?"

"No. That I've scared a fella so badly he didn't shake my hand before leavin'."

She laughed at his statement. "Just how often do you have to contend with reavers searching for gold?"

He gave his shoulders a shrug. "Not often. Once every two or three years. But I learned a long time ago that it doesn't pay to be uncooperative. Let them dig a few holes, kill them with kindness, and by the time they leave, you're all fast friends. Works every time. Phineas used to quote an old proverb: 'What can the enemy do when the friend is cordial?' But Gus, did you have to invite them back?''

Her smile widened. ''I don't think you'll have to worry about their ever coming back. They'll be too afraid they'll have to eat more of my stew. Did you see the expressions on their faces after they'd tasted it?'' She mimicked the face the Tooth had pulled, then, reacting to Elijah's grin, she clapped her hands over her mouth and dissolved into gales of laughter. She doubled over and shot upward again, spun in a drunken circle toward the house, then collapsed to the ground with her back braced against the siding. Her eyes teared, her side ached, and her giggles were following so close upon each other that she couldn't catch her breath. She heard Elijah rumbling with his own laughter, and when he landed on the ground beside her, she leaned into his arm and began crying all the more. The laughter purged her of her earlier anger and irritation. The tears seemed like a baptism of sorts—washing away what had come before to prepare her for a new beginning.

''Gus,'' Elijah choked out on the tail end of a guffaw. ''How'd you think to add all that salt to the stew?''

She howled with another peal of laughter then stopped abruptly. Dragging her hand down her cheeks to dry her tears, she boosted herself away from his arm and looked up at him with innocent, unblinking eyes. ''I . . . they deserved to be taught a lesson for their rudeness. So I . . . obliged them. And you were wonderful, Elijah, pretending to like it as much as you did. That was quite clever on your part. But how did you know to play along with me?'' She hoped the question would divert their conversation away from the subject of salt, but when Elijah furrowed his brow in concentration, she suspected her goose was cooked.

"I'm not entirely stupid, Gus. I know what's enough and what's more than enough. What I can't figure is, how did you empty nearly the whole damn saltcellar into that stew without them seein' you? That stuff can get rock hard sittin' in that container. How'd you hammer it out without anyone noticin'?"

Her dark eyebrows winged upward in what she hoped was a virtuous expression. "Unmitigated luck?"

He shook his head. "You'd need more than luck. Those reavers would have to've been asleep to miss somethin' like that. Either asleep or not there at all."

She felt hot blood rise to the surface of her flesh to stain her cheeks. Riven with guilt, she looked away from him but she couldn't run away from the words he spoke into the silence.

"The salty stew wasn't intended for the reavers at all, was it, Gus? It was meant for me. Rudeness is rudeness, whether it comes from a bunch of reavers or from the man you married."

She bowed her head thinking that, once again, she had ruined everything.

"Guess I deserved to be taught a lesson."

It was the last thing she ever expected 'Lijah Payne to say. She turned back to face him. His head was bowed. When he looked up, he didn't avert his gaze as was his custom, but locked eyes with her, more gentle than she had ever seen him.

"I don't keep a lot of pretty words in my head, Gus. And the ones I do know don't always come out right. I guess you've heard a bellyful of them since you came.

I'm not tryin' to be ornery, but I mean to tell you, it's damn hard learnin' the right words to fill the quiet again. A man gets set in his ways when he spends so much time by himself, but that doesn't mean he likes bein' set in his ways, or that he minds a creature makin' a few changes here and there, gradual like. And it sure as hell isn't proof that he doesn't like a creature. Takes time gettin' used to anything, Gus.''

Although steeped in third-person narrative, Elijah's speech nonetheless struck her with its conciliatory tone, so much so that she felt compelled to make a mild concession herself. ''You don't deserve all the blame for these past few days. I've been told by people who consider themselves authorities on the subject that I'm next to impossible to live with, so it doesn't surprise me that you're experiencing difficulty.''

''How come you didn't mention that in your reply to my advertisement?''

''How come you didn't mention the lighthouse, or the rescues at sea, or the buried treasure that some people seem disposed to kill for?''

Elijah nodded sagely. ''I guess we're even.''

Augusta tucked in her lips. ''Mmmm, not quite. You didn't tell me a lot more than I didn't tell you.''

''That so? Well, here's somethin' you can tell me.'' Reaching his hand toward her face, he rubbed a finger along her cheekbone, then held it up for her perusal. ''How come you wear this white stuff all over your face? What is it, chalk?''

Uncomfortable that he should mention something so personal, she looked away from him. ''It's not chalk. It's . . . it's powder.''

"But why do you wear it? Doesn't it hurt?"

She was self-conscious that he should isolate her defects and want to discuss them, but the fact that he thought powder could be painful tempered her embarrassment. "It doesn't hurt. And I wear it because . . . because that's what Philadelphia ladies do when they want to disguise nature's flaws."

"Flaws?" He touched a knuckle to her cheekbone and glided it tentatively toward the outer corner of her eye. Her breath slowed at his touch. Her heart thumped so loudly against her ribs that she feared she might deafen him. "What flaws does this face have?" He feathered his knuckle halfway across her brow and down her nose, then ever so gently traced the outline of her lips from corner to corner. "I don't see any flaws." His voice grew husky. "Everything looks to be in the right place. And I don't see any scars, or moles, or warts."

Her face felt numb where he'd touched her, and for the first time in her twenty-four years, she felt giddy. "I have freckles," she confessed in a burst of honesty.

His amusement turned to laughter. "That's why you paint your face white as a scrubbed hammock? Because you've got freckles? What's wrong with freckles? Hell, Gus, *I've* got freckles."

"I know," she said in a whisper of breath. "I saw." He was suddenly so quietly intense that it unnerved her, but she couldn't tell whether he was shocked or flattered by her admission. "I'm sorry," she continued. "I shouldn't have said that. I seem to have acquired this knack for saying the worst possible thing at the worst possible time. It comes from . . ." And when no words came, she shook her head. "To be honest, I don't know where it comes from."

Catching her chin in the palm of his hand, he coaxed her face upward. "You're an original, Augusta Payne. Dressed the way I was today, I'm surprised you didn't catch an eyeful of something more than just my freckles. Philadelphia gentlemen probably don't work with their limbs uncovered, do they?"

She felt lulled by his voice, drugged by his eyes. Unable to locate her tongue to form a reply, she shook her head.

"I didn't think so." With an unhurried motion he smoothed his thumb over the contour of her chin, then pressed it vertically atop her lips. His gaze dropped with provocative slowness from her eyes to her lips, then back to her eyes. Parting his lips, he moistened them with the tip of his tongue. "I'm sorry if I embarrassed you with my nakedness today, Gus, but I hope I didn't shock you beyond repair. I know it's sometimes unpleasant for a woman to look at a man's body."

She wanted to tell him that his body was quite the most pleasant thing she had looked upon in nearly a quarter of a century, but she was still having problems with her tongue. And besides, she was sure such an admission would be considered brazen by even the most liberal of gentlemen. "I'm not . . . I mean . . . you're my husband, Elijah."

He dwelled on her face as if he'd somehow forgotten. "Aye," he whispered. "I am that."

She thought she felt his hand tremble, but before she could be sure, he drew his hand away from her face and marked the position of the sun in the sky. "I've gone and wasted the entire day, and here it's almost time to head back up the cylinder. I've got chores that need doin'."

"What you need is sleep," she corrected as he lumbered to his feet. "You've managed only two hours since yesterday morning."

"Too much to do, Gus. Tomorrow morning'll have to be soon enough. You want a hand up?"

She pondered the open palm he offered her, thinking that today hadn't been wasted at all. They had found common ground and built bridges from her world to his, from her being to his. That wasn't wasteful. That was miraculous. She placed her hand in his, not surprised to feel the power that surged through his arm as he drew her to her feet. His flesh was warm, his palm callused, and when she would have withdrawn her hand from his grasp, he circled his fingers around her wrist, holding her close for longer than he needed. She bowed her head, eyeing the bond of their flesh, knowing that beneath the flat of his thumb he could feel the wild tattoo of her pulse. It seemed something a woman should hide from a man, but she could no more hide this than she could fly.

"What would you have done had those reavers been cut from different cloth?" she asked without looking up at him. "What if they had refused to leave the island, or if they had actually used their gun? There were three of them and only one of you. What could you have done?"

With his thumb he stroked the inner flesh of her wrist, as if memorizing its softness. "You didn't have to worry, Gus. If they'd gone afoul, I'da had their guts for garters."

"You'd what?"

He shook his head as he released her hand. "Don't ask." He took a reluctant step away from her. "I'm gonna head down to the beach to see if those fellas have really gone, and then I'm gonna fill in those holes we dug, and then I'll come back here, quick milk the cow, and head up the tower.''

''You can do all that before the sun sets?''

A fire kindled in the depths of his eyes as he took measure of her. ''There's more I'd do before sunset if I'd the time, Gus.''

The look singed her, leaving no doubt as to what he referred. She blushed, she fidgeted with the ringlets at her temples, but she could think of no coherent comment to make in reply, except ''You'd best remember your shovel, then.''

He snapped his fingers. ''Right. And you'll feed the chickens?''

''Chickens. Oh, Lord! Chickens! I completely forgot! One of them escaped this morning, and I haven't found her yet.''

Elijah calmed her with a gesture. ''She's probably tryin' to find a secluded place to lay her eggs. Don't worry. She'll turn up.''

''If the reavers don't mistake her for an Indian and—''

A shot rang out in the distance.

''—shoot her.''

They looked toward the forest before exchanging grim looks with each other. Elijah rubbed the back of his neck. ''I keep my meat cleaver in the pantry, Gus. You got a recipe for chicken soup?''

—8—

Leaning her shoulder against the frame of her bedroom window, Augusta slid her hand beneath the nightgown that served as a curtain and angled it away from the sash. She could see the lighthouse beacon from this window, if not the tower itself, and she wondered if Elijah was keeping a calm watch, or if he, like herself, was wearing a path in the floor with uncharacteristic pacing.

She couldn't sleep. There was no clock in the house save for the sundial carved into the windowsill in the parlor, so she had no idea of the time. But she suspected it was quite late, perhaps past eleven. She had retired for the evening twice already, and twice had gotten up to stare at the beam given off from the lighthouse. Falling asleep had never been particularly difficult for her, but she had never before experienced the kinds of emotion that preyed upon her tonight.

She pressed the back of her hand to the slant of her cheekbone, and in her mind's eye relived that moment when Elijah had touched his knuckle to her flesh, touching her as if her much-heralded imperfections meant nothing to him. He had stroked her cheek, but her reaction played now as a warmth in the center of her breastbone and a soft pressure in her loins. She knew well the ways of a man when he was displaying gentlemanly disinterest in her, but Elijah's overtures did not bespeak a lack of interest. She was not blind. For the briefest moment he had looked at her in a manner in which she thought no man would ever look at her. He had wanted her as a man wants a woman, as a husband wants a wife, and it unsettled her. She had spent so many years defending herself against the hurt of rejection that she found it difficult to relax her guard. She wanted to be accepted, to be loved, but she didn't know if she was capable of giving herself freely to Elijah Payne. It would entail such risk, such courage. She'd never thought marriage would require her to be courageous, but she realized it took a great deal of courage to bare oneself emotionally, spiritually, and physically to another person. The prospect was frightening, but . . .

Her lips curved into a subtle smile. He had caused her to stir. Not with flowery words or fancy gifts, but with a look, a touch. To capture that feeling again—the exhilaration, the anticipation, the closeness—she knew she would be willing to risk everything.

Everything.

Turning away from the window, she removed her wrap from the foot of the bed and flung it over her shoulders. She lit the candle on the bureau, then, lifting the sconce into her hand, made her way through the house, like a wandering spirit in search of human warmth.

At the sound of creaking wood, Elijah set aside his whittling and stood up to peer out the tower glass. There was no moon tonight, so the darkness into which the tower shot its long shaft of light was black as the Earl of Hell's riding boots. He squinted into the blackness and cocked an ear to listen. Wind battered the thick triangles of glass and whistled through the small ventilation ports cut into the baseboard. He curled his toes with the cold and frowned when he heard another unfamiliar groan of wood.

What the hell? He wheeled around to eye the three semicircular levels of lamps and reflectors that comprised Devilstone's light. He knew the oil reservoirs were more than adequate and he'd just finished trimming several wicks. With a practiced glance, he scanned each of the twenty-one lamps. The flames were at the correct levels, the glass chimneys were soot-free, and the reflectors—which Phineas Payne had always likened to barbers' basins—twinkled with a bright silver sheen. Nothing out of order. And if there was nothing wrong with the lamps, he had little to worry about.

Shrugging, he looked away from the light and rubbed his eyes. Black and white spots danced on the backs of his eyelids, attesting to the brightness and intensity of the Argand lamp flame. The spots also proclaimed the hazard of staring into the flame too long, for it always took him a good five minutes to recover from his temporary blindness. Shaking his head as if that might assist the cure, he found his chair again. But he didn't reach for his whittling right away. Blind men were better at carving thumbs than they were at carving wood. And he rather liked his thumbs. It'd be hard to whittle without them.

He held his palms up before his face, rotated them, then noticed for the first time that the backs of his hands were red as boiled lobsters. That's what he got for working out in the sun all day. He wondered if the rest of him was as red as his hands, and thinking it made him aware that his shoulders actually felt scorched and his forehead seemed to be shrinking against his skull. Hell, he was burning up! His neck had been warm for some time now, but he'd attributed that to the thoughts he'd been having.

He'd never advertised for a wife before, and Augusta Mayhew had proven something of a shock. She asked more questions than any woman he'd ever met. She was quick-witted and sharp-tongued and didn't act as if she intended to listen to anything he had to say about anything. He admitted that that aspect of her personality irritated him, but there was another aspect he admired. She didn't seem afraid of man, beast, or the elements. She certainly hadn't shown any trepidation with the reavers, which he found rather remarkable. Any other woman might have swooned, but Gus just got more feisty. He liked the idea of a woman giving as good as she got. It was kind of humorous. But he suspected it would always be humorous when she did it to *other* people, and not so funny when she did it to him.

He shook his head comically. She was a strong-spirited little thing, and a woman needed to be strong to survive on Devilstone. He'd already buried two wives; he didn't want to bury another. But as Gus had said, he seemed to have trouble with his wives living.

A rash of goose bumps peppered his flesh as he dwelled on that thought. The bitter taste of long-forgotten guilt filled his mouth. She would ask about his wives again, and one day he would have to tell her. But what would happen when she discovered the truth? He suspected she would find more cutting words than narrow-minded and contrary to rain upon him. Why did she have to ask so many questions? Why couldn't she be happy as Mrs. Elijah Payne without having to drag the past into their marriage? Lydia and Eliza had never asked questions. They'd been more docile, the way he figured all women should be. But not Gus. Gus even wanted to sail into Lustre's Gate. And he could just imagine the hell that would break loose if any of the villagers caught her ear and told her what they knew about the wickie of Devilstone Light.

It made his stomach grind into knots.

Gus seemed sensible enough. Maybe she wouldn't believe the tales. But what if she did? Would she try to leave him?

He bowed his head and traced a line in his palm, unable to fathom spending more years by himself on this island. Gus accused him of working too hard and too much. Couldn't she understand that his work was the only thing that had kept him sane over the years? If a man worked himself senseless, he wouldn't have time to think how lonely he really was. He wouldn't have the time to remind himself that he was a prisoner on this island and always would be. He wouldn't have to think about what would happen to him if he were gone from this island for even one night. If Gus left him, he wouldn't be able to chase after her. He'd have to let her go, and he didn't want to do that. He liked having her around. He liked her cooking.

He liked poking fun at her female logic. He liked looking at her, touching her.

He took a deep breath as another blast of heat raced up his neck. This afternoon he'd wanted to do more than just touch her cheek. But he'd reminded himself, reluctantly, that Augusta Mayhew was a lady, and even if she was his wife, it didn't give him the right to use her physically for the singular purpose of slaking his desire. He wanted her to feel comfortable with him before he took her to his bed. It might take a week. It might take longer. But he was willing to wait. He'd waited six years for another wife. A few more days wouldn't make that much difference.

If she got to know him better, perhaps she would feel less self-conscious when they finally did come together. She might be less tense, less nervous. He could extend that consideration to her for a time. He could deny himself any husbandly pleasure until Gus was ready. Only an animal would bed a woman he'd known only two full days. He wanted to show Augusta that he was made of finer stuff than that, and when she saw this side of him, maybe she'd be better able to reject anything she might hear from the residents of Lustre's Gate. So he would postpone his pleasure if it meant that, in future, she would pledge him her loyalty and her heart.

Creeeeak.

He shot out of his chair and in three quick strides was standing above the hatch that led to the watchroom on the floor below. He blinked to clear his vision of persistent blind spots, then lifted his brows when he found himself looking down into Gus's upturned face.

"Gus? Jeesuz, I didn't know what was down there. What're you doin' up? How come you're not in bed?"

"I couldn't sleep. May I come up?"

Her candle flame highlighted the soft rises of her face and shaded its hollows, making of her countenance an image so lovely to behold that he couldn't refuse her. "I guess it's about time you saw the lantern anyways. Yah, c'mon up. But blow out your candle and leave it on the table down there. You can't climb up the ladder with a candle sconce in your hand."

She ascended the ladder from the watchroom to the lantern without difficulty, and when she was halfway through the hatch, Elijah straddled the opening, fit his hands around her waist, and swung her up onto solid flooring. Minus her corset she felt wonderfully soft to him, her waist small and yielding, her hips full without being fleshy. And the braid that trailed down her back was so long and thick that he guessed if she unplaited it and let it hang loose around her, it would veil her flesh like a cloak. The image was so provocative that he quick let go her waist, crossed his arms over his chest, and clamped his hands beneath his armpits so they'd be out of harm's way.

"So this is where you spend your nights."

Her nightgown was a full white thing that covered her from neck, to wrist, to the middle of her calves. He didn't find it particularly alluring, but the idea that she was as naked beneath her nightgown as he was beneath his shirt made his blood hum in his chest. Two satin ribbons secured the gown at her throat. With his eyes he caressed those ribbons, toying with them, flirting with them, slowly unlooping them so he could slip his fingers beneath the placket and part—

"The lamps are so bright." Augusta shielded her forearm over her eyes and looked to Elijah for confirmation, causing him to startle out of his trance. He regarded her vacantly. He'd been so preoccupied, his ears had stopped functioning, but he managed to pull her last word out of the air.

"Bright? Yah." He nodded toward the lamps. "Each one of those lamps burns as bright as seven candles. Don't look directly at them. They make your eyes crazy."

Dropping her arm, she looked curiously about the room. "What exactly do you do up here all night?"

"A little bit of everything, I guess. Keep a watch for founderin' ships. Trim wicks. Adjust the lamps. Keep the oil reservoirs filled and the reflectors clean. Dust the apparatus if it needs it. Whittle plugs for lobster claws."

"Whittle what?"

He indicated the pile of wood shavings on the floor by his chair. "You ever see a lobster plug?"

"I've never seen a lobster."

"Never seen a lobster! Gus? Where've you been all your life?"

"Philadelphia," she replied as he took several long strides toward her.

Hunkering down by the chair, he sorted through the shavings, plucked something from the pile, then stood up before her. "*This* is a lobster plug." He rolled it around in his palm so she could see. It was narrow—about an inch and a half long—shaped like a wedge with a tapered point, and made from pine. "If you stick these in the lobster's thumb joints, they'll hold his claws shut. It's a lot easier handlin' the little cusses if you don't have to worry about them snippin' your fingers off at the base."

"They can do that?" She peered up at him with eyes that were round in disbelief, making him realize he hadn't noticed the color of her eyes before, but in the lantern light they looked to be of a greenish brown cast. Pretty eyes, he thought, with lashes as black as her hair.

"They can do that," he answered, wondering what it was about her tonight that made her look so appealing. Something was different. He just couldn't figure out what. "Devilstone lobsters can be mean buggers, but you can't beat the taste of them when they're hot boiled, fresh cracked, and swimmin' in butter. I'll have to catch you one so you can see for yourself."

"I'd like that."

He thought he should look away from her, but his eyes seemed unwilling to follow the directive from his brain. She was much too pleasant to look upon to cause him to turn away. However, her nearness was making him acutely aware that he hadn't had a woman for six years, and that his desire could not be as easily suppressed as he'd hoped. He made a fist around the lobster plug and searched for something to say that would divert his thoughts. "Phineas used to whittle. Not pine so much as other things. Whale ivory, mostly. And then there was always the occasional whale's tooth that Cap'n Crowley would bring him. He'd dig out an old sail needle and jackknife and spend weeks scrapin' and etchin'. Reminded him of his whalin' days on the other side of the world."

"Your father was a whaler?"

"He was that, until the stink of the tryworks got so thick in his nostrils that everything began smellin' like rendered blubber. So he hung up his harpoon and decided to find a place with a sweeter smell."

"A place with a smell of woodland pine and salt air,"

she recited. "It seems Phineas Payne and I were drawn to Devilstone Island for much the same reason."

Elijah eyed her queerly. "How come you remember that advertisement so well, Gus? It was just a bunch of words."

She smiled into his face, a soft, gentle look that warmed him from the neck down. "To you, it was a bunch of words. To me, it was a piece of my future. How could I forget anything so important?"

Not knowing how to reply to that, he simply stared at her, thinking that at any moment he was going to drown in her eyes.

"I suppose it was Phineas who taught you how to use the harpoon?"

Elijah nodded. "I've heard tell that Phineas was the best damn harpoonist who ever sailed a floatin' stinkpot."

"And the ivory and whales' teeth that he carved. What did you do with them? I'm surprised you don't have a whatnot in the parlor to display them."

"Phineas wasn't the showy sort. After he finished somethin', he'd stow it in the attic. Everything's still up there in the same trunk, along with the daily logs he kept for the lighthouse. You ever wanna see them, I could show you what trunk they're in. He did nothin' but the finest kind of work."

She smiled at the pride in his voice. "You miss him very much, don't you." It was statement not question.

"Sure. He was practically the only person I ever saw for twenty years. When he passed on, it was as if . . . as if . . ."

"—as if the sun had set with no hope of ever rising again. You realize that your parent's death marks the end of childhood forever, and whether you wish it or not, nothing will ever be the same. It's like dying your own little death.''

Elijah regarded her in awe. ''Why's it so easy for you to put my feelin's into words?''

''Maybe because I've had occasion to feel the same things, and think the same thoughts. I know a person can become so devastated by the death of loved ones that he can become hardened to death. To other people he might appear compassionless. But I suppose people involved in dangerous occupations might have to control their reactions in order to survive. They're not compassionless. Only cautious.''

To Elijah it sounded as if she was trying to rationalize his behavior the night the seaman had died. He had no objection to that, but he had no wish to discuss survival or death. Not tonight.

Into the awkward silence that lengthened between them, Augusta asked, ''How long was your father lightkeeper on Devilstone?''

''A long time. He bought the island from Massachusetts in 1797 when Maine was still just a district of the Commonwealth. Paid three dollars and fifty cents for it, which was quite a sum in those days. Some of the residents of Lustre's Gate helped him build the lighthouse, but he built the main house all by himself and kept addin' on sheds as the years passed.''

''And what of your mother? You've never mentioned her.''

Panic flickered in his eyes. Wrenching his gaze away from her, he knelt down and quickly began to scoop wood shavings into his hand.

"I never knew my mother, Gus. If you're ready to head back down the cylinder, maybe you could take these with you and—"

Bam!

The outside glass shuddered. Augusta shrieked. Elijah sprang to his feet, body alert and eyes searching. He threw an arm around Augusta's shoulders, drawing her against him, then took a slow step toward the window. At about chest level he saw the blood smearing the glass. He reached out a finger to test the integrity of the panel, and when he discovered that no crack had formed, he patted Augusta's shoulder.

"It's all right, Gus. It was just a bird. Sometimes that happens. They try to fly right into the fire, but the glass stops them first." He could feel the tension leave her arm, could hear her breathing return to its normal cadence.

"I'm sorry I screamed, but I . . . it frightened me."

She fit neatly beneath his arm, making him aware what a tiny little thing she was. He felt the press of her hip against his flank, the sharpness of her elbow against his rib. She held her wrap tight across her bosom as if shielding herself from other dangers that might be lurking in the night. But he wondered if she realized the only real danger she faced was from him. He glanced down at the crown of her head. The flesh of her center part was pale as the cotton of her nightgown, and for a forbidden moment, he wondered if the flesh he couldn't see was as pale as the flesh he could. He curled his fingers around the cap of her shoulder, liking the way she fit against his body.

"Funny thing how some birds are attracted to the light," he rambled on. "Phineas used to compare them to the birds who'd fly into the fires at whalin' stations. Fire birds, he called them."

"Is the glass damaged? Did it break?"

"A bird's gotta be pretty damn big to break this glass. That one was too small to cause any damage. The only thing he did was make enough noise to scare the bejesus out of you." He fingered the soft yarn of her wrap. She laughed at his comment and turned in his arm, accidentally slashing her elbow across his ribs.

"Aghh!" He grabbed her elbow, sucked in his breath with the pain, and eased himself gently away from her.

"Elijah?" Her hand flitted up and down, not knowing where to touch him. "Are you all right? Did I hurt you?"

He forced a smile as he touched his fingertips to his ribs. "I'm fine," he rasped out. "Just sufferin' from a dose of too much sun. Come mornin', I suspect I'll be right as rain again."

She cocked her head, slatting her eyes at him. "Is the rest of you as red as your face?"

"Dunno. Haven't looked." As an afterthought, he elevated his hands. "Backs of my hands are."

"Is it very painful?"

"Stings some."

"And I suspect it will sting worse by morning. Do you have any vinegar handy?"

He frowned at the request. "Vinegar? Kinda late in the evenin' to be thinkin' about cleanin' windows, isn't it, Gus?"

"It's not for the windows. It's for your sunburn. Vinegar will soothe the sting."

He screwed his mouth to the side and rubbed his jaw. His eyes mirrored his distaste. "I dunno. How much of that damn stuff would I have to drink before it would do any good?''

Augusta rolled her eyes toward the ceiling. "How does a man reach the age of twenty-eight and know so little about sunburn remedies?"

"If a man is smart enough to remember to wear a shirt while he's workin' in the sun, he doesn't have to fret about sunburns *or* remedies. And you didn't answer my question. How much vinegar do I have to drink?"

"Elijah, you don't have to drink the vinegar at all. You're supposed to apply it to the surface of your skin, wherever the flesh is burned.''

He lifted his brows. "That so? I don't have to drink it? Well, if that's the case, I just happen to know where I can find some in the watchroom. You wait here. I'll be right back.'' He bent down to scoop up his wood shavings again, and once the floor was clean, disappeared down the ladder. Augusta wandered toward the glass. Looking upward, she found the place where the bird had struck the tower, and lifting her hand, touched the glass. On the outside of the window, clinging to the hideous stain of blood, was a solitary feather that looked as soft and wispy as a fern frond. She bemoaned the loss of the bird, but had no idea how to prevent something like that from happening again. There were times when the laws of nature seemed grossly unfair. That simple curiosity could kill was a harsh reality to embrace.

And what of her own curiosity? If Elijah chose never to tell her about Lydia and Eliza, could she abide that? Could she live with the fact that he was even unwilling to discuss his own mother? He said he hadn't known her. It was common enough that women died in childbed, but if she'd been wife to Phineas on this island, and had given birth to Elijah on this island, where was her grave? All the markers in the cemetery bore an inscription of some kind. If they were valid, it proved there were no females buried on Devilstone other than Lydia and Eliza. So where was his mother's body? It had to be somewhere, unless . . .

A startling thought took hold of her. *Unless she's not dead at all. Unless she's still alive.*

"Here you go, Gus."

She pivoted around as Elijah vaulted off the ladder. "One bottle of vinegar." He strode toward her, brandishing a long-necked, dark stoneware bottle. "What do you want me to do? Splash some of this on my hands and face?"

"And anywhere else that needs it."

He hesitated, the humor draining from his face as he realized how much of his body was in need of treatment. "Yah. Right." He held the bottle against him, rubbing the cork with his thumb. "Look, Gus, I can take care of this. Why don't you crawl back under the kelp and see if you can get some sleep."

"It's a messy task. I don't mind helping."

He didn't respond. He merely stood there, looking uncomfortable. Augusta studied his face with some amusement.

"If I didn't know better, I'd guess your hesitation indicated a sense of modesty. Might I remind you that you were unclothed for the better part of the day? You won't be showing me anything tonight that I didn't already see this afternoon—and in better light."

But he knew something had changed between them in

the past few hours. This afternoon she had been safe from him. Tonight, she wasn't. Tonight, he wanted her, and stripping the clothes from his body wouldn't ease the situation.

"Are you shy of a sudden?"

"No, I'm—" He wanted to say honorable; that he wouldn't take advantage of a woman he barely knew, even if she *was* his wife. But he thought it best left unsaid. "No. I'm not shy. Here, hold this." He thrust the bottle into her hand, then, steeling himself against temptation, he yanked his shirttails out of his breeches and peeled the garment over his head.

His torso blazed a rich, vivid red. Augusta winced at the imagined pain. "You're redder than the famed Mayhew hair."

"The what?"

She shook her head and indicated the chair. "Never mind. Just sit down so I can apply something cool to your poor skin. You may have just created a new color in skin tones."

While he sat, she adjusted her wrap to hang like a scarf around her neck rather than a shawl around her shoulders. With her hands freed up, she unstoppered the cork on the vinegar bottle, set it on the floor, then stepped around Elijah's chair where she could have access to his back. She poured a small amount of liquid into her right palm, and with a "This might be a little cold," splashed it onto his spine.

"*Aghhh!*" His torso stiffened. His arms locked in place. "This your idea of revenge for havin' to walk shoeless over cold floors the first night you arrived?"

"This is nothing," she said, mimicking the words he'd

used that night. "Wait until February." She splashed more vinegar into her palm, then, more slowly than before, drizzled it over the rise of his shoulder blade. His muscles didn't relax, but at least they didn't grow more rigid. "Better?"

"No."

She massaged the liquid over his flesh with her fingertips. "You're spleeny."

"Damn right."

His back was wider than her forearm was long, a back so solidly formed that it seemed cast from rock. It was smooth, and hot, and beautiful, and touching it seemed to set her palm aflame.

"I smell like a dish of pickled beets," he grumbled.

"There's nothing wrong with the way you smell." And as she worked her way upward from his waistband to his shoulder, she remembered her brothers-in-law and the smells she had come to associate with them. Charles, the undertaker, had always smelled of dead flowers. Harvey, the librarian, had smelled like an old book. And both Godfrey and Stanley had wreaked of the macassar oil they used in their hair. But Elijah smelled neither dead, nor old, nor oily. He smelled like fresh air and sunshine. He smelled manly, and wonderful.

Her hand grazed his shoulder, drifting over the freckles that marred his flesh. His shoulder was thick and hard, and as she shaped her hand around it, she slowed the motion of her palm, savoring the feel of him, his strength, his hotness.

Her throat felt suddenly dry. She cleared it with effort. "Bend your head forward so I can do your neck."

He bowed his head, and when he did, his hair parted

of its own accord, baring the paler flesh of his neck. His hair was nothing like her own. It was neither frizzy nor unruly, and it didn't seem to have a separate will of its own. It winged forward over his face like silk fringe, long and sleek and freshly washed, and the way it caressed the curve of his neck made her ache to caress him in a like manner, to touch him as a wife might touch him, without fear or hesitation. "Your neck doesn't seem to have suffered as much as the rest of you. I suppose the length of your hair provided some protection. I . . . I think I'll do your arms now."

Hearing her intent, Elijah lifted his left arm out in scarecrow fashion for her, praying that she would finish what she was about quickly. He was a man of strong resolve, but even he had limits beyond which his self-control would cease to function. She was touching him in places no female had touched for six long years. The motion of her hand was setting fire to his nerve endings; the gentleness of her fingers was making him crave her touch on that part of his body that had thickened with his desire and was even now straining against the confinement of his breeches. He kept his head bowed and his eyes closed as she smoothed the liquid over the swell of his biceps, circling around to the underside of his arm, lightly stroking flesh he had never thought sensitive—until now. He shivered at the pressure of her fingertips, and when she skimmed a hollow of flesh close to his armpit, he felt a sensation so exquisite course through him that he gritted his teeth to prevent himself from moaning with the pleasure of it.

"I'm sorry the vinegar is so cold, 'Lijah. I don't mean to make you shiver."

His reply was a silent nod. *Hurry, Gus. Just hurry*. And

she seemed to heed his unspoken plea, for no more than a few seconds later she was lowering his arm to his side.

"If you'll look up, I'll do your face."

He threw his head back. She had stepped between his parted knees and was standing so close he could smell the starch of her nightgown. With a gentle hand she fanned his hair away from his face. "My sisters have hair like yours."

"Two-toned and ragged?"

"No. Glossy. And beautiful."

That she would consider anything about him beautiful caused him to blush beneath his sunburn. "Men aren't beautiful, Gus."

She sprinkled more vinegar onto her fingers and avoided looking into his eyes as she smoothed it over his cheek. "Some are." Her expression was so serious that he noticed the flesh between her brows split into two vertical creases, and as he studied her countenance, it suddenly occurred to him what was different about her tonight.

"So *this* is what Augusta Payne really looks like," he marveled.

She snatched her hand away from his face and pressed the backs of her fingers to her cheek, looking as though she found it truly painful that he should mention anything about her looks.

"Gus. I'm not pokin' fun."

She lowered her eyes self-consciously. "I'm sorry you weren't able to marry one of the younger Mayhew daughters. They have perfect complexions, and perfect hair, and perfect smiles. They swoon perfectly, and flirt perfectly, and would never be so bold to look a man straight in the eye. I chided you for not telling me everything about yourself or the island, 'Lijah, but it's you who could chide me for being less than honest. I never told you that, in a family of swans, I was always considered something of a toad. You married a toad.''

Had she not sounded so downtrodden, he might have laughed, but intuition counseled him this was not a time for levity. Reaching up, he drew her hand away from her cheek. ''Are we discussin' freckles again, Gus?''

She nodded.

''Were you the only creature in Philadelphia born with freckles?''

''I was the only one in the Mayhew family born with freckles.''

''And tell me again what's wrong with them?''

''It's in every piece of ladies' literature you'll ever read. They're unsightly. Splattered across a woman's face, they give her an uncomely appearance. They make a woman wholly undesirable.''

He suspected they were discussin' an issue more vital than freckles here, but he wasn't sure what the issue was. ''Are you jealous of the way your sisters look, Gus?''

''Jealous? I love my sisters. It would be unchristian of me to be jealous of them.''

But it might be human, he thought. And he wondered what it must have been like for Augusta, living in a house where she would never measure up to the ideal. He wondered how a child would be affected if her defects were constantly brought to the fore and paraded about for public comment. She would probably grow up critical and rough-edged, he theorized, and would try to hide her imperfections behind face powder or a hand raised to her cheek. He had thought his new bride sharp-tongued and fearless, but perhaps she was more fragile than he realized.

He squeezed her hand and gave it a gentle shake. "Look at me, Gus. Not at the floor. At my face. There. That's better. I'm gonna say this, and I'm gonna say it only once. I like the way you look without that damn powder all over your face. It makes no damn's-odds to me what they think in Philadelphia. You're on Devilstone now. Anyone who's anyone on Devilstone has a few freckles to boast about. That was one of the other requirements I meant to list in my advertisement: 'Woman must come equipped with own galoshes and freckles.' They make you look real, Gus. They make you look as if someone sprinkled little grains of sand all over your face."

She cringed at the analogy. He shrugged. "I guess that's not what you wanted to hear. I told you I'm not good puttin' pretty words together. But I happen to like sand, Gus. It's a lot easier on the feet than rocks or barnacles."

She fixed him with a pathetic look that slid gradually into a smile. "What you lack in eloquence, you make up for in simplicity. Thank you for that, Elijah."

"You're welcome. Now, are you gonna finish slappin' that stuff on my face, or do I have to sit here and wait for my skin to go up in smoke?"

"I'm sorry, I'm sorry."

He pressed his thumb into the center of her palm and gave her hand a final squeeze before releasing it. "Maybe you can get to my forehead next. Everything between my hairline and eyebrows feels dry as a widow's kiss." He was beginning to appreciate the soothing effect of her remedy. His back already felt less inflamed. If only he could ask her to soothe the place on his body that required the greatest relief.

"You've had so little sleep in the past two days, 'Lijah. I don't understand how you're able to stay awake."

He closed his eyes as she moistened his brow. "Have to stay awake. Don't want the superintendent of lights to dismiss me for neglect of duty. And sleepin' on watch is one sure way to neglect my duty." But his eyelids suddenly felt so weighted he wasn't sure he could open them again. She touched every part of his face with her hand—eyebrows, temple and cheek—seducing him into relaxation, lulling him into quiet repose. Exhaustion settled into his limbs on cat's feet. She elevated his chin, spreading more vinegar over the dark stubble below his jaw. Her hand was so cool; his flesh was so hot. He suffered a wrenching in his loins as she anointed his throat with long strokes of her fingertips. And when her fingers dipped toward his collarbone, he covered them desperately with his own, flattening her hand against his neck so she could feel the quickening of his pulse against her palm.

"Your hand feels so good," he said in a hoarse voice. He stroked her fingers with a shy hand, torn between resolution and desire. He opened his eyes, allowing his gaze to linger on the crisp white sleeve of her nightgown, then higher, to her shoulder, where her knitted wrap hung in long folds to her waist. With his free hand he reached upward to finger the wrap, then, grasping its fringed end, flung it off her shoulder.

His eyes roved the length of her. He saw the fullness of her bosom limned beneath the hang of her nightgown and for a powerful moment felt himself being drawn to her like a fire bird to fire. He craved to touch what he could not see; to taste what he could not feel. He inhaled a slow breath, then with his eyes burning holes in his sockets, he shaped a tentative hand to the curve of her waist.

She was so small from front to back that even the waistband of her drawers added only slight thickness to her form. She felt delicate as a piece of shell, but it was a delicacy tempered by a woman's strength, a woman's shape. And that shape became more apparent as his hand gathered in the blousiness of her gown, elongating pleats and folds against the full round swell of her breast. The cotton strained, seeming to chafe her, but it could not flatten the thick bud of flesh that stood proudly erect beneath it, thrusting so far outward that he could see its wine-dark color beneath the cotton's whiteness.

"Jeesuz, Gus." He shook his head in an attempt to marshal his emotions. Light-headed and heavy-limbed, he wrested his hand from her waist and nodded toward the vinegar bottle. "Maybe you'd better let me finish up what you started." The thought of her hand stroking his naked chest was near driving him to madness.

"I can finish."

"No." He snatched the bottle from her hand. "You can't. And don't go gettin' all breezed up. It's for your own good . . . and mine too. We'll both feel better in the mornin' because of it."

"Because of what?"

"Because of . . . for not . . . for not doin' what I'd like to do right now. Dammit, Gus, a man can abide just so much."

"So much what?"

"Temptation! A man can abide just so much temptation!'' Without a care for spillage or waste, he upended the vinegar bottle, pouring the contents over his chest. With an ungentle hand, he spread the moisture across his flesh. ''I'm no monk.'' His chest hair darkened and curled with the dampness, and reacting to the roughness of his own touch, his nipples grew small and tight.

''I'm not asking you to be a monk,'' Augusta whispered.

His hand stilled midmotion. In the lamplight her eyes were softly green, and when she looked at him with those eyes, an emotion so electrifying passed between them that it lifted the down of the back of his neck. She stepped away from him and fumbled to draw her night wrap back over her shoulder. Her movements were awkward. She looked discomfited. But he said nothing to ease her awkwardness; he did nothing except sit and stare, his emotions in complete disarray.

''Perhaps you should go back to the house for a while, Elijah. You . . . you look so tired. I could stand watch for you for an hour or two so you could get some sleep. Truly, I'm so wide awake I might as well volunteer for duty. I wouldn't be able to sleep if I went to bed now anyway. Maybe by the time you wake up, I'll be in more of a mood for sleep. You might as well take advantage of the opportunity. That's one of the reasons I'm here, isn't it? To relieve you?''

His face was haggard as he nodded. ''To relieve me. I don't think you'll ever know how much I need to be relieved tonight, Gus.''

''Then you'll sleep for an hour? The bed is already warm.''

With that he stood up, unable to defend against any more of her torment. ''An hour isn't so very long, is it?''

She shook her head. "Just tell me what's expected of an assistant wickie, and I'll do it."

Whether the origin was physical or emotional, he was suddenly so bone-weary he could hardly stand, but he grinned at her despite his exhaustion. "The oil reservoirs are full, and I finished trimmin' the wicks no more than twenty minutes ago. Everything should be all shipshape and Bristol fashion for a while. All you gotta do is keep an eye skinned for any trouble offshore. The first sign of anything suspicious, you come and wake me up. But it's a fair night tonight. I'm thinkin' you'll be treated to a pretty quiet watch, at least for an hour."

"I'll be fine," she assured him. Grabbing his shirt from the back of the chair, she thrust it at him. "Go now, before you drop."

"You sure you're gonna be all right up here by yourself?" he asked as he shrugged into his shirt.

"I'm sure." She shooed him toward the ladder, following behind him as he went. "You'll see. You'll be proud of me."

He slid a foot onto the ladder. "The way you handled yourself with those three fellas today, I'm already proud of you."

She beamed at his praise. Elijah laughed at her expression.

"You look like you're glowin' from the inside out."

"I am."

He grinned a crooked grin. Elevating his hand toward her face, he sketched a line from her temple to her jaw with a solitary finger. "Doesn't surprise me. I don't think anything about you is gonna surprise me anymore. See you in an hour or so."

She watched him disappear down the ladder. When he

was gone, she spun around in an exuberant circle, braid swinging and night wrap flapping. She imagined taking him back to Philadelphia with her, promenading him before her sisters, watching intently as they turned green with envy. Ole Augusta might have frizzy hair and eyes that were a placid hazel, but she had a husband who was more beautiful than any Mayhew ancestor who had ever lived, and that gave her something to crow about.

She slouched into Elijah's chair. With a warmth of feeling coursing through her, she angled the back of her head against the stayrail and closed her eyes, savoring her private feelings. She'd never thought herself capable of enticing a man, but tonight Elijah had been enticed, and it filled her with expectancy. Her flesh tingled from her breasts to her loins, and she thought if this was the secret that all married women shared, it was indeed something to be whispered about. So perhaps when Elijah wasn't tired and when he wasn't on duty, he'd be more inclined to succumb to temptation.

Tomorrow would do nicely.

She raised her head every so often to peruse the darkness beyond the lighthouse, but naught seemed amiss. Her limbs cooled after a space, so she hugged her wrap closer about her shoulders. Her eyes began to feel grainy. She yawned, and blinked, and settled more comfortably into the chair. She made a cursory survey of the lamps, then tried to blink the subsequent blind spots from her eyes, but they would not be blinked away.

She closed her eyes, waiting for her vision to clear, and while she waited, she did something unforgivable.

She fell asleep.

—9—

The wind whispered across her cheek as she sat on the edge of the cliff above the storm beach. With an idle hand she drew circles in the grass, clockwise then counterclockwise, big then small, and then what she touched suddenly moved. The earth rumbled and shook. She leapt to her feet to escape, but the ground beneath her gave way like a trapdoor and she was falling . . .

. . . *faaaalllling* . . .

Her head snapped forward, waking her with a jerk.

She threw her head back reflexively. Her eyes shot open. With her heart lodged somewhere in her throat, she gaped at her surroundings, unable to perceive where she was for a full half-second before her memory flooded her consciousness. The lamps. The tower. She remembered where she was now, but—

"Dear God, I fell asleep." Panic riffled through her. Still dazed, she catapulted out of her chair and threw a bleary gaze into the night. Her vision was fuzzy. Doubling her hands into fists, she scrubbed the sleep from her eyes. How long had she been dozing? She squinted into the brightness of the lamps and their reflectors, wondering if Elijah would need to tend them soon. How long had he been gone? If she hadn't fallen asleep herself, she might be better able to gauge the time, but now she had no idea.

She worried her lower lip as she peered again into the darkness. Should she go back to the house to fetch him? What if he had overslept? What if he'd been asleep for hours? She rubbed a crick in her neck.

What if they both had?

A queasy feeling settled in the pit of her stomach. She couldn't tell him about her lapse of duty. She couldn't. She'd told him she would give him cause to be proud of her. He wouldn't be proud that she had fallen asleep. Knowing Elijah's regard for duty, he would find it unforgivable, and so would the superintendent of lights. And both men would be right. Her breach of responsibility *was* unforgivable. She could vow never to fall asleep on watch again, but the fact remained that if anyone found out about her transgression this evening, Elijah could very well be dismissed.

Guilt settled atop her queasiness.

He would be so disappointed in her. How could she face that? She had survived everyone else's disappointment in her. She didn't think she could survive Elijah's. So . . . she wouldn't tell him what she'd done. In this instance she suspected her silence would cause less harm than her honesty. As for the lamps and their immediate care, she couldn't leave that to chance. She needed to fetch Elijah before something unthinkable happened.

Not waiting to contemplate the matter further, she climbed down the ladder to the watchroom, located the matchbox on the wall, lit the candle sconce she'd left on the table, then descended the circular staircase to the base of the tower. She stayed close to the cylinder wall, where the angle of each step was wider, but even with the wall for support she found the descent a dizzying one. Her footfalls became so uncertain that the arches of her feet began to tingle, but despite her anxiety, she pressed onward.

Once reaching the floor of the lighthouse, she passed into the connecting storage shed, where the large barrels of whale oil were housed, then continued wending her way through the entire series of adjoining sheds until she reached the house. She offered up a silent prayer of thanks that Elijah hadn't climbed the tower to find her dozing. After nearly a quarter-century, perhaps her luck was beginning to change. She tiptoed through the kitchen and parlor and, after crossing the threshold into the bedroom, held the sconce high to cast light on her sleeping husband.

The bed was empty.

The covers were more rumpled now than when she'd left, which indicated Elijah might have been resting earlier. But where was he now? "Elijah?" She frowned at the shadows hovering in the corners of the room. Had he gone outside to use the convenience?

Suspecting that to be the case, she crossed back into the parlor and gazed out the window on the west wall of the house.

Nothing looked to be afoot. There was no errant light on the path leading to the outhouse, no oblique shadows wandering in the darkness. More curious now, she stepped back from the window. "'Lijah?" The floorboards squeaked beneath her slight weight as she walked back to the kitchen. She couldn't imagine where he was, unless . . . unless he had gone back to the tower at the same time she had made her way to the house. If he had cut across the yard instead of going through the sheds, she wouldn't have seen him. Which meant *he* could be wandering about the tower now wondering where *she* was.

Rolling her eyes at the obvious mix-up, she hurried back to the lighthouse the way she'd come and, with a quick but guarded step, began reclimbing the tower stairs. Twenty-five feet up, her quick step slowed to a trudge. Fifty feet up, gasping and winded, she staggered into the watchroom and leaned, panting, against the wall. "'Lijah?" She studied the ceiling, expecting to hear her husband's footsteps, but from the room above her, there was naught but silence.

"Are you up there?"

Silence.

Where on earth was he?

Unable to answer her own question, she decided there was little for her to do but climb back up to the lantern and wait. He would have to come back sometime. Wouldn't he?

A little more than an hour later, he did.

"I think I slept longer than I said I would, Gus. Hope that didn't cause you any problem. How come you're lookin' at me so queer?"

"Because I went back to the house over an hour ago

and you weren't there. You weren't anywhere. It was as if you just . . . just disappeared.''

He laughed as he turned away from her to inspect the lamps. ''I don't know where you were lookin', Gus, but I was in bed the whole time. I didn't even get up to use the convenience.''

''I held my candle above the bed, Elijah, and you weren't in it. There are many things I am not. Nearsighted is not one of them.''

''But sleepy is. You didn't fall asleep on me and dream the whole thing up, did you?''

She stared at his back as he lifted the lid of one of the oil reservoirs. ''No, I . . . I didn't fall asleep. And I didn't dream anything up. You weren't there when I went to fetch you.''

''Why'd you come to fetch me?'' And even as the last word left his mouth, he wheeled around. ''Was there trouble off the ledge?''

''No. But I thought you'd been gone long enough. I was getting nervous about the lamps.''

''No need to, Gus. They were fine. Still are. But I'm not so sure about you. I think you're havin' pipe dreams on me.''

She diverted her gaze toward the window. White-faced seals and missing bodies. Was her imagination running completely amok? But it had seemed so real. She was sure she hadn't been dreaming. So what was the explanation?

She didn't know. She simply did not know.

''You can head back to the house now, Gus. And I tell you what. Seein's how you were up so long tonight, why don't you plan to sleep later in the mornin'. I'll get my own breakfast.'' She shrugged as he guided her toward the ladder. ''You did a fine piece of work tonight, Mrs. Payne. Looks like my position on Devilstone is safe for at least another night. Get yourself some sleep and quit havin' those pipe dreams.'' He ruffled her hair with a playful hand as she negotiated the ladder, but when he returned to stand before the tower glass, his playful hand clenched into a fist, and the eyes that Augusta had seen smolder with passion only a short time earlier suddenly darkened and filled with fear.

She found the kitchen garden where Haydon Crowley had told her she'd find it—on the near side of the stand of spruce that flanked the cobblestoned beach. It occupied an area no larger than the space allotted for the graveyard, and thrived with such greenery that it amazed her.

She'd been unable to sleep late as Elijah had suggested. Her inability to explain his disappearance the night before had weighed so heavily on her mind that she'd slept only fitfully the remainder of the night and had risen the moment the sun washed the darkness from the eastern horizon. She'd found her way to the garden even before Elijah had come down from the tower and headed back to the house now with a basket full of onions and carrots for use in her chicken soup. She traversed the footpath that bordered the shore, for the coolness of early morning was less apparent with the sun on her face. The island's interior paths were too densely foliated to allow the sun's penetration. She'd followed one of the interior paths to the garden a half hour earlier and was still shivering from the effects.

Her steps were unhurried as she picked her way along the footpath. Long blades of grass, heavy with dew, overhung the path. And as she brushed past them, they bent against her hem, painting her skirt with ribbons of moisture. Beyond the garden, she passed a wasteland of rounded stone and fractured ledges that formed a horseshoe-shaped cove. She paused for a moment, thinking of the soap and towel she had packed in her basket. She'd thought to bathe in a warm tidal pool this morning, but she was coming to realize that Maine mornings were not conducive to stripping off one's clothes. Yet she wanted to be clean for Elijah in case—a secret smile touched her lips—well, just in case. Thinking that the tidal pool at the reef might be better suited to her needs, she forged onward.

The sun was peaking higher in the east, drenching the water with reflections that glowed as brightly as the lamps in the tower and were equally blinding. She shielded her eyes against the glare, but not before colored spots began leaping before her vision again. It seemed temporary blindness played a large part in island life.

She navigated up a hillock and down the other side, past the burial point and around a sharp bend that allowed her a view of the reef in the distance. From where she stood, the surrounding rocky beach was on the same level as the island, but as she walked, the island rose, the beach dipped, and the surf, upon greeting thicker walls of bedrock, grew more surly. She could see that the reef was partially submerged, somewhere around half-tide, but she had no idea whether the tide was coming in or going out. She as yet lacked Elijah's experience for judging such things.

She didn't cross the natural bridge to the reef immediately. She waited at the entrance, trying to gauge what the tide was doing, but it seemed an impossible task. The entire rock formation was wet and steaming, which led her to believe that the tide was on its ebb. But she had no intention of submerging herself in a tidal pool only to learn that she had guessed wrongly. So she waited, and watched, and amid a profusion of seaweed hugging the reef, she saw a dark shape rise and fall, disappear, then appear again on the crest of a wave.

It looked like a head. A human head. But when it bobbed higher and slithered around, she saw that its face wasn't quite human. It was irregularly shaped and barnacle white, and its eyes were black as midnight.

"Seeing things, am I? Seeing things, my foot." Unable to quell her excitement, she skidded down the path onto the rock bridge so she could better view the seal. It dived below the water, a fluid shadow swimming parallel with the shore, but instead of vanishing the way it had two days earlier, it popped up again and seemed to look straight at her, beckoning her with its dark eyes.

"I don't understand," she whispered, shaking her head. "What do you want from me?"

It plunged downward. She could see its streamlined body below the surface of the water, propelling itself away from the reef. It twirled and broke the surface, gliding on its back. It found her eyes again and stretched its neck, as if pointing toward something in the distance.

"Follow you? Do you want me to follow you?"

It made a sound she'd never heard before and launched itself so deep she could no longer see its shadow. When it reemerged, it was farther still from the reef, but it remained in the same spot for long moments, as if waiting for her.

"I'll follow you, then, if that's what you want. But I only hope I know what I'm doing." She scrambled back up the path and, with the seal in clear sight, raced along the marginal way, paralleling the creature's movements. "I see him," she kept repeating to herself. "I actually see him. I am not a crazy woman." As she approached the narrow beach that Elijah had nicknamed the Gulch, however, she lost sight of his head, so she stopped to scan the water.

Her eyes darted back and forth. Where was he? She studied the long slants of granite that dipped toward the sea, then hastened farther along the path so she could view the actual beach. She saw the roof of the outbuilding as she approached, and when she paused in a place directly overlooking the narrow strand, she spied something she hadn't been expecting to see.

Facedown in the sand, above the waterline, was a body. A man's body.

Logical thought flew from her head. Mindless of the danger, hem flying and stones sliding beneath her feet, she pelted down the incline and charged across the sand. Grunting with effort, she levered her hands beneath his hipbone and shoulder and rolled him onto his back.

She pressed her ear to his chest.

His heart was beating.

He was alive.

"Will he be all right, do you think?"

Elijah pulled the counterpane high to the man's chin before motioning Augusta into the parlor. He closed the bedroom door behind him.

"I can't see where he's hurt that much, Gus. No bleedin'. No bruises. Nothin' feels broken. I can't even figure why he's out cold as mutton, unless he hit his head on somethin' before he got washed ashore. But if that was the case, he'd be dead right now instead of takin' up room in my bed, wouldn't he?''

"I don't know. I've never found a body washed up on a beach before. I don't know what to think.''

He escorted her into the kitchen and straddled a chair as she walked to the sink. "I can't figure out where he came from. If he survived that wreck two nights ago, he'd be in a lot worse shape than he's in. And I didn't see any wreckage that he might've been hangin' on to, did you?''

"No. No, I didn't.'' She dippered water into a basin, set the basin in the sink, then one by one placed her carrots into the water to soak. Elijah raked his fingers through his hair as he watched her.

"'Course, not much flotsam ever washes ashore from wrecks on the Devil's Elbow. The tide wants to carry it this way, but there's a fierce current runnin' east of the island that latches on to everything and sends it clear to the mainland. We might get a few spars thrown our way now and again, but not very often.''

Augusta removed a carrot from the basin and with a stiff-bristled vegetable brush began scrubbing grit from its surface. "What other explanation is there?''

"Beats me. Unless there was trouble last night while I was off watch. But you were up in the tower and you already said you didn't see anything. Right?''

Her hand slowed over the carrot. Warmth prickled her cheeks. "Right,'' she said in a soft voice.

"So I don't know how in hell he got here, or when. Looks like we're just gonna have to sit on our thumbs 'til he comes to, so he can tell us what happened.''

She applied the brush halfheartedly to the carrot. Guilt sank to the bottom of her stomach like ballast stones.

"You're bein' awful quiet, Gus. You all right?"

She threw a quick look over her shoulder and favored him with a wan smile. "I think I'm a little shaken is all. He frightened me. I wasn't expecting to find anything human on the beach this morning."

"Good thing you happened by when you did. Lord only knows how long he might've stayed there 'til I found him. You probably saved his life, Gus."

Not me, Elijah. The seal. But she didn't want to mention the seal yet. Other concerns were more pressing at the moment, not the least of which was, had a ship foundered while she was asleep last night? One man had survived, but had her negligence sent others to their deaths? Weak-kneed, she leaned into the sink for support. Only one person could answer that question, and he was lying unconscious in the bedroom. She shuddered to imagine the tale he would tell when he awakened.

The ponderous weight of guilt in her stomach grew unbearable. She inhaled a courageous breath. "Elijah, I—"

"No need for modesty, Gus. That fella's damn lucky, and when he wakes up, I'm gonna tell him so. 'Til then, I'm gonna drag the trundle bed into the parlor so I can catch a few winks of sleep. There hasn't been so much activity around here for a century. It's like salts through a goose. Happens at once." He heaved himself out of his chair and slid it back under the table. "You plan on fixin' that chicken soup for dinner?"

She parted her lips, vacillating between the need to confess and the need to preserve her favorable image in her husband's eyes, if only for another hour. Conceding to cowardice, she held up the carrot for his observation. "That's why I dug up the vegetables."

"Good girl. Nothin' like hot chicken soup to set a half-drowned man to rights again. You all done scrubbin' that carrot?"

She looked from the carrot to him. "Yes. Why?"

"Thought maybe I could eat it for breakfast. There's been so many bodies turning up around here lately, I haven't had time for an honest sit-down breakfast. I don't mind tellin' you, I'll be glad when the commotion dies down so things can get back to normal. Can I have that carrot or not?"

She held it out to him. "It's not much of a breakfast, Elijah. I could prepare something more hearty if you'd prefer."

He grasped the end of the carrot, but instead of lifting it from her hand, he slid his forefinger along its length until his fingertip grazed her thumb. Almost shyly he lowered his eyes to her hand, and then with a tender motion that belied his size and sometimes gruffness, he feathered his touch over her thumbnail and down the flesh that was still beaded with water. "You don't have to do that, Gus. You've got plenty to keep you busy this mornin' without havin' to bother with me. I'll just eat my carrot and offer up a prayer that I can get an hour's sleep before the next body shows up."

The water on her flesh dried beneath the slow strokes of his finger. Anticipation filled her lungs, for his overture was reminiscent of what they had shared last night. But her anticipation soon became diluted by the subtleties of reality. It seemed indecent to be thinking about the intimacies of the flesh in broad daylight. It was difficult submitting to desire when you were being devoured by guilt.

Bridling her embattled emotions, she eased her thumb from beneath his finger and thrust the carrot firmly into his palm. "You need your sleep, Elijah. Eat your carrot and go to bed." But she said it kindly, so he smiled with his mouth, leaving his eyes to mirror feelings that ran deeper, and hotter.

"I'm goin', I'm goin'. I'll close the door between the kitchen and parlor so you won't have to listen to my snorin'."

"Do you snore?"

He shrugged his big shoulders. "Don't know. Haven't had anyone around here to tell me one way or the other. But I'll assume the worst and close the door anyway."

"Does your sunburn feel any better?"

"Some. It doesn't seem to burn so much anymore. Truth is, I haven't had time to think about it yet this mornin'. But your vinegar helped. Thanks. Guess I'll have to walk down to the beach to wash the smell off sometime today."

She quickened at the thought of Elijah's flesh being washed by the surf, touching him in all the dark, wondrous places she ached to touch. Turning back to the sink, she dipped her hands into the basin of carrots, thankful for the cooling effect of the water. "Yes, that's . . . that's probably advisable. And maybe while you're down there, you'll see—" She hesitated. She'd already decided she wasn't going to mention the seal, so what was she doing bringing the subject up now?

"I'll see what?"

She snatched a carrot from the basin and applied the brush to it with sudden vim. "Maybe you'll see nothing even vaguely human. You told me that visitors were a rarity on Devilstone, but you've had more unexpected company in three days than I had in the entire seven years I cared for my parents. How do you explain that?"

"Maybe word leaked out about your cookin'. Or maybe it's some damnable curse that just keeps throwin' obstacles in the way of a husband gettin' to know his wife. Don't know, Gus. I'll have to think on it while I'm asleep."

She heard him crunch down on his carrot as he walked toward the parlor door, and though she knew he needed his rest, she suffered a pang of regret that he was leaving. His presence stirred so many untapped emotions within her. She felt so alive when he was near that when he left, she seemed to dry up with lifelessness.

After she finished scrubbing the carrots, she cut them into slices, peeled and sliced the onions, then set the chicken to boil in the kettle. She heard no snoring from the parlor, no noises from the bedroom, but she worried over the man in each room. She worried what one would say, and how the other would react. She knew it would be better to tell Elijah the truth beforehand. She was taking a terrible chance by waiting, but she couldn't bring herself to destroy the illusion he seemed to have built around her. She wondered if he would find any debris washed ashore when he went down to the beach to bathe. She wondered how she would react if she discovered that by staying awake last night, she might have prevented a tragedy from happening.

"I'm going to make myself sick," she whispered, desperately seeking diversion. She gathered her carrot and onion peels into a bowl so Elijah could compost them later, then, having run out of spring water, she held her hands up for inspection. Her fingernails were tinted orange. Elijah was going to smell like soap and sea water. She was going to have orange fingers that smelled like onions, unless she wanted to walk all the way down to the beach to wash them.

It was then she remembered the rain barrel.

Shaking her head for having forgotten this other source of water, she removed a clean linen towel from a drawer in the pantry, grabbed the soap from the kitchen sink, and headed out the side door.

The rain barrel sat in the bend of the L where the sheds between the main house and tower angled together. There was more mud than grass surrounding the barrel, and when Augusta saw the volume of water in it, she concluded that Elijah had positioned it at the precise spot where it would receive the greatest amount of runoff from the roof. *Efficient,* she thought. But she wondered if there wasn't something he could do about the mud.

With a hesitant hand she skimmed several dead insects off the surface of the water, then, removing the dipper from where it hung on the side of the barrel, she plunged it into the water and poured the contents over one hand, then the other. She set the dipper on the ground while she lathered her fingers and palms, and when she thought her hands sufficiently clean, she dippered more water over them and let them air out to dry. The day was warmer now, so there was no sense dirtying a towel when the air would work as well as linen.

She paced about the barrel as she flicked her fingers dry and opened her senses to the sounds that had become part of her existence. The creak of the weather vane as the wind spun the crossbar west and south, west and south. The shriek and cry of sea birds soaring above. The inexhaustible roar of breakers pounding the storm beach, sounding much like one of the great waterfalls of the world, ever rushing, ever booming. The wind blew a skein of her hair across her lips, and when she tasted the cook-fire taste of those single strands, she stopped short, wondering how she had ever allowed herself to slip into such a wretched physical state. She tested her scalp with her forefinger, and when she felt grit clinging to her roots, she made a moue with her mouth and began stripping her hair of its combs and pins. The knot of hair at the back of her neck began uncoiling of its own volition. She wrapped her hair ornaments in her towel and set them on a nearby step, then shook the remaining coil loose, fanning her fingers through the dark mass to separate the strands.

Rainwater. She'd never washed her hair in rainwater, but pondered if it would render her willful locks as lustrous as Elijah's. She sighed to herself. "One can hope."

She unlooped the clear glass buttons that paraded down her bodice from throat to waist, snugged out of her sleeves, then tied them at her waist. Not bothering to remove her corset, she threw her hair over her head and poured dipper after dipper of water over it. When it was soaked through, she knelt down on a grassy spot and began to lather her scalp with the kitchen soap. She scrubbed and lathered and scrubbed. Soap suds started drizzling down her neck. Boosting herself off her knees, she returned to the rain barrel, filled the dipper, bowed her head low, and poured the rinse water over her hair.

Torrents of water streamed down both sides of her neck,

drenching the soft cotton of her chemise and the boned cotton of her corset with equal measure. She slapped her left hand over her eyes and blew soapy water from between her lips.

A door opened and closed behind her.

She cocked her head in that direction. ''Who's there?'' She swiped the heel of her palm across both eyes, trying to rid them of soap, but the suds kept streaming down her nose and sliding beneath her lids. And it burned. She heard footsteps. Someone running.

''Jeesuz, Gus, gimme your hand.''

The water dipper flew from her grasp. Elijah seized her wrist and slapped her hand onto a part of his body that was warm and bare. ''Scratch, Gus. As hard as you can. Damn, I feel like a flea-bitten dog.''

''I have soap in my eyes!''

''Finish scratchin' my back, then I'll take care of you! Jeez, this itch is about to drive me crazy. Damn sunburn. Ahhh, there. Right there.''

Head still bent and eyes pressed shut, she scratched the prescribed section of flesh in the same manner that a child might scribble on a clean sheet of parchment—wildly and hurriedly.

''Not so hard!''

''You said—''

''A little higher to the right. Under my shoulder blade. That's it.'' He sighed his relief once, twice, and after a space, she felt the muscles in his back go slack. He sighed again.

''My eyes, Elijah!''

In the next instant, she was scratching air. Groping blindly for a handhold, she whacked her knuckles on the side of the barrel. She tried to shake the sting out as Elijah straightened up her torso and pushed her hair back from her face. She heard the dipper plunge into the barrel. She heard water slosh and splat onto the ground, and then she felt his hand on her face, guiding fresh water into her eyes.

"You've got enough suds here to scrub a whale, Gus. Quit squirmin'."

Lips tightly compressed, she groused at him with inarticulate nasal and throat sounds. *"Mmm gttng wtt!"*

"I'm sorry if you're gettin' wet, but the water's gotta go someplace. Bend down now and let me give your hair a proper rinsin'. Hold your hands over your eyes so you don't get any more soap in them."

She bent over, face buried in her hands. Elijah tossed her hair forward, then, with the expertise of a man who was no stranger to the intricacies of female toilette, he rinsed the soap from her hair, thoroughly, painlessly. Under his direction, the water streamed onto the ground rather than down her neck. The soap scattered and dissolved rather than float into her eyes. She felt him gather her hair into his hands and squeeze, ridding it of moisture, and then he was twisting the strands into a long coil, eliminating whatever excess remained. She dried her face on the backs of her hands, and when still he kept twisting, she motioned him to stop. "If you twist that any more, you're going to force my eyebrows off my face! They're sitting over my ears as it is now. Can I have that back, please?"

She grasped the coil with both hands and tugged. Elijah let go but girded a steadying hand around her upper arm as she lifted the long rope of hair over her head. It slapped wetly against her back, making her wince. Elijah bent his head so he could look her straight in the face.

"Looks like your eyes got sunburned. Did we get all the soap out?"

"I think so." She rubbed her eyes with her fists, and when she elevated her arms, she presented a picture so appealing that Elijah could not draw his eyes away from her.

The neckline of her chemise was cut square and low across her bosom. The garment appeared to be made of stout cotton cloth, but it was so drenched with water that the now limp fabric fit her flesh like a skin fits too-hot milk. Her flesh was nearly as white as her chemise and looked to be softer than the most delicate of sea mosses. Her corset pushed her bosom upward, creating such exaggerated fullness that the spectacle dazzled Elijah into near-paralysis. His eyes roved the provocative shapes underlying the wet cotton. His palms, still moist with water, began to sweat. He could see that her flesh still maintained its youthful tightness, that her breasts were full and heavy, and that her nipples were long as his thumbnail and thick as the top of his baby finger. They pressed boldly against the cotton, lifting the wet cloth into a shape so visually stimulating that Elijah surrendered all pretense of control. Blood roared in his ears and pumped to his loins.

"That's better," said Augusta, posing her fists alongside her cheekbones while she blinked residual tears from her eyes. She saw Elijah through the blur of those tears, and when she marked the attention he was leveling on her, she dropped her gaze to her bodice and lifted a modest hand to shield herself.

"No." He took a step closer to her. "Don't hide from

me, Gus.'' He lifted her hand away from her breast, then with two fingers touched the flesh that swelled above the neckline of her chemise. His breath soughed between his teeth, hot and anxious.

The kitchen door swung open. Elijah looked up. Their unknown guest stood in the doorway.

''Damn.'' Grabbing Augusta, he shoved her behind the protective bulk of his body, then to the stranger called, ''You shouldn't be outta bed! Go ahead back. I'll be right in.''

The man peered quietly at Elijah, then after a long moment stepped aside and closed the door behind him. Elijah spun around to face Augusta, standing so close to her that his knees brushed her skirt. ''Gotta go.'' But having said that, he thrust his hands beneath her armpits and lifted her high against him—so high that he could press his mouth to the hollow of her throat. With the tip of his tongue he licked water droplets upward from the dip in her throat to the underside of her chin, and as she slid downward against his chest, she felt his warmth against her wetness, his strength, his power. He kissed the rounded angle of her jaw, then forced her head back as he crushed his mouth against the curve of her lips.

Her breath mingled softly with his. His roughened jaw scratched her flesh, but she felt no discomfort. She felt only awareness of this man, of his mouth, his heat. Sensations began whirling in her head. A thickness filled her ears, muting the creak of the weather vane and the cry of the gull. And for one perfect moment, on this island where the surf roared like a waterfall, she could hear nothing save for the whisper of Elijah's breath and the thud of his heart against her breast.

Her bones turned to air. Her limbs felt light as dandelion spores floating above the earth. The back of one shoe slid off her heel, dangled from her toe for an instant, and fell unnoticed to the ground. Then, as quickly as he had picked her up, he set her back on her feet and prized his mouth away from hers. She caught her breath and swayed backward against the rain barrel.

"Come into the house when you're ready, Gus. We've got a heap of questions to ask that fella. Thanks for scratchin' my back." Leaving her where she stood, he hurried across the grass and raced up the two stairs to the kitchen door. Augusta stared numbly into the distance. She blinked once, twice, then thrust out her bottom lip and blew a long puff of air into her face.

"You're welcome," she said to the distant wood. But her voice didn't sound like her own voice. It sounded breathless, and her words sounded slurred. As she slouched against the rain barrel, waiting for her bones to return to their former density, she pondered why no one in the history of the Western world had ever thought to warn unsuspecting brides about the way it *really* was between men and women.

She wondered why no one had bothered to tell her that kissing made you deaf.

—10—

"What do you mean you don't remember? You're here, aren't you? I wanna know how you got here." Elijah sat a chair by the side of the bed, grilling the man who lay weakly against the pillows Augusta had just plumped for him. "Some pelican flyin' by didn't just up and spit you out."

The man shook his head, causing a shock of black hair to fall over his forehead. His face was thin and angular; his eyebrows formed a slender, finely shaped ridge across his face. His eyes were small but so startlingly blue that one couldn't look into his face without focusing on them immediately. He appeared to be several years older than Elijah—a man of refinement and intelligence who looked rather awkward wearing the nightshirt Elijah had provided him. He fixed Elijah with a look of utter frustration. "I have no recollection, I tell you. It's as if I'm in the middle of a snowstorm and can see neither where I've been nor where I'm going. I don't know how I arrived here."

"You had to've been on some sailin' vessel. Were you part of that wreck two nights ago?"

"I told you, I—"

"What about your name? You forget that too?"

"Elijah." Augusta's voice cut through the exchange with quiet authority. She placed her hand on her husband's shoulder. "Our guest has been through quite an ordeal. I don't think badgering him will improve his memory."

Elijah stiffened his spine against the chair's vertical slats. "Never heard tell of anyone *forgettin'* his name, or not rememberin' how he got from one place to another."

"I have," she said. She removed her hand from Elijah's shoulder and circled her fingers around the mushroom-shaped finial that decorated his chair. Her voice was wistful. "When my parents had their accident seven years ago, my father hit his head on the cobblestones in the street. For days after that he couldn't remember anything—his name, my name, where he lived. His physician said it was an uncommon condition but it had been known to happen in certain instances where people had suffered blows to the head. He also said that in his experience the loss of memory was almost always short-lived. It was in my father's case. It's much like . . . like staring into the flame of a lantern and being struck temporarily blind." *Or kissing a man on a summer's morn and being struck temporarily deaf.*

Elijah slanted an eyebrow at her. "Are you makin' this up, Gus?"

"I would never, *ever*, confect stories about my father, Elijah Payne, and if you—"

"All right. I believe you. You don't need to turn the air blue on me." He fired a look at the black-haired man. "Did you hit your head?"

"How do you expect him to answer that when he can't even remember his own name?"

"The man can speak for himself, Gus. Did you hit your head?"

Augusta rolled her eyes toward the ceiling. She couldn't understand his surliness. He'd acted more cordially toward the reavers than he was acting toward this poor unfortunate. Then again, he'd acted more cordially toward the reavers than he'd acted toward *her*, so maybe this was merely his way. When faced with a threatening situation, he was hospitable. When faced with an unthreatening situation, he was hostile. It made no sense whatsoever. She wondered if this was an obscure rule in the wickie's code of conduct that he had taken to heart. Or perhaps this was what happened to a man who kept company with no one but himself for so many years.

When the man made no attempt to answer, Augusta answered for him. "The only thing he has *hit* is you in a sour mood. His memory will return. He just needs time, and quiet, and some hot chicken soup." She offered the man her most charming smile. "Isn't that right?"

"I don't know, Mrs. Payne, but I sincerely hope so."

"I'll make you a cup of tea with honey to tide you over until dinner, and *you*"—she clamped her hand around Elijah's elbow, urging him to his feet—"need to take that bath you were talking about earlier. If you'll excuse us, sir. I'll be back with your tea in a minute." She herded Elijah out the door and into the kitchen, and after closing both doors behind her, confronted him, feet apart and hands riding her hips.

"Are you this rude to every man who has the misfortune of washing ashore on this island?"

"Did you see that fella's eyes, Gus?"

"Of course I saw his eyes. He has beautiful eyes. But what does that have to do with your rudeness?"

He looked taken aback, then, "He has small eyes. Phineas always said you can never trust a man with small eyes."

"Oh, honestly. If I made a statement of that caliber to you, you'd tell me I was talking nonsense."

"Phineas was never wrong about people. In his whole life he was never wrong. I'm tellin' you, I don't trust that fella in the other room, and if Phineas were alive today, he wouldn't trust him either."

"Because of the size of his eyes."

"You're gonna be wearin' that smirk on the other side of your face when you learn the truth about that jeezer."

"And you're going to owe him an apology when you discover that all your suspicions are completely unfounded."

"Did you get a look at his hands? They're soft as a cow's udder. Not a callus on them. Probably never done an honest day's work in his life."

"A man does not have to sully his hands to do an honest day's work."

"In my book he does. And believe me, this fella remembers a lot more than he's ownin' up to."

"How do you know that? From the size of his ears?"

"No. From what he said. How does he know what it's like bein' in the middle of a snowstorm unless he's actually suffered through one? He might not remember how he got washed up on Devilstone, but he remembers snow.''

Recalling the man's comment, Augusta frowned. ''You're right. I never would have made that connection. Quite astute, Mr. Payne. But whether he's seen snow or not, I still think you're treating him unfairly. He's not a criminal.''

''And how do you know that, Mrs. Payne? From his 'beautiful' eyes?''

Augusta twitched her lips in annoyance. ''Why are you getting so upset?''

''I'm not gettin' upset!'' His chest swelled. The veins bulged in his temples. ''But I'm warnin' you, if that fella so much as breathes out the wrong side of his nose, he'll be answerin' to me.''

''Shhh! Do you want him to hear you?''

Elijah glared in the direction of the bedroom. ''What I want is for that fella to be outta my bed and off my island. Don't cozy up to him, Gus. He's just passin' through.''

She shook her head as he stormed off to the pantry. He reappeared a moment later with a towel slung around his neck. ''You'd best set aside some time to wash the man's clothes. He'll be needin' clean duds for travelin' back to the mainland. And I want you to steer clear of him while he's here. He might've forgotten his name, but I'll wager he hasn't forgotten how to use his rudder.''

''His rudder?''

Elijah drew up in front of her and jabbed a long finger in her face. ''Don't pretend you don't know what I'm talkin' about, 'cause I can tell by the gleam in your eye that you do. You serve him his tea and then you get the blazes outta that room. Understood?''

She answered him by nipping at his finger, but he snatched it out of harm's way before her teeth found flesh. She leveled a stubborn look at him. "I will do whatever needs to be done, and I will thank you to keep your finger out of my face. Now, is there anything else you'd like to say before you leave, Mr. Payne?"

"One thing."

"Which is?"

He elevated his hand to her face, and in a complete change of mood fingered the wisps of hair that were curling at her temple. "Your hair's pretty hangin' loose like that, Gus. Makes a man wanna touch it." He curled one tendril behind her ear, then as if remembering himself, withdrew his hand and scratched his palm self-consciously. He was halfway to the door before she called softly behind him.

"Don't forget your soap."

Snapping his fingers, he made a detour for the sink, grabbed the soap, and was quickly gone. She watched him pass by the kitchen window. His mercurial moods confounded her, as did his unpredictability. But she felt herself being drawn inexorably to this man who boasted two former wives and a mother with no grave.

Loosening her hair from behind her ear, she twined it slowly around her finger, and as she watched his head disappear from sight, she touched the finger to her lips . . . and smiled.

Pronouncing their guest too weak to get up, Augusta served him his noon meal on a tray and urged him to spend the remainder of the afternoon in bed so he could regain his strength.

Pronouncing himself two hours behind schedule after he

bathed, Elijah caught an hour's sleep, then ate his noon meal in the tower while washing lamps and polishing reflectors.

Augusta ate by herself in the kitchen. She pronounced her chicken soup to be one of her better creations, so good, in fact, that she decided to serve it for supper as well. After eating, she baked two loaves of bread and a squash pie to supplement the evening meal, then, while the bread was baking, she walked outside to the cliff overlooking the storm beach and peered in the direction of the Devil's Elbow.

The man's loss of memory had postponed her day of reckoning with Elijah, but it hadn't lessened her guilt or anxiety. One part of her *wanted* the man to remember so she could learn the truth and be done with it. Another part of her hoped he *never* remembered so she wouldn't have to face the consequences. She despised feeling so ambivalent. It made her feel cowardly, and cowardice was not a word common to her vocabulary.

As she continued to muse, the wind gathered her hair in its fist and blew it into wild black streamers over her left shoulder. Laughing at the phenomenon of having unbound hair blow across her face, she chased it with her hands, and once she'd corralled the errant strands, she began twisting them in the same manner that Elijah had twisted her hair earlier when it was wet. Thoughts of him caused her to glance upward at the tower.

He was watching her. He was standing behind the tower glass looking down at her in the same way that the god Zeus might look down on his minions from atop Mount Olympus. But there was nothing fatherly in Elijah's gaze. It was the gaze of a man who craved something he was being denied. It was a gaze that made the flesh of her instep prickle with sensation, for if he could read into her heart, he would know that she craved the same thing.

The black-haired man was already seated at the kitchen table when Elijah went in for supper early that same evening, but the man's presence was not the only thing different about the room. The table was covered with white linen. There were china plates and bowls at each place setting—translucent white things with dainty pink flowers painted all over them. And in the center of the table was a vase filled with dark pink rhodora. Bewildered, Elijah slowed his steps and indicated the table with a sweep of his hand. "What the hell's all this about?"

The man's eyes darted from Elijah to the table and back again. "I don't know what you mean."

"The china, the tablecloth, the flowers. Why is all this stuff here?"

"I presumed this was the manner in which you and Mrs. Payne were accustomed to dining."

Elijah scowled at him. "Right. Where's Gus?"

"Mrs. Payne asked me to vacate the bedroom so she could dress for supper."

"She was already dressed. Why'd she need to change?"

Augusta swept into the room like a runaway hen. "I'm glad you've come in, Elijah. I'm just about ready to serve." She didn't stop long enough for Elijah to get a steady bead on her, but he managed a look-see anyway. She'd left her hair down and brushed the wings back from her face, catching them with a satin ribbon at her crown. She was moving too fast in the opposite direction for him to see the front of her gown, but the back was green as a ship's sidelight, and the material rustled and swished as she walked. China, tablecloth, flowers, and Gus dressed up to the nineteens. Not too hard to see what she was tryin' to do, or who she was hopin' to impress. He glowered at their guest and thrust an angry finger at the china teapot on the table.

"Draw yourself a cup while I wash up. In fact, draw all of us a cup. The activity might help jog your memory."

"I'll be happy to pour the tea, Mr. Payne, but I believe you're being overly optimistic to think that so simple a task could have any bearing on the present status of my memory."

A glazed look crept into Elijah's eyes. "Right," he said in response. "Excuse me." He strode to the sink, his ears still ringing. He had a feeling this was gonna be a very long meal.

By the time he finished washing, Augusta had ladled out the soup and was standing beside her chair, slicing a freshly baked loaf of bread. "I hope you don't mind eating chicken soup twice on the same day," she was saying to their guest. "In years past, I've noticed that fowl doesn't keep as long as other things, so it's best to eat it quickly."

"I don't mind in the least, Mrs. Payne. I've always found chicken soup to be quite pleasing to my palate."

Elijah yanked his chair out from the table and sat down heavily. "Chicken soup ring a few bells, does it?"

The man looked confused. Elijah tapped his spoon on the corner of his bowl. "Chicken soup. How do you know you like chicken soup?"

Augusta stopped slicing to stare at the man.

"I . . ." He threw a desperate look between husband

and wife. "I really don't know. But I'm sure I do. Do you suppose this indicates an improvement of sorts?"

"It probably indicates some sort of slipup, but don't let it bother you. My guess is you'll make plenty more. If you're through slicin' that bread, Gus, why don't you anchor your stern so we can get started."

Augusta smiled sympathetically at the man, sorry that he had become the object of Elijah's wrath. "You must forgive my husband's ill humor, sir. He's not like this all the time. Only when he chances to open his mouth."

Elijah regarded her blackly, but she ignored him in favor of tugging on her apron strings and lifting the ruffled bib over her head. The man popped out of his chair and raced around Elijah, who whipped his head from right to left following the man's flight.

"Where the hell're you goin'?"

He pulled Augusta's chair away from the table, then stood patiently behind it while she rid herself of her apron. Elijah slatted his eyes at him. "Somethin' wrong with the chair you were in? Maybe you wanna try mine out too before you finally decide where you wanna sit."

"Allow me, Mrs. Payne," the man said in a quiet, courteous tone.

Elijah watched in awed silence as Augusta gave her head a gracious bow and allowed herself to be seated. It made the flesh high on his cheekbones grow warm with blood. The stranger knew exactly what to do and Augusta knew exactly how to respond. It was as if they were a pair of bookends, perfectly matched, perfectly created to complement the other.

The man circled around the end of the table again and sat down.

"Pass the salt," said Elijah.

Augusta obliged by thumping the saltcellar onto the table in front of his plate. "My husband has an uncanny appetite for salt," she explained to the man seated across from her. "Please don't follow his example when seasoning your soup."

The man waved off the offering. "I've swallowed enough salt recently to last me until I expire. And if it hadn't been for the appearance of you kind people, I probably would have swallowed a good deal more. It's quite a miracle that you happened by when you did. If I haven't thanked you before, I'd like to do so now. Thank you, Mr. and Mrs. Payne. I will forever remain in your debt."

Elijah snorted as he dipped his spoon into the soup. "Don't waste your breath thankin' me. I had nothin' to do with your miracle. It was Gus who found you. Thank her."

"Is that true, Mrs. Payne?"

"Well, I . . . I was the one who spotted you on the beach, yes, but it was Elijah who carried you back to the house."

"But you were the one who found me." There was reverence in his voice, adoration in his eyes.

Augusta looked slightly embarrassed. "Actually, you shouldn't be thanking me. You should be thanking the men who landed on the island yesterday. If they hadn't shot our hen, I wouldn't have walked down to the garden this morning to dig up vegetables. And if I hadn't walked down to the garden this morning, I wouldn't have passed by the Gulch. It was mere coincidence that I found you."

"It wasn't coincidence," he corrected her. "It was destiny."

Elijah rolled his eyes back in his head. "Pass the bread."

Augusta obliged him before addressing their guest.

"Do you believe in destiny, Mr. . . . ? Do you know, this is terribly awkward not having a name to affix to you. Would you object if we—if we made something up until your memory returns?"

What about bonehead? Elijah thought.

"I wouldn't object at all, Mrs. Payne."

"And I wouldn't object if you called me Augusta."

Elijah frowned. "What's wrong with him callin' you Mrs. Payne? That's your name." Then, turning dark eyes on the man, "And I'd hate like hell for him to forget it."

"Mrs. Payne is much too formal. I'd prefer Augusta."

"Well, *I'd* prefer Mrs. Payne."

"Fine." Unruffled, she smiled at their guest. "You may call me Augusta. You may call my husband Mrs. Payne."

The man sniggered. Elijah made a spike of his tongue and jabbed it into the side of his cheek.

"Now, sir, what shall we call you? Are there any names that come readily to mind?"

He looked thoughtful, then shrugged. "Perhaps you could suggest something appropriate."

"I could suggest some names that are *in*appropriate. Charles. Harvey. Stanley. Godfrey."

Elijah cocked his head at her. "Sound like regular names to me. What's wrong with them?"

"They're the names of my sisters' husbands, and from what I can observe, our guest in no way resembles my sisters' husbands."

"You have four sisters, Mrs. Payne?"

"Four sisters and eight nieces and nephews. All younger. All living in Philadelphia."

"You must find it extremely difficult being away from them."

Lifting her spoon, she trailed it idly through her soup. "Actually, I didn't see my sisters that often in Philadelphia. They were understandably busy with their own homes and families and didn't have a great deal of time to devote to an old-maid sister or bedridden parents. They visited frequently among themselves, but . . ." She tried to maintain her smile, but it wavered and finally broke. She bowed her head as if to hide her face, and seeing this, Elijah felt impelled to extend a comforting hand across the table to her, but she regained her self-possession before he could make the gesture. She looked up again, eyes bright and smile neatly in place. "Our family was something of an oddity in Philadelphia. All four of my sisters are twins. Amelia and Amanda are a year younger than I am. Alberta and Albina are two years younger."

Which was startling news to Elijah. "You've got twins in your family, Gus? I've never heard of a family havin' even one set of twins who survived. And here your family's got two. How come you didn't tell me sooner?"

"You've never asked me anything about my family. I assumed you weren't interested." She stated it as a simple fact, without malice, but her words made Elijah feel as if he'd just been whacked between the face and eyes with a bow oar. Hell, he'd asked her about her family, hadn't he? He strained his memory, recalling fragments of conversations about curtains, and freckles, and lobster plugs and fire birds. But he couldn't remember asking her about her family. He couldn't remember asking her anything about herself, except why she used so much powder on her face. He'd spent a lot of time dancing around questions about his wives and mother. Maybe he should've used some of that time to ask Gus some simple questions about her life in Philadelphia. It didn't sit well with him that in a space of five minutes she had revealed more about her family to a complete stranger than she'd revealed to him in four days. It made him uncomfortable with himself.

It made him feel the fool.

"Well, I, for one, would take great pleasure in hearing more about your lineage," said the black-haired man. "And more about Philadelphia. Perhaps I've visited Philadelphia. For all I know, I could well reside in that fair city."

Elijah ground a carrot between his teeth, wishing the man was there right now.

"I'm sure if you lived in Philadelphia that no blow to the head could erase your memory of the place. It has tree-lined streets, and cobbled walks, and the summers are unbearably hot. I grew up on Spruce Street . . ."

She talked through four bowls of chicken soup, one loaf of bread, and a serving of squash pie. Elijah didn't bother keeping track of what everyone else ate, but he kept track of everything Augusta said, from stories about the lemon paste she'd used to fade her freckles, to anecdotes about her father trying to find a peaceful place to smoke an occasional cigar. When she finished one story, their guest would ask the precise question that would prompt another story, so she would remember, and laugh, and in turn cause the stranger to laugh.

Elijah asked no questions throughout the meal, but the conversation proceeded uninterrupted without him. In his whole life he could never remember envying another person, but this evening he found himself envying this man who conversed so easily with his wife. The man might not remember his own name, but he sure had a talent for asking questions that didn't rile Augusta. Elijah had yet to learn that trick. In fact, that would be the real miracle—if he could learn to speak to Gus in a way that would create harmony rather than discord. For men like the stranger, it seemed a natural gift. For men like himself, it seemed an impossibility.

"It's close to six o'clock, Elijah. Shouldn't you be milking the cow and heading up to the tower?"

Her question startled him out of his abstraction, and only when he blinked did he realize that he'd been staring at her so intently that he'd probably determined how many freckles she had on her face. "Yah, I, uh, I guess I should be headin' on outta here."

"I'm surprised you've sat this long." Then, to their guest, "He usually swallows his food whole, then runs off to do chores before I've even served myself."

There was a loud clink as Elijah set his fork down on his empty dessert plate. Sure he'd run off those other nights, but it was hard being alone in a room with a creature and not knowin' what to say to her. It was a whole lot easier just gettin' up and leavin'. But tonight he didn't want to leave. He wanted to listen to Augusta's recollections, to learn who she was and where she came from. And though he'd complained before about her constant yammering, he could find no cause for complaint tonight. Tonight, her voice gave him pleasure and her laughter reached out to him like a beacon, drawing him near. Tonight, he wished Geraldine could milk herself.

With reluctance he slid his chair away from the table.

"I've monopolized the entire dinner conversation, and

we have yet to think of a name for you," said Augusta in apology to the stranger. "Elijah, help me think of a name for him before you leave."

Elijah trained a knowing look on the man. "Jonah."

"Jonah." She nodded. "That might be acceptable. Strong. Biblical. And I suppose you could draw several similarities between what happened to Jonah and what happened to our guest."

"What happened to Jonah?" asked the man.

"Jonah was a Hebrew," said Elijah. "The Lord bade him go to Nineveh, but he ran from the Lord and boarded a sailin' ship to Tarshish. So the Lord sent out a great wind on the sea, and the mariners on the ship cried out to their gods to save them. But the wind didn't cease. They cast lots to see which of them was causin' this evil to fall upon them, and the lot fell upon Jonah. So the mariners asked Jonah what he had done to deserve such punishment. They plied him with questions." Questions that Elijah began flinging at the man as if he were the biblical Jonah. " 'What is thine occupation? Whence comest thou? What is thy country? Of what people art thou?' Simple questions. Questions a man might ask any stranger." His voice held an edge that could have cut through stone, but the man did not flinch.

"Did Jonah tell them the truth?"

"He did."

"So what did they do to him?"

Elijah stood up and looked far down his nose at the man. "They threw him overboard."

"Oh."

Elijah began gathering up his empty dishes.

"He failed to tell you the end of the story," said Augusta. "Jonah didn't drown. The Lord prepared a great fish to swallow him up, so he lived in the fish's belly for three days and three nights, until the Lord bade the fish spit Jonah onto dry land. Which he did."

Upon hearing the ending, the man did flinch. His expression grew introspective, then alarmed. He focused on a single point on the table linen, then squeezed his eyelids shut, seemingly unable to bear the vision that had come to mind. "I remember a . . . a fish, or . . . or some kind of sea creature. It was dragging me through the water."

Elijah raised a skeptical brow in Augusta's direction, but with a single meaningful look she warned him to keep his silence. Shaking his head, he started for the sink. Behind him the man continued to talk, and remember.

"The water was . . . paralyzing. I . . . I couldn't move my limbs. But the creature was—it was beneath me somehow, swimming on its back, and I could see its face." He opened his eyes and stared at Augusta as if he wanted her to assure him that he hadn't lost his mind. "It had a face as white as this table linen."

A crash echoed through the room. Augusta jumped. The man cursed. And Elijah stared down at the shards of translucent china that lay scattered at his feet. "Jeesuz, Gus, I'm sorry. They . . . they slipped. I—" He lifted his hands in a helpless gesture.

Augusta popped out of her chair. She gaped at the remnants of her mother's china.

"I'll clean it up," said Elijah.

"No. You're in your bare feet. Just step around it. I . . . I'll clean it up."

"I'm sorry," he repeated, but she didn't seem to hear him. She looked too stunned to hear anything else. But he was thankful for her preoccupation. It allowed him to escape without offering any explanations, because he knew if he didn't escape, he would smother.

Augusta sank down onto her heels and, sliver by sliver, gathered the broken china into her palm. The man whom Elijah had christened Jonah joined her.

"Your husband certainly effected a hasty retreat. Does he make habit of dropping your good china and flying out the door?"

Augusta grabbed the man's wrist. "I've seen the creature. But it isn't a fish. It's a seal. A white-faced seal."

The setting sun lent a warm pink glow to the watchroom. Elijah inked his quill pen and made an entry in his logbook.

August 1, 1831
Found a man's body washed ashore this a.m.

He dipped his quill again, wondering what more he should say. Should he say he didn't trust the man's motives? That he didn't believe him? Or should he simply admit something more basic? That he didn't like what happened inside himself when he watched Gus and the stranger getting on so well. It made him feel cloddish that he couldn't speak like the stranger, or ask fancy questions like the stranger. It was a feeling that was foreign to him. One he didn't like. But hell, words had never done him any good. Words didn't rescue men from sinking ships. Brawn and will rescued men. *Action* rescued men. He was a man who lived by action, not by words. So maybe it was time to act with Augusta. Maybe he was doing them both an injustice by postponing their physical union. They had years ahead of them to become familiar with each other. Maybe what was needed now was a show of action that would impress upon Augusta's mind exactly who she was.

His wife.

He nodded at his decision. That's exactly what was needed. Consummation of their wedding vows as soon as possible. But what of his other problem?

He set his quill down. Propping his elbows on the table, he pressed the heels of his palms against his forehead as if he could stop Jonah's words from echoing in his head. *I remember a fish or a sea creature dragging me through the water. A fish or a sea creature. A sea creature* . . .

Dear God, it was starting all over again.

Elijah milked Geraldine early the next morning and rushed back to the house in the hopes of catching Gus still abed. He imagined kissing her awake, then carrying her to the watchroom in the tower, where he would officially, and at some length, seal the bonds of their marriage. It had been many a year since he'd lain with a woman, so anticipation lightened his step as he vaulted up the stoop and threw open the door to the kitchen.

Augusta was elbow deep in dishwater; Jonah was lifting a plate out of the rinse water to dry; and throughout the room there wafted the smell of griddle cakes and maple syrup. Elijah skidded to a halt just inside the door, disappointment draining through him. "You're up. And dressed."

Augusta backed away from the sink so she could see

him around Jonah. "Morning. We've already eaten, but I left griddle cakes for you in the oven."

"The oven?" He shot a look toward the hearth before looking back at Augusta. "You goin' someplace?"

"Jonah wants to see where I found him, so I'm going to take him down to the Gulch."

"Right now?"

"Well, not this very moment. After I finish the dishes."

Without uttering a word, Elijah took long strides across the room and set the milk bucket on the table. Augusta glanced at him over her shoulder. "Is there something you'd rather I be doing?"

He eyed the mass of dark hair that fell to the small of her back. He imagined roving his fingers through its thickness, draping its length over her naked shoulder. She was dressed in blue today—a pale blue that was so easy on his eyes he found it hard looking away from her. "You go ahead. I suppose with a guest to entertain, you gotta do what you gotta do. Don't let me stop you." But he figured they wouldn't be gone more than an hour. Maybe when they got back, if he set Jonah about sweepin' the tower stairs, there'd still be time for him and Gus to . . .

"If you really don't mind our going off, I think I'll add a few more sights to our tour—the reef, the garden."

Elijah's enthusiasm turned suddenly sour. "Why don't you go ahead and show him the whole damn island while you're at it?"

"Well, I—" She looked at Jonah. "Would you have an interest in seeing the whole island?"

"If you would have the good grace to show me, Augusta, I would only be too happy to accompany you. Besides, I should learn my way around your island. I could be stranded here for quite a long time, couldn't I?''

I wouldn't count on it, thought Elijah as he glowered at the man's back. *I wouldn't count on it at all.* Grabbing the bucket by its handle, he headed off to the bedroom to dump the contents into the milk pan. "Mind the weather. Wind's changed. It'll probably be rainin' before long.''

Augusta bobbed her head to peer out the window. "But the sun is shining!" She waited for a reply but received no answer. She shrugged at Jonah. "How can it rain if the sun is shining?''

Jonah nodded sagely. "It won't be the first time your husband has been wrong, will it, Augusta?''

She graced him with a nervous look and returned quickly to her dishes.

By force of habit Elijah usually awoke at noon, but when he drifted awake later that day and squinted out the parlor window, he was unsure how long he'd slept, for the sun was no longer visible. It wasn't raining, as he had predicted. Instead, the southwest wind had ushered in a fog so thick that it appeared to Elijah as if the entire island was engulfed in dense white smoke. Yawning, he rubbed his eyes and tossed his legs over the side of the trundle bed. Still groggy, he hung his head for a moment, wondering why he didn't allow himself more time for sleep now and again. But not this afternoon. Nope. This afternoon he had wood to split, brightwork to polish, a barn to muck out, and a wife to bed.

"A wife to bed." He grinned to himself, liking the inclusion of this task into the day's routine. He began whistling a lewd sea ditty as he pulled his shirt over his head, then stopped midsong when he realized how hushed the rest of the house was. Either Jonah and Gus were being exceptionally quiet, or they simply weren't anywhere within spitting distance. He lifted a curious brow. Had they ever returned from their earlier hike around the island?

"Gus?" He struck out for the kitchen. It was empty. He scratched his head. Where in hell was she? She should've been back hours ago. "Hey, Gus, are you here someplace?" He walked through every shed between the house and the tower, and once inside the tower, yelled up the spiral stairs. "Gus? Jonah?"

The answering refrain was silence.

He shook his head. Where else could they be? The barn?

Barefoot and coatless, he walked out into the fog. It was a chill fog, an oppressive fog. It swirled around him, dampening his hair and flesh, blinding him with its whiteness. Fogs were like this on Devilstone. They weren't like the bridal-veil mists that plagued the mainland. They were thick as blackstrap molasses and pressed so heavily against your face that they seemed bent on suffocating any man who dared hazard his way through them.

Elijah could see no more than two feet into the distance, but the terrain was so familiar to him that he found the gate to the stone fence with little difficulty. He followed the fence around to the barn, lifted the horizontal bar from the double doors, then dropped it back into place. How could they be in the barn if the door was bolted from the outside?

Turning around, he cupped his hands around his mouth. "Aug*uuuu*sta*aaaa!*" The fog distorted the sound, muffled it, made it sound as though it were coming from a different direction. It was like yelling into a box of cotton wool. "Auguuustaaa!" He lowered his hands to listen.

There was no answering call. There was only eerie stillness.

He wandered back to the stone fence and climbed over it. In fog this thick, if a body didn't know the lay of the land, he could easily walk off the edge of the cliff or fall into a ravine. The thought of Gus in a broken heap on the rocks was suddenly more chilling than the fog. It wouldn't be the first time a killing fog had claimed a life on Devilstone. But by damn, it wasn't gonna claim Gus.

"Gus!" Anxiety quickened his step. He found the forest path through the swirling mist and set off down the winding incline at a jog. Damp pine needles stuck to the bottoms of his feet. He waved his arms before him to clear the mist, but to no avail.

"Gus!" He listened for the sound of her voice.

Silence.

And he wondered if perhaps this wasn't meant as punishment for him. Since she'd arrived, he'd done nothing but harp at her for having too much to say. He wouldn't mind having her bleat at him now—if only he could find her.

"Hallo!" He went from a jog to a run. Fear prickled the back of his neck. What if she'd been caught on the reef when the fog rolled in? She might have plunged to her death trying to escape across the natural bridge. Or she might have waited on the reef and been swept away by the tide. The tide was a brutal reminder of the sea's ruthlessness. He, more than anyone, could attest to that.

"Gus!" His lungs burned with exertion, with fear. He stumbled over an exposed tree root, then caught his foot in his hand and hopped around one-legged to ease the pain. Moisture stung his eyes. In the distance he could hear the muted rush of surf over the cobblestoned beach, and then, by chance, he thought he heard something else.

He let go his foot. Cocked his ear.

"Gus?"

He waited, listened, and from somewhere within the fog heard a faint, ". . . jah!" Panic seized him. He spun one way, then the other. Where the hell was it coming from? Ignoring his stubbed toe, he hobbled down the path toward the beach. Just beyond the tree line, he stopped to yell again. "Gus! Where are you?"

As if from the far end of a tunnel, he heard a "Here!"

He looked left and right. Here? Where the hell was here? "Say again!"

"Here! . . . house!"

House? Boathouse. She had to be by the boathouse. He ran toward his right, following the path that fronted the tree line. He prayed she wasn't hurt, that he'd be given another chance to prove himself to her. "Hang on, Gus! I'm comin'!"

At about the place where he knew the boathouse to be, he veered from the path, sliding down bedrock, charging through the sand, and leaping over several driftwood logs to reach the building whose outline he could barely define in the fog. "Gus?" He saw a splash of color against the building's gray shingles. It was blue. Pale blue. And it had Gus's voice.

"We *never* have fog like this in Philadelphia, Elijah. Isn't it amazing?"

She was standing serene and tidy with her back pressed comfortably against the boathouse. On her lips she had the nerve to be wearing a smile. She opened her hand for his perusal. "Look what I found. Blueberries! You didn't tell me there were blueberries on the island. Here." She plucked one from her palm and held it up for him. "Have one."

He disregarded the berry. He stared into her face. Her cheeks were rosy, her eyes bright and animated. She wasn't hurt. She was exuberant. He didn't know whether to kiss her or throttle her. Bracing a hand on either side of her face, he forced her head up and drilled a look into her eyes. "Why didn't you come back? Jeesuz, Gus. You have any notion what you just put me through?"

She blinked as if surprised by the tone of his voice. "I couldn't *see* to go back!"

"Then you should've headed back sooner!"

A vertical crease appeared between her brows. She looked startled, then hurt. "I would have! But it happened too quickly. I . . . it seemed more sensible to stay in one place and wait for the fog to clear. I don't know your island, Elijah. I might have found my way back to the house, but I might have killed myself trying, too! Is that what you want? Because if it is, I can still try to accommodate you!" Her lip began to quiver. Her eyes welled with tears, and Elijah, knowing he had said the wrong thing again, drew her to him and cradled her head against his chest.

"No," he whispered against her hair. "I don't want you dead. But Jeesuz, Gus. Don't scare me like that again. Not knowin' where you were, wonderin' if you were hurt. It made me a little crazy." She felt so soft and supple in his arms that it stirred images of how she had looked by the rain barrel yesterday, her corset lifting her breasts high, her chemise clinging wetly to her flesh, taunting him with the long, incredible thrust of her nipples. His body responded to the image. Desire surged through him, thickening the flesh between his legs.

Augusta pushed away from him, her eyes defiant, her voice terse. "You shouldn't have bothered worrying about me. I might not be the hearty, fair-dispositioned wife you advertised for, but you'll never be able to accuse me of lacking good sense. It's the essence of my character. Some women are outrageously pretty. Others are outrageously sweet. *I* am outrageously sensible. What are you grinning at?"

He backed her against the wall, and when she looked as if she might flee, he braced an arm on either side of her, blocking her escape. He bowed his head against hers, touching his forehead to the point of her widow's peak. "How did you manage to get rid of your friend?"

"I didn't get rid of him. He wandered off while I was picking blueberries. I don't know where he went."

A smile pulled at his mouth as he whispered a kiss over the flesh at her hairline. "Good. Maybe the tide'll carry him off."

"Elijah! That's a hateful thing to say."

"Yah, but it's true." He angled his head until his lips found the outer corner of her eye. "I didn't find you to argue with you, Gus. I'm tired of arguin'." He tasted the dampness of the fog on her flesh and wondered if the flesh beneath her pale blue gown would taste of the same dampness. "I want to touch you." He breathed the words against her temple in a hoarse, husky whisper. His heart filled his chest with its beating. He felt the glide of her palm on the back of his arm, as if in consent, and feeling her response, he touched her side and smoothed a finger along the outer curve of her breast.

His breathing quickened. His fingers trembled. And in the swirling mist, lust overcame reason. He forced her head back with his mouth and buried his face in the angle that blended her jaw and throat. He worked his finger from the side of her breast to its underside, then, in a gesture of husbandly boldness, shaped his hand around her fullness. Her soft woman's flesh swelled against the hollow of his palm, filling his hand, whetting his desire.

"Augusta? Hello out there! Augusta? Are you here?"

It was Jonah's voice, and he was so close that Elijah could hear his every word distinctly. He stilled his hand. Against the warm flesh of Augusta's throat he made a hissing sound. "Damn the man." He lifted his head and dropped his hand and when he squinted in the direction of the tree line, he spied movement within the fog, followed by the emergence of a disembodied shadow that kept chattering as it approached them.

"I was picking mushrooms in the woods and had an absolutely fiendish time finding my way back out when this fog rolled in. Ghastly stuff. I don't know how you're able to contend with it, Payne. Lucky for me I have a decent sense of direction, else I might have been wandering around lost all day." He strolled to within five feet of them and stopped short when he saw Elijah draped around his wife. He blinked his surprise. "Am I interrupting something?"

Elijah scowled. There had to be something he could do to get rid of this fellow.

He wondered if murder would be too obvious.

Murder was beginning to look better and better as the day wore on.

Elijah was silent through most of the noon meal, but his eyes drifted to Augusta so much that her cheeks seemed to acquire a constant blush. He lit a cigar after the plates were cleared and watched her through the cloud of smoke that floated about his head. He had already eaten one dessert, but his encounter with Gus this morning had definitely put him in the mood to sample another.

"I have to go out the barn to do some cleanin' up this afternoon, Gus. Might be a good time for me to show you how to milk Geraldine. You interested in comin' along?"

But before she had a chance to reply, Jonah jumped into the conversation. "You milked the cow once today already, didn't you, Payne?"

"Yah. What of it?"

"Well, how can you milk her again so soon and expect her to produce anything? You'd be better to wait 'til after supper. Give her a chance to let her milk down. Augusta won't learn anything if you take her out there now."

Elijah frowned into the man's face. *Oh, yah?*

"Is that true what he says?" Augusta asked.

"Yah." Elijah's frown became more ominous. His eyes remained fixed on Jonah's face. "I suppose it is."

Jonah held up his hands in his own defense. "I know what you're going to say. You're going to ask me how I know so much about bovines. I swear to you, I don't know. It's just something that popped into my head."

I'd like to pop you in the head, Elijah thought.

"There's really no problem," said Augusta, walking to the table to better address her husband. "I'll set time aside after supper tonight to go with you." Her smile held such warmth and promise that he was glad he was sitting, because he felt himself go weak in the knees. A few hours. Just a few more hours. He doubled his fist beneath the table in victory.

"If it's all the same to you, Payne, I wouldn't mind accompanying you to the barn after supper too. Who knows? It might be the very stimulus I need to help me remember something. You don't mind, do you?"

Murderin's too good for the man, thought Elijah as he trudged up the tower stairs early that evening. *He deserves to be gelded.*

An hour in the barn hadn't helped Jonah's memory one whit. But it had helped Elijah, who kept remembering what he could be doing with Gus if not for Jonah's presence. He'd spent an agonizing hour watching Gus milk out Geraldine's quarters. Every time she stroked downward on a teat; every time she worked the milk down with her curled fingers; every time she forced the milk out the end of the teat, he imagined his own release, and it was hell.

He winced as he lifted his foot to the next stair. His groin was so sore that it rendered his every movement a lesson in pain. He hadn't realized a man could sustain himself physically for a solid hour. Neither had he realized that the aftereffect would be so excruciating.

He groaned aloud as he took the next stair. At this rate, he estimated reaching the lantern around midday next Tuesday. *I'm gonna kill him,* he thought, but if not that, then maybe he could just make him *wish* he were dead.

When he climbed the next stair, he was smiling.

"Thank goodness that horrendous fog is nowhere in sight this morning. So, Augusta, what exciting ventures do we have planned for the day? I think I'd like to explore the seaward flank of the island. I saw a bit of it from the woods yesterday, and it looked interesting enough to bear further investigation.''

Augusta peered at their guest over the rim of her mug. *Seaward flank?* Who in the world used terms like seaward flank? She set her mug down and eyed him suspiciously. ''Why?''

''Why? I'm sorry, I don't exactly understand. Why what?''

''Why do you want to explore the seaward flank of the island?''

''To look for the seal, naturally. You did say you've seen the creature only by the reef. Well, I think we should broaden the area of our search so we can prove to your husband that neither one of us is crazy.''

But she didn't think that was the real reason. Ever since yesterday when he had wandered off in the fog, she had begun to wonder about him. His loss of memory seemed not to affect him emotionally at all, which seemed odd to her since her father's short memory loss had tormented him to near-insanity. Jonah seemed much too relaxed. If she had lost *her* memory, she suspected she would exhibit some degree of anguish. Jonah only wanted to explore the seaward flank of the island, which led her to conclude one thing. ''Are you looking for Bunker's treasure? Because if you are, I regret to inform you that it's not here.''

''Bunker? Who's Bunker?''

''Mornin', you two.'' Elijah banged his way into the kitchen through the woodshed door. Augusta clung to him with her eyes, remembering the way he had kissed her yesterday, the way he had touched her. And suddenly, remembering wasn't enough. She wanted to be alone with this man who was her husband. She wanted to be his wife.

"Good morning. Shall I start dishing out your breakfast?"

"Not yet, Gus." He set his milk bucket on the table and walked around to his chair. "I think I'll just sit a spell. Catch my breath. You can pour me a mug of tea, though." And when his mug was full, he leaned back in his chair, looking more amiable than he had since Jonah's arrival. "I suppose you two are expectin' to live in one another's pockets again today."

She wanted to tell him no, but since it was her duty to see that Jonah was properly entertained, she could do little but admit the inevitable. "Jonah wants to see more of the island."

"And naturally I would be most honored if your wife would accompany me. She has such a talent for conversation. She makes me feel quite welcome here."

She sidled a hopeless look at Elijah, who drummed his fingers idly on the table. "Since you two are gonna be hyperin' around outside, I think I'll give you a bucket and let you fill it with periwinkles for me. We can steam them and eat them for supper."

Augusta was skeptical. "You want us to eat a bucket of flowers for supper?"

"Periwinkles, Gus. Snails. They're all over the rocks on the beach. You've probably seen them but didn't know what they were. About the size of acorns and nearly the same color."

"In Philadelphia we kill snails. We don't eat them."

"Hell, they're good. The best place to find them is on

the cobblestoned beach at low tide. Just pick them right off the wet rocks. I'll show you how to cook them later.''

She made a moue of distaste. ''The flowers sound more appetizing.''

''It's low tide right about now, so you'd best head out. There's a bucket in the woodshed you can take with you.''

She was getting the distinct impression that he was trying to get rid of her, but she didn't understand why. ''I'll serve your breakfast before I leave.''

''I've got two hands, Gus. No reason I can't serve myself.''

His insistence disturbed her. Was he angry with her? Had she done something wrong? ''Then I'd better wash up the dishes. I can't leave a messy kitchen.''

''I'll clean up. *You* collect the periwinkles. I've been thinkin' about steamed snails all night.''

He'd been thinking about snails all night. She'd been thinking about him. That seemed about normal for the two of them. ''Very well. Since you're being so insistent, I'll leave.'' She stood up, her feelings more bruised than she was willing to admit. ''Jonah? Are you coming?''

As the man made to rise, Elijah reached across the table and clapped a hand on his forearm, forcibly restraining him. ''Ole Jonah's gonna do me the honor of havin' a smoke with me this mornin'. Aren't you, Jonah?''

Unable to move his arm, Jonah sank back into his chair. He cleared gravel from his throat with a nervous cough. ''Yes. I, uh, I suppose I am. But I must warn you. I don't know whether I smoke or not.''

Elijah grinned widely. ''I'll teach you.''

Augusta looked from one man to the other. She didn't

trust them alone with each other. Or, better stated, she didn't trust Elijah not to kill Jonah. But she could do only so much protecting, and she wasn't going to stay where her presence wasn't wanted. She crossed glances with Jonah. "Don't be long. I'll be waiting for you on the beach."

She fetched her snail bucket in the woodshed. Elijah's voice drifted in to her from the kitchen. "Damn fool. You're supposed to light the other end. Here. Take a swig a my tea. It'll settle your nerves."

If she hadn't been expecting Jonah, she would have hiked her petticoats to her knees to avoid dampening her hemline. But given his impending appearance, she conceded to modesty by allowing her gown to hang properly, albeit wetly, around her ankles.

"Ouch." She lifted the foot whose heel was being stabbed by sharp-edged pebbles and found purchase for it on a smooth ellipse of stone. She'd removed her shoes and stockings and left them above the high-water mark, but she regretted that decision now, for she found the beach impossible to negotiate in bare feet. Next time, she'd let Elijah collect his own periwinkles. The rugged lay of the beach never seemed to bother *his* feet.

With her bucket a quarter full in front of her, she hunkered down and began plucking more snails off the rocks. She held one up to her face for closer observation and was surprised to see a dark head poking out from the shell. It had a pale yellow mouth and tiny horns and was incredibly foul looking. "He actually eats these things?" Shivering with disgust, she tossed it into the bucket with the others she'd collected, then paused to consider the low waves that scalloped the shore with floating lace. It was so peaceful here that she could almost feel the harmony that existed between earth and wind and sea. Watching the ebb and flow of the tide, listening to the rhythmic wash of waves —it made her feel as if there were no problems in this life except those of her own creation. And when fitted into the scheme of the world, her problems seemed so insignificant.

Her eyes strayed to the boathouse, to the place where Elijah had pressed her against the wall yesterday. With the back of her hand she touched the underside of her jaw, remembering the feel of his mouth on her flesh, the hotness of his breath. Her bosom still tingled from the imprint of his palm, and for a wicked moment, she wondered where else he would have touched her if Jonah had remained lost. She wondered—

''Ohh!'' She shot upward as an errant wave licked her toes. But once on her feet, she found herself being caught around the waist and knees and swung high into a pair of strong arms. Her shriek echoed up and down the beach. Her left shoulder slammed into a rock-hard chest. She saw a flash of sun-streaked hair and dark eyes, but before she could gasp her relief, Elijah forced her head against his arm and kissed her mouth with a hunger that left her senses reeling. And he continued to kiss her as he carried her toward the upper reaches of the strand, never faltering in his step, his strides long and purposeful.

His hair grazed the slope of her cheek. She swept it back toward his face, then clung tightly to its length as she draped her wrist around his neck, holding him close. His face obscured their surroundings. Her lips grew numb from the hard pressure of his mouth. Her loins constricted, flooding the secret places of her body with moisture and warmth. Near the tree line, he set her aright on a flat rock that was of a height with his calves. The granite was dry and gritty on the soles of her feet, but she was standing so high she could feel the slant of his hipbone pressing into hers. And when he shaped his hands around her buttocks and crushed her against his pelvis, she felt something else.

His breath shortened. He elevated one foot onto the rock for balance, then unlooped her arm from around his neck and flattened her fingers against his inner thigh. With his fingers still atop hers, he angled his pelvis a hairbreadth away from her, then glided her hand between their two bodies so she could know the fierceness of his desire.

His hardness filled her hand from heel to fingertip. She hadn't supposed any man to be so long, or thick, but the fact that he was only heightened her arousal. Emboldened, she roved her fingers along the straining ridge of his flesh, and feeling this, Elijah drew the tip of her tongue into the warmth of his mouth, sucking gently, savoring the taste of her.

Sensation washed over her like grains of sand falling through an hourglass. Elijah's fingers were suddenly at the waist of her bodice front, unfastening hooks and eyes with fevered intensity until her bodice lay open to him. "Jonah might come," she whispered against his mouth, but in answer Elijah swooped her into his arms, stepped behind the concealment of the rock, and laid her on the mossy surface of the ground.

"Not very likely." Leaning back on his haunches, he stripped his shirt over his head and tossed it aside, but before she could question him further, he had straddled her hips and was kissing her again. He entwined his fingers with hers and angled her hands above her head, nesting them against the soft black mass of her hair. His mouth singed the soft flesh of her lips. She could taste his impatience, could feel it in his straining muscles. For a fleeting moment, he lifted his face away from hers. He took scorching measure of her from her lips to her eyes, and when he saw the willingness in her gaze, he became a man driven.

He released her hands then parted her bodice front, exposing her flesh to the soft breath of the wind and the softer touch of his fingertips. With a solitary finger he stroked the pulse in her throat. She knew he felt the strength of that pulse when he smiled and placed his palm full over her chest, as if reassuring himself that the rapid beating of her pulse replicated the desire in her heart.

His hand warmed her through the batiste of her chemise. He did not fumble to remove her underlinens, but merely shaped his hand over the fullness hidden beneath her cotton bodice. His hand was big, but even lying on her back she could feel herself filling the deep hollow of his palm with her woman's flesh, could feel her breasts beginning to ache for the warmer touches of his mouth.

He glided his palms down the length of her corset, impressing her flesh with the feel of ribbed whalebone. She watched him as he slid lower on her legs, watched the sleek glide of his hair against his cheek, watched the play of his wondrously big hands as they unfastened the button fly of his breeches. He eased her petticoats over her knees, then higher. She felt his weight flattening the white muslin of her drawers against her legs. She felt the wind skate over her bare shins and kiss her toes, cooling the flesh that was not being warmed by Elijah.

Wedging himself between her thighs, he skimmed his fingers along the split crotch of her underlinen, parting the material. His explorations tickled, but when he touched her with a probing finger, she held her breath. Finding the deep, slick hollow of her flesh, he guided himself into her opening and, with an exacting thrust, filled her with the long shape of his man's body.

The sensation wasn't what she'd been expecting. She lifted her hips and bucked with the pain. Tears starred her eyes, and seeing this, Elijah lowered himself atop her and kissed away the tears that floated outward from the corners of her eyes. "I won't hurt you, Gus," he whispered. "I promise." Balancing himself on his palms, he began to move his hips with slow, rhythmic thrusts that neither hurt nor chafed her. And as he moved, she felt her flesh yield and stretch, softening the initial pain of his intrusion. The ends of his hair swept lightly against her face. Lifting her arms, she caught the wings of his hair in her fists and clung tightly as the rhythm of his strokes quickened. He drove deeper and deeper into her body, igniting sensations from her breasts, to her loins, to her calves. She caught her breath and let it out, slowly at first, then faster, until her gasps were keeping pace with his. She pulled downward on his hair, opening her mouth to the warmth of his kiss. And whether from the friction, or the fire, or the quickness of their bodies, when he claimed her lips, a blinding heat swept over her, causing her to shudder against him and cry softly into his mouth. After two more thrusts he shuddered also, more strongly than she, and she felt his flesh pumping within her, anointing her with his seed.

He kissed her long and deeply then. His lips were hot. Her lips were cool. But like earth and sea, they were joined, for once, in harmony.

—12—

"Tell me something, husband." Elijah sat with his back braced against a nearby pine, cradling Augusta in the angle formed by his chest and bent knee. Lacing her fingers with his, she elevated his right hand to her mouth and kissed the rise of his first knuckle. "What monstrous thing have you done to Jonah?"

"Hmm?"

"Why hasn't Jonah interrupted us? You forced him to smoke too much, didn't you? He got sick on the fumes, didn't he?"

"Nope. But that's a damn good idea."

"'Lijah!"

He tossed his head back with laughter, then smiled a wicked smile. Disengaging his fingers from hers, he smoothed a fingertip along the slant of her collarbone. "I suspect that at this very moment, ole Jonah is listenin' to the sounds of thunder.''

''Thunder?'' She looked skyward, and when she did, he touched his thumb and forefinger to either side of her windpipe and stroked slowly upward to the underside of her chin, then down again. She swallowed with difficulty. ''How can he be hearing thunder when there's not a cloud in the sky?'' Her voice was breathless from his touch, which caused him to smile.

''It's localized today.'' Gliding his fingers toward the cap of her shoulder, he found the ruffled edge of her chemise and traced its border beneath the opened front of her bodice jacket. ''The only way you can hear it is if you're warmin' the seat in the convenience, which I imagine Jonah's been doin' for some time now. Can you stow this thing someplace?'' he asked, indicating her bodice jacket.

''He's ill, then? But not from smoke?'' She looked concerned as she untied the tabs that anchored her bodice to the waistband of her skirt. ''Do you suppose he's suffering some aftereffect from his ordeal?''

He helped her shrug out of her jacket before cradling her against him again. ''I suspect he's sufferin' from the tea I suggested he drink to calm his nerves.''

''The tea? What was wrong with the tea?''

''Wasn't anything wrong with it . . . until I dropped some aloe powder into it.''

Her eyes grew round and owlish. ''You didn't.''

He slid the wide strap of her chemise over her left shoulder. ''I did.''

''But aloe powder gives you—'' She blushed rather than say the word.

''I know. That's why he's holed up in the privy.''

"You're terrible."

"I think desperate describes it better. He'll recover." He skated a knuckle across the pale flesh that was framed by the ruffled border of her chemise, then, with that same knuckle, he feathered a touch down the length of her breastbone, to the place where her bosom strained against the cotton that overlaid it. "Are you sorry, Gus?"

Distracted by the hand that lingered at her breast, she shook her head. "I'm not sorry we did what we did, but I would have preferred you leave the purgative out of his tea."

Elijah slid his fingertips beneath the edge of her chemise. "Who knows. Sittin' there on the roost might improve his memory. Nothin' else has worked so far."

"He'll remember when he wants to remember. And he'll tell us who he is and why he's here when he has a mind to, and not before. That seems to be the way with men, doesn't it? They tell you what they think you should know, and nothing more. Why do you suppose men find it necessary to be so secretive? I don't understand what they're so anxious to hide."

"The truth, I suspect."

"But why?"

"Because the truth isn't always pretty, Gus. Sometimes lookin' back at the truth can shred a man's innards like a grapplin' hook."

She was silent as he traced the underside of her ruffled border with his fingertips, dusting her flesh with the provocative touches of his own. "Is that why you won't tell me about Eliza and Lydia? Because the truth is too painful?"

A fretful look crept into his eyes as he studied the play of his fingers beneath her chemise. "I've had two wives die on me, Gus. You think that's somethin' a man can be proud of?''

''No. But if you don't talk about your wounds, you'll never allow them to heal.''

''Never had anyone to sit and listen to me after Phineas passed on. Couldn't very well walk around the island talkin' to myself, could I?''

''You're not alone anymore, 'Lijah. I'll listen to you. I *want* to listen to you.''

And when he saw the sincerity in her eyes, he nodded. ''I suppose you have a right to know, don't you? All right, then, if that's to be the way of it. But don't go throwin' any of this in my face later. You're wantin' to know, so I'm gonna tell you.''

He seemed to settle in then. He stilled his hand and with his four fingers plucked idly at the tiny folds of her chemise ruffle. ''We found 'Liza some ten years back. Her ship hit the ledge in an October fog and went down faster than a lead line. We were able to fish her outta the water, but everyone else drowned. Just like the other night. She was in pretty rough shape when we found her. She'd swallowed a basinful of water, and a block 'n' tackle had caught her square in the face. Broke her nose and—'' He cringed with the memory. ''Never mind. You don't need to hear what else it did. But she lost her sight because of it. Phineas and I doctored her as best we could. She was a little thing like you, Gus. Thin as a widow's weddin' ring and only sixteen. Hell, she was hardly outta the egg. And layers shy. She'd been on her way to Boston to become a kinda schoolmarm for some rich fella's brood. But with her eyesight gone, she knew she wouldn't be any use to the man, or anyone else for that matter.''

Augusta shook her head. "Did she have no family she could go home to?"

"She had an aunt in Castine, but she was too weak to go anywhere. Phineas thought it best that she stay on Devilstone, but he didn't think it proper that she be alone with just the two of us men, so he decided I should marry her. That made it more proper in his eyes."

"Did you want to marry her? Bless my stars, you didn't even know her." Which was a ridiculous statement, she realized, considering he hadn't known Augusta Mayhew either when he married her.

"I didn't have much say in the matter. I was eighteen years old and did what the man told me to do. Phineas sailed into Lustre's Gate for the preacher, so he came out and married us. But 'Liza was so sick, you could already see the dark angel on her shoulder. We did what we could for her in the time she had left. I never . . . we never came together like a man and wife should, but I used to read to her while she was in bed. From the Bible, mostly. Sometimes I'd read to her hour after hour until my throat would just dry up like an old leaf."

Augusta bowed her head, remembering how dearly her mother loved hearing a good story, and how vehemently Amelia protested about having to do it. "You were kind to her, Elijah. She could have found no better husband. I'm glad you were here for her."

"She died three months after we were married. Just stopped breathin' one mornin'. Poor 'Liza. Doesn't seem fair." He paused for a space, as if contemplating the senseless loss of life. "Phineas died two years later, in 'twenty-three. Then it was pretty damn lonely around here 'til Lydia showed up."

"Did you rescue Lydia from a foundering ship too?"

He grinned. "Lydia rescued herself. She was a survivor, that one was. She was a passenger aboard a schooner carryin' ice to South Carolina. A couple of cousins of hers owned the vessel, so they gave her permission to accompany the crew to Charlotte, where Lydia had relatives. It was March, and a freak lightnin' storm sheared the mainmast of that schooner clear off. The crew thought they could reach a port with only the foremast sails, but Lydia didn't trust the way the ship was bein' tossed around like a pea on a drum, so she decided to bail out."

"In midocean?"

"It was nighttime, and Devilstone's beacon was lit, so she knew there was safety not too far away if she could reach it. She grew up on Penobscot Bay, so she knew how to row a boat. The crew lowered one of the ship's boats for her and off she rowed for Devilstone. Made it, too, though she did have a few words of complaint to voice about the current. Said it was easier to bend an oar on Penobscot Bay than it was out here in the middle of nowhere."

"So what happened to the schooner?"

"Don't know. It either made it or it didn't, but it didn't founder on the ledge. I would've seen that."

"And Lydia just showed up at your door?"

"Nope. She showed up in the barn while I was milkin' Geraldine. Scared me so bad I nearly fell off my stool. She was quite a woman."

Suppressing a twinge of jealousy, Augusta brushed her fingertips across the golden hairs that dusted his forearm. "What was she like?"

"She was a worker. Always willin' to lend a hand.

Never complained. She took everything with an even strain. I never had much call to have words with Lydia.''

Unlike your third wife, thought Augusta, who was beginning to see herself as willful and shrewish in comparison. Perhaps the twins had been right about her, after all. She worried a wisp of his arm hair with her index finger. ''I suppose she was quite pretty.''

''Pretty? I don't know if a body could ever look at Lydia and call her pretty. She was . . . impressive.''

''What does that mean?''

''It means she was nearly as tall as I am, Gus. She was wide across the shoulders and beam and probably weighed more than a barrel of whale oil. She had a bump on the bridge of her nose and eyes that were too far apart, but she was so damn friendly. And she took a fancy to Devilstone right away. Said it smelled a lot better than Penobscot Bay at low tide.''

Augusta arched one brow as if to dispute him. ''I rather guess it was you she took the fancy to and not Devilstone Island.''

Elijah shrugged. ''Whatever the reason. After she'd been here a couple of weeks, she asked me how I'd feel about takin' on a wife. Said she couldn't promise me any babies, but she knew a thing or two about cookin' and cleanin', so if I'd be happy for the company, she'd be happy to stay.''

''Just like that? I mean . . . didn't she have family obligations? People who would miss her?''

''She was a widow lady. Never had any children, so I expect she could do pretty much what she wanted. She was thirteen years older'n me, Gus. Lydia knew her own mind.''

"Thirteen years older?" Which, to Augusta, seemed an oddity beyond comprehension. She gaped into his face. "You agreed to marry a woman thirteen years older than yourself?"

He nodded.

"But why?"

"Hell, why not? I didn't have any better offers pendin'. She was here, and she was willin'. I wasn't about to turn her out. Why're you lookin' so thunderstruck?"

"Because I've never known a man to marry a woman older than himself. In Philadelphia, a man always marries a much younger lady. In Philadelphia, *I* was considered old, Elijah."

"You? Gus, you're only twenty-four. That's not old." He dipped his fingers beneath her chemise and with quiet expertise lifted her breast above its cotton confinement. Her flesh was shell white and veined with pale threads of blue. Her nipple was the color and texture of her tongue, and it lay exposed above the ruffle of her chemise, long and thick, like an offering to him. He stroked it lightly with the pad of his forefinger. His voice became gravelly. "Twenty-four is just right."

What he was doing to her with his hand was making her thirsty for him. She leaned more heavily against his slanted thigh, flesh tingling. Lydia had been thirty-five when Elijah had married her. Compared to that, Augusta wasn't spinsterish at all. She wasn't old and withered. She was practically youthful. And somehow, thinking it made it so. Elijah's voice grew more husky. He began stroking her tongue-colored flesh with two fingers.

"We sailed into Lustre's Gate to have the preacher splice us. We got along real well, the two of us did. While I milked Geraldine in the evenin', Lydia would light all the lamps in the tower for me. One evenin' when she was climbin' back down the stairs, she must've caught her toe in the hem of her petticoat. I don't know how far up she was when she stumbled, but I found her at the base of the staircase when I came in.''

''Was she—''

He nodded in answer to her unspoken question, knowing he had to stop there. Any more, and he'd be tellin' too much. He couldn't allow that to happen.

''How terrible for you, 'Lijah.'' The unhurried stroking of his fingers was causing her loins to pound, her ears to buzz. She tugged at the cotton of her chemise, trying to bare more of her flesh for his touch. She closed her eyes and sank her teeth into her bottom lip as he drew lazy circles around the base of her nipple.

''It was more terrible for Lydia.''

''Why did you feel you couldn't—*Unhhh.*'' She moaned the sound as arousal peaked within her. Opening her eyes, she locked gazes with him. She was breathless, her mouth dry. ''Why couldn't you tell me? There's nothing sinister in what happened. Elijah, you were being so secretive, I began to imagine you did away with the women, that you only married them for their money.''

He allowed himself a smile. ''Nothin' that complicated, Gus. A man doesn't like to talk about his failures. Makes him feel less a man.''

''But it wasn't your fault.''

''Whatever happens on this island is my fault. It's my island. I take responsibility for what happens on it.'' His eyes grew serious. He stopped the motion of his hand and lifted it to his lips. He sucked his forefinger deeply into his mouth, drew it out slowly, then pressed the wet tip to the rounded peak of her breast.

Her shoulder twitched. A spasm erupted in her loins. Her eyes rolled back in her sockets.

"I want you, Gus." He leaned forward and kissed her mouth long and greedily, then whispered against the corner of her lips, "But it's too soon yet. You're gonna be sore enough without my addin' to it again so soon."

"I'm not sore."

"You will be if I don't use some restraint." But when he saw the disappointment in the soft green of her eyes, he relented. It pleased him that she wanted him as much as he wanted her. "All right, Gus. There's other ways. There's ways a Philadelphia lady couldn't even begin to imagine. But we need to go easy with you. There's no hurry now. We've got the rest've our lives."

She opened her mouth to him. He filled it with his tongue, then lifting the hem of her petticoat, he touched the inner flesh of her thigh with his fingertips. *We've got the rest've our lives,* he told himself, as gently and without haste, he set about showing her what pleasure the wickie of Devilstone Light could bestow. *As long as we stay on the island, we've got the rest've our lives.*

They returned to the house with Augusta's bucket brimming with seawater and snails.

"The door's latched on the convenience," said Elijah as they passed by the structure. "Hmph. I would've expected our guest to be in there all day. Maybe he's tryin' to sleep it off. Hate to tell him, but sleep isn't gonna help what he's got one bit."

They didn't find Jonah asleep. In fact, they didn't find

him at all. He was absent from house, sheds, and cylinder. With his expression settling into a curious scowl, Elijah sat down on the kitchen stoop, knees parted and forearms braced across his thighs. "Where do you suppose he's gotten off to now?"

Augusta tented her gown around her legs and sat the grass to the side of him. She looked stricken. "What if he saw us?"

"Trust me. He couldn'ta gone too far from that privy in his condition."

"He said this morning that he wanted to explore the seaward flank of the island."

"The what?"

"Seaward flank. That's the term he used." She heard stubble chafing flesh as Elijah rubbed his jaw.

"Seaward flank isn't somethin' a man pulls outta the air, is it? Especially when the man claims he can't remember his own name."

"Do you suppose he's looking for gold?"

"Could be. But it's queer him showin' up here the day after we get rid of those other three fellas. Like I told you before, we get treasure hunters on Devilstone once every two or three years, not twice every two or three days."

"I asked him this morning if he was searching for Bunker's gold. He appeared not to know what I was talking about."

Elijah guffawed. "Were you expectin' he'd tell you the truth, Gus?"

"Well, yes. That would have been the honorable thing to do."

He laughed again as he heaved himself to his feet. "It's a good dryin' day today. Why don't you wash the man's duds for him. If we get a ladies' sea tomorrow, maybe I'll just load the man into the yawl and dump him at Lustre's Gate.''

"I thought you never sailed to the mainland?''

"My sailin' to Lustre's Gate is about as rare as a tooth in a turkey, but under dire circumstances, I've been known to relent.''

She wondered how she could portray bare windows as a dire circumstance. "Do you suppose I could sail in with you?'' A few yards of yellow gingham might be worth a bout with seasickness.

"The yawl only carries two, Gus. Besides, you'll need to stay here to light the lamps for me in case I'm late comin' back. Don't look so glum! After tomorrow, we won't have to sneak down to the beach to do what we should be doin' in bed.''

She sighed. And once she removed her nightgowns from the bedroom windows, there wouldn't be any way to prevent other people from *seeing* what they were doing in that bed, either.

Men.

It was midafternoon when Jonah finally reappeared. Augusta had volunteered to wash the glass chimneys while Elijah polished the reflectors. Having completed that task, they were beginning instruction on how to adjust and light the wicks, when Augusta glanced out the tower glass. "There he is! He's just coming out of the forest. And he's carrying a bucket.''

Elijah walked up behind her and placed his hands on her shoulders. "What in hell is he doin' with one of my buckets? Next thing you know, he'll be walkin' off with the parlor furniture.''

Jonah waved to them as they emerged from the lighthouse. "Augusta! Payne! I was rather baffled by your disappearance this morning! Where did you go? I searched everywhere for you!"

"Never mind where we were," Elijah called out as he bore down on him. "Where the hell've *you* been?"

Jonah set the bucket on the ground. "You said you wanted periwinkles, so periwinkles are what I've brought you."

Elijah peered into the bucket to find it a quarter full. "You were gone an awful long time. What else've you been doin'?"

"Sitting and staring, mostly. Trying to piece together the fragments of a shattered memory. To no avail, however. My life still remains a complete mystery to me."

"You're well, then?" asked Augusta, wondering why he wasn't weak from the purgative.

"Never felt better. In fact, if it's all the same to you, Payne, I wouldn't mind indulging myself with another of your fine cigars. Would you care to join me?"

Elijah slatted his eyes at the man. "Yah. Why not. Go ahead in. I'll be right there."

"What happened?" Augusta whispered when he had gone. "I thought your purgative would have incapacitated him."

"It should have. I don't know what went wrong."

"He probably saw us."

"Don't worry the matter."

"But what if he did?"

"Then the man'll die happy." He trailed his thumb down the curve of her throat. "If he saw the same thing I saw, he caught an eyeful of the best-lookin' piece of female flesh this side of the Mississippi."

She didn't know whether she should be stunned or flattered by his comment, but as the afternoon wore on, she decided to be flattered. Hearing him voice sentiment that he thought her attractive was heady stuff. It made her feel like one of the green-eyed, red-haired Mayhews.

It made her feel pretty.

Late that afternoon, Elijah transferred the periwinkles from bucket to kettle and steamed them just until the disc at the end of the shell fell off. Augusta melted butter and provided sewing needles with which they could pick the snails out of the shells, so they spent the supper hour picking, dipping, and chewing.

"What do you think of them?" Elijah posed the question from behind an ever-rising pyramid of empty shells.

"They look disgusting," said Augusta, "but they're palatable. Actually, I think I'm tasting more of the butter than I am the snails."

"I would truly relish a meal of clams and mussels tomorrow," said Jonah. "I'll even volunteer to help with the digging."

Elijah focused his attention on the man. "Mussels don't need to be dug, and you're not gonna be around here long enough tomorrow to eat a meal."

"I'm not? Where am I going?"

"Back to civilization. I'm thinkin' you need more help than we can give you, so I'm takin' you to Lustre's Gate tomorrow. Maybe someone there will recognize your face and ship you back to where you belong."

"A rash measure, don't you think, Payne? If you would allow me to remain a few more days, I'm sure I'd start remembering something."

Elijah flashed him a stiff smile. "I insist."

"But—"

"Finish your snails. They're the last taste of shellfish you might get for a while."

"Augusta? Are you going to allow him to do this to me?"

Her immediate response was silence. She no longer felt he was being entirely honest with them, which made it easier to believe he had arrived on Devilstone as a consequence of something other than shipwreck. Perhaps she would never learn who he was and how he had arrived, but if there had been no shipwreck, and she was sure there hadn't been, she had no reason to feel guilty about falling asleep in the tower. If Jonah stayed, however, there remained the possibility that Elijah could still find out about her failure of duty. She was willing to go to any length to prevent that from happening—even agreeing to the man's banishment. She couldn't suffer her budding happiness being destroyed by a complete stranger.

"Devilstone is my husband's island," she said after a few moments. "Whatever happens here is his responsibility, so if he thinks it best that you return to the mainland for care, then I'm afraid I must agree with him. I'm sorry if that interferes with your scheme of things, Jonah."

He arched his brows nonchalantly before jabbing his needle into a periwinkle shell. "It doesn't interfere with anything. If the two of you are so adamant about being rid of me, then I'll be happy to leave. Never let it be said that I stayed where I wasn't wanted." But Augusta suspected that this, too, was less than the truth.

After the last snail had been plucked and eaten, Augusta gathered the shells into one bucket and started to head out the kitchen door with them.

"Where you goin' with those things, Gus?"

"I thought I'd toss them over the side of the cliff."

"Why don't you just leave them outside the door there. I've been noticin' it's pretty muddy around the rain barrel. I think maybe I'll crush the shells and spread them on the ground out there. Might make it easier on your feet next time you decide to wash your hair."

She smiled at the kindness. "That's thoughtful of you, Elijah. Thank you." He nodded and turned away awkwardly, which caused her smile to deepen. Despite the fact that neither of them was comfortable giving or receiving compliments, they were making slow progress in that direction. At least it was a beginning. "I'm going to collect eggs. I'll finish cleaning up when I get back."

Elijah retrieved a cigar from the box that sat atop the cupboard. "I suppose you want a smoke," he said to Jonah.

"Thank you, no. I wouldn't want to impose further upon your generosity."

Pulling a match from the matchbox, Elijah drew the wooden stem through the emery paper that wreathed the head. A flame ignited on the tip of the matchstick. "Never let it be said that I was stingy with my cigars." He lit the cigar and doused the flame. "I suppose you'll be wantin' to tag along while I milk Geraldine."

Jonah stood up. "Your demonstration yesterday evening was sufficient, thank you. I think since this is to be my last night on the island, I'll simply take an evening walk."

"Yah. Why don't you do that. If you go down by the shore, though, watch out for crabs. They usually come out in battalions this time of day lookin' for food. If you get too close, they might mistake you for a tasty morsel and drag you back into the water with them. But if that happens, I'll be spared a trip to Lustre's Gate tomorrow, won't I?"

Jonah hesitated, nervous skepticism etched on every feature of his face. "I don't for one minute believe you." He crossed to the door, but before leaving, turned. "Perhaps your wife would care to join me. I'll ask her."

Elijah blew an angry stream of smoke at the ceiling. "Yah. Why don't you do that." The door closed. Elijah squinted into the smoke. "Coward. Phineas said you can never trust a man with small eyes."

He finished smoking his cigar before heading out to the barn. He filled Geraldine's feed trough with grain, then, while she ate, began milking out her quarters. Five minutes later, with two quarters emptied, he heard the sound. It was a soft *plopping* sound, as of an acorn falling into a bed of pine needles. He looked over his shoulder, his eyes scanning the interior of the barn. "Somebody there?"

No response. He continued milking.

Plop.

He stilled his hands and slatted his eyes. It was getting closer. He looked toward the hayloft. "Won't do you any good throwin' rocks at me, you miserable cuss. You're goin' to Lustre's Gate tomorrow even if I've gotta bind and gag you!" He worked the remaining milk down the cow's teats, and when he was done, he slid the bucket to the side and stood up.

Thwack.

"Ow!" His hand flew to the crown of his head. Pain erupted at the roots of his hair. He searched the ground for the offensive projectile and amid the wood shavings by the feed trough found not a stone but a periwinkle shell. He snatched it up and smothered it in his fist. He glowered at the hayloft. "It's a long way to the ground from up there, fella, but maybe the sudden stop'll improve your memory.'' He stormed across the barn to the hayloft ladder and began climbing the rungs with such anger that the loft began to shake. He pulled himself to the top, then stopped to scan the hay bales that were stacked before him, bales that were shipped out to him from Lustre's Gate each year. ''You can try to hide your ugly face from me, but it's about to get uglier.''

He heard a rustle of straw, then from behind several stacks of hay saw two more periwinkle shells rainbow to the ground. Elijah shook his head at the man's stupidity. Remembering the shell in his fist, he lobbed it over the hay bales.

''Ouch!''

He frowned at the voice. ''Gus?'' Straw scattered before his hurried footsteps. He turned the corner of the stacked hay to find his wife rubbing the top of her head.

''You don't play fair, 'Lijah Payne. That hurt.''

''Gus, what the hell're you doin' up here?''

''I remembered something I wanted to ask you.''

The situation suddenly struck him as so humorous that he began to laugh. Grabbing a bale from the surrounding stacks, he flung it onto the floor and sat himself down atop it. ''All right. Ask away.''

She toyed with the hooks of her bodice jacket as she leaned against the wall. ''There are dates on all the markers in the graveyard except for two—Eliza and Lydia. Why didn't you make note of the years when they died? It seems so neglectful to me. Did you do it for a reason?''

''You mind my askin' how long you've been worryin' about this?''

''Ever since the day we buried the seaman.''

''Well, you should've asked sooner. Might've saved yourself some concern. I didn't make note of the dates

because it seemed like a waste of time carvin' out somethin' I'd always remember. A man doesn't up and forget
the years his wives died, Gus. Now, you have any more
questions? Lamps have to be lit in about fifteen minutes.''

"I have a comment."

He gave her a ''hurry up'' sign with his hand.

''You lied to me.''

His palms went cold. A chill crept up his spine.

''You said I'd be sore.'' She parted the front of her
bodice jacket as she walked toward him. She was naked
beneath her jacket—no chemise, no corset, just soft,
shapely flesh that was more erotic than any vision he could
ever have imagined. She stepped between his parted thighs
and, roving her fingers through the silken length of his hair,
drew him close. "I'm not, 'Lijah. I'm not sore at all."

He slid his hands beneath her bodice jacket, shrugged
it off her shoulders, and coaxed the sleeves down her arms.
She heard the cadence of his breathing quicken. His tongue
curled around the long, stiff peak of her breast before he
drew it between his lips and into the hotness of his mouth.
The warm, moist touches of his tongue as he plied and
stroked this most sensitive part of her, the pressure of his
lips as he gave suck to her flesh, made her feel bound to
him wholly and intimately, without embarrassment or self-
consciousness. She arched her back as he glided his hands
up the ridge of her spine and down again, to the button at
her waistband.

He unfastened the button with deft fingers.

The skirt slid low to her hips.

She was wearing no underlinen.

He shaped his palms to the flesh and bone of her hips
and rasped against her breast, ''Gus, Gus, you're makin'

a madman outta me.'' He whispered kisses along the heavy underside of her breast, and with a mouth that was warm and eager, worked his way downward from there.

Augusta's cry some minutes later caused Geraldine to moo out her alarm. The cry was shrill and uncontrolled, the kind of cry that bespoke madness . . . or bliss.

She watched the two men pile into the yawl and set sail for Lustre's Gate early the next morning. The sea was calm; the winds fair. Elijah told her if the wind didn't change direction, she could expect him back in nine or ten hours, but to Augusta, nine or ten hours without her husband suddenly seemed forever. Something entirely unexpected was happening to her, something she thought would never happen.

She thought she was falling in love.

She filled her day with busy work. She weeded the garden and dug up a bunch of carrots, beets, and a half-dozen small potatoes for later in the week. She bathed in the shallow, sun-warmed tidal pool on the reef and looked for the white-faced seal among the rocks, but he was nowhere to be seen today. Like Jonah, like Elijah, he was gone.

She picked buttercups and daisies on her way back to the house and arranged them in a jar on the bureau dresser to brighten the room. In the parlor, she stripped the linen from the trundle bed and checked the sundial etched into the windowsill. *Ten o'clock*. Seven more hours until Elijah returned.

She regarded the homeliness of the parlor—the plain chairs, the bare floor and mantel. There had to be something she could do to improve the ambience of the room. Embroidered pillows for the chairs? Flowers on the side table? Something decorative for the mantel. Seashells perhaps? Or . . . or . . .

Of a sudden, her mind came to light on Phineas Payne. ''Scrimshaw.'' What had Elijah said? His father had packed away his scrimshaw in a trunk in the attic. This seemed the appropriate time to unearth some of it.

The roof of the attic was low and slanted, and the room itself was as ordered and inelegant as the rest of the house. Elijah had stowed her three trunks at one end of the room. At the opposite end were two smaller trunks, which she assumed to be Phineas's. Unstrapping the leather bindings of one trunk, she threw back the lid.

The inside was remarkably tidy, with each item having been separately wrapped in clean white cloth. She unfolded one small bundle to discover a series of various-sized iron spikes whose points were slightly curved. In another was an ivory penholder with a whale carved in relief on the base. She found a plain, round ditty box that was stuffed with hanks of cotton thread, sewing needles, and an ivory thimble, and much to her delight, she also unwrapped a wheeled piecrust crimper whose ivory handle was carved in the shape of a dolphin. *Where are the whale's teeth Elijah was talking about?*

Removing another bundle from the trunk, she unraveled the cloth, and when the object within was revealed, she set it on the floor, staring at its design, unable to touch it, for with jackknife and sailmaker's needle Phineas Payne had sculpted a sea creature. He had used lampblack to darken the creature's long, sleek body and round eyes, but he had left the face untouched so that the natural ivory showed through.

Phineas Payne had sculpted a seal.

A white-faced seal.

When twilight began to wash the eastern horizon, Augusta climbed the stairs to the tower and lit the twenty-one Argand lamps, but her mind was not on the business of lightkeeping. Her mind was fixed on the ivory figurine in the front pocket of her apron. Pulling the wickie's chair close to the lantern glass, she sat down and, with a reluctant hand, removed the seal from her pocket.

The workmanship was extraordinary. Phineas had cut thousands of tiny grooves into the ivory to represent the creature's fur. He'd carved broad, flat flippers and delicate ears that were no bigger than the shaft of her embroidery needle. He had even made minuscule ridges from the seal's nose downward to depict whiskers. She had no doubt this was the same seal she had seen by the reef, which meant that Phineas Payne had seen it also. And if Phineas had seen it often enough to carve its likeness, why was Elijah going to such extremes to deny its existence?

The situation was making less sense to her now than it had before. Why couldn't Elijah admit the seal existed? She had seen the creature twice. Jonah claimed to have been rescued by him. Phineas carved the creature in ivory. Could all three of them be suffering from imaginations gone amok? She didn't think so. But neither could she understand why Elijah would rather accuse her of having defective eyesight than concede the creature's presence on the island. It lacked the same logic as his refusing to leave the island overnight. What did he think was going to happen to him if he allowed himself to accept the seal's existence? Was he reacting out of fear? Good Lord, what could he possibly fear from a seal?

She traced a fingertip along the blackened grooves of the creature's body. There were still so many unanswered questions surrounding Elijah. He had said himself he found it difficult engaging in conversation again, so she suspected it would be a while before he answered all the questions she needed to ask him. His telling her about Lydia and Eliza had been a start, but she didn't know if she was willing to wait indefinitely for him to flesh out the rest of the picture for her. She wanted answers, and she would prefer to have them now, even if it meant incurring her husband's ire.

"Gus . . . ss . . . ss! You up there . . . re . . . re?" Elijah's voice echoed up the length of the cylinder to startle her out of her reverie. Thrusting the seal back into her pocket, she popped up from her chair and hurried to the hatch in the floor.

"I'm here!" She heard his feet thumping on the wooden stairs, softly at first, then louder and louder as he climbed higher up the spiral.

"Are you standin' by the ladder up there?" He threw out the question as he crossed the watchroom floor. "If you are, move away from it and stand with your back facin' the hatch. I've got somethin' I don't want you to see just yet."

And *she* had something he probably *never* wanted to see, but she stepped away from the hatch as he requested. "All right. My back is turned."

The ladder creaked with his weight. The floor deflected slightly as he walked up behind her. "You can turn around now."

She turned around slowly. "Welcome back," she offered. He stood three feet away from her with his hands hidden behind him.

"It's good to *be* back. Would've been here a damned sight sooner if it hadn't been for my cussid companion."

"He gave you trouble?"

"Did he ever. That aloe powder kicked in today. Made a helluva mess. Gonna have to burn the bucket I carry in the yawl."

She winced. "Did he suspect anything?"

"Yup. He accused me of feedin' him bad periwinkles. He wasn't too lively when we finally made landfall. I pointed out Reverend Pleadwell's house and told him the good reverend would do what he could for him. I've gotta admit, Gus, I'm not sorry the man's gone." He tilted his head to observe her. "You must've had a busy day. You look kinda—I dunno—tired. Preoccupied."

She shrugged off the accusation, not yet ready to broach the subject of the seal. "Having you away from the island is a little wearing on the nerves. Anything could have happened to that little boat on the open sea, couldn't it? I could have been a widow before I'd enjoyed another day of being a wife."

Elijah looked surprised by her statement. "You enjoy bein' my wife, Gus?"

She compressed her lips, then smiled despite herself. "I'm learning to enjoy it. We still have a great deal to discover about each other, though. I think once we're able to sit down and talk freely about—"

"I have somethin' for you."

She thought it necessary to continue what she was saying, but he looked so pleased with himself that she didn't have the heart to spoil the moment for him. She cocked her head as if trying to peek behind his back. "Am I supposed to guess what it is?"

"Can if you want."

"Is it something you bought?"

"Yup."

"In Lustre's Gate?"

"Yup."

There was only one thing she wanted in Lustre's Gate —a bolt of yellow gingham—but she was afraid that saying it aloud might put a jinx on it. "Is it . . . for the kitchen?"

He nodded. Excitement began welling within her.

"Is it yellow?"

His eyes lost some of their glitter. "Yellow? Hell, Gus, they didn't have yellow. I had to get you blue."

"Blue is fine. I like blue. Oh, Elijah, you didn't!" She rose up on her toes and steepled her hands over her mouth in anticipation.

"Yup. I did." He swung his arms out from behind his back. In his hand he held not a bolt of gingham, but a bowl made of pressed glass. It was cobalt blue with diamond diapering all over the outside and a deep gouge on the rim. It was quite the most garish piece of glassware she had ever had the misfortune to encounter. She sank down slowly onto her heels. She lowered her hands from her mouth.

"It's . . . it's . . ."

"It's supposed to replace the bowl I broke the other night. I tried to find somethin' with little pink flowers plastered all over it, but this was all they had in the way of bowls. I could've bought you one without the chip in it, but this one was thirty cents cheaper with the chip. I figured you'd appreciate the bargain. And for no charge at all I can use a little sharkskin to smooth that gouge right out. Have it lookin' good as new for you." He beamed at his offering. Augusta struggled to find her voice.

"It's . . . Words can't describe how . . . how very interesting it is."

He was quiet for a moment. His face grew suddenly somber. "You don't like it."

"No. I mean yes, I *do* like it." She removed it from his hand and held it before her face to observe it from all angles. It wasn't yellow gingham, but it proved he'd been thinking about her—and thinking kindly. She couldn't fault him for that. Perhaps his demonstrations of thoughtfulness would never meet her expectations—like his deciding to hang a wedding garland to welcome her rather than cleaning out a drawer for her possessions. But she was beginning to find his unpredictability rather endearing. And funny. She suspected that life with Elijah Payne would never lack for surprises. "This is the finest gift that any man has ever given me, Elijah." Which was not an untruth, considering no man had ever given her a gift before. "But it's too pretty to eat out of. Maybe I'll just set it in the middle of the kitchen table and fill it with something cheery."

"You really like it?"

She cradled her hands around the bowl as if it were the world's greatest treasure. "I really like it."

Stepping close, Elijah lifted her chin and planted a soft, smoldering kiss on her mouth. "I'm glad," he said, kissing her eyelids shut. With an anxious hand he smoothed his palm over her hip, then dipped his fingers over the flat plane of her stomach, encountering something unwieldy in her apron pocket. "What's this?" he asked, fingering the contour of the thing.

She stilled his hand. She could mention the seal now and destroy the warmth of his mood, but it seemed too dear a price to pay for curiosity. She was too anxious for his affection to deprive herself of that luxury. She would mention the seal eventually, but not now. She couldn't do it right now. "It's nothing. A seashell." With her hand atop his, she guided his fingers toward the place where she most craved his touch. "But it's broken, so I'll have to find another."

He found the place and pressed his fingertips gently against it. "Plenty of seashells on the island."

"Hmmm." She caught her breath as he began a slow, rhythmic dance with his fingers.

"Gus?"

"Hmmm?"

"I didn't tell you before, but they've got glasses to match that bowl."

The weather held for the next several days. It was weather typical of an August in Maine—warm days accompanied by cool nights. It was a time when Devilstone rang with unaccustomed laughter. A time when a Philadelphia spinster and a Maine wickie could while away the hours by lobstering, clamming, and falling in love. A time so spellbinding that it blinded them to the shadows of the past that were gathering ever so slowly about them.

"This is hard, Elijah."

"Where's your spirit of adventure?"

"I feel quite graceless."

"Keep your knees a bit more apart. Thatta girl. Back straight. Curl your hands around the tip there. Not too tight. All right, now. Very slowly, Gus. Stroke. Stroke."

The blades of her oars splatted against the surface of the water, spraying them from both starboard and port sides. Elijah sloughed water from his face. "The trick is to drag the blades *vertically* through the water, Gus. You're usin' them too much like spatulas."

"I'm hopeless."

"Slow, not hopeless. Let's try it again."

"I'm getting blisters." She held up her right hand so he could see the welt that was forming between her thumb and forefinger.

"Poor Gus." Leaning forward off his seat, he steadied her oar, grabbed her hand, and kissed the weal that was

bubbling her flesh. He returned to his seat in an instant.
"All right. Again."

She scowled as he reclined lengthwise across the thwart,
hands behind his head and bare feet propped against the
gunwale. "Why do I have to learn to row a boat?"

"'Cause it's a good thing to know how to do, especially
for a body livin' on an island. Concentrate on what you're
doin'. Keep the blades vertical. Short, choppin' strokes."

The thole pins rattled.

Plop. Splat.

Elijah backhanded spindrift from his nose and cheeks.
"You suppose you could do that one again, Gus? You
missed a spot here on my cheek."

She stuck her tongue out at him. He reached for her
foot and gave it an indulgent shake. "I recognize that
tongue. It's the same one that was lickin' my earlobe this
mornin' and my—"

"'Lijah!"

He laughed at her outrage. She steadied her oars, looking
as if she might whack him with one of them. "You never
mind about my tongue. You shouldn't be saying things
like that in broad daylight."

"Who's gonna hear?"

"*I'm* going to hear. And it might convince me to become
more selective about where I allow my tongue to roam. I
don't think all married ladies do the things you're teaching
me to do, Elijah."

"They do them, all right, Gus. But my guess is, they
don't do them half as well." He circled his fingers around
her ankle, a touch so sensuous that it lifted the down on
the inside of her thigh.

Plop. Splat.

She wriggled her foot free of his grasp. "You make me sound like a shameless tart, 'Lijah Payne. Now, mind your hand, else I won't be able to concentrate."

He braced his hands behind his head once again. She squared her oars and stared at his bare toes. "Do you ever wear shoes?"

"Nope."

"Not even in the winter?"

"Nope."

She lowered her oars. One plunked into the water. The other skated backward. "Why not?"

"Why don't I wear shoes? 'Cause they hurt my feet. Always have. More comfortable goin' without."

She squared her oars again. "How do you avoid frostbite in the winter?"

"I wrap animal hides around my feet. Hides don't constrict like shoe leather. You makin' any progress there? The tide's gonna have us beached in two minutes if you don't bend your back to it." Then, in a more suggestive tone, "I've seen what you can do on dry land, Gus. You've got a lot more energy than you're showin' me here."

She rolled her eyes at his continued insinuations, then doused him with one whack of her starboard oar. He shot up, feet drenched. "Aw c'mon, Gus. We've got half the Atlantic in here with us now. Leave the other half where it is."

His discomposure made her laugh. She enjoyed teasing him; enjoyed knowing she could pester him mercilessly and still have him willing to accept more. It seemed a bond that might exist between friends. And she smiled to think that this man who was her husband could also become her friend. He set his cold, wet toes atop her feet, extracting from her a shriek of protest that was deafening in volume.

"You . . . you . . . !"

"You need some serious help here, Gus. Hand over the oars. No! Don't let go. I'm gonna show you the rhythm, and you're gonna follow my lead. Blades vertical to the water. Now, with the ends here, pretend you're drawin' rainbows in the air. Like this. Stroke. Stroke. That's it." Under Elijah's capable guidance, the boat started making progress away from shore. Augusta concentrated on keeping the oars vertical and their motion synchronized. "Sometimes if you don't think about it too much, the motion just comes naturally—like other bodily functions which we won't mention in broad daylight 'cause someone might overhear."

She sighed her exasperation with him. He gave her a wink. "You're gettin' it, Gus."

And, to her amazement, she was. Elijah let go the oars, but she continued rowing, steadily albeit awkwardly. Her delight became apparent as her strokes grew more efficient. "Not too bad for a person who had included boat rowing as the last item on her list of new things to learn."

"What did you have on the top of the list?"

"Whistling. I want to learn to whistle."

He looked puzzled. "Why?"

She looked puzzled back. "Because I don't know how."

"Kind of an odd thing for a creature to want to learn, isn't it? Don't think I've ever heard a female whistle."

"That doesn't surprise me. But it's a wonderfully cheery thing to do, so I'd like to learn."

Elijah wet his index finger, then raised it above his head. "Wind's calm. You wanna learn now?"

"What, pray tell, does the wind have to do with anything?"

"Ask any shellback, Gus. Whistlin' in a calm will bring a favorable wind. But if you whistle in any kinda wind, you're invitin' a hurricane."

She smiled into his sun-bronzed face. "Sounds to me as if the wickie of Devilstone Light is a trifle superstitious." His eyes registered such disquiet that she was immediately sorry for her comment.

"It's not superstition, and I'm not superstitious."

But she suspected he was. This man who risked his life plunging through ten-foot waves to rescue strangers had an unnatural fear of what would happen to the wind if he whistled into it. "Very well, you're not superstitious. Teach me to whistle, then. I believe I'm intelligent enough to master two skills in one day." She drew her oars into the boat and sat with her hands folded studiously in her lap. Elijah leaned forward, elbows on his knees and hands dangling between his parted thighs.

"Show me what you can do so far."

She puckered her lips and blew outward.

Elijah dragged his sleeve across his face. "Your spittin's great. The whistlin' part needs work." He reached his hand toward her face and squeezed her cheeks gently. "Make like you're a fish. Pucker your lips. Yah, just like that. Now, stick the tip of your tongue behind your teeth without touchin' anything. Kind of in the middle of that space where your teeth aren't touchin'. Now whistle me the first stanza of 'What'll We Do with a Drunken Sailor.'"

Her eyes widened. "I was *not* raised on the afterdeck of a derelict ship."

''All right, all right. Whistle me something I might recognize.'' He ducked his head out of range of her mouth. She began pushing air in staccato bursts around her tongue. When she was done, he lifted his head.

'' 'Three Blind Mice.' ''

''Mozart's 'Menuet and Trio in G Major.' ''

He gave her a long look out the tail of his eye. ''Right. Can't figure out why I didn't recognize it. I think we better try somethin' else.'' He squeezed her cheeks again. ''Pucker up. Yah. Right about like . . . that. You have your tongue where it's supposed to be?''

She nodded.

''Good.'' And, leaning far forward, he kissed the exaggerated shape of her mouth with such passion that she completely forgot what she was supposed to be doing with her tongue. He coaxed her off her seat and wedged her between his legs, and as the boat drifted aimlessly about Devilstone Island that afternoon, he indeed taught her to master another skill, but it had little to do with whistling.

They divided the work in the lighthouse between them so they could devote more time to the business of learning to be husband and wife. On an afternoon when the tide was low, they dug clams from the tidal muck of the cove and caught lobster in the shallow water near the rocks. Elijah baked them in a deep hole on the cobblestoned beach, lining the bottom of the hole with rocks and covering their catch with seaweed and kelp. He demonstrated his prowess at skipping stones while the food cooked, and though he instructed Augusta how it was done, she discovered she was no better at skipping stones than she'd been at whistling. He cradled her against him near the place where they'd first made love and played idly with the dark strands of her hair. And she felt contentment in all its sweetness wrapping itself around her, drawing her into the timeless web of life on Devilstone Island. Sometimes they spoke; sometimes they didn't; but always, they were aware of each other and the feelings that were taking root deep within them.

Elijah cracked open the lobsters on the rocks, then spent most of the meal throwing stones at the herring and ring-billed gulls that gathered overhead. He fed Augusta her first taste of butter-dipped lobster and felt himself grow hard with desire when she sucked his fingers into her mouth with the lobster. The meal was lost to him from that moment on, so that when the feast was over, he stripped off his clothes without preamble, exposing his desire to her in all his naked magnificence. Her mouth tasted of butter and lobster; her flesh was sweet where the butter had drizzled onto her chin, so he licked her flesh clean with the tip of his tongue, savoring the taste of her as he unlooped her bodice buttons. He undressed her with the quickness of a man possessed, and when they both stood naked, he scooped her into his arms and began running with her over the round, sea-washed stones toward the water. Augusta kicked and screamed and giggled. Elijah charged into the frigid water, kicking up spume all around him. When he was waist deep, he graced her with a mischievous smile, and in the next instant they were both submerged, their flesh in shock at the paralzying cold.

He shot upward once again, dripping and invigorated, and when Augusta screamed her indignation, he smothered her protest with his mouth and carried her back to shore.

He stood her on their blanket and smoothed the wet strands of her hair away from her face. With a fingertip she touched the dark strip of hair that arrowed downward below his navel. He was like the earth, hard and angular and more physically beautiful than any man she had ever seen. She looked down at the arching length of him, then took him in her hand, allowing her fingertips to linger and stroke until they touched the hard, swollen sac at the root of his phallus. She formed her palm around its fullness, then bent her head forward to kiss the flesh of his breastbone.

He shivered with the touches of her mouth, with the pressure of her hand. Then, without encouragement, she lay down on the blanket and opened herself to him.

He filled the space between her legs with his body and parted her flesh with his own. The friction of their bodies dried the seawater from their flesh. His wet hair fell forward, dripping onto her shoulders, but he bowed his head and sucked the beads of moisture into his mouth. He moved within her slowly, flawlessly. She lifted her hips to meet his thrusts, and then, in a fevered rhythm of entwined limbs, he took her to a place that was hot and explosive, a place of desert thirsts and heated flesh, a place made wondrous by the unspoken thrill of newly formed love.

On August 6, Augusta baked herself a blueberry cake to celebrate her twenty-fifth birthday, and though she had once fostered a desire to bake a cake and eat it all herself, she now took great delight in sharing it with her husband. She even fed a small piece to Geraldine. She played a birthday salute to herself on her violin. Elijah applauded her performance, though secretly he wondered why all her musical offerings sounded like "Three Blind Mice" to him. Geraldine made known her opinion of the recital by running into the barn.

Elijah expressed regret that she hadn't told him of her birthday sooner. "Might've had time to make you somethin' special if I'd known, Gus."

"You brought me my glass bowl back from Lustre's Gate. That's birthday present enough." But what she really wanted was to hear him speak the words that no man other than her father had ever spoken to her. She wanted to hear him say, "I love you."

When she climbed the tower early that evening, she found Elijah sitting at the table in the watchroom penning an entry in his logbook. Crossing the floor to him, she stood behind him, rubbing the back of his neck, then parted his hair with a finger and placed a warm kiss on his nape. She peeked over his head. "What are you writing?"

He moved his hand so she could see for herself. " 'August 6, 1831,' " she read aloud. " 'An oily sea tonight. Celebrated Gus's birthday today.' "

"Anything else you wanna add?"

Only that I love you, she admitted shyly to herself, not quite having the courage yet to say the words aloud. "What's an oily sea?"

"It's the way the water looks when there's a squall brewin'. Bad weather tonight, I suspect."

Remembering what happened last time there was foul weather, she felt a sudden queasiness in the pit of her stomach. "I hope nothing untoward is in the offing."

"No way of knowin' that 'til it happens."

Diverting her attention from what might lie ahead of

them later in the evening, she focused on the pages of the logbook. "Do you have an entry for every night?"

"Yup. Every night since August 23, 1799. Not all in this book, mind you. Like I told you before, most of the old logs are in the attic. Phineas used to get a lot more wordy than me. I tend to keep the facts short."

Augusta flipped through a few pages at the beginning of the book. " 'January 25, 1830. A villain snowstorm. January 30, 1830. A Saturday night, very cold. February 12, 1830. A heavy gale of wind to northwest.' " She nodded good-naturedly. "You could say those facts were short."

"I told you I wasn't good with words."

"Your prowess in other areas completely makes up for your deficiency where words are concerned."

He made a *tsk*ing sound with his tongue at her comment. "Augusta Payne, what would the ladies in Philadelphia say if they could hear you?"

"I don't care what they'd say. I don't live in Philadelphia anymore. What they think isn't important."

But Elijah wondered if she was trying to convince him . . . or herself.

The squall breezed up around eight. High winds buffeted the tower with such force that Augusta swore the top of the tower was swaying. Rain began falling in horizontal sheets, driven by the wind and illuminated by branches of lightning that sliced through the night sky. Thunder crackled overhead; white-capped breakers boomed against the storm beach far below them. Elijah circled his arms around Augusta's waist as she stood at the window, peering at a world that seemed to be spinning out of control.

"You wanna go back to the house?" he whispered against her earlobe. "It's not too invitin' up here tonight."

She shook her head and covered his big hands with her own. "I'll stay. It's just a little frightening."

He tightened his embrace and fixed his chin atop the crown of her head. "Didn't think you were scared of anything, Gus. Not afraid to answer a man back. Not afraid of treasure hunters with guns. Not afraid to leave home and family and begin a new life with a man you've never seen."

"You make me sound courageous."

"You are."

"No, I'm not. You're the courageous one, Elijah. You're the one who rescues people from sure death. You do what you do for reasons that are good, and positive. I do the things I do because in most instances I feel I have nothing to lose. That's not being courageous. That's being cowardly. I always thought my sisters were the cowards because they refused to accept responsibility for my parents' care. But they weren't the cowards at all. I was. I was a coward for not demanding they remain at home to help. So I allowed them to leave one by one, because it was easier to be rid of them than to listen to their complaints, and I became the dutiful daughter—the one who would happily forfeit every moment of her youth so everyone else could flourish. I . . . I should have felt privileged to take care of my parents, 'Lijah. There where times when I did, but at other times I felt put upon, and abandoned, and I stayed for no admirable reason. *You* would have remained because you would have felt as if you were doing something good, and positive. *I* remained because no one else would. So I'm not courageous.

Everything that anyone has ever said about me is true. I'm selfish and froward and . . . Oh God, I'm a horrible, *horrible* person!''

Elijah turned her around in his arms, wondering what had brought all of this on. While thunder burst around them, he hugged her against his chest, trying to calm the sobs that suddenly wracked her body. ''Gus, honey, you're not a horrible person. C'mon, now. Listen to me.''

She shook her head vehemently. ''I am. You . . . you don't know.'' She inched away from him and stared at a spot in the center of his chest. ''There was a night years ago, just . . . just like tonight. There was rain and thunder, and lightning was dancing all around the house. Storms usually passed quickly. But not that night. It just sat above the house exploding with thunder that shook the house. I was so afraid, Elijah. Storms had never bothered me, but the one that night was so different. I knew the lightning had to strike the house. It was everywhere. And it was incessant, blazing at every window. I went down to the parlor and sat in the rocking chair, watching the rain and the lightning. And do you know what I was thinking?'' She dashed tears from her cheeks. ''I was trying to decide which of my parents I would try to save if the house caught fire! Neither one of them could walk. I wasn't sure if I could carry even one of them down the stairs. But I knew I had to be prepared, and I hated my sisters for it. I hated them for not being there to help me, for leaving me all alone. I hated them for putting me in a position where I would have to make a decision like that! It's a sin, 'Lijah. It's a sin for anyone to hate as much as I hated that night!''

Elijah folded her in his arms and began swaying from hip to hip, slowly, calmly, trying to soothe her with the motion of his body. "And ever since then you've despised yourself, haven't you, Gus? You despised yourself for resentin' your sisters, because a good Christian would never resent anyone. Never mind how much you sacrificed or how fine a job you did. You allowed yourself to think ill of your sisters that night, so you became a bad person. It's one of the reasons you came here, isn't it, sweetheart? You thought by comin' to Devilstone you could run away from your guilt. But it followed you here, didn't it? A body can run away from a lot of things, Gus, but I don't think a body can ever run away from himself."

He cupped the back of her skull in his hand. "And you're wrong about not bein' courageous. It takes a lot of guts to admit what you just admitted. It takes guts to admit it to me, and even more to admit it to yourself. But you're not a bad person, Gus. Man alive, you're a God-blessed saint compared to a lot of people."

"I'm not a saint. I'm . . . I'm mean-spirited and . . . and horrible!"

His voice grew soft. "I wouldn'ta fallen in love with a horribly mean-spirited person."

Her sobs caught in her throat. She looked up at his face, her eyes red-rimmed and moist with tears. "You love me?"

"Been meanin' to tell you. Guess now's as good a time as any. I love you, Augusta Payne."

"But . . . but why? How can you love someone who has so little goodness in her heart?"

"What you did for your parents all those years shows your goodness, sweetheart. Doesn't matter that you had bad days when you would've liked to run away. The important thing is, you didn't. You stuck it out when no one else would. That alone entitles you to a few days of hatin' the world and everything in it. What you've forgotten is that actions speak louder'n words. Doesn't matter about the words or feelin's you hid inside. It's your actions that counted. You've got nothin' to be ashamed of, Gus. Fact is, you've got reason to be damned proud. You're loyal and hardworkin'. You're a damned good cook, you make people laugh, and you're not afraid to look a man straight in the eye. Can't think of any more reason than that for a man to love a creature. Except maybe to know that the creature loves the man in return.''

She searched his face with eyes that were suddenly bright and exuberant. ''I do, Elijah. I love you so very much.'' She hugged him so tightly that he gasped for air.

''Whoa! You can loosen up some, Gus. I'm not goin' anywhere.''

''Promise me you won't. Promise me you'll never leave me.''

''I don't have to promise, sweetheart. I'm as likely to leave you as I'm likely to leave Devilstone, which goes to say, not likely at all. We're gonna be here forever, you and me, Gus. And no one or nothin'll ever change that.''

She reveled in the power of his embrace and felt his love surround her heart in the same way that the cocoon had once surrounded her spinster's body. ''I don't want anything to change, Elijah. I want us to be as happy for the rest of our lives as we are this very moment.''

''We will be, Gus. I promise you.''

The promise lasted until the next day, when the man they had named Jonah returned to the island.

—14—

It was early the following afternoon when Elijah began digging a shallow grave for two fire birds that had smashed into the tower glass after the storm had ceased the night before. Augusta sat on the grass with her knees drawn to her chest and her arms circling them. She squinted upward to peruse the top of the tower.

"Couldn't you devise some type of screen around the outside of the lantern to catch the birds when they fall, Elijah? Colliding with the glass probably stuns them, but it's the fifty-foot drop to the ground that does them in. If you could prevent them from falling, they might have a chance to survive."

Elijah drove the blade of his shovel into the ground, then leaned an elbow on the handle and followed the direction of Augusta's gaze. He poked his bottom lip out in thought, then nodded in agreement. "Might work. That ledge at the base of the lantern is about two feet wide. If I ordered some heavy wire, I suppose I could rig up some kind of screen around the exterior there to catch the birds before they fall. Good thinkin', Gus. I just hope when the buggers come to, they don't try the same thing all over again.''

''Will you order the wire from Captain Crowley or from the supply ship from the mainland?''

''Probably be best to order it from . . .'' His eyes riveted on the forest. ''Well, will you lookit that.''

Augusta dropped her arms from around her legs and twisted around to find Jonah heading in their direction. Her stomach felt queasy of a sudden. It seemed a kind of omen that he had returned. A bad omen. ''What do you suppose he wants?''

''I dunno, but I'll wager it's nothin' we wanna hear.''

He walked with a spry step, with purpose—as if he knew exactly who he was and what he wanted. This was not the same man she had found at the Gulch. This man didn't have beautiful blue eyes. He had predator's eyes, and she feared that she and Elijah had been singled out as the prey. She doubled her hands into fists, clinging symbolically to the threads of happiness that had woven themselves around her.

Cupping his hands around his mouth, Elijah shouted at the man, ''I got rid of you once! What the hell're you doin' back here again?''

Augusta boosted herself onto her feet and brushed off the back of her skirt with a few swipes of her hand. As Jonah neared them, she took her place by Elijah's side.

''Payne. Augusta. Good to see you again.''

Elijah scowled. ''Not if you're askin' me, it's not.''

He wore a fine suit of clothes, different from the ones he'd washed ashore in. His trousers were black and unwrinkled, his coat light colored and sporting. He wore a dark-green waistcoat and a shirt whose standing collar had stiffened points that showed on his cheeks above his cravat. In his hand he carried a beaver-top hat whose brim he kept smoothing nervously between his fingers. "I believe I owe the two of you an explanation. Could we go inside to talk?"

"I happen to be busy here," said Elijah. "So why don't you just do your explainin' right where you're standin', then leave. Some people in these parts actually work for a livin'."

"I work too, Payne. But my work is somewhat different from yours. Allow me to introduce myself." He extended his right hand toward Elijah. "My name is Strawn. Wilfred Strawn. And I work for the United States government. For the military, actually."

Elijah stared at the man's hand until Strawn returned it self-consciously to his side. "This somethin' you're just rememberin', or did you know it all along?"

"I imagine this is something I should apologize to you about. I knew all along, but there was a reason why my charade was necessary."

"The government in the habit of sendin' employees into the field who lie like flat fish?"

"I assure you, no. But in this instance, the lies were essential. If my report came back with an unfavorable recommendation, my superiors would have preferred that you remain totally ignorant about our interest in Devilstone Island."

"What report?" asked Augusta.

Strawn began worrying the brim of his hat again. "The report that I came here to write. The military is looking for a secluded, easily defendable area to serve as the base for an operation that has been assigned the highest degree of secrecy. We've surveyed a dozen islands, and Devilstone seems to be exactly what we're looking for. I speak for President Andrew Jackson when I tell you that we're prepared to purchase Devilstone from you for three thousand five hundred dollars, which will earn you a profit of almost one hundred thousand percent over its original price of purchase. We're enabling you to leave Devilstone a wealthy man, Payne, with plenty of capital to establish yourself anywhere you want. Maybe even buy yourself a pair of shoes."

"Three thousand five hundred dollars?" repeated Augusta. It was a vast amount—enough to buy a home in Philadelphia and curtains for every window. But Elijah seemed not to be sharing her enthusiasm.

"You come snoopin' around my island, writin' secret reports for secret operations, and now you tell me you're gonna do me the big favor of buyin' my island so I can buy myself a pair of shoes?" He speared Wilfred Strawn with a fearsome, black-eyed look. "Not . . . very . . . damn . . . likely. Now, if you're through yammerin', get the hell off my island."

"I urge you to accept my offer, Payne."

"And I urge *you* to show a clean pair of heels while you're still able."

"Maybe I haven't made myself clear on the subject. I'm not here asking you to accept my offer. I'm here to tell you that the government intends to acquire Devilstone Island with or without your consent. Our offering you recompense for your loss is a mere courtesy. We would hope you would cooperate and go peacefully, but if you refuse, we're prepared to use force."

"And maybe I didn't make *my*self clear on the subject," Elijah challenged. "*I'm* not the one goin' anywhere. *You* are."

Augusta curled her fingers around her husband's arm. "Elijah, perhaps we should discuss this before you—"

"This is none of your concern, Gus. Stay out of it."

"You should listen to your wife, Payne. I expect she knows you can't do battle with the government and hope to win."

"I *own* this island, Strawn, and neither you, the military, nor President Andrew Jackson himself has the power to make me leave. Go ahead. Draw the battle lines. But you'd better prepare yourself for a damned good fight."

"Give it up, Payne. You can't win."

Elijah tightened his fist around the handle of his shovel until his fingers were bleached the color of bone. "You're trespassin', Strawn. And right this second, I'm not feelin' too kindly toward trespassers."

Wilfred Strawn took a step backward. "It seems rather futile my debating the matter with you further when your mind is so closed to discussion. I'll be back in a few days with a notice of eviction. That should put a damper on your belligerence."

"I've got a harpoon in one of my outbuildings that's killed slicker fish than you, Strawn. You show your face on Devilstone again, I promise you, you'll be wearin' that harpoon between your third and fourth ribs."

Wilfred Strawn managed two more quick steps backward. Fear lurked in the pale-blue depths of his eyes.

"They won't like this when they hear about it in Washington. You can't threaten a government man."

"I just did." Elijah yanked his shovel out of the ground and grabbed the haft as if he might hurl *it* instead of his harpoon. "Now, if you've got a boat waitin' for you, you'd better run to catch it. Word is, when it comes to throwin' deadly projectiles, my aim is kinda . . . accurate." When he hefted the shovel to his shoulder, Wilfred Strawn turned tail and ran. "And don't come back!" Elijah shouted after him.

He flung the shovel to the ground. "I told you the man wasn't to be trusted, Gus. I knew it from the moment I set eyes on him."

Augusta folded her arms across her chest and pinched her eyes into round little balls. "Is that the excuse you're using to explain your rudeness?"

"Rudeness? The man wants to steal my island from me! What did you want me to do? Invite him to tea?"

"Not rudeness to *him*, Elijah. Rudeness to *me!* Did it ever occur to you to ask my opinion about whether we should accept his offer or not? I live here too. I should have just as much say in the matter as you."

"Last night you said you never wanted anything to change. Sounds to me as if somethin' has changed already. Your mind!"

"That's not true. I never want anything to change *between* us. *Between* us. I want to spend the rest of my life with you, Elijah, but it doesn't matter where as long as you're there beside me."

His face turned ugly. "Well, it matters to me."

"I love Devilstone, but that doesn't mean we can't be happy someplace else."

"You wanna sell out for thirty pieces of silver, Gus?"

"No, I don't. But I think we owe it to ourselves and future generations of Paynes to sit down and calmly talk this out."

"You can talk all you want, but my mind's already made up."

"You . . . you pigheaded man! You're about to wage war on the government of the United States! The military, Elijah! Think about it. Strawn is right. You can't win!"

"Then I'll die tryin', won't I?"

Frustration caused tears to well in her eyes. "Why won't you leave this place?"

"Because it's my home!"

"There's more to it than that! Tell me, Elijah! What in God's name are you afraid of?"

His eyes grew black and steely. "I'm not afraid of anything." Looking mean as a storm cloud, he turned away from her and headed for the lighthouse.

"You *are* afraid! If you weren't so afraid, you wouldn't always be running away when I ask you to open your heart to me!" She chased behind him as he entered the shed that abutted the tower. "Talk to me, Elijah. I want to help. I'm your wife. I love you!"

He grabbed a stack of clean linens and a box of tripoli powder off a wall shelf. She could sense his anger in the tightness of his movements. "I will not be ignored!" she railed at him. "If you wanted to marry a woman who would sit by passively while you withdraw into yourself, then you should have stipulated that requirement in your advertisement! Or better still, perhaps you should have responded to someone else's letter of inquiry! Tell me,

Elijah, just how many women did I beat out for the privilege of being slighted by you? Twenty-five? Fifty?''

He confronted her, seeming averse to answering her question.

''Tell me!''

A muscle began pulsating in his jaw. ''Yours was the only response I got.''

Of all the replies he could have made, that was not the one she was expecting to hear, but it had the same paralyzing effect on her as the numbing cold of the North Atlantic. She felt the heat from her agitation drain from her face. Her lips went cold. She thought he had *chosen* her over all the other women who had made reply to his advertisement. She surmised he had found something so appealing in her response that he'd decided she was the only applicant with whom he could spend the rest of his life. That she'd had no competition seemed to cheapen the entire process of selection. He had chosen her not because she was special but because there had been no one else *to* choose. She had become Mrs. Elijah Payne not by choice, but by default.

A knot of emotion began vibrating in her throat. Last night she had felt so beautiful, so loved. Today she felt like a Philadelphia spinster again—insignificant, worthless. And she suddenly wanted to be as far away from the object of her humiliation as she could possibly be.

Elijah saw the fire leave her eyes, to be replaced by a look so tormented that it filled him with self-loathing to think he was the cause. ''Gus.'' He lifted his hand in supplication. Augusta regarded it in the same manner that he had regarded Wilfred Strawn's hand, and when he ventured a step toward her, she swung away from him and raced out the doorway.

"Gus!" He charged after her, stopping at the threshold to watch her flee toward the forest, petticoats flying and hair streaming behind her. He'd never intended to tell her how many inquiries he'd received. He didn't think it was the kind of information she needed to know. But he'd gone and done it now, hadn't he? He slammed his fist against the doorframe. "Dammit, Gus." Why did she have to ask so many questions? Didn't she know the answers would only hurt her? He didn't want to hurt her. He loved her too much for that. But the damage was already done, so now he was going to have to figure out some way to repair it. But how? He had a history of ruining things, not making amends. How was he gonna set things to right again?

"I'm sorry, Gus," he said as he watched her disappear into the forest. And quite suddenly, the thought of losing Devilstone paled in comparison to the thought of losing this woman whom he had come to love. "I'll find some way to make it up to you."

By suppertime, he'd thought of the very thing.

She was still angry with him. He could tell by the way she was flitting around the kitchen, pretending she was too busy to notice he'd come inside. He washed up at the sink and, amid the tense silence that surrounded him, prepared himself to wear down her defenses.

"Smells good," he called over his shoulder. "What is it?"

There was a long pause, followed by a terse "Soup."

"What kind?"

"Hot."

He dried his hands and walked to the table. At least she

was talking to him, even if it was only one word at a time. She set the soup tureen on the table, then lifted her apron over her head and draped it over the back of a chair. Elijah stepped around the corner of the table and held her chair for her.

Augusta stopped dead in her tracks. She lifted a curious eyebrow, then, without uttering a word, took her seat and began ladling out the soup. Elijah took his place at the head of the table.

"Looks awful good, Gus."

Augusta remained silent.

He dipped his spoon into the soup. "I never meant to hurt your feelin's this afternoon. If I'd known the truth was gonna affect you like this, I would've lied. Sometimes it just doesn't pay a man to be honest with a creature. But you had me fooled. I thought when you were harpin' at me before to be honest with you, that you really meant it. I guess what you should've said was that I should be honest with you as long as I didn't tell you somethin' you didn't wanna hear."

Her nose twitched slightly, but she didn't look at him.

"Did you ever stop to think that maybe I got only one reply because it was meant to be that way? It could've been the Good Lord's only way of makin' sure I didn't foul things up. If I only get one response, then I can't possibly choose any other woman except the one I'm *supposed* to pick—the one the Good Lord was tellin' me would have a big enough heart to love me despite all my faults and vices."

Her lips twitched, but still she didn't look at him.

"I might've gotten a thousand responses, Gus, but you can't tell me I wouldn't of chosen you anyway. Can you?"

She dragged the tip of her spoon through her soup.
"No."

"The way I figure it, God took a shortcut and spared
my eyes some strain by not havin' to read through all that
extra mail. God thinks like a Mainer sometimes. He wanted
me to save my eyesight for better views—like Gus smilin',
and Gus laughin', and Gus tryin' to keep a straight face."

She angled her face away from him.

"And I'm sorry I snapped at you in front of Strawn.
I'd no right to do that. You're my wife. You've got a say
in what happens around here too. I guess I've just been
too long by myself. Time was when I never had to consult
with anyone about anything. I'll try to improve, Gus, but
it could take time. Perfection takes a lot of work."

She angled her face slightly toward him again. He
watched her features soften as she contemplated his words.
Considering her own experiences in her quest for perfection, he was hoping she would tell him that faultlessness
wasn't necessary—that she loved him just the way he was.
That she loved him even when his foot was occupying his
entire mouth. He eyed her hopefully.

"Soup's getting cold," she said in a low voice.

Elijah's shoulders slumped. "Are you ever gonna talk
to me in whole sentences again, Gus?"

She shrugged.

But shrugging wasn't good enough. He wanted his wife
back the way she'd been this morning, when she had loved
him with her hands and pleasured him with her mouth.
There was only one recourse left. Much as he hated to do
it, he'd have to play his trump card. "I've been thinkin'.
The sail into Lustre's Gate the other day wasn't so bad. I

got back with plenty of time to spare. Maybe if the weather holds tomorrow, I could take you for a look-see at the mainland. Maybe even sashay you by Biddle's Dry Goods Emporium. Wouldn't doubt that he might have a bolt of some kind of fancy cloth that you could use to dress up the windows in the kitchen here.''

She fixed him with a long, suspicious look. "You're trying to bribe me.''

"Damn right. Is it workin'?''

She looked away, chin high, lips pinched, expression thoughtful. "Throw in some chintz for the bedroom windows and you have yourself a deal.''

Augusta discovered that travel in Elijah's yawl was much less debilitating than travel in a larger vessel. When they docked at the main pier of Lustre's Gate late the following morning, she wasn't even queasy.

"Why do they call it Lustre's Gate?'' she asked as she watched Elijah secure the bow painter around a stake driven into the floating wharf.

"It's 'cause of that channel of rocks we passed.''

She looked back toward the mouth of the harbor. A reef of boulders formed an impenetrable wall halfway across the inlet. It reminded her of the reef on Devilstone.

"Townfolk say the seawall is kind of like a gate. It allows smaller fishin' vessels by, but it's too narrow for some of your foreign ships of deeper draft. They have to anchor outside the seawall and off-load cargo onto smaller vessels. It's too bad. The village is a deep-water port, but it doesn't do anyone any good 'cause of the damn gate.''

He helped her out of the yawl, then followed behind her

as she climbed the steep gangway to the stationary pier. "Gangway won't be so steep when we head back. Tends to level out when the tide rises."

At the top of the gangway, she shook the wrinkles out of her skirt, fluffed the poufs of taffeta at her shoulders, straightened her straw bonnet, and hooked her gloved hand around her husband's elbow. Elijah laughed at her primping. "Don't get too fancy on me, Gus. This is Lustre's Gate, not Philadelphia."

The main thoroughfare of the village bore little resemblance to Philadelphia. The street was paved with neither cobblestones nor brick. Rather, it was a simple dirt road along which barefoot boys chased wooden hoops with boisterous yells and slender rods. Elijah guided her along the side of the road, where picket fences stood as white and starched as soldiers at attention. She regarded the houses behind the fences with keen interest, deciding they were unique for their sameness, for though they varied in size and shape, there was not a clapboard that was painted other than white, nor a shutter that was other than black. It was almost as if there existed in Lustre's Gate an inherent fear of appearing the least bit different, outwardly at least.

"The houses are all the same," she whispered out the corner of her mouth.

Elijah nodded. "All the same, but all different. Just like the people."

As they continued to walk, she noticed some of the differences. Flat roofs sported rooftop walks and hexagonal cupolas whose sides were encased in glass. Where roofs were sloped, railed widow's walks extended from second-story bedrooms, there to overlook the harbor below. *The same but different,* she thought, noting that the houses blended so well with each other that their individual presence seemed conspicuously obscured. She wasn't aware that far down the street behind her, the children who had been rolling hoops had stopped their game to gather into a tight circle. She couldn't hear their whispered voices or see the fingers they pointed at the wickie of Devilstone Light.

They left the view of the harbor behind them as they rounded the corner toward the business district and Biddle's Emporium, which was their destination. The main street of Lustre's Gate was much quieter than any street in Philadelphia. Tidy shops lined each side of the street, but pedestrian traffic was nonexistent. The only sign of humanity Augusta could find was a man who was sweeping the wooden walkway that fronted a shop farther up the street. He was aproned from neck to knees and was jerking a broom from side to side as if it were an uncooperative dance partner.

"Do you know him?" she asked Elijah.

"Name's Higher Cookworthy. He owns the general store."

She looked left and right at the signs displayed over the doors of the other establishments. "Let's see, you have a confectioner, a book binder, an apothecary, a comb maker, a banker, a jeweler, an auction and commission store, and . . . that's all I can read from here. Except for the barber-surgeon's pole down by Mr. Cookworthy. I gather that's an establishment you don't frequent often."

"Don't see much sense in spendin' good money to cut somethin' that's only gonna grow back."

She shook her head at him. "You have an odd way of looking at things, Elijah Payne. You'd better show me where Biddle's is located before you change your mind about my curtains.''

''Gave you my word on that, Gus. Not likely to go back on my word.''

He escorted her down the wooden walkway to the establishment located directly opposite Cookworthy's General Store. Augusta read the sign that hung above the storefront. '' 'Biddle's Dry Goods Emporium.' '' Then, lowering her gaze to the door, she read the smaller sign that hung from the door glass. '' 'No Bare Feet Allowed.' '' She slanted a downward look at Elijah's bare toes. ''I suspect if you set one foot inside this door, your welcome will be less than rousing.''

Elijah scowled at the sign. ''I never noticed that hangin' there before.''

''Have you ever been inside Biddle's?''

''Never had need.''

''That might explain why you've never seen the sign. I imagine the proprietor is trying to protect himself against an invasion of barefoot children with hoops and rods.''

Elijah looked from his feet to the sign again, not quite believing it hung there. Augusta patted his arm in sympathy.

''I'm sorry you can't come inside. Do you want to wait for me out here?''

He raked a hand through his hair, looking uncomfortable with her suggestion.

''You needn't look so worried, Elijah. I assure you, I'm much more proficient at purchasing cloth than I am at rowing boats.''

He stuck his hands deep into his pockets and stepped away from the door, but the look of unease remained.

"You'll have to hurry, Gus. We don't have as much time as I thought we had."

"You weren't in a hurry ten seconds ago."

He made no reply. Angling his head to the side, he peered through the storefront glass. "Doesn't look like there's any customers in there. Maybe Biddle can wait on you right away. You know what you want?"

"Exactly."

"Then I'll head across to Cookworthy's to buy some wire for that screen we were talkin' about. I'll be back here in about fifteen minutes, so you'd best keep an eye skinned for me. You have money?"

She dangled her reticule before him by its drawstrings. "Sufficient."

He nodded, but seemed unwilling to leave.

"Why are you so nervous of a sudden, Elijah? You act as if you'd prefer I not go in there by myself. Should I have reason to be wary of Mr. Biddle?"

He turned his back on the store and focused on the wooden walkway across the street. Indecision played across his features. "Gus."

"Yes?"

He paused, eyes narrowing, then shook his head. "Nothin'. Pick out somethin' pretty—somethin' you can be happy with for a long time." And then he sprinted down the stairs to the street without so much as a good-bye. She threw a perplexed look at his retreating back, wondering if there would ever come a day when she would truly understand this man who was her husband. Sighing, she curled her hand around the door handle of Biddle's Emporium and depressed the brass tongue.

A bell tinkled overhead announcing her arrival, but she

saw no proprietor to greet her. For a moment she stood motionless, then, with growing excitement, began skimming tables and shelves with her eyes. On one table sat a wealth of ladies' leghorn bonnets. On another a fine display of gaiter boots, French Morocco walking shoes, kid buskins, and children's shoes of the latest styles. Passing by the main counter, she paused to read the labels on an assortment of perfume packets that could be tucked into bureau drawers and handkerchief boxes to scent their contents. Jessamine, verbena, lilac, geranium. The bureau drawers on Devilstone all smelled like seawater, but she doubted that Elijah would appreciate wearing any article of clothing that made him smell like a flower.

She strolled randomly between two long tables that dazzled her with an array of cloth the likes of which she had never seen in Philadelphia—rept and corded cashmeres; plain, shaded, and fancy mous de laines; cotton velvet in plain colors and patterns; shot, chiné, and striped glacé silk; and gingham in every color and variety—Earlston ginghams, seersuckers, muslin grounds, crossover stripes, umbrella ginghams.

"Most of that arrived last week," said a man who appeared suddenly from a back room. He was a rotund man, bald and rosy-cheeked with spectacles that sat slightly askew on his nose.

"I should have come in before you received your shipment. My husband is coming to fetch me in fifteen minutes. I don't think I can make a decision that quickly. Your selection is too overwhelming."

The man laughed as he came to stand beside her. "Never seen you in here before, ma'am. You and your husband visitin' someone in town?"

"We sailed in from Devilstone Island actually. My name is Augusta Payne. I'm recently married to Devilstone's lightkeeper."

He couldn't have looked more surprised had she told him she was married to Noah and had recently arrived on the Ark. The man folded his arms across his chest and backed against the near table. He regarded her over the tops of his spectacles. "So the wickie has taken himself another wife, has he? Did you wash up on shore like the rest of them?"

She wasn't sure how to interpret his tone, but she decided to be civil until otherwise provoked. "My husband advertised for a wife in the *Philadelphia Inquirer*. I answered the advertisement."

"Philadelphia? Well, he couldn't have gotten farther away from Lustre's Gate if he'd been trying."

"No, he couldn't." Then, on a whim of curiosity, "Isn't it sad that he couldn't have found a wife right here in Lustre's Gate."

He drew his brows together in a long white ridge over his nose. "Sad? Just how much do you know about your husband, Mrs. Payne?"

"I know that he's brave, and good, and inordinately stubborn when he wants to be."

The man nodded. "He's indeed brave. No one can take that away from him. Like Phineas in that respect."

"You knew Phineas?"

"I helped him build that lighthouse on Devilstone. Phineas was a fine man, and a good friend. It was a sad day when Phineas Payne died."

"At least he left behind a son who could assume his lightkeeping duties for him."

The man said nothing. He pushed himself away from the table and coaxed his spectacles up his nose. "I never introduced myself, ma'am. The name's Josiah Biddle. Now, what can I help you with today?"

But Augusta wasn't ready to close the door on their discussion. Josiah Biddle was privy to information about Elijah—information she expected would allow her a better understanding of her husband. Information she deserved to know. "I found some of Phineas's ivory carvings in the attic last week. He possessed quite an extraordinary talent."

"He whittled my Martha a piecrust crimper some years back. Martha's gone now, God rest her soul, but I still have the crimper."

"I discovered a crimper too, but it's much too elegant to use. I also found a penholder, and the most delightful carving of a seal. I'd guess Phineas used lampblack to darken the body of the seal, but he left the face completely white. I have no idea why he would do something like that, unless he ran out of lampblack, which seems highly unlikely."

Josiah Biddle smacked his lips. "So he carved the seal, did he? Doesn't surprise me. His whole life changed after his run-in with that creature. And he didn't run out of lampblack. The seal always had a white face."

"You've seen it, then?"

"Years ago, everyone saw it. He lived right here in the harbor."

"But not anymore?"

Biddle shook his head. "Not since that lunatic fisherman took a shot at him. Man was crazier than a loon. Wasn't from around here. Didn't understand the way it was with the seal."

"The way it was? I'm not sure I understand either."

"I suppose you wouldn't, being from Philadelphia. The Abnaki had a name for the white-faced seal. They called him Chakwa. According to their lore, he was possessed of mystical powers."

A chill raced up Augusta's spine. She wanted to know the truth, but for the first time she began to wonder if she would be able to accept it once she heard.

"The Abnaki believed it was a great blessing to have a white-faced seal living in their harbor. The seal sang haunting songs for everyone's pleasure, and he sometimes saved drowning victims by dragging them to shore."

Augusta leaned into a display table for support. Wilfred Strawn claimed to have been rescued by a seal, but Wilfred Strawn had told them nothing but lies.

"The seal's presence in the harbor was thought to protect the harbor and to assure a bounty of fish in the surrounding waters. In return for the creature's protection, the Abnaki vowed that no injury would ever befall the seal. If a man harmed a white-faced seal, his punishment would be swift and terrible. The seal was sacred to the Abnaki."

"But, I assume, not to the white man."

"Not to all white men. When the Abnaki moved their village inland and the first white settlers took their place on the coast, the seal stayed right there in the harbor, watching over everything."

"But—" Augusta tried to calculate mentally. "How old would that make the seal?"

"Well over two centuries."

She nearly laughed at the absurdity. "A seal can't possibly live that long." Then, less skeptically, "Can it?"

"Not usually. But if you believe the Abnaki lore,

Chakwa wasn't any ordinary seal. According to the legends, if the creature remained in the same place, faithfully protecting it, there wasn't anything to prevent him from living forever. But if he ever left the harbor, even for a night, legend said he'd die.''

Augusta frowned. What he was saying struck an all-too-familiar chord. Was it Abnaki legend that somehow accounted for Elijah's unnatural attachment to Devilstone Island? Good Lord, what kinds of stories had Phineas Payne filled his son's head with?

"The fishing was always good around Lustre's Gate, but some years back the herrin' started running in the harbor. Herrin' business was a good one, but some of the locals began complaining that the seal was eating all their profits. Seals have a powerful liking for herrin'. All the villagers knew the Indian lore about the seal, so no one was willing to do anything about the situation, except one fisherman from away. He said all the lore about the seal was hogwash, so one morning he rows out into the harbor and shoots the creature. Phineas was in town buying supplies and saw the whole thing from the main pier. He jumps into his boat and sets out to rescue the seal, if there's anything left of the poor creature. He finds him among the rocks of the seawall with a lead ball buried in his flesh above his right flipper. So Phineas loads him into his yawl and carries him back to Devilstone.''

"But what about the legend? If the seal leaves the harbor, he's supposed to die.''

"The way Phineas figured it, the seal was bound to die anyway. He was just trying to ease the pain of it. But wouldn't you know? Phineas dug that lead ball out and nursed that seal right back to health again.''

"Did the villagers do anything to the fisherman who shot him?"

"Didn't have to. Within the week, the man got tangled in his fishing nets and drowned."

A prickly sensation crept up the backs of Augusta's arms. "A swift and terrible punishment," she whispered.

"Since that day, the herrin' have never returned to Lustre's Gate, and neither has the seal. The villagers have since come to think that maybe the one incident precipitated the other."

Augusta worried the inside of her cheek. But there was a white-faced seal on Devilstone. Was it the same seal, or a different one? "Do you know what happened to Chakwa after Phineas nursed him back to health?"

"He never said directly. We just figured he let him go."

"He never mentioned ever seeing the seal again?"

"Never. But the odd thing was, the next time Phineas sails into the harbor, he's got himself a baby."

"Perhaps he simply found it indelicate to discuss his wife's condition with anyone."

"Phineas was a bachelor all his life. He never married."

Augusta stared into Josiah Biddle's eyes, knowing now why there was no marker for Phineas Payne's wife on Devilstone Island. But if Phineas had no wife, then . . . "Where did the baby come from?"

Biddle shrugged. "All Phineas ever said was that he found the baby washed ashore on the beach and that he intended to raise him as his own. Decided to call him Elijah."

For a long moment, Augusta lapsed into introspective silence. That would explain why Elijah tried to avoid talking about his mother. How could he discuss the woman if he didn't even know who she was? Her heart went out to him for the anguish he must have suffered because of it. "Was there any attempt made to try to find the baby's parents?"

"Don't know how we'd ever find that out. The only way that baby could have washed ashore was as the result of a shipwreck, and there weren't any wrecks recorded that entire summer."

"So how do you justify the child's appearance?"

"We don't. But I imagine we've all got our own ideas about what really happened."

"For instance?"

Biddle smoothed his palm over the crown of his bald pate. "Well, there's some that say there was a wreck in the area that we never found out about, and that the baby washed ashore on some flotsam. Then there's those who claim the baby was a gift from the sea—Chakwa's way of thanking the wickie for saving his life. And then there's still others who say the baby is really Chakwa in his human guise."

Augusta stood very still. Her instep began to tingle. "What do you mean, 'human guise'?"

Biddle looked confused, then nodded. "I guess I never said before. When the seal was living in Lustre's Gate, sometimes we'd see him swimming in the harbor, and sometimes we wouldn't. The Abnaki always claimed that when you couldn't see him, he was walking the earth in the form of a man."

The door to the emporium opened. The bell jangled crazily, prompting Josiah Biddle to raise his hand in greeting to an elderly man who dawdled into the store on two gimpy legs and a cane. "Morning, Alden!"

"What's that?" The old man lifted a hearing trumpet to his ear and aimed it at Biddle.

"I said, 'Morning, Alden!' "

The old man shook his head. "Not done yet. Just got here."

Josiah Biddle laughed indulgently. "Will you excuse me for a moment, Mrs. Payne? Why don't you look over my selection of yard goods and I'll be right back to help you."

Augusta nodded, but the bolts of cloth to which Biddle referred began swimming before her eyes in a kaleidoscope of color. The man was implying that . . . that Elijah . . . Dear God, what he was suggesting was insanity. Sheer insanity. Her husband was flesh and blood, not . . . not . . . She pressed her gloved fingertips to her brow, thinking herself about to be quite unwell. *Air. I need air.*

Gliding one hand along the edge of the table for support, she hastened down the length of the aisle and rounded the corner toward the door. Biddle's voice rang out behind her.

"Mrs. Payne? Please don't leave! I can help you now."

She heard his footsteps thumping across the floor in her direction, but she was faster. She pulled the door open, sending the bell into fits of chaotic jingling, then rushed out into the morning light where tales of centuries-old seals and their human counterparts remained Indian legend rather than reality. She hurried across the walkway and down the three wooden stairs to the street, and only then stopped to catch her breath. "Thank you, Mr. Biddle, but you've helped quite enough for one morning." It made perfect sense to her now why Elijah resisted sailing into Lustre's Gate. Given the villagers' opinion about his origins, they probably treated him as if he were a carnival freak. There were times in Philadelphia when she had felt decidedly freakish. It pained her to think that Elijah might have suffered the same torment. It made her want to fold him in her arms to protect him from cruel looks. It made her want to leave Lustre's Gate as quickly as possible.

Lifting her skirts, she half walked, half ran across the main street to the general store. The door flew open as she set foot on the walkway, and when she looked up, Elijah's big body was filling the doorway.

"Gus?" He stopped short, looking down at her as if she had sprouted another head. "You done already? I thought you'd take so long I'd have to send someone in to drag you out by your toenails. Where's your cloth?"

She looked down at her empty hands, realizing for the first time that she had fled the store without making a purchase. "I . . . He didn't have any gingham."

"Couldn't you find somethin' else you liked besides gingham?"

"No. He had a very small selection. It was quite disappointing. I'll simply have to make do with the sprigged muslin I brought with me from Philadelphia. Are you ready to leave?"

He stepped away from the portal of Cookworthy's, allowing the door to close behind him. Looped around his left shoulder was a heavy coil of thick wire, which he shifted to a more comfortable position for carrying. He peeked at her beneath the brim of her bonnet. "You all right, Gus? You're white as a pan of milk."

She touched the back of her gloved hand to her cheek. "You're probably witnessing the color of disappointment."

But Elijah looked troubled. "You sure that's all it is? Biddle didn't . . . He didn't say anything to you, did he?"

His unease was so palpable that she felt an overpowering need to comfort him with the only words she suspected would work. "Of course he said something to me, Elijah.

He said, 'Good morning,' and 'May I help you,' and all the other phrases that proprietors of such establishments are supposed to use.''

''But he obviously didn't use the right ones, because he let you get away without buyin' anything.''

She felt a twinge of something warm and vital pull at her heart as she looked up into her husband's face. He had agreed to take her to Lustre's Gate knowing full well what could happen while she was here. Her learning what the villagers thought about him could destroy her trust, her love. But she wasn't going to allow that to happen. He had risked much by bringing her here. She intended to repay that kindness by ignoring the gossip and showering him with love instead of mistrust. He had accepted her for what she was. She owed it to him now to respond in kind. They were alike, the two of them. Odd birds with rough edges and misshapen angles. They didn't fit in everywhere, but that didn't seem to matter anymore.

They didn't need to fit in.

They had each other.

''Did I just say somethin' funny that I didn't hear?'' Elijah asked. ''How come you're smilin' like that?''

''Because.''

''Because why?''

Stepping close to him, she stood on tiptoes, wound her hand around his neck, and planted a kiss in the center of his mouth. ''Because I love you.''

His face turned redder than the petals of a wood lily. When she stepped back, he looked left, right, and over his shoulder, then grabbed her by her elbow and scurried her along the walkway. ''Jeesuz, Gus, you want the whole town to see?''

"I don't care if the town sees. I don't need to hide the fact that I love you. Why are we walking so fast?"

"Jeesuz, it's broad daylight."

"You don't mind *talking* about it in broad daylight."

"Talkin' and doin' are two different things."

"We've *done* it in broad daylight, too."

"Not on Main Street in Lustre's Gate, we haven't."

"Everyplace but."

He rolled his eyes and kept walking. "Jeesuz."

"I've embarrassed you, haven't I?"

"I don't get embarrassed."

Just like you don't get jealous or superstitious, she thought. She smiled to think how human he was, how incredibly, irrationally, wonderfully human.

She sat huddled in the stern of the yawl on the way back to Devilstone. They spoke little during the four-hour journey, lulled by the soft hum of wind through lines and sail. But she watched Elijah during those hours and began reflecting upon the odd circumstances that had made her his wife. And in one instance she realized she owed a debt of thanks to the villagers of Lustre's Gate. Had it not been for all this nonsense about Phineas and Chakwa and an orphaned baby, Elijah probably would have found himself a wife in Lustre's Gate and *she* would still be a spinster in Philadelphia.

That was the bright side. The darker side was how these misguided whisperings had affected the villagers' perception of Elijah, and how Elijah had responded to them. She would guess his reclusiveness stemmed directly from his earlier experiences in Lustre's Gate. But why hadn't Phineas set things to right with the villagers about the child? Why hadn't he taken it upon himself to prove that Elijah and Chakwa were not one and the same? Recalling her confrontation with Josiah Biddle, however, she realized she could ask the same question of herself. Why hadn't *she* challenged the man's theory? It would be so easy to disprove. All she would have to do is point out that . . . that . . .

Point out what? That Elijah swore the seal didn't exist? That she had never seen the seal at any time when Elijah was near? That on the morning when she had fallen asleep in the tower and Elijah was nowhere to be found, Wilfred Strawn claimed to have been rescued by a white-faced seal?

She grew quiet, uncomfortable with the bend of her thoughts.

Coincidence. All coincidence. But her mind began lighting on other coincidences that had seemed insignificant until now. How did she explain Elijah's tolerance of salt? Was it bizarre tolerance or a natural craving? And his feet. Why was he unable to abide shoes? An odd abhorrence, or did it go deeper than that? Could a creature of the sea bear to have its feet bound while on land? She frowned as she regarded her husband's bare feet. *Perhaps not.*

A cold fist tightened around her vitals. Seeming to sense her eyes on him, Elijah turned his head and gave her a lazy wink, and it was then that she became aware of a final coincidence, and she wondered why she hadn't made the connection before.

His eyes were soft, and sooty, and nearly black, and she had seen them before. Buy they weren't the eyes of anyone human.

Dear God, they were the eyes of the white-faced seal.

—15—

"I'm sorry you had to come back empty-handed," said Elijah as he followed her into the bedroom an hour later. "But at least I found some wire. Maybe we can start riggin' up some kind of screen tomorrow."

Augusta removed her bonnet and hung it on the wall peg next to Elijah's work shirt. "Whatever you like."

"I know somethin' I'd like."

She pulled off her gloves, stuffing them into her reticule, then hung the reticule on another peg. As she started to turn, she felt the hardness of Elijah's body behind her and then the warmth of his mouth on the back of her neck. "I'd like you, Gus," he said in a husky whisper against her ear. He smoothed his palms down the length of her arms, then folded her arms across her chest, holding her tightly, solidly in his embrace. "I'd like you right now."

She twisted her head away from his mouth, her nerves too frayed to countenance his nearness. "Please, Elijah."

"Please what?" He nuzzled the flesh below the hang of her earlobe. "Please hurry?"

Her neck grew hot as he drew her lobe into his mouth, sucking gently on its fullness. She couldn't make love to him. Not now. Not when she was so beset by doubts about who he was, what he was. She closed her eyes, struggling with the sensations that his touch provoked. "Please stop." But she said it more harshly than she intended. He responded by lifting his head and regarding her profile with one part curiosity and a great deal of surprise.

"Is this the same woman who a little more than a spit ago kissed me on my mouth in the main street of Lustre's Gate?"

"The trip back seems to have upset my stomach," she lied. "I'd feel better if you weren't squeezing me."

He loosened his grip and turned her around in his arms. "I'm sorry, sweetheart. You should've said somethin' before. Can I get you somethin' for it? You wanna lie down?"

She shook her head, unable to look him square in the face. "I just don't want to be squeezed."

He dropped his arms to his sides. "That can be arranged."

But the tone of his voice had changed. He sounded disheartened, hurt. *I don't want to hurt you, Elijah, but I need answers. And I know if I ask, you won't give them to me.*

"I don't imagine you're gonna wanna eat if your stomach's slidin'."

"I don't imagine. But I'll throw something together for you if you like."

He nodded and threw a hand out in the direction of the barn. "Maybe I'll just head out to milk Geraldine while you're changin'. You want me to unbutton your dress before I go?"

"No!" She backed against the wall, looking as if she would scream if he touched her. Elijah searched her face.

"Jeesuz, Gus, what's wrong with you?"

"Nothing. I . . . I just don't want you to touch me right now."

His eyes lengthened to dark slits. His jaw tightened into a hard angle. "You afraid if I unfasten a few buttons, I might lose control of myself?"

She said nothing.

"Are you?" A muscle pulsed in his cheek. His voice grew loud, gruff. "Answer me, dammit!" And when still she said nothing, he speared her with a look that made her wince. "I've never taken a woman against her will. I'm sure as hell not gonna start with my own wife! What the blazes has come over you?"

She lowered her gaze, wanting to tell him but fearing his reaction. Looking disgusted, Elijah clenched his fist. "I suspect you'll get tired of holdin' up that damn wall sometime. Lemme know when you do."

He left the room then, his back stiff with anger. She had wanted to learn the truth. Now that she knew one man's version of it, however, she wished she'd never heard any of it. And as she listened to the sound of the kitchen door banging shut, she wondered what she had sacrificed for a bolt of yellow gingham that remained on the display table at Biddle's Dry Goods Emporium.

* * *

She couldn't look at him at supper without her imagination running wild. She knew she should discount everything she'd heard today as romantic fantasy, but some elements of the fantasy were too real to discount. When Elijah climbed the tower that evening, she raced down to the reef to see if she could find the white-faced seal, but the creature was nowhere to be seen. She wasn't sure why it was so important for her to see the animal again. She already knew he lived somewhere in these waters. What seemed more imperative was that she see him in Elijah's presence, which would ultimately disprove any theory the villagers had confected about Elijah and the white-faced seal.

The Abnaki claimed when the seal wasn't swimming in the harbor, he was walking the earth in the form of a man. Surely, Phineas Payne had determined long ago that there was no connection between the seal he had nursed back to health and the baby he had found. Or was she merely hoping he had made that determination?

How would she ever know?

She scanned the eastern horizon, where darkness began melting into the evening sky. Elijah would be making his daily entry in his logbook about now. What would the day's entry read? *Sailed into Lustre's Gate. Gus acting strange.* Or would he merely note the direction from which the wind was blowing? Phineas, no doubt, would have recorded the day's proceedings at length. But Elijah—

The logbook! The daily log. Phineas had kept detailed accounts since— What had Elijah said? August of 1799. And they were all packed away in the attic. Had he recorded the events of twenty-eight years ago on the pages of those books?

She searched the dark Atlantic waters with a wary eye. If he had, she needed to know. Half-truths and conjecture were making her insane. Whatever he had written, no matter how improbable or implausible, she needed to read.

But what if the truth is something you can't live with? an inner voice prodded.

She turned her back on the reef and began the trek back to the house. "Then at least I'll know what I'm dealing with. That's better than knowing nothing at all."

She waited until dark before she climbed the stairs to the attic. Not being entirely comfortable with what she was about to do, she deemed her snooping better left to the realm of darkness. Besides, Elijah was less likely to intrude upon her if he was busy keeping watch in the tower. She cupped her hand around the flame of her candle as she ascended the staircase, and after she gained the room and crossed to Phineas's trunks, she set the sconce atop the trunk where she had found the carving of the white-faced seal. She had returned the figurine to its rightful place among Phineas's possessions several days ago. It had seemed a safer place to keep it than the pocket of her apron. She wondered now why she hadn't thought to peruse Phineas's logbooks then. It might have provided fodder with which she could have refuted Mr. Biddle's accusations.

Unstrapping the leather bindings from the outside, she lifted the lid, and in the removable tray that spanned the length of the trunk, she found a series of books stacked neatly together, spines facing upward, all bound in pigskin-colored leather cloth that was embossed with black numerals. In the dimness of the light she squinted to read the spine of the first book. "Seventeen ninety-nine through eighteen hundred." She regarded each consecutive volume, determining that each book covered a period of two years. Twenty-eight years ago would take her back to the volume for—"Eighteen hundred three through eighteen hundred four," she muttered, removing the book from where it was wedged.

The leather felt soft to the touch. When she opened the cover to the first page, she was struck first by the clarity of Phineas's script, then by the length of the passage he had penned. She skimmed his words of January 1, 1803, discovering what he had eaten that day, what chores he had performed, what the weather had been like, how many vessels had passed by the island, and a host of other details that bore no relationship to the business of lighthouse keeping. Phineas's account read more like a journal entry than a log entry, but she supposed it was one vehicle he had found with which he could combat loneliness.

For the next ten minutes, she leafed through pages in search of an entry that mentioned the white-faced seal. On a page dated July 2, 1803, she discovered what she'd been looking for.

Took the yawl into Lustre's Gate today but sailed back to Devilstone with more than just supplies. Some damn fool pumped a lead ball into the white-faced seal right there in the harbor. I dug the ball out with my jackknife. Thought the creature would ring eight bells before I got him to the island, but he's lived long enough for me to stitch him up. Don't know whether he'll last the night or not. That's some nasty gash he's got over his flipper. This should never have happened. Leave it to some outsider wanting to make a profit to upset the balance of things. Don't know what's going to happen in the village now with the seal gone. Maybe if he recovers, he'll swim back to the harbor again. Makes me a mite squeamish having him here. No one's ever even touched him before that I know of. I kinda wish I hadn't been the first, but someone had to help the poor animal. I wonder what the Abnaki have to say about a man who tries to save a white-faced seal but fails? Nothing bad, I hope.

Augusta read the entries for the next several days, finding that, to Phineas's amazement, the seal improved with every passing hour.

I can't understand it. He's healing awful well for an animal who's supposed to be as old as he is. If someone shot a hole that big in me, I'd be dead by now. Maybe there's something mystical about this crazy seal after all. It's getting so a man doesn't know what to believe anymore.

And then the following day:

His appetite is back, and then some. I'm having to spend a good part of my day fishing just to keep the creature's belly full. The gash over his right flipper is still pretty fierce looking. Don't know if his fur will ever grow over it again. I suppose I should feel put out for having to spend so much time caring for him.

He's taking time away from my chores. But it's kinda nice having him here. Never knew that looking out for someone else would make a man feel so good inside. When I talk to him, he looks at me like he knows what I'm saying. Once he's fully recovered, maybe he'll decide not to swim back to Lustre's Gate at all. Maybe he'll decide to stay here. Truth is, I wouldn't mind at all.

But on the next day, July 8, everything changed.

When I got back from fishing today, he was gone. I was keeping him in the boathouse on the beach so I wouldn't have far to haul water to him. He must have found his way to the water at high tide. I'm glad he was well enough to leave, but it kinda leaves a big hole in things around here. I'd gotten used to his being here. He was someone to talk to. Guess I'll just have to get used to being alone again. I wonder if he'll end up back in the harbor at Lustre's Gate? Whatever the outcome, I'm going to miss him here on Devilstone.

She followed the ebb and flow of his emotions through the following days:

I keep checking the boathouse to see if he's come back. I can't quite reconcile the fact that he's gone . . .

. . . I thought I saw his head bobbing in the water near the reef today. Turned out to be just a rock . . .

. . . Is it possible he could have died? I can't believe

he would just disappear like that and never show his face again.

. . . It's so quiet here. I wish he'd come back . . .

The depth of his loneliness became a painful thing for her to continue reading. She skimmed the text of what he had written until she came to the entry for July 11.

Good Godfrey Mighty, I think I'm a father. I found a baby washed up in the Gulch this morning. A baby boy. He was naked and squalling, and I can't understand why he wasn't blue with cold, though the weather's been fairly hot of late. Can't figure out where he came from or how he got here, but I'll keep him until someone comes by to claim him. The little fella has some set of lungs on him. Cripes, what do I know about caring for babies? Good thing I've got Geraldine. Least I'll have something to feed him until he starts sprouting teeth. If he stays that long.

Frowning, Augusta reread the last three sentences. *Geraldine? It couldn't possibly be the same Geraldine they were still milking, could it*? Skipping several pages, she continued to read.

He's a good baby. I've rigged up a kinda harness for myself so I can carry him around with me while I'm doing chores. He seems to like that. I've named him Elijah after my father. Having the baby here is nice, but the seal squirted me a lot less.

Augusta laughed at Phineas's humor, though she imagined it had been no easy task for him to provide care for a baby when he had no idea how to do it. It must have been a trying experience for both of them. She flipped slowly through subsequent pages, finding interesting tidbits of information as the night wore on.

September 15, 1803—Took Elijah to Lustre's Gate with me today. Attracted a lot more attention than I wanted. Everyone wanted an explanation about Elijah, and I couldn't give it to them. I suspect they'll start making up their own stories about where the baby came from. I don't think I'll want to hear what they finally concoct. They can be a superstitious lot in the village. They tell me the seal hasn't returned to the harbor since I took him to Devilstone. I think he must be dead. Bought me some ivory at Cookworthy's while I was there. I have a grand idea for a new carving. They tell me the fisherman who shot the seal is dead. Good enough for him.

July 8, 1804—Of all things and after all this time, I saw the seal this morning while Elijah was napping. He was swimming down by the reef. I got as close to him as I could but he kept his distance. He saw me, though. It seemed to me that he looked right through me with those big black eyes of his. And call me a fool, but his face kinda looked happy. Can seals smile? Hell, I just thought of something. It was a year ago today that he disappeared. I wonder if that's supposed to mean something. I guess it means he didn't die. I'm glad. Wait until Elijah gets a gander at him. He won't know what to think. Elijah said his first word today. "Salt," of all things.

"So the seal didn't die and Phineas spied him while Elijah was sleeping." Augusta sighed. "Nothing has changed much, has it?" She scanned the weeks and months that followed. Through Phineas's eyes she saw Elijah take his first step, catch his first fish, throw his first pair of shoes over the cliff. "Goodness, he really didn't like anything on his feet." And she felt the love that developed between father and son—love, and like, and respect. They became inseparable, but every so often Phineas would make a comment that led her to believe he lived in great fear that Elijah's real parents might one day come for him.

I would have to give him up if they could prove he was their child. But giving him up would be like cutting out my heart while there was still breath in my body. My life would no longer be worth living. Maybe I should limit our trips to the mainland. The fewer people who see Elijah, the less chance anyone will have of recognizing him.

That entry was dated May 20, 1808. A month later, on June 20, she read the following:

Things seem to be getting worse for Elijah in the village. The older children are taunting him and calling him Chakwa. Sounds to me as if they've all made up their minds about where he came from. On the way back to the island, he asked me what the word meant. No sense trying to pull the wool over the boy's eyes. I told him the Abnaki lore about the white-faced seal and explained that the boy's appearance at about the same time the seal disappeared has convinced some of the villagers that there's a connection between the two. "Is there?" says he. "The villagers are a bunch of damn fools," says I. "There's no connection at all." "Have you seen the seal since I came to live with you?" says he. He looked so terrified, I decided to stretch the truth some. "The seal's dead," says I. "I haven't seen him for going on five years now." Which was an outright lie, but a lie that needed telling. I've seen the seal several times over the past five years, but always while Elijah was somewhere else. That's not something the boy needs to hear. It's a queer happenstance for sure. "Phineas," says he, "you told me God left me here on Devilstone so you wouldn't be lonely anymore. Does that mean I have a real mother and father somewhere else?" It's the question I'd been dreading these five years. "That's what it means," says I. He looked thoughtful for a time. "I don't think I want to visit Lustre's Gate anymore," says he. "I don't want anyone taking me away from you, Phineas. I want to stay here with you forever and ever." It's not what I thought he'd say. But hearing him say it made me feel blessed. It seems Elijah isn't as likely to leave me as—

She turned the page.

"Have you found what you're lookin' for yet?"

At the sound of Elijah's voice, her heart leaped into her throat. She slammed the book shut and fired a horrified look at the place where the stairway from below cut a long, rectangular opening into the center of the room. Elijah had yet to reach the top of the staircase, so only his torso was visible above the level of the floor. He carried no lantern, no candle. The whiteness of his shirt seemed a beacon in the darkness, but the shadows of the room clung to his features, masking his face.

"I couldn't figure why the sudden change between Lustre's Gate and Devilstone." He climbed the last few risers. The staircase was so solidly built that the wood didn't creak beneath his feet. She realized it was why she hadn't heard him approach. He walked toward her with a slow, measured pace. "Why would you kiss me in front of Cookworthy's and not want me to touch you four hours later?" He stopped before her. "Biddle told you, didn't he?"

She stared at the space between his feet. "Yes."

"I never should've taken you in there. Once I saw that sign on the door, I should've turned you right around and headed back to Devilstone. I never should've let you go in there by yourself."

"Did you intend to hide the rumors from me forever?"

"If I could."

She smoothed her fingertips over the logbook's leather cloth. "How did you know I was up here?"

"I saw the light shinin' through the attic window. If you wanted to go snoopin', you should've thought to cover the glass."

She clutched the book to her breast, then, mustering her courage, looked far up the length of his body to his face. "Have you read any of this?"

"Why should I? I already know what Phineas thought. He thought the same thing the whole village of Lustre's Gate thinks."

"That's not so, Elijah. I haven't seen any evidence of—"

"He *lied* to me!" Clenching his fists, he began pacing before her. "He told me the seal was dead. I remember the day he told me, but years later we hauled a seaman out of the water who claimed he'd been carried away from his sinkin' ship by a white-faced seal. All those years the man had been lyin' to me!"

"He lied because he loved you!"

"He lied because he believed the stories the villagers told. He believed his son was a . . . a freak!"

"He doesn't say anywhere in his journal that he believed those stories."

"Then you haven't read far enough. A man lies when he wants to cover somethin' up. Phineas wanted to cover up what he couldn't explain. And he couldn't explain why he never saw me and the seal together at the same time."

She inhaled a deep, calming breath as she watched him pace. "If you knew the seal existed, why did you jump down my throat when I told you I saw him? Why did you make me think I was seeing things?"

He slowed, then stopped, then fanned his fingers through his hair, forcing the unruly strands back from his face. "Because after Phineas passed on, the seal went out of my life. I never heard the creature mentioned for eight long years. Not until you came along. I thought it was all over. I didn't wanna believe the whole thing was startin' over again. Jeesuz, I still don't."

"Did you ever share your doubts with Phineas?"

"Once." He looked upward, concentrating on a spot amid the rafters. "I asked him what would happen if I ever left Devilstone. I wanted him to say, 'Hell, nothin'll happen to you.' I wanted him to tell me I'd still be alive the next mornin' if I left. But he couldn't do that. He just got this pained look in his eye, like he wished I hadn't asked, and then he tells me that he expects I'll be wickie on the island even after he swallows the anchor, so I don't need to worry my head about it.''

''Is that the only answer he ever gave you?''

''It was the only one he had to give me. Sometimes what a man doesn't say is more important than what he does say.''

It made sense to her now why Elijah refused to leave Devilstone and why he would fight Wilfred Strawn for control of the island. If he had come to believe the Abnaki lore, he wasn't fighting for a piece of property. He was fighting for his life. ''I'm sorry, Elijah.''

''Sorry about what? That you read Phineas's logbooks? That I caught you readin' them? Or sorry that you married a freak?''

''You're not a freak!''

''If you believed that, you wouldn't of pulled away from me in the bedroom. You didn't believe what Biddle told you at first, but on the way back you convinced yourself that there was some truth to what he said. And now you can't deny it. Just like Phineas couldn't deny it.'' His voice grew low, despairing. ''Just like I can't deny it.''

Augusta bowed her head. She lowered Phineas's journal to her lap and flattened her palm against the cover as if it might provide comfort. ''I don't know what to believe anymore.'' The ensuing quiet pressed against her eardrums, making her head ache.

''I won't make you stay here, Gus. If you wanna leave Devilstone, you're free to go. You can leave with Strawn when he comes back. I'm not gonna keep you here against your will.''

She peered up at him, thunderstruck by his suggestion. "I don't want to leave you, 'Lijah."

"You should! Jeesuz, you should run from this island as fast as your feet'll carry you. Because if you don't . . ." He bit back the rest of his sentence. Anguish rode every feature on his face.

"If I don't, what?"

His flesh strained over his cheekbones and around his mouth. His eyes looked so black they seemed to be tunneling to the back of his skull. "Because if you don't, I could kill you, Gus. I could kill you just like I killed Lydia."

Her heart began to pound. She swallowed slowly. "You told me Lydia fell to her death down the cylinder stairs."

He nodded, then, turning away from her, began to pace again. "She fell all right, but when I found her, she wasn't dead. She was a little dizzy and was already gettin' a knot at the base of her skull, but other than that, she seemed fine. She went to bed early that night, 'cause her head started to ache. The next mornin', I found her in bed and . . . she wasn't breathin'. She was dead."

Augusta boosted herself to her feet and stood with her heels pressed close to Phineas's trunk. "What you're telling me is that Lydia died as a result of her fall." She had braced herself for some lurid confession, not so blatant a revelation of innocence. "Why are you blaming yourself for that, Elijah? What could you have done to prevent it?"

"I could've taken her into Lustre's Gate for help. I should've known, Gus. I should've seen how hurt she was. But I didn't want her to be hurt. I wanted her to be well, so I'd have an excuse not to leave the island. The lamps in the tower blind me sometimes, but the night that Lydia

fell—that night I was so blinded with fear that I didn't see
what I should've seen. I could've saved her, Gus, but I
let her die. And if you don't leave with Strawn, I might
one day let the same thing happen to you!''

His expression was so tortured. He looked so alone. She
imagined she had looked the same way on endless occasions when she'd been caring for her parents. If only there
had been someone there to hold her hand, to tell her that
everything would be all right, to assure her that she wasn't
alone. Elijah needed that reassurance now, which presented her with two choices. She could allow herself to
be consumed by the doubts that Josiah Biddle had raised
and Phineas Payne had not disproved, or she could ignore
the rumors and gossip and give her husband the kind of
support that no one had offered her when she'd needed it
most. The plea in his eyes wrenched at that part of her
that had never been able to deny duty. But more than that,
his vulnerability made her want to be strong for him. He
had once saved her from drowning. Perhaps tonight, in
another way, she could do the same for him.

Her mind made up, she grasped Elijah by his elbow and
directed him to the chest that contained Phineas's ivory
carvings. "Sit down."

"I haven't got time to sit. I've gotta get back to—"

She swung him around forcefully and plunked him down
onto the trunk. "First, you sit."

So sit he did, albeit reluctantly. "Nothin' you say is
gonna change anything."

She paid no heed to him, but following his earlier example, began to pace. "When I first came to this island,
I thought we had very little in common, but now I think
we're not so different after all. A short time ago you

accused me of punishing myself because of the way I felt about my sisters. Well, you've done the same thing, Elijah. You've been punishing yourself for Lydia's death, when you had nothing to do with it! And now you want *me* to leave because you're afraid the same thing might happen again. You told me I might have run away from Philadelphia but I'd never be able to run away from myself. The same thing applies to you, Elijah, only *your* idea of running entails your sending *me* away. If I go, nothing will change here. You'll still be consumed with doubts about your link with the seal. You'll never stop wondering who you are, what you are.''

''That just seems to be the way of it, doesn't it? I'll handle it, Gus. I always have. I expect I always will.''

''How? By remaining a prisoner on Devilstone Island?''

''If that's what I have to do, yes!''

''But you don't *have* to remain a prisoner! I can help you.'' She expected him to say that the only way she could help him was by leaving, that he didn't want her help.

But he said none of those things. He slatted curious eyes at her and in a gravelly voice asked, ''How?''

She was so stunned by his response that initially she could think of nothing to say, but as her astonishment faded, she began to see solutions more clearly. ''I could finish reading Phineas's logbooks. I have fourteen years' worth of entries left to peruse. He might have said something in some later account that might be of value to us.''

Elijah shook his head. ''You can read all you want, but my guess is, you're not gonna find out anything more than you already know.'' Which reminded her of something she had read that she hadn't understood.

''Elijah, Phineas mentioned Geraldine's name in one of

the first entries of his log. I'm certainly no expert on bovine life expectancy, but isn't twenty-five years rather a long time for one cow to give milk?"

"Damn near impossible, I'd say."

"Then how do you explain Geraldine's being on the island since 1803?"

He gave her an odd look. "We've probably had a dozen cows on Devilstone since 1803, Gus, but we've always called them Geraldine. A man can waste a lot of time havin' to come up with new names all the time."

"Same name, different cows?" And when he nodded, she focused on his face, suddenly enlightened. "Do you think . . . Could that be what's happening with the seal? What if Chakwa isn't a two-centuries-year-old seal? What if he only *looks* like the same seal? Think about it, Elijah. Chakwa could be different seals who happen to be possessed of the same trait. And what if it's not a he? What if Chakwa is female? She could be passing on her white face to all her pups."

He didn't look hopeful, but neither did he look discouraged. "So what if the seal is female? What does that prove?"

"By itself it proves nothing. What we need to establish is that the seal who supposedly protected the harbor of Lustre's Gate for two centuries isn't the same creature that I've seen near the reef on Devilstone. If the seal isn't the same, I believe we could conclude that the legend of Chakwa is purely myth. And if that's so, then you, my love, have no reason to fear leaving Devilstone."

He laughed then, but there was a grimness to his laughter. "And how the hell are you gonna figure out if it's the same seal or not? I've lived here twenty-eight years, and I haven't seen the creature once. Not once!''

"But I have. And if I can get close enough to him, maybe I can see if he still bears a scar over his right flipper. That's where Phineas dug out the lead ball. If there's no scar, then the legendary Chakwa is no legend."

"Sounds easy enough, doesn't it? But from things I've heard, the only person who ever got close enough to the seal to touch him was Phineas, and that's because the seal was hurt."

"What about the people who claim to have been rescued from drowning by the creature?"

"Like Strawn, you mean?"

She nodded, realizing that Wilfred Strawn was privy to information that could be critical to them. "What Strawn knows could either vindicate or condemn you, Elijah. You disappeared the night Strawn washed ashore. I know you said you were sleeping, but you weren't. You were gone. Strawn claims to have been saved by the seal. Your being gone that night might indicate—" She paused, unwilling to verbalize the exact words. "It might indicate what you don't want it to indicate."

"Great. So what do you suggest I do? Kill Strawn to keep him from talkin'?"

"No. But I think we should glean the truth from him. You were so angry with him the last time you saw him that you never bothered to ask how he actually arrived on the island the night I found him. If his story about the white-faced seal was a lie, then wherever you were that night, it wasn't in the ocean dragging Strawn to shore. You were someplace else, and so was Strawn."

"So you think there's hope."

"Until we can prove otherwise, there's always hope. And we have options, Elijah. I can look for the seal. We can talk to Strawn. I can finish reading Phineas's journals. We'll find the answer somewhere."

"All this fuss over a creature I've never seen."

Augusta's eyes brightened. "Stand up. I want to show you something."

When he moved away from the chest, she opened the lid and dug out the small bundle she'd replaced only days earlier. She unraveled the cloth from the figurine, then placed the ivory in Elijah's palm. "Allow me to introduce you to the white-faced seal."

Elijah elevated his palm. There was awe in his eyes as he studied the carving from every angle. "So this is what he looks like." He turned the carving right side up and upside down, then wrapped his fist around it and stared it square in the face. "Jeesuz, Gus, he's got my eyes."

Early the next morning, Augusta packed up Phineas's logbooks and headed down to the reef. She spread a blanket on the ground just above the natural bridge, then, for the duration of the morning, alternated between keeping a lookout for the seal and reading the rest of Phineas's journals. Elijah had begged off joining her. "If I'm there with you, Gus, you'll never see the creature. I can guarantee it. Besides, after I get some shut-eye, I wanna start workin' on that screen for the tower. I'm tired of buryin' dead birds."

She read for hours, until her vision started to blur, but to her supreme disappointment, Phineas's accounts revealed nothing significant other than the fact that his son had been the delight of his life. That, she suspected, was something Elijah already knew. Sighing her frustration, she rubbed the bleariness from her eyes, and when she looked up, she saw an elongated shadow just below the surface of the water to the left of the reef. She stood up, her gaze riveted on the shadow, her palms suddenly moist. She hurried across the natural bridge, then picked her way over the rock formation to the edge of the water, where seaweed undulated on the tide. The shadow glided beneath the water's surface, parallel to the reef. Twenty feet to her right, it nosed out of the water, exposing its white face above the cold blue of the surf.

"Here, boy." She hunkered down and extended her arm toward the seal, beckoning him toward her. "I'm not going to hurt you, but I need you to come closer. Please." The seal swam five feet closer. Augusta wished she'd thought to bring a fish with her so she could use it as bait to lure the creature. "Come on, boy." She tried to whistle, which seemed to daunt the seal rather than entice him. He bobbed higher out of the water and stared at her curiously, once again impressing upon her how very human his face appeared. "Won't you please come closer?"

As if in answer, he dived below the surf, leaving a concentric ring of ripples to mark his point of entry. Augusta shot upward. "Don't you dare disappear on me! This is very important!"

When his head bobbed up again, he was farther away. "This isn't a game! If you care one whit for what happens to Elijah, you'll let me look at your flipper!" While he treaded water in that one spot, she clambered over the uneven surface of the reef until she reached a point that was opposite him. But once she gained the area, the seal dived again, leaving her choking on frustration. "Why are you taunting me?" She scanned the water for shadows, but he was too far away now for her to track his movements. Turning her back on the water, she climbed to the highest point on the reef, hoping the higher elevation would allow her a wider range of vision.

It did.

Opposite her right shoulder, she spied sails in the distance—sails that looked to be on a direct tack for Devilstone Island.

Wilfred Strawn removed a sheaf of papers from the satchel he carried and thrust them at Elijah, but Elijah merely lifted an indifferent brow. "Get your papers outta my face, Strawn."

"They have the authorization of President Andrew Jackson, and they *demand* your departure from this island."

"I already made it clear to you that I'm not goin' anywhere."

They were gathered in one of the sheds that adjoined the lighthouse. A crude carpenter's bench occupied one corner of the room, and it was here where Elijah stood, straightening, cutting, and weaving the wire he'd bought in Lustre's Gate. He had already fabricated a section of screen that was five feet long and a foot and a half wide. It was composed of three transverse wires through which he had woven shorter, vertical lengths of wire every three inches. Placing a length of wire on a small chopping block, he grabbed his hatchet and with a downward stroke sliced it in two. Augusta watched Strawn's eyes widen at the force of the stroke.

"I have a bank draft here for thirty-five hundred dollars,

Payne. If you have any sense at all, you'll take the money, pack your belongings, and leave. I told you before, you can't fi—"

"You told me before that a white-faced seal dragged you to shore the night Gus found you." Elijah set aside his hatchet and reached for a pair of pincers. Looking uncomfortable, Wilfred Strawn took a step backward.

"I, uh, I had to say that."

"Why?" asked Augusta.

Strawn directed his attention at her. "Because that's what my immediate superiors *told* me to say. They said if I mentioned something about a seal with a white face, it would make my story sound more convincing to Payne."

"What immediate superiors?" demanded Elijah.

"I'm not at liberty to tell you that."

"Why the hell not?"

"Because government agents are duty bound to protect—"

"How did you arrive on the island that first night, Mr. Strawn?" Augusta interrupted.

Strawn hesitated. "Two associates of mine sailed me out that night. They left me on the beach, then sailed back to the mainland."

"And how did you know that someone would find you in the Gulch?"

"I didn't, but I knew that someone would have to find me sometime. I planned to wait on that beach for a space, and if no one came by, to try another beach that wasn't so secluded. I figured time was on my side. I could explore and take mental notes until someone happened by. And as you already know, Mrs. Payne, I didn't have to wait long before I saw you walking along the path."

"You saw me, but why didn't I see you?"

"As I remember, the sun was bright that morning. Reflections off the water can sometimes blind a person. You were looking east toward the sun. I had the advantage of looking away from the sun."

She thought of the anguish she had suffered thinking there might have been a shipwreck the night she'd dozed off. "So there was no shipwreck," she said, ticking points off on her fingertips. "There was no near-drowning, no white-faced seal, no truth to anything you told us. Have you any idea of the anxiety you and your untruths caused us, Mr. Strawn?" Her voice became so strident that he took another step backward.

"I don't appreciate your tone, Mrs. Payne."

"And I don't appreciate you and your associates toying with our lives!"

His chest puffed up with indignation. "I don't have to explain anything to you people! I work for President An—" He gulped down the rest of his sentence as Elijah grabbed him by the front of his shirt and lifted him one-handed into the air.

"You've got this annoying habit of repeatin' yourself, Strawn. You already told us who you work for. President Andrew Jackson. Well, you do me a favor, and next time you see Mr. Jackson, you tell him the wickie on Devilstone Island doesn't take kindly to the government sendin' weasels to spy on him and his wife. I don't like your lyin'; I don't like your papers; and I don't like you." His fist was wedged so tightly beneath Strawn's chin that the man began to gasp for air. Augusta took three quick steps to Elijah's side and placed her hand on his arm.

"Let him go, Elijah. He's already told us what we need

to know. Your suffocating him won't accomplish anything."

"It'll rid the world of one more government weasel." Strawn's face began to look like an overripe cherry. He began flailing the air with his arms. Gritting his teeth savagely, Elijah dropped him to the floor and watched him stagger backward against the wall, clutching his throat.

"You're a lunatic, Payne!" He choked down air as if it were in short supply, then with a shaky hand straightened his shirtfront and cravat. "You're dangerous!"

"Damn right. So dangerous, in fact, that if you've got any sense at all, you'll take your papers, pack up your satchel, and run like hell back to where you came from. I'll even help you." Turning back to his workbench, he picked up Strawn's papers, tore them in half, then quarters, wadded them into a ball, then hurled the ball at Strawn's feet. "Your papers."

"You can't mutilate government property and get away with it, Payne."

"I suppose you're gonna tell me I can't mutilate government employees and get away with it, either."

Alarm reshaped Strawn's features. Elijah reached for his pincers again, and when he saw Strawn shield his face with his forearm, he laughed. "If I wanted to do real harm, I wouldn't have to resort to pincers. I'd use my bare hands." And saying that, he grabbed the length of wire he'd cut minutes before, wove it through the transverse pieces of his screen, and attached each end to the lateral wires by clamping one to the other with the pincers. He lifted the screen, nodding his satisfaction.

"This section's done. I'm gonna head up to the tower to see if I can figure some way of securin' this thing to the ledge below the lantern. When I climb back down, Strawn, I expect you to be gone.'' With screen in hand, he made his way toward the shed door. Strawn peered down at the wad of paper at his feet, then, with sudden resolve, kicked it across the floor and took up stride behind Elijah.

"I've been threatened by bigger men than you, Payne."

Elijah continued walking—through the shed that housed the whale oil for the lamps, then into the lighthouse. Augusta chased behind both men, her nerves tingling with fright.

"If you don't talk to me, Payne, there'll be other men who'll come! And they'll have more than papers with them to convince you to leave!"

Elijah began climbing the spiral stairs two at a time. Strawn followed close at his heels.

"You're nothing but a wickie, Payne! You can't battle the government. We always win. Always!"

Elijah had just turned the first corner in the cylinder, about fifteen feet up, when Strawn reached forward and seized the end of the wire screen. "Don't walk away from me when I'm talking to you!" He yanked hard on the wire in an attempt to force Elijah to stop, but Elijah kept climbing. So he yanked again, and this time he exerted so much effort that the wire broke away from the screen. He windmilled his arm for balance, but his backward momentum was so great that he had time only to holler his surprise before he was tumbling down the spiral stairs . . . down . . . down . . . mimicking the fall that had killed Lydia Payne six years earlier.

—16—

Augusta's scream echoed all the way to the top of the tower. Elijah vaulted back down the stairs to find Strawn lying at the foot of the staircase like a marionette whose strings had been slashed. Blood oozed from his eyebrow and nose and lip, and his head was crooked at an odd angle.

"Oh, Jeesuz." Elijah searched for a pulse. "He's still alive." Crouching down beside him, he eased Strawn's head away from the wall, but when he removed his hand from the back of the man's skull, his fingers came away moist with blood. Panic riffled through Augusta. She placed a steadying hand on her husband's shoulder.

"Carry him into the house. Quickly."

Elijah laid him facedown on the kitchen table so Augusta could locate the wound on the back of his head. In length it measured half the size of a sewing needle, but it was extremely deep and was discharging enough blood to cause her serious worry. "Have you ever stitched a wound before, Elijah?"

He shook his head.

"Neither have I, but I think one of us might have to. Look at this."

He blew a stream of air between his teeth after he'd taken his look. "Can we stitch him up around all that hair?"

"We'll probably have to cut the hair, then shave as much as we can from around the wound."

"Better get started, then."

Working side by side, they washed, shaved, and stitched the gash in Strawn's head. That done, Elijah turned him onto his back so Augusta could tend the cuts on his face.

"Watch out for his stitches," she cautioned. "Here, put this towel under his head." She pressed her fingertips together. Her flesh was sticky with his blood. "His blood is like honey." She doubted they'd ever be able to rid the table of the stain.

Elijah watched in silence as she pressed cold compresses to Strawn's eyebrow and lip. "You think he'll be all right, Gus?"

She wanted to say yes, but considering what had happened to Lydia Payne, she didn't dare voice any optimism. "I've never treated injuries like this before. I don't know what the implications are."

He nodded, then, thrusting his hands deep into his pockets, crossed the floor to the window. He seemed suddenly dispirited, glum. "I wonder if his immediate supervisors are waitin' for him on the beach."

"They'll need to be told, Elijah. And if they're there,

you'd best fetch them. I think the safest place for Mr. Strawn right now is on the mainland, where someone with a knowledge of medicine can tend him. We . . . we don't want to take any chances with his life.'' She crossed glances with him, suspecting he knew very well what she was trying to prevent.

He gave his head a nod. "I'll see to it." But when he returned twenty minutes later, he appeared more gloomy than when he had left. "Looks like he sailed out by himself. There's a yawl on the beach but no sign of anyone who might have come with him."

Augusta walked to the sink and quietly began scrubbing the stain of blood from her hands. "That doesn't leave us many alternatives, does it?"

Elijah stood over Strawn's body, his gaze lingering on the bruises that scarred the man's face. "Lydia didn't look anything like this when she fell. There wasn't any broken skin. No blood. She seemed fine. Twelve hours later, she was dead."

Augusta dried her hands, then returned to the table to stand opposite her husband. She smoothed her fingers over Strawn's brow. "The irony is, when he first came to us, he claimed to have no memory. When he regains consciousness now, he truly might have no memory."

"*If* he regains consciousness. I dunno, Gus. I've seen lots who look better, but not many who look worse." He was silent for a moment, then, "The damn fool!" His outcry was one of rage, of hopelessness. "Why'd he have to come back here? Why couldn't he've left us alone?"

Augusta bowed her head. She couldn't look at his face. His anguish was too painful for her to endure.

He heaved a sigh, then, in a more composed voice, said,

"It's up to me now, isn't it? This man wants to rob me of my home, maybe my life, but I'm gonna have to take him to the mainland to make sure he doesn't lose his. How's that for fairness?"

"Maybe it wasn't meant to be fair, Elijah. Maybe it's just the way it's supposed to be."

"What do you mean by that?"

"Do you remember how devastated I was the day you told me that mine was the only response you received to your advertisement for a wife? I thought I'd become your wife by default, but you told me to look at it another way. You said that maybe it was God's way of making sure you made the choice He wanted you to make. If you're given only one option, you can't possibly make the wrong decision."

"So?"

"So maybe the same principle applies here. Maybe the only way you'll ever disprove the theory about you and Chakwa is by leaving the island, and maybe the only way the Good Lord could make you do that is by allowing you only one option where Wilfred Strawn is concerned."

"Sounds pretty farfetched."

"Wilfred Strawn is giving you a chance to rid yourself of your demons, Elijah. If you don't take advantage of the opportunity now, you might never be given another chance. You can be free, sweetheart. We both can."

He nodded halfheartedly. "And what if I can't make it back tonight? What if I'm gone from Devilstone and the legend is true?"

She rounded the table. Grasping his right hand, she cradled it beneath her chin. "It's not true. You'll come back to me, Elijah. I know you will."

An hour later, she was standing outside the boathouse on the cobblestoned beach, waiting to bid him farewell. They had made a bed for Strawn on the floor of the yawl close to the transom, then bundled him in woolen blankets. He still hadn't regained consciousness, but his pulse was strong, which gave them reason to be hopeful. Elijah pushed the yawl out of the boathouse on the greased track-way, then stepped to the side where Augusta was waiting for him. Circling his arms around her, he hugged her tightly to his chest.

"You'll be all right by yourself for a while?"

"I'll be fine."

"You'll remember to milk Geraldine?"

"I'll remember."

"And you won't have any trouble fillin' the oil reservoirs and lightin' the lamps?"

"I won't have any trouble."

"Promise you won't fall asleep on duty again?"

Her muscles tensed. "How did you know that?"

"Always could tell when a woman was tryin' to hide somethin'. Just be a good wife and try not to do it again." He kissed the crown of her head, then embraced her with such vehemence that she thought he would squeeze the air from her lungs. She gasped out his name, and in reply he lifted her chin and kissed her mouth with all the passion and desperation of a man who would never live to see another sunrise. "I'm so afraid if I let you go, I'll never see you again." He whispered the words against her cheek, and when she looked up at him, she saw the deep blackness of his eyes well with tears that began to spill onto his cheeks. "I love you, Gus. No matter what happens. I'll always love you."

His tears flowed without shame, touching her as no gesture could. That this gruff, unmannered man could shed tears over her was a happenstance she never thought to witness. No one had ever cried over her before. Perhaps no one had ever loved her as much as Elijah.

Bending his head close to hers, she kissed the tears from his cheeks and eyelids, then pressed a feathery kiss to the warmth of his mouth. "Nothing will ever keep us apart, my love. Neither myth, nor legend, nor lore. Be safe, and hurry back to me."

He tied Strawn's boat to the stern of his yawl on a long tether. From the cobblestoned beach Augusta watched him sail away—watched until the white of his billowing canvas became a mere mote on the edge of the earth.

The island was quiet without him. It made her poignantly aware how much she delighted in his company, how empty her life would be without him. It was a thought she couldn't bear.

She worried that she'd fall asleep in the tower that night. She worried that a vessel might founder on the ledge. She worried that something dreadful might happen to Elijah's yawl on the way back to the island. Minus Elijah's calming influence, it seemed there was no problem small enough to escape her worry.

The wind shifted that night. It whistled through the ports in the floor of the lantern and whipped the surf into a lather of white-crested waves. It howled up and down the tower and beat at the windows—so loudly that Augusta knew she wouldn't be able to hear Elijah's footsteps if he climbed the stairs to the cylinder.

But he didn't climb the stairs that night, and when dawn broke the following morning, she realized he might never climb the stairs again. The coming of dawn would have decided his fate. Wherever he was, he knew now if the legend was myth or truth. So until she was informed, all she could do was wait.

It was intolerable.

She slept little that day in favor of maintaining a constant vigil in the lighthouse. But she saw no sails on the horizon, only white horses prancing on the crest of waves and flocks of migratory birds winging southward. She tried to imagine what winter would be like on Devilstone Island. She tried to imagine a winter without Elijah.

The wind persisted during the day and increased in velocity toward evening. It was a fierce squally blow—the kind that could capsize yawls in a trice. She told herself that Elijah was too wise a seaman to venture back in this weather. She blamed the high seas for his absence. She blamed the high winds for his absence. She blamed everything except the reason she dreaded most.

Dawn of the following day brought calmer winds and a gentler sea. With the weather presenting no impediment, she expected he would set sail for Devilstone this morning. She milked Geraldine and collected eggs, then raced down to the cobblestoned beach to await his return. She sat near the place where they'd first made love, and every so often dozed against the tree where he had cradled her against him. Each time she awoke, she expected to see his canvas sail dotting the horizon, but the horizon remained unblemished.

From the position of the sun, she judged when the hour of noon arrived, then one o'clock, then two. *He should be back by now*, she told herself. She walked to the reef to search for the seal, somehow convincing herself that if the seal were alive, Elijah was safe. She wandered out to the farthest point on the reef, meticulously scanning the waters, but she saw no shadow gliding beneath the surface, no white face, no seal. She considered the lore that had built up around the seal. Mr. Biddle had implied that the creature protected the harbor of Lustre's Gate. *Protected it from what?* Foul weather? Attack from the English? Was the seal supposed to protect the harbor, or the people who earned their living in the harbor? Had the creature protected Devilstone? Or had it merely protected Devilstone's inhabitants? Was it the creature's doing that Elijah had never been harmed when he'd rescued people from the Devil's Elbow? Was it the creature who had protected him from the savagery of the Atlantic? That Elijah had never been hurt seemed uncanny, unnatural. But if she allowed herself to believe the superstition, then given the present circumstances, she would have to admit that . . . that . . .

"I won't admit it!" she screamed at the horizon. "He's coming back to me!" Then, more softly, "He has to."

Weariness dogged her steps as she made her way up to the lantern that evening. She penned her entry in the logbook, then lit the twenty-one lamps of Devilstone's beacon. She stood at the glass, willing Elijah's sail to appear, but in the distance all she could see was a low bank of clouds rolling seaward off the mainland. It moved like an army of infantrymen, gliding on invisible feet, crawling in stealth, in silence. It camouflaged the horizon with its albino coloring, then spread over the water, slithering inexorably toward Devilstone. It flattened the water beneath its oppressive mist. It enveloped the sea in its eerie stillness, and when it reached Devilstone, Augusta watched it snake toward the tower, swallowing the forest treelimb by treelimb. She remembered the other fog that had shrouded the island. Then it had seemed fascinating. Tonight, alone in the tower, she found it a threat with which she had no wish to contend.

It muffled the sound of the breakers that crashed into the storm beach. It was thick, and white, and cocooned itself around the tower. It seemed an unfriendly fog, one that would smother her if she ventured into its depths, so she sat her chair in the lantern and rained defiant stares at its haunting intrusion. She sat, and watched, waiting for the fog to lift, waiting for her husband to return.

Unable to see either moon or stars, she could not mark the change in their position, so time seemed to pass not at all. The only way she knew the hours were passing was from the stiffness that attacked her bones from sitting overly long in Elijah's wooden chair. Wincing with the discomfort, she stood up and stretched, then walked behind the lamps to peer in the direction of the forest. There was such blackness outside the tower, such stillness. Her heartbeat was the loudest sound she could hear. Her heartbeat and—

She cocked her head to listen. What was the other sound? Flapping? Yes, wings flapping. But it sounded like a great many—

The glass imploded with such violence that it hurled tiny shards across the room. She ducked her head and covered her eyes, but the screech of injured birds made her wheel around toward the lamps. She saw feathers, and blood, and not just one bird but a half-dozen sprawled on the floor, broken and writhing. And still they came, one after the other, crashing into other panes of glass—big migratory birds, blinded by the fog and lured by Devilstone's beacon. "No!" Augusta shrieked. But her scream could not prevent the nightmare from continuing, or two more birds from launching themselves through the hole in the lantern glass, flying straight at the blazing light given off by the twenty-one Argand lamps.

The lamps fell like dominoes. Metal reflectors and oil reservoirs clanked onto the floor. Glass chimneys shattered. And flames began to spread, riding on the flow of the spilled whale oil. In an instant the floor was aflame, then the table, and she began to smell the stench of burning feathers. She covered her nose and mouth. Her eyes stung with the smoke. She coughed into her hands, wanting to douse the flames, knowing she *must* douse the flames, but realizing she had no means of preventing the fire from spreading. The only thing she could do was run, and run quickly, before the lantern was completely engulfed in flames.

Hugging the exterior wall, she circled around to the hatch in the floor and climbed down. A fit of coughing beset her as she reached the watchroom. Doubling over with the spasm, nostrils and eyes burning with fumes and smoke, she headed for the spiral stairs, and in the darkness made her way to the ground. Her eyes began to tear. Her throat was scratchy. It felt as if it was closing on her. She ran out into the fog and looked up at the tower.

The lantern was completely aflame, like a monstrous torch, and the flames were spreading downward, feeding on the dry wood of the cylinder's interior. She could hear it hiss and pop—could see embers floating in the mist, hot and glowing. Ash rained down upon her. Outside the open doorway of the tower she felt a quick rush of air, as if the

fire were sucking up great drafts of Devilstone air to feed
it.

It's going to burn. It's all going to burn. She dragged
her hand across her eyes, and when she glanced at the
sleeve of her gown, she saw pricks of blood staining the
material—blood marking the places where slivers of glass
had embedded themselves in her flesh. Above her she heard
another pane of glass explode. Shielding her head with her
forearms, she ran farther away from the tower, farther into
the mist. She knew the dampness of the fog would have
little effect on the fire. It was burning too hotly to be
extinguished by anything but a downpour, and that event
seemed unlikely. If only the sheds weren't attached to each
other! Perhaps then the house would be spared. But there
was nothing to prevent the blaze from racing from shed
to shed, and then to the house.

Thank God there was little breeze. At least the barn and
the woodland would be safe. But as she watched flames
shoot out the window at the base of the lighthouse, she
remembered what was stored in the shed that directly adjoined it, and she felt her mouth dry up with sudden fear.
*Whale oil. That shed contains barrel upon barrel of whale
oil.* Would it explode? Or when the barrel burned, would
the oil simply become a river of flame, igniting everything
in its path? The month of August had been relatively dry,
so the grass could go up like straw. And if the grass caught
fire, nothing was safe. Not the forest, not the barn, not
Geraldine . . .

Geraldine. Good Lord, how was she going to save Geraldine?

In the glowing mist, she ran in the direction of the stone

fence, threw open the gate, and headed for the barn. On her way past the henhouse, she unlatched the door and roused all the birds from their roosts. She didn't know where they could go to escape the fire, but they would have a better chance of survival if they weren't locked up in their coop. She looked back at the fire as she raced for the barn. The roof of the first shed was in flames. How much longer before the barrels of oil started to burn?

She lifted the bar that secured the barn door, opened the doors wide, and hurried inside. Unsure of her footing in the darkness, she located Geraldine's stall and fumbled with the latch on the gate until she was finally able to work it free. The cow was asleep in her stall, unaware that Devilstone was threatening to burn around her. "Up you go, girl." Augusta clapped her hands in a quick rhythm. Geraldine, newly awakened and stubborn, let out a lazy moo. Augusta yanked on the collar around the creature's neck. "Come on, Geraldine! I wouldn't be here if the situation wasn't serious! I have to get you out of here." And as if the cow understood exactly what she was saying, she heaved herself to her knees, then her hooves, then allowed Augusta to lead her into the barnyard.

The entire lighthouse was ablaze now, burning like a sinner in hell. The roar of the fire was more terrible than a hurricane wind, and even from the barnyard Augusta could feel the heat emanating from the blaze. Geraldine grew skittish with the smoke, the fire, the fog, and Augusta wondered if her attempt to save the animal wasn't futile. She led her to the easternmost corner of the barnyard and scratched the space between her ears. "This might be the safest place for you to be, girl. I'll leave the gate open and I won't tie you up. If the grass catches fire, you might have to dodge the flames, but you'll have more of a chance here than you would if I tried to lead you someplace you didn't want to go.''

Geraldine mooed again. Augusta gave her a final scratch and offered a silent prayer that she was doing the right thing. She looked back at the lighthouse. The tower and sheds had become an inferno that was spewing ash like a blizzard spews snowflakes. And from the first storage shed she saw flames pour over the grass and knew that the wooden casks containing the whale oil had finally burned. She deemed it her signal to seek refuge.

The fog glowed with the eerie light from the fire. Able to see more clearly now, Augusta hurried out the gate, then followed the path that Elijah had led her along the first night she'd arrived on Devilstone. She could sense where the edge of the cliff was, so her footsteps were sure as she made her way along the eastern perimeter of the island. If the entire island went up in flames, she realized there was only one place where she would truly be safe, and that place wasn't on the island. It was on the water.

With the inferno far behind her now, the darkness and mist began crowding in on her. She slowed her pace. Her footsteps became more cautious. At the place where she knew the rescue boat to be housed, she groped with her foot to find the wooden walkway, then inched her way down the ramp. She used the boulders on her left as a guide, trailing her hand over their surface as she walked. She found the steps without falling down them, then, after groping her way along another ramp, spied the oblique outline of the boathouse. Finding the door, she rushed inside. She paused for a moment to gain her bearings. She knew there were candles and matches on the wall shelf to her left, beside the bucket of axle grease. Walking in that direction, she located what she needed, lit the candle, then jabbed it onto the iron point of a hook that was driven into the wall.

She stared at the rescue boat with some trepidation. Elijah had shown her how to release it down the slip and how to row the thing. All she had to do was row it around the lee of the island toward the cobblestoned beach and remain offshore until the fire either burned down the island or burned itself out. Given the uncertain path of the flames, it seemed the wisest choice to make—the only choice to make.

She crossed the short space to the winch and released the crank on the drum, just as Elijah had demonstrated. That done, she climbed the four stairs that flanked the boat and cradle, stepped over the gunwale, thrust her two oars between their thole pins, then seated herself on the center thwart. She readied herself. She inhaled a deep breath. She positioned her hands correctly around the oar grips. She gnawed on her bottom lip. Then, letting go her left oar and grasping it with her right hand, she leaned to port and pulled back on the lever that rose above the gunwale.

The boat jerked, then rattled, then, like that first night, careened headlong into blackness. Thumping into the surf made her teeth clack, her tailbone ache. But there was no time to dwell on physical discomforts. She had to maneuver the boat away from shore before the surf carried her onto the rocks.

The sea was calm. Almost too calm. It was as if someone had poured gallons of palm oil over the surface to quell the waves. She supposed the fog was to blame. The fire had started as an indirect result of the fog, but it was because of the fog that she had an avenue of escape. She would have been quite helpless with ten-foot waves tossing her about. She recalled Elijah's instructions. *Knees apart. Back straight. Blades vertical. Short, chopping strokes.* Squaring her oars, she lowered them into the water and stroked . . . stroked. She could feel the press of the water against the blades, could feel the boat move as she forced the blades against that pressure with short, chopping strokes. With the grips she drew little rainbows in the air to maintain a smooth rhythm. *Keep your strokes synchronized,* she told herself. *Blades vertical. Now pull. Pull.*

Thirty feet from shore, she lifted her port oar, stroked twice with her starboard blade, and angled the boat in a direction to follow the leeward shoreline. It was an effort keeping the boat a safe distance from shore, for she could feel the incessant pull of the tide beneath her. It was perhaps more effort than she was prepared for. After a while the constant battle with the tide took its toll. The muscles in her arms grew sluggish. Her palms started to ache. She grew short of breath. She lifted her oars for a moment to rest, and when she did, the boat angled its head toward the mainland and began carrying her away from the course she had set, slowly at first, then more quickly.

Too late, she remembered the current that flowed on the eastern side of Devilstone—the current that swept wreckage away from the island rather than toward it.

Dipping her blades into the surf again, she struggled to turn the boat around. She pulled on the oars, fought against the power of the current, but no matter how hard she pulled, she could do no better than to stay in the same place. "All right," she finally gasped. "You've won." Exhausted, she lifted the oars into the boat. The current would carry her to the mainland. If the sea remained calm, she would have no difficulty arriving on shore unharmed.

Retrieving a blanket from the locker behind the stern thwart, she wrapped it around herself and settled in for a long night. The fog was all-consuming. She drifted through it like some unearthly wraith, floating on the current until she could no longer see the glow of fire on Devilstone Island. She wondered how many miles she had drifted. She wondered if the fog would ever lift. She wondered why Elijah wasn't here to console her. She was trying to be brave, but she was in desperate need of consolation.

Huddled beneath her blanket on the center thwart, she'd just begun to doze when she saw the lights in the distance. There were two of them—a green light to her left, a red light to her right. *Ship's running lights*. But was the ship headed toward her or away from her? She tried to recall the rhyme Elijah had taught her: 'Red to red or green to green, no danger can be seen. Red to green and green to red, there's a vessel dead ahead.' If her boat had been outfitted with running lights, her red light to port would face the ship's green. Her green to starboard would face the ship's red. *Red to green and green to red*—which meant . . .

Good God, it was headed straight at her.

"Stop!" She shot upward, crisscrossing her arms over her head, but the fog muted her voice as thoroughly as it shrouded her presence. She wrenched the starboard oar out of its thole pin and waved it high in the air. "Stop! Can't you see me?"

The ship cut steadily through the water, drawing closer and closer. *It's not going to stop. It's going to cut me in half.* Terror seized her. Thrusting the oar into the water, she began to use it like a paddle. Her boat started to spin in a slow circle. She looked up.

The bow of the ship loomed above her.

She felt the impact at the same time that she heard the hideous rending of wood. It threw her against the side of the boat and catapulted her over the gunwale, and then she was being surrounded by a cold tomb of water that blinded her with its blackness. She felt the numbing cold assault her temples. She felt her lungs burn with the pain of trying to hold her breath. She clawed at the water and thrashed with her legs, but when her throat constricted, the Atlantic crept into her mouth and up her nostrils, and then, mercifully, she felt nothing else.

The sun was warm against her cheekbone and ear, but the rest of her body felt chilled. She lacked the energy to raise her eyelids, so she simply remained the way she was, facedown on what she suspected was a feather tick. Nearby she heard the screech of a gull and the unmistakable rush of tidal water, and in a moment of confusion, she wondered if she was outside. But why would anyone be foolish enough to set a feather tick outside where it might get rained on?

She heard movement close by, then, quite suddenly, felt something cold and moist nuzzling the angle below her jaw. She lifted her hand to swat it away, but when her fingertips encountered fur, tired or not, she forced her eyes open.

His face was so close to hers that his whiskers tickled the corner of her mouth. His fur was soft, his nose moist, and when he started licking her cheek, she snapped her eyes shut reflexively. She giggled even though it hurt to laugh and hurt to breathe, and with her left hand caressed the slope of his head. Opening her eyes again, she stared into his white face, just now beginning to remember what had transpired the night before.

She raised her head slightly, eyeing her surroundings. She wasn't inside on a feather tick. She was lying on the sand on the same slice of beach where she had found Wilfred Strawn. She was on the eastern shore of Devilstone, at the Gulch. *But how did I get here?*

The seal made an *aarwk*ing sound. Augusta brushed her palm down his neck. The last thing she remembered was the red and green running lights of the ship whose bow had rammed her boat. She'd been thrown clear of the boat, but the water had been everywhere. The water, she realized, should have been her tomb.

Overcome with awe, she peered into the creature's eyes. "Do I owe you my life?" she whispered. "Was it you who saved me?"

He stretched his neck, playfully chasing her hand as she trailed it over his shoulder and down toward his right flipper. His pelt was full and thick, but its thickness could not mask the heavy ridge of scar tissue she could feel underlying the fur. The creature's coat had grown back, but he still bore the scar where Phineas Payne had dug the lead ball from his flesh.

She swallowed slowly. "Chakwa." The legend wasn't myth. It was true. Chakwa was real, and Elijah—*Dear God, what of Elijah?*

Seeming to sense her disquiet, the seal tilted his head and looked her straight in the face, and in an odd alignment of facial features, appeared, for the briefest of moments, to smile at her.

A knot of emotion vibrated in her throat. "Elijah?" Her

eyes starred with sudden tears. One trickled down the slope of her cheek. Unexpectedly, the seal leaned forward and brushed the tear away with his nose, much the same way she had kissed away Elijah's tears three days earlier.

The comparison left her cold. She boosted herself onto her hands, and as if frightened by the movement, the seal recoiled, heaved himself onto his flippers, and started slinking toward the surf. Augusta rolled onto her hip. "Don't go!" But the seal gained the water and splashed headlong into the low waves that washed the beach. "Elijah? *Don't leave me!*"

She clutched her ribs in pain. Every bone, every organ in her body was screaming out its misery. And then, from behind her, she heard a man's voice.

"I've found her! She's here! She's alive!"

Looking over her shoulder, she saw a man scrambling down over the rocks toward her. He looked vaguely familiar, and as he approached, she realized why.

"Captain Crowley." Her voice afforded him a scratchy greeting.

"Praise be, Mrs. Payne." He bent down and helped her to her feet. "We thought you were a goner for sure." He brushed sand off the lower half of her gown while she attacked her bodice, but the gown was still damp, so the tiny granules stuck like pieces of burr. "We've been looking for you a good two hours, ma'am. After this pass, I was about ready to agree with your husband that you'd burned up in the tower."

She grabbed Crowley's shoulder. "Elijah is here? He's alive? He's not dead?"

"He's here, ma'am. But by the way he was starin' at the ruins on the top of the cliff when I left him, he looked like he wished he were dead. I'd best get you up there as soon's you're able.''

''I'm able now.'' She took a painful step forward, then clutched onto Crowley's arm for support. ''If you'll help me.''

He assisted her up the gravel path to the marginal way, then walked beside her as they cut through one of the interior paths of the woodland.

''Why didn't he come back?'' Augusta asked the captain of the ship *Windlass*. ''Why was he gone so long?''

''The way he tells it, ma'am, when he sailed into Lustre's Gate with that Strawn feller, he got some pretty suspicious looks thrown his way. The two fellers who were with Strawn accused Elijah of God knows what—foul play and everything else. So they refused to let him outta their sight until Strawn was well enough to talk. 'Course, Strawn woke up that night and cleared the boy of blame, but by then the wind was too squally for him to sail back. Those two friends of Strawn felt bad about not lettin' him head back when he wanted, so they put him up in the same rooming house where they were stayin, in the same room as one of the fellers, and when that feller wakes up in the middle of the night and looks toward Elijah's bed, he finds it empty. He gets up, searches all through the house for him, and can't find him.''

Augusta felt dazed. ''What night was that, Captain?''

''I reckon that was last night, ma'am. So the man heads back to his room to wait for 'Lijah, lights a candle, and an hour later in walks 'Lijah, naked as the day Phineas found him and sound asleep. Without as much as a howdy-do, he crawls back under the kelp and keeps on sleepin'.

Did you have any notion that the boy walks in his sleep, Mrs. Payne?''

''No. None at all.'' But it would certainly explain what had happened to him the night he had claimed to be sleeping and wasn't. At least, for all practical purposes it would explain it. She thought back to yesterday. ''Why did he spend that extra day in Lustre's Gate? What prevented him from heading back yesterday?''

''Seems there was a small problem with the yawl. We suspect it was some youngster's prank, but the boat was half full of water before anyone noticed there was a hole chopped in the bottom of it. In my day, youngsters weren't so malicious. So 'Lijah had to set about gettin' the thing repaired before he could start back. I moored outside the harbor late yesterday afternoon. I'd intended to sail to Devilstone to deliver that gross of wicks I'd promised the boy, but one of my crew got word of a death in the family, so I let him off in the closest village where he could catch a stage inland. And then the fog set in, so I decided to stay put for a while. When I saw 'Lijah in town, I offered him a ride back to the island, and he was more than willin' to take me up on it. He was some worried about you, ma'am. So we headed out of the village early this mornin' even before the fog lifted.''

She stopped to catch her breath, wondering if it had been the *Windlass* that struck her boat in the fog.

''You can imagine our reaction when we neared the island and saw a cloud of smoke hanging over the place. Had all I could do to keep 'Lijah from jumpin' over the side and swimmin' ashore. And when he saw everything burned and still smokin', and no wife, well, I can tell you,

Mrs. Payne, it wasn't a pretty sight. But it's a miracle the whole island didn't go up. The tower and house can always be rebuilt, but you'd be hard-pressed to replace the trees.''

The devastation wrought by the fire became apparent as she emerged from the forest. What had been a complex of buildings the night before was now a smoldering pile of rubble and ash. The stench of burned wood cloyed at her nostrils. The grass was charred in a wide arc. It was a heartrending sight, but even more heartrending was the sight of Elijah as he stood before the ruined buildings. His back was facing her, but she could see that his head was bowed, his shoulders were slumped, and he was still as death.

''He's been standin' like that since we got here,'' Crowley whispered. ''I think I'll go round up my crew while you say your hellos. You two young'uns don't need Haydon Crowley breathin' down your necks.''

She would have run had she been able, but she could manage nothing more than a slow hobble on weak legs. Two feet behind him, she stopped. ''Elijah?''

For a long moment he remained still, but then he elevated his head, paused again, then pivoted around slowly. He stared at her without seeming to see her. His flesh looked haggard, gray. ''Gus?'' He lifted his hand to her face, touching his fingers to the angle of her jaw as if assuring himself that she actually stood before him. ''I thought you were dead, I thought the fire had . . .'' His voice broke. She held his palm to her cheek.

''I couldn't prevent what happened, Elijah. A flock of birds flew at the beacon in the fog. The glass broke and the lamps overturned. I'm sorry I couldn't save anything. I'm sorry—''

"You're sorry?" His eyes grew more lucid, and before she could stop him, he had plucked her off her feet and was whirling her around faster than a child's top. "You're alive, Gus! You're alive!" He spun around with her, and squeezed her, and showered kisses on her neck and face, and when he finally set her on her feet again, she had to lean against him for balance. He hugged her against his chest and smoothed his hand down the tangled mass of her hair. "I'm never gonna let you outta my sight again, Gus. No more. From now on, wherever I go, you go, and wherever you go, I go."

"No matter where?"

He set her slightly away from him and probed her face with eyes that no longer appeared tormented by wonder and worry. There was a calmness about him now. Elijah Payne looked at peace with himself. "Nothin' happened to me in Lustre's Gate, Gus. Just like you said it wouldn't. I left Devilstone for three days, and I'm still alive to talk about it. It was all a passel of lies. If the lore'd been true, I'd be dead. What you said about Chakwa bein' different seals has to be the way of it. There isn't any two-centuries-old seal. The legend isn't true, Gus. It just isn't true."

She parted her lips, then closed them again. She could tell him what happened to her last night. She could tell him of her encounter with the seal on the beach. But what purpose would that serve other than destroying the fragile peace he had discovered? Perhaps there were times in a person's life when peace of mind was more important than knowing the truth. This, she realized, was one of those times.

"You've got a funny look on your face, Gus."

She nodded. "It's the look of a woman who's extremely

happy to have her husband back whole and healthy. I love you, Elijah.'' Unable to suppress her tears, she circled her arms around his waist and held him close. The future held such hope. They could begin again.

They could begin today.

''We've got company, sweetheart. You wanna turn around for a minute?''

Drying her eyes on the heels of her palms, she angled herself away from Elijah without leaving his side. When she looked toward the stone fence, she saw Wilfred Strawn making his way toward them. He was unshaven and rumpled looking and was brushing bits of straw from his coat as he walked toward them. ''The cow is all milked out for another few hours.''

''Geraldine survived the fire?'' Augusta's amazement knew no limits. ''She's all right?''

''She is now,'' answered Strawn, ''but she was feeling pretty bloated when we found her. That's one lucky bovine. And I guess I'm one lucky government agent.'' He favored her with a sheepish look before continuing. ''I asked Captain Crowley to allow me to accompany him out here so I could thank you in person, Mrs. Payne. I, uh, I wanted to express my gratitude for all you did for me. For stitching up my head, for offering to remain here alone so your husband could take me to the mainland for medical attention.'' He nodded at the destruction behind them. ''I'm sorry about what happened here. I feel as though it was partially my fault. If I hadn't fallen down those stairs, your husband wouldn't have had to leave, and maybe his presence would have lessened the damage the fire caused.''

Augusta shook her head. "I doubt that anyone's presence would have changed the outcome of the fire."

"But still, I hold myself responsible. And I'd like to make it up to you in some way. The only way I can think of doing that is by giving you back your island. The government can find someplace else to build its project. I'll just tell them that my first estimations were incorrect. It'll be my way of saying 'thank you and I'm sorry for all the trouble I caused.' "

Elijah cleared his throat. "What if we don't wanna take it back? Hell, Strawn, the place is no good to us now. Where're we supposed to live? In the barn with Geraldine?"

"Well, I—"

"Never mind. You can have the island. In fact, I'll *give* it to you. That all right with you, Gus?"

She blinked her surprise. What was he saying? Where would they go? What would they do? He was obviously so enthralled with his newfound freedom that it was making him reckless. But who was she to deny him his first taste of impracticality? "It's fine with me."

"Good." He pumped Wilfred Strawn's hand in a gesture of agreement. "You just got yourself an island, Strawn."

"In that case, I'll have another bank draft drawn up for you."

"No need. I don't want your money."

Augusta slanted a meaningful look at her husband. Freedom was one thing. Impoverishment was quite another. "Elijah, perhaps you should accept Mr. Strawn's offer of recompense."

"We'll manage, Gus. Always have. Probably always will. One thing I wanna know, though, Strawn. What's this project you're talkin' about? And I don't care if it's supposed to be a secret. If I'm givin' you my island, I'd like to know what you intend to do with it.''

Strawn thought for a space, then nodded. ''If you'd excuse us for a few minutes, Mrs. Payne, I believe I can tell your husband what he wants to know.''

Elijah kissed the top of her head. ''Meet me at the burial point, sweetheart. We have some good-byes to say before we leave.''

She was pacing beside Phineas's grave when he joined her, and even before he said a word, she began spouting her thoughts. ''We could go back to Philadelphia. It won't be easy. We'll have to impose on my sisters for a while, but after I collect the rest of the inheritance that's due me, we could find a little flat somewhere. I could take in sewing and laundry until you found something you enjoyed doing. But there's one monstrous drawback.''

''And what's that?''

''You'd have to wear shoes.''

He laughed at the serious expression on her face. Taking her by the hand, he walked her to the far corner of the cemetery plot. ''We don't have to live in Philadelphia, Gus. Fact is, we can go anywhere and do anything we want.'' Bending over, he removed a large rock from the mound covering the grave marked ''Drowned Man—1816.''

Her eyes widened in sacrilegious horror. ''What are you doing?''

He set the rock aside and bent down to retrieve another. ''You ever had a hankerin' to do somethin' you've never done before, Gus?''

''I already did it. I got married. Elijah, put those stones back. Have you lost your mind?''

"Nope. I think I might've just found it." When he'd removed a half-dozen rocks, he knelt down, shoved his hand into a small aperture beneath the remaining pile of stones, and pulled a burlap pouch into the open. He pitched it at Augusta, who hopped out of the way, letting it drop to the ground.

"Get that thing away from me!" But when she glanced at the place it had landed, she didn't see the human remains she'd expected to see. She saw gold. Round, heavy, gold coins that had spilled out of the pouch and onto the ground. She stared at the coins, completely and utterly speechless.

"There's lots more where that came from. I suppose Haydon can lend us a few sea chests to stow it away in."

Augusta crouched down. She lifted one of the coins. "What is this, Elijah? Where did it come from?"

"Bunker's treasure, Gus."

"But . . . but you said—"

"Hell, you don't think Phineas could've lived on this island all those years and not found it, do you? I thought it was kinda clever, him buryin' it in the cemetery the way he did. Even your most black-hearted of reavers has more respect than to defile the grave of a drowned man."

"But . . ." She felt light-headed. "Elijah, you're rich."

"I know that."

"You . . . you have more money here than you can ever spend in one lifetime, and yet for twenty-eight years you allowed your house to go without curtains?" It suddenly struck her as so wonderfully absurd that she started to laugh. She threw one of the coins at Elijah, then another, and then they were locked in each other's arms, in laughter, in tears, and in love.

—EPILOGUE—

It took Haydon Crowley's crew longer to transport Geraldine onto the *Windlass* than it took Elijah and Augusta to pack their belongings. They had nothing other than their gold to take with them. Augusta bemoaned the loss of Phineas's logbooks and carvings. Elijah bemoaned the loss of six good cheroots that he had yet to smoke. But standing at the rail of the *Windlass*, they realized they were fortunate not to have lost each other.

"Elijah, can you give me a hint about what the government is planning for Devilstone?"

"Oh, that." Elijah rolled his eyes. "Damn fools. I suppose they're gonna have to prove it for themselves, but I can tell them right now that, no matter what they do, they're never gonna get an iron ship to float."

"Iron ship?"

He pressed a finger to his lips. "Not too loud, Gus. It's supposed to be what Strawn called 'top secret.' "

As they left Devilstone Island behind them, Augusta turned wistful. "Do you think we'll ever see it again?"

"Maybe some years down the road. But I've got me a notion to buy us a big ship and sail to the South Seas to see all those places Phineas always talked about. You feel cold to me, sweetheart. Lemme get you a blanket out of the cabin." He left her standing alone at the rail. She looked back at the island, remembering the beauty and timelessness of the place, and decided they would return.

One day.

On the storm beach of the island known as Devilstone, a white-faced seal watched the ship *Windlass* fade slowly in the distance. Phineas Payne's son was gone, but instinct told the creature the black-haired woman would watch over the boy just as Chakwa herself had watched over him these many years. As she continued to watch the ship, a very human tear escaped from one of her very human eyes, and when she could no longer see the vessel, she dived deep into the Atlantic for the last time—into the water known for its numbing cold and savage tides.

Up and down the coast of Maine, the seal was never seen again.

GET
LOVESTRUCK!

AND GET STRIKING ROMANCES
FROM POPULAR LIBRARY'S
BELOVED AUTHORS

*Watch for these exciting
romances in the months to come:*

December 1989
SAVAGE TIDES by Mary Mayer Holmes
SWEPT AWAY by Julie Tetel

January 1990
TO LOVE A STRANGER by Marjorie Shoebridge
DREAM SONG by Sandra Lee Smith

February 1990
THE HEART'S DISGUISE by Lisa Ann Verge

March 1990
EXPOSURES by Marie Joyce

April 1990
WILD GLORY by Andrea Parnell

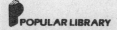

POPULAR LIBRARY